Christopher J Walker was born in Sheffield in 1969. Some 36 years later he has surpassed all expectations by remaining alive and relatively healthy. An office job veteran, Christopher also considered careers in the military and law enforcement, both of which met with spectacular failure during the selection process. Now firmly entrenched behind a desk, he does his best to transcend his 9 to 5 existence by writing novels. He still lives in his beloved Sheffield with his equally beloved wife Sharon.

Saturday Knights is his second novel.

www.christopher-j-walker.com

The author has also published

"Chasing **TROY"**
Published in 2005 (Vanguard Press)
ISBN 1 84386 099 6

Cover Blurb of *"Chasing* **TROY"**

A hapless private investigator with a drink problem.
An erratic service droid with more gadgets than James Bond.
A feisty space courier on a never-ending adrenaline trip.
An ape-man assassin hooked on mangos.
A telepathic dung beetle.
A troop of gung-ho military droids.
A secret of mind-boggling importance.

The universe has managed to drag itself as far as 2105. It's a
disagreeable, dangerous, noxious place, but all the same it's in
danger - serious danger. The chase begins on the grubby streets
of Cosmopolis. TROY is in the open and everyone wants it, even
those who don't know what it is. From the authentic Wild West
town of Steersville to the hazardous jungles of Fangoza, TROY
is pursued across the galaxy in a textbook display of organised
chaos. Only one man can save the day and unfortunately it's
Rick Venison, quite possibly the most inept human being alive,
helped and hindered in equal measure by E-type, his trusty
service droid.

Can he save the universe before it self-destructs?

Maybe - as long as he's back for last orders.

SATURDAY KNIGHTS

Christopher J Walker

SATURDAY KNIGHTS

Vanguard Press

A CIP catalogue record for this title is
available from the British Library

The photo of the author on the back cover by
kind permission of Mike Leng, Photography.

ISBN-13: 978 1 84386 284 0
ISBN-10: 1 84386 284 0

*Vanguard Press is an imprint of
Pegasus Elliot MacKenzie Publishers Ltd.*
www.pegasuspublishers.com

First Published in 2006

**Vanguard Press
Sheraton House Castle Park
Cambridge England**

Printed & Bound in Great Britain

Dedication

For Mum and Dad – for everything

ACKNOWLEDGEMENTS

Thanks to Sharon, my wife, for believing, for continuing to put up with me and my nonsense, but most of all for just being there.

Once again, my thanks to The Greaves, my official proof-reader, for wading through yet another weighty tome – one of the few things he does quietly.

Thanks to Phill McManus, a man with neuro-kinetics way above normal. The website looks great, bud.

Thanks also to all those involved at Rosemount Estate in New South Wales and South Australia for your inspiration. You helped me go places I wouldn't normally go.

And finally, a big thank you to the late, great genius, Ray Charles, who kept me company throughout the whole trip.

CHAPTER ONE

"Old age is like everything else.
To make a success of it, you've got to start young."

Theodore Roosevelt

3am – a murky alley somewhere in Cosmopolis.
Whispered voices.
Belch!
"Will you *stop* that?"
"Sorry Mr Tanner, I can't help it, I burp when I get nervous!"
"I've never heard anything so ridiculous, why don't you just bite your nails like everyone else?"
Belch!
"Sorry, it's a childhood thing."
"Have you seen a specialist about it?"
"Yeah, there's nothing they can do."
"Well try and control it will ya? We're supposed to be hiding!"
Belch!
"OK, I'll try."

Pug Tanner was a career criminal and had, after achieving the enviable status of being his own boss, promoted himself several times over the last ten years. He was the kind of guy you'd enjoy getting drunk with but wouldn't buy a used car from in a zillion lifetimes. Starting out as a petty thief at the age of twelve, he had risen to the lofty heights of professional burglar by his eighteenth birthday. Now twenty-two he was an established villain, specialising in the hijacking of security vans, which for some insane reason tended to make their runs during the dead of night when they were far easier to knock over. He had thus far managed to avoid The

Joint[†], but this had little to do with his skill as a crook and far more to do with the utter shambles that was the Cosmopolis police force.

He was out on one such job tonight, waiting in the alleyway between Top Topper's Pizza Emporium and Zeke's Auto Shop. After careful research and planning he knew the local branch of Fatcat Banking was expecting a delivery at exactly 4.30am and their van (hopefully bulging with crisp dollar bills) would be passing the alley en route.

Pug usually worked alone as a) he didn't trust many people and b) he got to keep all the money he stole. But tonight was different and this is where the problems had started.

With Airbag Mick.

At first, Pug had assumed the nickname was nothing more than a playground tag that had stuck over the years, but as the night had worn on he had been left in no doubt as to the origins of his companion's unfortunate label. The introduction of Airbag Mick had come about like this – a friend of a friend had begged Pug to take Mick along on his next job, assuring him that despite still sporting his criminal 'L' plates he was a capable thief who just needed some professional guidance. Having been somewhat flattered Pug had accepted but, as they lay in wait for the van, he was already regretting his decision to bring along an amateur.

Belch!

"For Pete's sake kid! Can't you at least try to stifle them? That last one nearly took my head off!"

"Not really, it only seems to make it worse, they kinda build up inside me until I let off one almighty…"

"Alright, alright, just do your best to keep them to a minimum," Pug moaned, shaking his head in despair.

He was seriously considering putting an end to this nonsense by knocking his apprentice out cold when the sound of an approaching vehicle drifted into the night air. The two villains tensed – this was it. "OK, its show time kid, remember I just need

---

[†] The largest maximum-security prison facility in Cosmopolis populated by the very worst the criminal fraternity has to offer. Celebrity villains such as Max 'The Axe' McTavish and Improbable Jake, the man who single-handedly caused the Cosmo blackout of 2098 reside here. Unfortunately for them (and every other inmate) a trip to The Joint is often a one-way ticket.

you to cover me while I do the business. This is usually a non-lethal activity so don't go shooting anyone unless I'm in serious trouble, got it?"

Mick nodded and let out another burp.

Creeping to the entrance of the alley Pug spotted the headlights of a vehicle in the distance. This *had* to be the target vehicle; no-one drove around this neighbourhood at 3am unless they were a) drunk, b) lost, c) looking for some violence-based fun or d) driving a Fatcat Banking security van. He retrieved a handful of homemade 'spikers' from his knapsack, six inch nails that had been welded together so no matter how they came to rest there was always at least one pointing upwards. As the vehicle (a Fatcat Banking security van no less) drew nearer he flung them into the road, smiling as he watched them scatter over the tarmac. "Get ready!" he hissed.

As planned, the van drove straight over the makeshift spikes, puncturing three of its four tyres instantly and went into a violent skid. Pug broke cover and raced towards the van which had come to a halt about twenty yards away. "Come on!" he cried.

Airbag Mick bounded after him, brandishing his laser pistol and trying manfully not to burp himself into oblivion. Pug had done this a hundred times and went through the routine with controlled non-lethal aggression. He subdued the disgruntled driver with minimal effort then attached a small explosive device to the rear doors of the van.

Belch!

"Nice work Mr Tanner. I must say it's a lot easier than I had expected."

"Don't fool yourself kid," Pug replied, "it takes years of practice. You might wanna step back while I blow the doors."

They retreated a few yards and Pug flicked the switch on his remote detonator, blasting the doors wide open but leaving the contents of the van undamaged. "Fetch the sacks kid; it's time to make a withdrawal."

Belch!

Mick scurried back into the alley. This was great! He'd agreed a five per cent cut of the takings and hadn't really had to do anything. Pug meanwhile was grinning as he looked upon the neatly stacked bundles of dollar bills wrapped in clear packaging– another smooth operation he thought, pleased he had given his gaseous pupil a flawless demonstration of professional thievery. "Come on kid," he bawled without looking round, "we need to get a move on before someone sees us."

No reply.

"Kid?"

Pug turned back to the alley with a feeling of slight unease. What was keeping him?

Then he noticed the burping had stopped.

He withdrew his handgun and took a pace forward, his slight unease snowballing into acute anxiety.

"Kid you OK?"

Airbag Mick stumbled from the confines of the alley and he was far from OK. He was gagged and his hands were cuffed behind his back – something had clearly gone terribly wrong. That something was Captain Uno, the city's number one crime fighter and all round American hero. Pug nearly collapsed from shock when he saw the veteran superhero emerge from the shadows. At nearly seven feet tall with muscles *on top* of his muscles, the Captain was indeed an awesome sight. He wore his usual outfit, the bright red all in one suit with silver gloves, boots, cape and famous Zorroesque cowl. The words 'Numero Uno' were emblazoned across his impressive chest in silver stencil. The whole imposing ensemble sent its own message – 'I am not to be messed with.'

"My congratulations on a unique approach sir. Most people use cash points at this time of night," the Captain said, smiling from ear to ear.

Pug was speechless and failed to notice the gun had begun to tremble in his hand. He knew the Captain was impervious to laser blasts, indeed, he had no known weaknesses whatsoever, except perhaps a tendency to hog the limelight every time a camera was pointed his way and a passion for imported beer.

"Thi…this isn't how it looks Captain!"

A pretty lame opener but all he could think of under the circumstances.

"Really? Then what are you doing? Checking the van for illegal aliens?"

The terrified hijacker did the only thing he could and took a shot at the advancing hero. As expected, the laser bolt ricocheted off the Captain, destroying the bulb of a nearby lamppost in a shower of sparks. In all the confusion Pug failed to spot the Captain wincing in pain. "Come along sir, just put the gun down and turn yourself in, there's no need for any more trouble," his adversary grunted, recovering slightly.

Behind Captain Uno's bulk Pug could see Mick rolling around on the ground and he suddenly remembered what he'd said about stifling his burps. Was there really a chance this kid could blow up in one awful explosion of indigestion? Unlikely – but it was the only card he had to play – so he played it.

"Wait! There's something you need to know. That guy behind you is in danger of exploding at any minute!"

"Oh *please!*"

"No, I'm serious he has a…a…wind problem. He could die if you don't untie that gag! You wouldn't want that on your conscience would you? I mean look at him, he's only a young punk. I don't think 'Captain Uno leaves suffocating youth to die in agonising pain' would make a very palatable headline do you? "

True – this would put a serious downer on the Captain's reputation as a humanitarian and bad press was something he avoided at all costs. There were no camera-wielding reporters in the vicinity but at the end of the day Captain Uno did have a name to uphold – with or without media coverage. He couldn't just ignore Pug's claims, however absurd they sounded. Against his better judgement he turned to look at the writhing teenager. In fairness he did look to be in a significant amount of distress.

"Are you alright chum?" he asked politely.

Mick could only gurgle nonsensically, the way one does when in danger of spontaneously combusting.

He really *is* in trouble, the Captain thought, but he would have to deal with the older crook before he investigated further.

When he looked back Pug had vanished.

Then the van roared into life and, with its one good tyre, started to pull away. "Why do they always run?" the Captain muttered and launched himself skyward.

Pug cursed as he willed the crippled van to go faster. If he were caught now he'd slide to the bottom of the career ladder and no mistake. He'd go from 'professional hijacker' to 'street punk' in the blink of an eye. He whimpered as he glanced in his wing mirror to see the silhouette of the Captain in hot pursuit. Everyone knew he could fly at dizzying speeds and catching up with this one-wheeled rust-bucket would be a doddle. Still he floored the accelerator and was astonished to notice his pursuer struggling to keep pace. Was he toying with him? That smug git! Just because he had super powers didn't mean he had to rub peoples' noses in it. To add to his annoyance, large bundles of hard cash were dropping from the back of the van. What a nightmare! Even if he did manage to escape he'd have little or nothing to show for it. Running into the Captain had been catastrophic – evading the Captain would be sensational - but escaping empty-handed would sour the achievement.

The chase continued for another twenty seconds until Pug heard someone or something land on the roof of the van. It would've been nice if the sound had been nothing more than a piece of falling masonry from one of the ramshackle buildings he was driving past, but this just wasn't Pug's night. Moments later a red and silver shape appeared outside the windscreen completely blocking his view of the road. The Captain struggled awkwardly on the bonnet until he was facing the panic-stricken driver.

"See how you like this!" Pug screeched, activating the van's windscreen washer jet.

Soapy water sprayed into the Captain's face and the wipers (on the maximum speed setting) buffeted his face from side to side, but still he maintained his hold. Unable to see ahead, Pug stamped hard on the brakes in another effort to dislodge the caped hero. The van slewed to a halt and the Captain finally lost his grip. Pug watched in amazement as his adversary bounced along the road, coming to rest in a motionless heap about thirty feet away. The temptation to drive over him was almost overwhelming but Pug was too surprised to react. Was the invincible Captain Uno in trouble? Had he actually managed to *hurt* him? He wasn't about to go over and ask and sprang back into action, hopping out of the van and making his way to the rear, praying there was at least one pile of cash left.

There was.

He dragged it towards the doors, satisfied he would at least make *some* money out of tonight's debacle.

WHACK!

Pug Tanner went sailing inside the back of the van, helped in no short measure by Captain Uno's left fist. One punch was all it took and the thief's lights went out immediately. The Captain stood just outside the vehicle, his hands on his knees, his breath coming in rasping gasps.

It didn't used to be this difficult.

Captain Uno had been the premier crime-fighter in Cosmopolis for many glorious years. Superheroes, vigilantes, call them what you will, were virtually non-existent in America's capital, which was surprising considering the inadequacy of its police force. It seemed most citizens of the great city were perfectly happy with the crime rate and provided they didn't become victims, were content to let it fester unchecked – after all, weren't cops supposed to deal with this kind of thing?

Of course they were.

Yet amidst the internal corruption, insufficient training and dwindling recruitment, they made little impact and it came as no shock when, back in 2080, they had welcomed the arrival of Captain Uno with open arms. Here was someone with whom they could share the burden and he didn't even want paying. Mayor Strada had assured his people the escalating crime wave would recede with the introduction of the charismatic hero and he had been spot on. For the last twenty-five years the crime level had been significantly reduced, thanks mainly to the efforts of Captain Uno and his young sidekick Gibbon Boy, so named after his unusually long arms, who had joined forces with the Captain in 2091.

But even superheroes have a shelf life and Captain Uno was fast approaching his sell-by date. Now pushing fifty, he had to accept the facts. Coming face to face with a crime fighter who, after a fifty yard sprint, was on the verge of collapse wasn't going to deter anyone; even the meekest of criminals would fancy their chances. The outfit was becoming increasingly tight and he was leaving dents in things when he sat down. The incident with Pug Tanner had been a prime example. It was time to throw in the cape. Gibbon Boy had moved to the Hula Archipelago (formerly Hawaii) in search of fame, fortune and hula girls, unhappy at being in the Captain's shadow all these years and the crime rate was down to a reasonable level. There was bound to be another (younger) vigilante just around the corner ready to take his place.

Cornelius Bleek, Captain Uno's true identity, had made a ton of money as the people's champion. He hadn't meant to, it had just happened that way. Every corporation worth its salt had wanted to use him to advertise their brands and the endorsements had come rolling in. Captain Uno bubble-bath, the Vigilante veggie-burger, Hero energy drinks, the list was endless; you could even buy a hover car called the Numero Uno. As an example to potential crime fighters he had donated a sizeable chunk of his wealth to charity, or at least it appeared sizeable, it was actually only a fraction of his personal fortune. And why not? *He* was the one risking his neck every night for the good of the people, so what if he made a few bucks while he was at it? Consequently, he knew he would be able to retire to a life of financial comfort once his caped crusading days were over.

And now they were.

As he relaxed in his Jacuzzi, Cornelius reflected on what had been a remarkable twenty-five years. Obviously, being bullet proof, laser proof, able to fly and possessed of unearthly strength had been a big plus in his quest for justice, but at the end of the day he was still only one man and he had made quite an impression on the criminal underworld of Cosmo. He was undoubtedly the most popular man in the country too, with an army of devoted fans and his own website on the supernet. But nothing was forever, his powers had diluted with age and he was now far from his peak. In fact, he was actually looking forward to some peace and quiet, the chance to chill out for once and spend some quality time on his luxury yacht.

His thoughts turned to just how he would announce his retirement. Nothing too schmaltzy or extravagant, maybe a public announcement in Liberty Square, with the police commissioner and the mayor by his side. Yes, that would be fine; perhaps the Cosmopolis Symphony Orchestra should be there to play him a farewell tune? However he decided to do it, he just hoped there was someone else in line to protect the good people of this fine city once he was gone.

CHAPTER TWO

"We must accept finite disappointment,
but never lose infinite hope."

Martin Luther King Jnr.

Eric Dorfler and Hank Halo had been best buddies for a long time.
They'd grown up in the same neighbourhood, gone to the same high
school, dated the same girls (usually at different times) and had, for
the last nineteen years, worked together at the Shovelbutt Mining
Corporation on the outskirts of Cosmopolis.

Hank was the larger of the two, six feet tall, broad shouldered
and a little clumsy, shedding a few pounds wouldn't have done him
any harm either. A former cop, now thirty-eight, he worked as a
security guard, checking people in and out of the main gate, making
sure everyone had their passes and keeping a wary eye out for any
trouble. He also had sole control of the red and white barrier that
barred the entrance and although he didn't actually move it himself
he had the final word as to when it was lowered and raised – a
crucial responsibility and one of which he was immensely proud.
Eric, a year younger, was a little more 'hands on' and was employed
as a driller, spending his days wearing earplugs and vibrating on the
other end of a turbo-charged mining drill. At five-feet nine he was a
stocky figure, very solid with a crew cut and just the slightest hint of
an approaching beer belly. Neither man was particularly gifted or
ambitious; they were standard, hard working middle class chaps,
good natured, honest and reliable.

Both were ardent Captain Uno fans.

It was Wednesday night and the two chums were where they
always were on a Wednesday night – Smiling Larry's Smashbowl[†]
Alley.

"Do you really think he's gonna quit?" Eric asked seriously,

[†] Very similar to regular tenpin bowling except the pins are made of
glass. It's a bit messier, but lots of fun and a great stress reliever.

retrieving his ball from the shelf.

Hank took a slurp of his beer, taking care not to drip any on his Captain Uno T-shirt.

"That's the rumour."

Eric lined himself up with the skittles at the far end of the alley.

"I still can't believe it."

He flung the ball towards the waiting glassware, it veered off to the right and ended up in the gutter.

"Unlucky pal," Hank sympathised.

"See? It's even affecting my bowling! I haven't managed a strike all night."

He took a seat alongside his buddy and retrieved his beer bottle. "This is serious Hank, I mean, who's gonna protect the city when he goes?"

This would have been a good opportunity to have a dig at the abysmal police department but Eric knew Hank had once been a cop and thought better of it.

"Perhaps we should try and a get a petition going?" Hank suggested, "y'know try and get him to reconsider. I know dozens of guys from the mine who'd sign up right away."

Eric guzzled some of his beer. When it came to drinking, Eric was a guzzler, not a sipper or a swigger, when he put a beer bottle to his lips you knew he meant business. He scooped up another ball and took up his position once more. He was trailing by over thirty points and had to get a strike in soon or Hank would surge into an unassailable lead.

Focus, focus.

Concentrating hard he swung his arm back, his eyes never leaving the transparent pins. "Maybe he's lost his powers or something?" Hank said, thinking out loud.

It wasn't an intentional attempt to put off his opponent but it did the trick nonetheless and Eric's second ball went the same way as his first. He kicked at the floor in frustration.

"Oh Hank, we gotta do somethin' man, I can't stop thinkin' about it! Look at that – my first nil scoring frame of the night, now when was the last time I did that eh?"

"October, last year."

"Yeah but I was drunk then remember?"

He flopped down next to Hank. "It's your turn bud."

Hank exhaled loudly.

"I don't think I wanna play, Eric."

"What?"

"I dunno, I just don't feel like it, not after hearing about Cap."

"Hey come on big fella, it's only a rumour. You said so yourself."

Hank drained his bottle.

"Let's take a break for a while and get another beer," he suggested.

They tramped over to the bar, the alley echoing to the sounds of smashing glass and roars of triumph. Eric ordered two more beers, leaning with his back to the bar he said:

"I tell you what, if he *does* quit, there'll be a crime spree, mark my words. I'll have to get a security system for the house and everything."

Hank didn't reply, he was still trying to come to terms with the prospect of a 'Unoless' world.

Lucas, the bartender returned with their drinks.

"Hey, you guys hear about the Captain?"

Eric groaned;

"Yeah we heard Luke, thanks for reminding us."

"I can't believe he's gonna quit!"

"Yeah, *we heard* Luke!" Eric said angrily, whisking the bottles off the bar.

"Hey lighten up Eric; it ain't the end of the world you know."

Eric spun around to face him.

"That's true, but it may be the end of Cosmopolis!"

Hank joined the debate and tried to dilute the situation.

"We don't even know if he *is* going to retire yet, so why are we even arguing ab…"

He stopped mid-sentence, his attention fixed on the TV behind the bar, which was switched on but had the sound turned down. The others followed his gaze. They saw what looked like a public rally of some kind, as though someone were campaigning for president. A small stage had been erected at the entrance to City Hall and the steps below were crammed with paparazzi and spectators. Behind the microphones on the lectern stood Mayor Strada, Spencer Arkwright (the police commissioner) and Captain Uno.

"Turn it up! Turn it up!" Eric blurted out.

Lucas obliged and the three of them watched in silence. They caught the tail end of the mayor's speech;

"...and so it is with a heavy heart that I turn the floor over to the one and only Captain Uno, for what may well be the final time."

There was a round of applause and jubilant cheers from the audience as the Captain, in full costume, approached the mike. Eric and Hank were dumbfounded, their worst suspicions were about to be confirmed, they watched on open mouthed.

"Good people of Cosmopolis," the Captain began, "at first I was unsure exactly how to announce my retirement. But after careful consideration I decided to do it here, on the steps of City Hall – 'on the streets' as they say, which is where I have spent most of my time. I deliberated over my decision to step down for several days and can assure you it was not something I found particularly easy or indeed welcoming. As you know, I've devoted my life to protecting the citizens of this proud city..."

"Turn it off," Eric said glumly.

"No, I want to listen," Lucas replied.

Hank was familiar with Eric's short temper and managed to grab him just before he launched himself over the bar. Lucas stepped back a pace, quite taken aback by the stocky driller's reaction.

"Alright, come on, just leave it!" Hank said, wrapping Eric up in a bear hug and dragging him away from the bar area.

"Tell him to turn it off Hank! I don't wanna hear it!" he shrieked.

The rumpus was causing heads to turn their way and Hank decided it would probably be a good idea to get his friend outside before someone called security. Maybe the fresh air would calm him down a bit.

It didn't.

Eric's frustration continued in the car park.

When it came to controlling his emotions, Hank was far more accomplished than his pal and even though he was bitterly disappointed at the news of his hero's imminent farewell he managed to stop short of physical violence. Unlike Eric, who was busy giving the nearest garbage can a kicking it would never forget. Hank watched from a safe distance, waiting for the assault to subside, keeping one eye on the door in case the racket drew any unwanted attention. Being a fairly fit individual, Eric managed to keep up the onslaught for a good ten minutes.

"Finished?" Hank asked eventually.

Eric delivered one last kick to the trash can which now looked more like an oversized, metal apple core. He was bathed in sweat and still extremely angry;

"We gotta do somethin' Hank," he gasped. "We can't just let him retire, it'll be open season for the law-breakers, there'll be no-one to stop them!"

"I know but what can we do?"

It was a fair question and it temporarily stumped the irate driller.

"*I don't know*! But we have to do *something*! You know what they say 'when the Captain's in town the crime rate stays down and when the Captain's absent the villains are rampant'. Do you wanna see that, man? You want it to be like the old days when people were afraid to walk the streets?"

"Of course I don't! But we're just two regular guys Eric – what can we possibly do about it? Come on let's go back inside and finish our beers eh?"

Eric stamped on the ground like a child in the fit of a tantrum.

"No! I'm not! I'm going home and when I get there I'm gonna find some way of making sure the city doesn't fall back into the hands of the criminal underworld!"

He stormed out of the car park. Hank held his arms out in supplication,

"Eric!"

He'd seen these moods before – Eric would usually sulk for an entire evening and then be right as rain the next morning. But they were talking about Captain Uno here, it wasn't some trivial bowling incident or unpopular policy at work – it was serious stuff. There was little he could do right now though and he decided to let Eric cool off in his own good time.

He'd be OK in the morning.

Hopefully.

CHAPTER THREE

"I used to be Snow White, but I drifted."

Mae West

True beauty[†] was hard to find in a city as grubby and noxious as Cosmopolis. However, there was one place you could find it, a place where splendour and loveliness was virtually guaranteed.

The Annual Miss Cosmopolis Tournament.

Once a year a few exquisite diamonds emerged from the city's towering rubbish heap to compete for the coveted title and spread a little elegance amid the dreariness. For one night the public could forget the pollution, crime and general apathy of the capital and focus instead on the glitz and glamour of the most prestigious beauty pageant the US had to offer. This being Cosmopolis, corruption was rife and the contest was rarely concluded without some kind of controversy splashed across the tabloids the following day. Bribery, political voting, underage contestants, illegal beauty enhancing drugs – you name it, the Miss Cosmopolis Tournament had seen it all.

And so had Eve Tendril.

A former winner on no less than three occasions and the only woman to win three years running (2065, 2066, 2067). Her natural charm, angelic features, dazzling green eyes, glossy, curly black hair and svelte figure had been an instant hit with the public (and the judges) and she had swept all opposition aside. The final victory had been somewhat marred with various accusations of skullduggery, more specifically several alleged sightings of the beauty queen with one of the panel judges in a hotel renowned more for its reflecting ceilings than its classy clientele. Naturally, these

---

[†] I guess this all depends on our definition of 'beauty'. After all, some people find a cluster of lampposts beautiful and even have the audacity to call it 'art', so to save any confusion we're talking about physical beauty here.

unsavoury stories had been hotly denied and the scandal had died down over time as the story slipped from the front page to the back page to obscurity. After failing to win an unprecedented fourth consecutive title in 2068, Eve had stepped down from the tournament and gone in to business for herself.

The beauty business.

For a three times Miss Cosmo winner, selling cosmetics was never going to be too difficult and her company 'You Beauty' (based in Cosmopolis) flourished impressively. Most of the city's inhabitants were in need of a good 'scrub up' and, in an effort to look as stunning as Eve; they had flocked to her stores in droves, eager to sample the new products. Consequently, Eve had become immensely wealthy, a millionaire by the time she was thirty, a multi-millionaire by thirty-five.

She was due to turn sixty this year and, given sufficient preparation time, could still look more glamorous than women half her age. Her business empire was firmly established and 'You Beauty' was the undisputed leader in the cosmetics industry with a network of stores across the planet. Not bad for a girl who had started her working life behind the counter of a Gruesome Burger drive-thru.

But despite her bulging bank account and global fame Eve was not happy – not in the slightest. Being hailed as the most beautiful girl in Cosmopolis had been a truly amazing experience, that cool radiance that had engulfed her, the realisation she had been Number One, Top Dog, the crème de la crème. Since quitting the tournament no sensation had come close to those heady times and there was little doubt that somewhere within a void remained. To add to her frustration, she was getting older and both her looks and her figure were beginning to fade – not even her own merchandise could stop it and as time wore on she was becoming increasingly bitter about the whole issue.

It is true to say that all the money in the world cannot buy you happiness, but it's very good at buying *off* unhappiness and comes in handy when you want to buy your own private tropical island – which was exactly where Eve had decided to spend the rest of her life. Her residence, lavish in the extreme and in keeping with her glamour puss style, had been built from scratch to her exact specifications. As well as boasting all the usual trappings of the rich and famous such as a gymnasium, swimming pool, sauna, three tennis courts and really big telly, she had also insisted that a full sized cosmetics laboratory be constructed a few hundred yards away. Eve was no scientist by any stretch of the imagination, but she preferred to have her staff bring all new products to her for approval – air travel did not agree with her and the smog and grime of Cosmopolis played havoc with her complexion.

For peace of mind the island was patrolled by a dozen Korellian mercenaries (commonly known as crocs), tough, no-nonsense bipedal reptiles who, for the right price, would shoot anyone you told them to. In the absence of any realistic threat they kept themselves amused by taking pot-shots at the jungle gorillas – an activity the gorillas found particularly infuriating. Eve also employed an army of domestic staff, chefs, beauticians, physical trainers and cleaners who waited on her hand and foot. In short she lived a life of pure luxury on her modestly named Perfection Island, dining on exquisite (but low calorie) cuisine, sunning herself by the pool and annoying the staff with petty requests whenever she grew bored. Having handed over the reins to the board of directors she had minimal involvement with the day to day running of the company, preferring instead to spend her time leafing through beauty magazines or attending industry award ceremonies (when she was sure she would win something).

It was 10.00am on Thursday August 4th and she was still in bed, munching on lightly buttered crumpets and scanning the pages of Gorgeous Monthly. A smile spread across her face as she read the news that one of her rivals, Cosmo Cosmetics had filed for bankruptcy after being forced to recall their entire range of mascara – its most lucrative line. The article went on to explain how traces of pepper had been found in the product, causing terrible side-effects. Industrial sabotage was being blamed for the disaster and a full investigation was apparently underway. Eve giggled maliciously and took another bite of her crumpet, she wasn't concerned, her people covered their tracks too well. The rest of the news was fairly mundane, a new anti-wrinkle cream here, a fresh diet programme there. Until that is, she reached the Trade Ceremonies page.

She stopped chewing.

After re-reading the article to make sure she hadn't misinterpreted it, she threw back the bedclothes and began to get dressed. So excited was she, she didn't even bother applying any make-up and with a final check in the reflectogram bolted from the room. The magazine lay on the bed, where she had left it, still open at the page that had caused all the commotion. The headline read:

MISS COSMOPOLIS TOURNAMENT SHOCKER!
AGE RESTRICTIONS ABOLISHED FOR 2105 AS NEW
ORGANISERS CAUSE A STIR!
THINGS COULD GET UGLY!

CHAPTER FOUR

"Time may be a great healer, but it's a lousy beautician"

Anon

Dr Max Ticklegrit was a chemist, a very talented chemist; in fact he was something of a Superchemist. Given a half-decent laboratory he could make just about anything *from* anything, which could be used to do anything to anything or any*one*.

The first person to spot his flair for science had been Eugene Balderson, his fifth-grade chemistry professor. He had given the class a routine homework assignment – to write an essay on how they felt chemistry could be used to improve the world as a whole. The papers had been marked the following week and Eugene had been a little perturbed by Max's submission, in which he had made constant reference to 'poisons', 'explosives' and 'viruses'. Feeling the child would benefit from a one-to-one session, the professor had kept him late after school one day to offer him some guidance and to channel the boy's obvious talent down a more appropriate route.

Max had not enjoyed it.

Indeed, he had stormed out of the classroom when his teacher had dared to describe his efforts as 'potentially irresponsible'. Eugene had seen these kind of kids before, gifted but headstrong, more interested in gaining knowledge than wisdom and even though his little tête-à-tête had ended on a sour note he hadn't been too worried.

Until all his hair had fallen out two days later.

With a surname like Balderson it hadn't taken long for the kids (and some of the staff) to find a suitable nickname for the unfortunate professor and although he'd been unable to prove it, he'd had a good idea as to the identity of the culprit. But being duped by a ten year old was embarrassing and consequently the matter had never been officially discussed.

Scalping his science teacher was just the beginning in a long line of 'potentially irresponsible' incidents for Max. As he progressed through high school and then college he found the best way to settle scores with his foes was by using his chemicals – turning people albino, teeth dropping out, impotence, warts, Max had a seemingly inexhaustible repertoire at his disposal. He also had no friends, a trait that had continued into later life. Graduating in the top one per cent of his class he had found a job with relative ease, as a chemist for an up and coming new cosmetics company called 'You Beauty'. By 2077 he had become Head Chemist, responsible for overseeing the formulation of all new products and in 2081 he became the youngest director in the company's history other than Eve Tendril herself. But position and salary were secondary considerations in Max's life, he liked nothing better than tinkering about in his lab, concocting new (and often quite disturbing) formulae.

Aside from his duties as a director, Eve had asked him to head up a new department – a small team of people who would be in charge of hampering the competition. Max had called it the Industrial Disruption Department and he was tailor made for the job as it provided an outlet for his 'potentially irresponsible' side. The recent collapse of Cosmo Cosmetics for example, had been one of his projects.

His appearance was as unsettling as the potions he created. He was hunched from years standing over a microscope, gaunt and pale with a pair of rimless glasses perched precariously on his beak-like nose. His subscription to the crazed scientist look was completed by the wild tufts of grey hair that sprouted, seemingly at random, from his scalp. And of course, there was his prized 'white' lab coat, a garment he had worn religiously for the last twenty years which bore the stains and burns of countless experiments.

He had been summoned to Perfection Island for a private conference with Eve, a trip he had made several times in the past and one he always disliked. Max was not an outdoor kind of guy, the heat, the insects and particularly those lumbering Korellians really tested his patience. He exited the hover car on the landing pad where he was greeted by one of the loathsome crocs and frisked thoroughly. Not for the first time Max wondered what a good dose of his recently perfected Pipecleaner Special (an industrial laxative) would do to the reptile. Happy that Max was not here to assassinate his employer, the Korellian led him into the main building, heading for Eve's private office, a room she reserved for only the most secret meetings. As he shuffled down the corridor Max pondered what seed of industrial disruption she would be asking him to sow. A lipstick that promoted cold sores? Lice infested hair mousse? Her imagination was his ammunition.

They arrived at the office door and the croc loped off, unaware Max was making obscene gestures behind his back. He knocked once and then entered, fairly confident she hadn't asked him all the way out here to discuss share prices. Eve was leafing through a magazine, sat behind a black marble desk that could also be used as a runway.

"Good morning Miss Tendril," Max volunteered as pleasantly as he could.

"Sit," she replied without looking up.

Max knew the routine, sit down and wait until she was ready to get down to business. Despite relinquishing her overall control she was still the boss, it just annoyed him that she felt the need to prove it every time they met. He took a seat and waited patiently.

Eve thumbed through her magazine for another three minutes.

"Have you heard the news?" she asked eventually, still refusing to make eye contact.

Max interlocked his fingers across his stomach, sat back and beamed with pride.

"Why yes I have. Cosmo Cosmetics has gone belly up. A tidy operation if I may say so, I particularly liked the part about..."

Eve laid down her magazine and looked him in the eye for the first time.

"No, no! I mean the *real* news."

"The real news ma'am?"

"The tournament! Haven't you heard?"

It was 8.30am on Friday, twelve hours ahead of Cosmopolis time; Max had had time for a cursory glance through the Cosmopolis Prattler during the flight, a coffee, a breakfast muffin and little else.

"Tournament?"

She gave a sigh of disapproval.

"Really Max you must pay more attention to your trade journals. I take it you're aware the Miss Cosmopolis Tournament has new organisers this year?"

At last she was talking about something he knew about.

"Of course, that outrageous publicity company from across the pond – oh what are they called? Ah yes, Out for the Lads & Co Ltd isn't it?"

"That's right, a rather crude outfit but do you know what they've gone and done?"

"Well if their most recent public event is anything to go by they've probably insisted on an all nude final."

Eve gave a short laugh.

"Nothing quite that drastic, Max. They've abolished the age restrictions."

The Superchemist was becoming irritated – what had this to do with him? There were important viruses awaiting his attention back at the Cosmopolis lab.

"So?"

"I'm going to enter."

"You're *what*?" he gasped, sitting bolt upright.

Had she lost her marbles? Age restrictions or not she didn't stand a chance, yes she was still very glamorous but against a group of late teens and twenty-somethings she'd be annihilated.

"Is that a problem?" she asked innocently.

Max fidgeted in his chair, he didn't like this one bit. Surely she realised the futility of it all, even if she didn't, he wasn't going to be the one to tell her. Eve Tendril's obsession with her own beauty was a well documented fact. She had even been known to fire people for commenting on the attractiveness of other women and Max enjoyed his job.

"No, there's no problem ma'am. I was just a little surprised, that's all."

"Why should you be surprised?"

The conversation was steering itself towards a cliff edge and Max desperately searched for a reverse gear as the room became decidedly warmer. Why was she pressing him so persistently?

"Er…I meant I was pleasantly surprised."

A look of concern spread across Eve's face.

"Are you thinking I can't win?"

Max groaned inwardly – he'd been expecting a new assignment, some devilish new scheme to bring down another rival. But this was turning into a disaster. What on earth did she want him to say? Conversation was not his strong point; he spent most of his time in a sterile, glass lab where the only banter was with himself.

He continued to squirm.

"Did I say that? I didn't say that did I? I'm sure you'll do very well."

"But you don't think I'll win do you?" she said narrowing her eyes.

What a nightmare!

"Ma'am I think you'll win comfortably," he lied, "in fact I wouldn't be…"

He stopped short as Eve suddenly smiled at him.

"You always were a supreme boot-licker Max. You don't think I've got a cat in hell's chance do you? And I agree with you."

"Ma'am?" he asked carefully, not sure if this was still some trick.

"Come on Max, if I were competing with women my own age then yes, I'd probably have a good chance but next to the cream of Cosmopolis beauty we both know I'd be a non-starter. It'd be like pitting the Peabody Tantrums[†] against the Rocksteady Raiders[*]."

Max couldn't quite believe his ears; he'd never heard Eve admit there were people out there more beautiful than her. Was she toying with him? Waiting for him to agree so she could fire him? He chose his words cautiously.

"What exactly are you trying to say Miss Tendril?"

"I'm saying I'm going to need some help if I'm to be crowned Miss Cosmopolis 2105 – and that's why you're here."

Max nearly slid off his chair with relief.

[†] The most inept team in the Bloodball league, perennial underachievers and relegation specialists.
[*] The current Bloodball champions and home of Slikkish Brillian, the greatest man to ever play the game.

CHAPTER FIVE

"All great ideas are dangerous."

Oscar Wilde

It took Eric a full two days to shrug off his sulk which, in an irrelevant coincidence, is the same amount of time it takes to shrug off a hangover when you've drunk too much Oska – a mind-bendingly potent alcoholic beverage.

Captain Uno had indeed retired despite his website receiving a flood of pleas from devoted fans and, with the job of maintaining law and order now back in the incapable hands of the Cosmopolis police dept, the crime spree had begun in earnest.

Hank hadn't even bothered trying to converse with his chum, he knew it was pointless and it wasn't until 5.11pm on Friday that Eric finally spoke to him. As usual all the workers were in a good mood. It was Friday afternoon, they'd finished their shift, been paid and were looking forward to the weekend. Hank, having given the order for the red and white barrier to be left up, waited by the main gates, trying to pick Eric out of the stampede. Their weekly routine was carved in stone and Friday night was boozing night, a chance for he and Eric to discuss the world over a few gallons of beer with perhaps an occasional Mindscrew* chaser - if they were feeling fruity.

"Over here big guy."

Hank spun round to see his squat pal stood behind him. The sulking session was clearly over; in fact he looked positively overjoyed about something. Fair enough it was Friday afternoon but not even the arrival of the weekend could make someone *that* happy.

"Hey bud, glad to see you've snapped out of it."

"Out of what?"

---

* Another potent alcoholic beverage but not quite on the same scale as Oska, i.e. you can still speak after downing two or three glasses.

"That mood you were in."

"Oh that! Yeah well, I've sorted it all out now."

Hank couldn't believe the change, he was absolutely *buzzing*. "Straight to Angelo's[†] is it?"

"Er...sure."

"Come on then, let's get movin'. It's chugging time and I'm buyin'."

"Are you OK Eric?" Hank asked tentatively.

"Never better bud, never better. Come on, I'll tell you all about it once I've got a beer in my hand."

Like most drinking establishments on a Friday evening, Angelo's was heaving, jammed wall to wall with punters revelling in that great Friday feeling. It was quite warm, in a smoggy kind of way, so Hank and Eric grabbed their usual table just outside the entrance. They could still hear the music and there was always the chance of witnessing some exciting street crime which provided an extra bonus. They sat back in their seats, waiting for Maria to arrive – not having to queue at the bar and having your own personal table were perks of being regular customers and they'd been coming here at 6pm every Friday for many years.

"So what's up?" Hank asked.

Eric smiled mischievously.

"Ah not yet bud, let's get a drink first."

Sure enough Maria appeared, extracting herself from the seething crowd inside. She too was beaming, but then again she always was – it enhanced her natural beauty and could easily render the average man speechless. Having spotted the two friends from the bar she had already brought two ice cold beers with her. This really was service with a *big* smile.

"Hi fellas. Gorgeous evening eh?" she said jovially, plonking the bottles down in front of them.

"Hi Maria," Eric replied giving her a wink, "you're looking even lovelier than usual tonight – new lipstick?"

"Why yes it is – new chat up line?"

"Did you like it?"

"I'd give it eight out of ten."

[†] Hank and Eric's favourite pub, cheap booze, good music and gorgeous Maria Valentino, the world's friendliest barmaid.

"If I ever get a perfect ten will you finally let me take you out to dinner?"

"If you get a ten you'll find out," she giggled and waltzed back into the pub.

"Groovy!"

Eric's all-time high score was nine and a half, which he had attained in 2102 following a remarkably astute observation about Maria's new shoes. Hank had watched the exchange in silence. He hadn't seen Eric this happy since they'd knocked the Scooby Brothers out of the State Smashbowl semi-finals two years ago.

"Alright, you've got your beer so what's going on?"

Eric took a long guzzle; draining two thirds of his bottle in one go, as all good guzzlers do.

"Well Hank old buddy," he said suppressing a burp, "I've been giving a lot of thought as to what we can do about the Captain's retirement. I trust you've already seen the papers? Cosmopolis hit by new crime wave and all that?"

Hank nodded then swigged his beer.

Since Captain Uno had stepped down almost every form of illegal activity had gone through the roof, there had even been the odd case of Pet-napping†, a crime most people had believed to be extinct.

"You're never gonna get him to change his mind Eric. You saw the speech; he's quit – for good."

Eric looked around him as though he were concerned about eavesdroppers, leaning close, his voice no louder than a whisper he said:

"I'm not thinking of reinstating him, I'm thinking more about…"

He double-checked the tables nearby – no-one was listening.

"…*replacing* him."

"Replacing him!" Hank cried.

"Alright, alright shush!!" Eric spluttered raising his hands to calm his friend down.

---

† Kidnapping the pets of rich people and holding them to ransom. The last known case occurred in 2078 when veteran movie star Jemima Shanks paid $2,000,000 for the safe return of her favourite goldfish Nero. Ironically, Nero died a week later at the hands of Delilah, Jemima's cat. What happened to Delilah is still a mystery.

Hank was getting drawn into the secrecy thing and he too leaned forward.

"Who are you gonna replace him *with*? Gibbon Boy's done a runner and the other few are just amateurs looking to make a name for themselves."

Eric took a deep breath.

"Well...I thought...*we* could do it. You and me."

For a moment Hank said nothing – he was too staggered to speak. Then he threw back his head and roared with laughter, quite unaware that Eric was grim-faced. He slapped the flat of his hand down on the table.

"Oh Eric, that's priceless man! Hank Halo and Eric Dorfler the dynamic duo!"

He went into another fit of guffawing.

"I'm serious Hank," Eric said evenly.

But his words were smothered by the raucous laughter.

"The Mighty Eric and his mythical laser drill!"

He was clutching his sides now and in danger of falling off his perch.

"I'm serious Hank!" Eric said a little louder, his anger on the rise.

Maria returned with another two beers.

"Two more cold ones, guys," she smiled.

She placed them on the table and was about to leave when Hank grabbed her arm.

"Hey Maria, do you think I'd look good in a cape?"

He cracked up in another side-splitting convulsion.

Eric's temper snapped.

"*I'm serious Hank!*" he screamed, slamming his bottle down with a bang.

Now nearby people *were* starting to listen in.

"Hey cool it fellas," Maria soothed, "I know it's hot but there's no need to get all irregular."

"Stay out of this Maria!" Eric snarled.

For the first time in nearly six years Maria's smile vanished.

"Fine! I will. And you can get your own beers from now on!"

She stormed off in a huff, the tray under her arm, her nose in the air.

Hank meanwhile had recovered from his hysterics and was staring at Eric in disbelief.

"There's no need to take it out on her, man! What's your problem anyway? You can't be serious about this superhero lark."

"I'm deadly serious!"

Fighting to keep the smile from his face Hank adopted a more rational (if a tad sarcastic) approach.

"Mate, I hate to be the one to tell you, but neither of us have any super powers. We're just regular people."

Eric took a gulp of his ale.

"OK forget it. I'll do it by myself."

He'd gone into spoilt brat mode.

"Eric – think it through will ya? We have no experience with this kinda thing."

"You used to be a cop!"

"That's different, cops are trained professionals (that was a laugh) they operate inside the law, they aren't vigilantes. And they can't fly!"

Eric folded his arms and looked away.

"So be it. You've made your decision, if you're too scared to be part of the Avenging Knights then that's fine."

"Avenging Kni…? Eric what are you *talking about*?"

"Sorry, I can't tell you now, it's a secret."

He drained his beer and stood up.

"Where are you goin'?"

"I've had quite enough of this conversation and quite enough of you Hank Halo. I'm going home. I'll see you on Monday."

"But what about Sunday night poker?"

"I'm gonna be busy. You'll have to find another partner."

Hank couldn't believe things were getting so out of hand.

"Eric, sit down and stop being such a baby!"

But Eric was very upset and equally determined. He tossed a few crumpled dollar bills on to the table.

"There's a couple of extra bucks in there for Maria, apologise to her for me will ya?"

And then he walked off, just as he had done in the car park a few nights ago, leaving Hank to digest the last few minutes. He sipped at his beer for a good forty-five minutes, wondering how on earth he was going to talk Eric out of his madcap idea. The very thought of them becoming crime-fighters was utterly ridiculous.

"Gone has he?"

Hank jumped as Maria came up behind him.

"Yeah, he's sulking. He asked me to tell you he's sorry for snapping at you by the way."

"What's eating him?"

Unsure whether he should reveal Eric's crazy plot Hank paused for a second. But then again, she really hadn't deserved to be spoken to like that.

"He's got some ludicrous idea about becoming a superhero."

Maria's winning smile returned.

"A what?"

"I know it's nuts isn't it? He wants me to be one too."

She was laughing now, the kind of laugh where it's hard to distinguish between genuine amusement and ridicule.

"*You*? A superhero?"

Ridicule – no doubt about it.

"Yeah, well you don't have to go on about it," Hank said feeling uncomfortable.

"Honey if you two become superheroes I'll take you *both* out to dinner!"

She melted back into the crowd, giggling to herself.

CHAPTER SIX

"No sensible decision can be made any longer without taking into account not only the world as it is, but the world as it will be."

Isaac Asimov

Life changing events sometimes hang on insignificant details. Details which, at the time seem completely trivial can often trigger far-reaching, momentous results. "If I'd had the cheeseburger instead of the kebab then I'd never have invented the particle bulb," – stuff like that. In this case, if Hank had caught a cab home from Angelo's instead of walking, the rest of his evening (and life) may have been very different. Not only would he have missed three separate street crime incidents (none of which he could do anything about) but he would also have returned to his apartment to find it as he had left it. Instead he had turned the corner into his street to be greeted by the ominous flashing of blue and red lights.

A Cosmopolis Police Dept patrol car was parked outside his apartment building – the Cliffhanger Cloudscraper. This could mean only one of two things, either the cops were lost and had stopped to ask directions or a crime had been committed in the vicinity some eight hours ago. He saw a cop stood at the entrance to the building smoking a cigarette and as he drew closer he realised it was none other than Murphy O' Flinn, an old pal from his days on the force.

"Hey Murph, what's up?"

Murphy crushed his cigarette underfoot (a blatant violation of the recently implemented littering laws) and shook hands, a big smile on his face.

"Hank! Buddy! Long time no see. How's the security guard business?"

"Oh not bad, fairly quiet – what's going on here?"

Murphy withdrew his notebook and flipped over a few pages as if he'd completely forgotten why he was here.

"Er...burglary. Real mess too, in fact it's more of a burglary/vandalism deal really."

"Which apartment?"

"Seven forty-six."

Hank was aghast.

"Murph! That's *my* apartment!"

"Is it?"

"Didn't you run the address through the database?"

"No...er...I'm still waiting for my database training. Well...er...bad luck bud, they've taken almost everything. I've got a forensics droid up there now checking for prints."

Hank leaned against the side of the building and gave a long sigh of frustration – he had finally become a victim of the escalating crime wave. Murphy, on the other hand, seemed completely indifferent. "Hey did you hear we raided the Cosmo Glue Corporation last night? Very exciting. Apparently they were bribing the government to ease up on legislation regarding toxic glue fumes."

"Arrest anyone?"

"A few, but it's unlikely we'll be able to make any of it stick!"

Murph slapped his thigh and laughed out loud, impressed with his own razor-wit humour.

"Murph I've just been burgled, I'm not really in the mood for jokes."

"Oh sorry Hank. Look, I know it's a bit late now but I recommend you get yourself one of those new burglar alarms, y'know the ones that you hook up to the electrified doormat?"

"Thanks Murph, I'll do that."

Their conversation was interrupted by the arrival of the forensics droid, tool kit in hand.

"Anything?" Murphy asked.

"I have scanned the entire apartment for prints and have only found those belonging to the occupant. The burglar forced the door using a crowbar and, judging by the graffiti, may have recently graduated from art college."

"OK well done, get back in the patrol car," Murphy replied.

He stuffed his notebook back into his pocket and clapped Hank on the shoulder.

"Well old buddy, looks like another case for the 'unsolved' pile."

"What? That's it? Aren't you gonna go up there and search for clues?"

"Are you kidding?" Murphy almost laughed. "What if the

burglar's still lurking around up there? Besides, the droid's checked it out and they don't often get it wrong, they're pretty sharp."

"Really? Then why is he trying to get into that ice-cream van?"

Murph whirled round. Sure enough the droid was attempting to open the door to one Signor Vanelli's ice-cream truck parked just behind the patrol car.

"It's this one you dope!" he blurted out, pointing to his car.

The droid mumbled an apology and clambered inside. "Look, I'll send a burglary expert over just for old times sake, that OK?"

"Yeah sure," Hank grumbled, knowing it would take at least a week for the 'expert' to arrive – if he ever came at all. He grunted a goodbye to Murphy and went inside.

"Some people," the cop said to himself walking back to his vehicle, "they never appreciate anything you do for 'em."

Murphy had been right – it was a mess. It looked like he'd just hosted a party for Irresponsible Hedonists Anonymous. Furniture was upended and smashed, graffiti (colourful and obscene) covered the walls and most of his electrical goods were gone. Even his bowling trophies had been taken, which annoyed him intensely. He stood and surveyed the carnage, hands on hips, shaking his head, wondering just where to start the clean-up operation, unaware his Dust-Zucker vacuum cleaner had also been swiped. For several silent minutes he just stood there and then, after a lengthy mental tussle, he went in search of the phone.

Thankfully it was still in working order, although he gave it a good clean first as he'd found it in the toilet bowl. He dialled and waited.

"Hi Eric it's me. Look, don't hang up! I need to talk to you. Can I come over now?"

A minor win on the inter-galactic lottery back in 2099 had enabled Eric to slip into that elite ten per cent of Cosmopolis citizens who actually owned a house. It wasn't big or fancy, just a semi-detached property, but it meant he didn't have to use elevators or share bathrooms and he was a good fifteen miles from the city centre where most of the criminals strutted their stuff. Naturally, he hadn't let the money go to his head and had ploughed a large portion of it into his modest abode.

It was past midnight by the time Hank arrived, he was greeted at the front door by Sixpack, Eric's well-weathered service droid. Unlike home ownership, droid ownership was quite common in 2105, many people had service droids to run their daily chores and a good second hand model could cost as little as one hundred dollars. Sixpack had been put up for sale after his former master had decided to upgrade and Eric had snapped him up for a very reasonable price. His original sunburst yellow paintwork had darkened over the years and the oil stains from his time under Eric's clapped out van had combined to give his exterior the look of an over-ripe banana. The blotched and slightly dented droid stood just over six feet tall with slender limbs and a variety of domestic appliances concealed about his person. His tinted anti-glare visor had jammed several months ago and was permanently activated, from a distance it looked as if he were wearing enormous sunglasses on his tubular head and, up close, gave the droid an air of menace. Until that is, he opened his mouth – Sixpack was quite possibly the most well-spoken service droid in the city.

"Good evening sir, please come inside."

"Is the 'shoes off' rule still in force?" Hank asked, crossing the threshold.

"Sir?"

"Do I still have to take my boots off?"

"Oh yes sir, the master is still very keen on household hygiene."

He slipped off his boots and waited in the kitchen while Sixpack went to find Eric. Deep down he harboured a smidgen of envy at Eric's home, he didn't begrudge him a single dollar of his lottery win, but whenever he came here it reminded him just what a dump *his* place was. He wondered if he'd always be an elevator user and a bathroom sharer. Eric appeared at the end of the hallway, the hostility was still there.

"So what's so important you have to come and see me in the middle of the night?" he asked, hands on hips.

"Calm down Eric, I'm actually here to discuss your idea."

"That's a bit of U-turn isn't it?"

"Yeah well, quite a lot's happened since then. Can we sit down and talk?"

Eric's tone softened.

"Of course, come into the lounge. Sixpack! Two cold ones for me and my friend here."

The droid made for the fridge as Hank and Eric went through into the sitting room. They sat opposite each other in Eric's comfy armchairs. "So what's changed your mind?" he asked.

"I've just been burgled."

Eric slapped his hand against the arm of the chair, genuinely upset.

"Aw dang man! I'm sorry to hear that!"

"It's not just the burglary though Eric. You were right, since Cap threw in the towel all hell's broken loose."

Eric knew this wasn't the time for the 'I told you so' speech so he focused on the positive.

"At least *you're* OK bud."

"Yeah I guess so."

Sixpack entered the room carrying two choc-ices.

"Beers Sixpack! – I meant *beers*!"

"I do apologise sir, two beers it is," he said hurrying from the room.

"Still having trouble with the slang then?" Hank asked, smiling.

"Yeah, but I think I've figured out why. I did some digging and traced his original owner; turns out he was the property of some university guy, an English literature professor no less. Seems he picked up the posh lingo. But don't worry I'm workin' on it. So you wanna be one of the Avenging Knights do you?"

Hank put his hands up.

"Whoa! One thing at a time man. I didn't come here to give you an unconditional 'yes'. I just want to know more about your plan."

Sixpack returned with the correct refreshments.

"Six could you fetch my *secret* folder please?" Eric asked, looking very pleased with himself.

"Secret folder sir?"

"Yeah, the one on top of the fridge."

"Certainly sir."

Hank looked surprised.

"You've got an entire folder?"

"Oh yes, I've been busier than you might think bud."

The secret folder in question, an A4 box file to be exact, arrived and Eric opened it up. "I've split it into different sections to make things easier. We've got Names, Costumes, Vehicles, Headquarters and Weapons – where do you wanna start?"

CHAPTER SEVEN

"If you have a talent, use it in every which way possible.
Spend it lavishly, like a millionaire intent on going broke."

Brenda Francis

While Hank and Eric were leafing their way through the Avenging Knights file thousands of miles away, Eve Tendril's plan to manipulate the 2105 Miss Cosmopolis Tournament was beginning to take shape.

The rules of the tournament were relatively straightforward. After an initial screening, accompanied by the usual flood of bribes, the hopefuls would be whittled down to just fifteen. Interviews would then be held to assess each contestant's attitude (as if that had anything to do with how beautiful you are), a process which would once again be rife with efforts to influence the judges. Finally, after disappointing a further five contenders, the televised final would be held between the ten most beautiful (and well-adjusted) women in the city. By attempting to add some spice to this year's show with the abolition of the age restrictions, the new organisers had made a rod for their own backs. Basically, if you were female and had been born in Cosmopolis you were in. As a result, tens of thousands of applications had been received and the staff at Out for the Lads & Co Ltd were already questioning the wisdom of their new ploy. Luckily for Eve they had decided not to meddle with the rule that allowed former winners to progress straight to the interview stage without having to be vetted.

Her plan was both simple and complex. Simple in theory (all she had to do was discredit the other contestants) and complex in practice (she had to do so without raising suspicion). Much to his annoyance, Max had been ordered to remain on the island and had been beavering away in the lab facility for the last twenty-eight hours. He was still not even close to creating the revolutionary beauty enhancing drug she had demanded although some specially requested chemicals were being flown in. Eve's attention had therefore switched to the likely finalists and this is where Cyrus Zifford entered the fray. She made a point of surrounding herself with gifted individuals, Max being a perfect example. Cyrus' particular field of excellence was deceit, dishonesty and treachery, indeed he was known throughout the company as Judas by many of the staff. Obviously he put these skills to work *against* rivals of 'You Beauty' whilst remaining ironically loyal to Eve and the directors. If you wanted to dig up some dirt on someone or blackmail them with a horrific secret from their past then Cyrus was your man. After Max, he was probably the last man in the company you would want to cross swords with.

Unlike Max however, Cyrus benefited from a healthy charisma, a disarming magnetism that he used to devastating effect – most people (particularly women) were too busy admiring his movie star good looks and immaculate designer suits to realise they were being fleeced. He had been with 'You Beauty' for over nine years and was pushing for a place on the board, which would be some achievement for a thirty year old, especially one with no formal qualifications to his name - at least none he had attained honestly.

He too had been whisked away from Head Office in Cosmopolis and was making his way down the corridor to Eve's private office on Perfection Island, the ever-present Korellian security guard plodding along by his side. Having graduated from the school of charm, guile and wit Cyrus didn't have much time for these reptilian brutes, he regarded violence as a last resort and if the fists *did* begin to fly he was quite adept at talking someone else into getting hit on his behalf.

"Nice uniform," Cyrus said casually as they padded down the corridor.

The camouflage-patterned combat fatigues could hardly be described as nice, especially when they were wrapped around something as unpleasant as a Korellian – but it was conversation. The croc grunted a response, which sounded like a thank-you. "Been working here long?"

"Just under two years," the croc growled.

Cyrus gave a sharp intake of breath – the kind you hear from a builder after you've asked him the cost of a loft conversion.

"Nearly finished then?" he said.

"Finished?"

49

"Well, Miss Tendril never keeps her island staff for more than a couple of years. It's a strict rotation policy she has, sticks to it rigidly apparently."

"Yeah but…"

"Still, big beefy guy like you is probably ready for some proper work eh? Getting paid a small fortune for lounging around in paradise all day must be a real bore for you, I mean it's not as if the place is overflowing with excitement and danger is it? This beautiful warm climate, the sun on the sea every day, comfy lodgings, nice food – dear me, you must be sick of it."

Korellians weren't the sharpest knives in the drawer and were not renowned for their intelligence. It was as if progression had decided to skip their species, indeed most crocs just assumed evolution was something that happened to other people and although this one was not as blunt as your average croc, he was still completely unaware he was about to open an account with the Cyrus Zifford Bank of Favours.

"Oh…er…well it's not so bad," the croc stammered, "I've had worse jobs."

Worse jobs?

Who was he trying to kid? This was a dream ticket. His wages were fantastic, indeed it would only be another three or four years before he'd be able to retire in relative comfort. As for the job itself – it was a doddle; no-one seemed remotely interested in bothering his generous employer. Cyrus continued to act casual – so, he was going for the bluff was he?

"Yeah, at least you've got a couple more months to enjoy it."

If crocs had one weakness (apart from their under-developed brains) it was their love of money, they idolised it above all else and the prospect of his income drying up in two months was making the security guard very uneasy. The office door was less than thirty paces away, he had to do something fast. Cyrus decided to apply a little extra pressure and began to whistle merrily.

"Actually," the croc said, slowing his pace a little, "I quite like it here."

"Really?"

"Yeah really. I don't suppose there's anything you could do is there?"

"Do?"

"Well, you've worked for Miss Tendril for a while haven't

you? Couldn't you, y'know, like put in a good word for me?"

Cyrus frowned but he was smiling on the inside – candy from a baby, he thought to himself as they reached the door.

"I'll see what I can do."

"Thanks Mr Zifford, I'd really appreciate it if you could extend my contract or something, even if it's only for another six months."

Most Korellians had a reputation throughout the universe as gruff, surly types with notoriously short fuses; when a Korellian voiced an opinion most people agreed with it, if they valued their health. In the space of sixty seconds Cyrus had wrapped this violent hulk around his little finger with the minimum of fuss.

"Leave it with me; I'll give it a shot."

The croc extended a meaty claw and shook hands.

"Thank you Mr Zifford, anything you need while you're on the island just let me know, Danzo's the name, Danzo Stax, I'm head of security."

"Alright Danzo, I'll be in touch."

He allowed himself a wry smirk as he watched the dull-witted Korellian, already overdrawn, lope off down the corridor, then he knocked on the door once and stepped inside.

CHAPTER EIGHT

"Nothing is particularly hard if you divide it into small jobs."

Henry Ford

Now that he had actually got Hank to listen to his idea in full, Eric was acting like a child with a new toy. He was supremely confident that after his friend had seen all the effort he'd put in he would be unable to refuse such a thrilling proposal. The fact neither of them had any experience of superheroism didn't deter him one jot – everyone had to start somewhere.

Knowing they could well be discussing the plan into the early hours, Eric had offered Hank a room for the night, which he'd gratefully accepted – after all, his own place was not exactly in five-star condition. Sixpack had been dispatched to the twenty-four hour mini-mart for some munchies and more beer although Eric had made it clear he didn't want their meeting to degenerate into a boozing session – for once the beer would be for refreshment, not inebriation.

They hunched over the coffee table as Eric turned to page one headed up Names. He took a slug of his beer.

"I thought we'd call ourselves the Avenging Knights."

Hank said nothing, just raised his eyebrows. "Y'see knights are bold, noble, tend to champion causes and are generally perceived as 'good guys'."

"Unless you're a black knight."

"That's true, but we're not going to be dressed in black, we'll come to that in the Costumes section anyway. The avenging part sounded cool cos...well...we're avenging all the victims aren't we? In fact now you've been burgled it's even more appropriate."

"Avenging Knights sounds good," Hank nodded.

He was beginning to warm to the idea a little but still had serious reservations about their own abilities, namely their complete lack of any super powers.

Eric leaned back in his armchair looking very happy with himself, the way you do after a particularly satisfying break of wind.

"Hank," he said with a wry grin, "do you have any idea how cool this is gonna be?"

"Cool?"

"They're gonna have to build extra prisons cos of us! Plus, we're gonna be invited to the very best parties, the Superheroes Ball, the Vigilante Awards. We're gonna be neck-deep in babes just begging for autographs."

"Is that why you're doing this Eric? To go to parties and get amongst the babes?"

He was well aware of Eric's terrible weakness for pretty girls, indeed, he was the only guy Hank knew who could get whiplash whilst driving when a babe wandered past. He sincerely hoped this wasn't Eric's only motivation - although he could think of worse reasons.

"Of course not. But it's a nice perk don't you think?"

Hank frowned disapprovingly and Eric decided to press on with the matter at hand. "Anyway, the Avenging Knights is just the group name, we have to have our own individual names too."

"Have you had any ideas on indiv..."

Hank stopped short as Eric turned the page to reveal two lists of names.

"I'm pretty sure I know which one I want for myself but see which of these peels your banana," he beamed, sliding the folder over to Hank. The list read as follows:

- Sir Hankalot (ties in nicely with knights theme)
- Hank the Tank
- The Hankinator
- The Crimson Crusader (see Costumes section)
- The Purple Paladin (see Costumes section)
- Stormy Knight
- Rough Knight

Hank scrutinised the list.

"Can I pick one of my own?" he asked, without really engaging his brain.

Eric looked crestfallen.

"Don't you like any of mine?"

He had obviously spent a significant amount of time on this

project and Hank didn't want to ruin things at the first hurdle.

"Well, I kinda like Rough Knight, but I don't think we should use our real names anywhere, after all, most superheroes have secret true identities don't they?"

"Good point," Eric said, perking up. He withdrew a notebook and pen and began scribbling down some notes. "So we'll put you down as Rough Knight for the moment then, unless you can come up with anything you like more, yeah?"

Hank nodded and then asked;

"What name did you choose for yourself?"

Sitting upright, Eric placed a fist across his chest and held his chin high.

"Sir Prize!"

Unfortunately, he caught his friend mid-swig, causing an unexpected jet of beer to shoot his way as Hank laughed and choked at the same time. "What's so funny?" Eric demanded angrily, wiping the beer from his face.

Hank had to think on his feet, which luckily for him, was not something he found difficult.

"It's just such a *great* name! Sir Prize as in 'surprise', which of course it would be if you were confronted by two mine workers in superhero outfits – wouldn't it?"

Just a bit.

The tension melted and Eric smiled again, he was clearly very proud of his new name, although Hank couldn't help thinking 'Sir Real' would have been more appropriate.

"Groovy! So – it's Rough Knight and Sir Prize, the Avenging Knights of Cosmopolis, now we just need to think up a name for Sixpack."

"Sixpack!"

"Yeah, he's our third member."

"Have you told him yet?"

"I've kind of mentioned it to him," Eric replied uneasily, which suggested he'd done nothing of the sort.

"Why do you wanna drag...er...bring Sixpack into this? He's got even less experience than we have!" Was it possible to have less than zero experience? "What's he gonna do – hoover them into submission? He doesn't know the difference between beer and ice-cream."

"I thought he'd be useful as back up and don't knock him, he's more resourceful than you think. I can probably swipe a few sheets of reinforced plasti-steel from the mine too, make him virtually bullet-proof and of course he'd be able to drive the Silver Steed."

"The *what*?"

"The Silver Steed - our transportation. It's not really silver but after a good polish it'll look like it, anyway we're jumping on to the Vehicles section and we mustn't get ahead of ourselves."

Hank was dumbfounded and could only stare at his colleague in complete bewilderment. Had he spiked his beer? Or was this all *really* happening?

"...of calling him Excalibot."

Poor old Hank was still reeling from the Silver Steed comment, his mind swamped with images of a giant metal horse galloping round the streets of Cosmopolis.

"Sorry?"

"Sixpack – I was gonna call him Excalibot."

Trying to focus on one thing at a time Hank replied;

"Surely Sixpack doesn't need a nickname, after all he's a droid isn't he? He won't mind if people know his real name."

"But they could trace him back to us Hank, there can't be too many droids in this city called Sixpack can there?"

The truth was Sixpack was the *only* droid in Cosmopolis called Sixpack so Eric had been spot on. There was a distant door closing sound from the kitchen.

"Why don't we ask him?" Hank suggested as Sixpack appeared in the doorway holding a grocery bag.

"OK let's do that. Six, remember that special project I was talking to you about yesterday?" Eric began.

The droid thought for a moment, unpacking the groceries on to the coffee table in silence.

"Ah yes sir, the road-sweeping enterprise."

"Road-sweeping?"

"Yes sir, I remember you saying we were going to 'clean up the streets of Cosmopolis'. You were very excited as I recall."

Hank suppressed a chuckle.

"Well that's not exactly what I meant Six, in fact the scheme I have in mind is actually very different, but I'll still be needing your assistance."

"Very well sir, as you know I am here to serve you in whatever way I can."

"Yes I know," Eric said patiently, "now this scheme, well, it's a little bit more involved than just sweeping roads. It's going to require…Six…what on earth are those?"

He was staring at the bag Sixpack had just placed on the table – the one with 'Carter's Munchies – Hi-Protein Dog Biscuits' written on the side. Again Hank covered his mouth to hide his smile.

"Munchies sir," Sixpack answered politely. "You asked me to go out and obtain twelve cans of beer and some munchies."

Eric buried his head in his hands.

"Sixpack, we don't have a dog, why would I want dog biscuits?"

"I must admit sir I was somewhat confused myself and could only assume that you were intending to purchase a domestic canine in the near future."

Digging into his pocket for some more money, Eric said:

"I have no intention of buying a pet now or in the immediate future, Sixpack, now please go back to the shop, take your dog biscuits with you and tell them you made a mistake. When you come back make sure you've got some snacks with you, preferably ones for human consumption like potato crisps or something."

Sixpack took the money, retrieved his Munchies and scuttled back towards the kitchen.

"You still wanna have him as part of the team?" Hank asked.

"It's just the slang bud, nothing else, he's very handy to have around. We just have to try and avoid using slang and he'll be OK." He returned his attention to the folder and flipped through to the next section. "We'll ask him about names when he comes back, meantime we need to address the next category – Costumes. You're gonna love some of my designs bud!"

Hank cracked open a fresh can of beer.

It was going to be a long night.

CHAPTER NINE

*"Honesty pays, but it doesn't seem to
pay enough to suit some people."*

F M Hubbard

Eve always treated Cyrus Zifford the way one should treat a
Vindaloovian* curry - with a degree of respect and a good deal of
wariness. She knew he was a supreme liar with a flair for deception
like no-one she had ever seen – she also found him devastatingly
attractive (which incidentally is where the curry comparison ends)
and this could throw her concentration off at times. Like most
people, she had terrible difficulty knowing when he was being
honest as most of his lies had seventy five per cent truth mixed in
with them. They sat opposite each other in her private office, as
usual Cyrus was wearing enough aftershave to knock out a
household pet.

"Good flight Cyrus?" she asked quickly, keen to get the
discussion going before he could start thinking up some clever
scam.

"Yeah not bad," he replied flicking a speck of dust from his
lapel. "It's amazing what people will do for you when they think
you're a member of the Jelluvish† Royal Family."

"Really Cyrus, must you try to con everyone you meet?"

"Keeps me sharp Miss Tendril."

Eve grinned – he *was* sharp, very sharp, which is why she
needed him. "What time is it here?" he asked.

---

* From the planet Vindaloovia, the curry producing capital of the
galaxy, famous for inventing the Bish Bash Rogan Bosh Gullet Stripper
– the hottest curry in the known universe.
† Jelluva is the capital city of the planet Squalorious, which despite its
name is one of the wealthiest planets in the galaxy and is populated by
billionaires. The royal family rule the entire planet with absolute
authority, often imposing heavy taxes on those deemed to be too rich.

"Almost 5pm."

He fiddled with his disgustingly expensive watch and set it to Perfection Island time. "Sorry I didn't have time to brief you before you left but I've got a rather interesting assignment for you."

"Let me guess. You want me to discredit as many of this year's Miss Cosmopolis finalists as I can without diverting suspicion on to you because you've decided to enter following Out for the Lads & Co Ltd's decision to abolish the age restrictions."

Razor sharp.

For a moment Eve was flustered – had her plan been leaked already? Then she reminded herself this was Cyrus Zifford she was talking to.

"Very good Cyrus, how did you know?"

"Well, if I'm not mistaken that magazine on your desk is the current issue of Gorgeous Monthly which, on page forty-nine, reveals details of this year's age restrictions being lifted. I simply assumed you couldn't resist another crack at the title." He paused to smile smugly, the way Sherlock Holmes never did but really should have. "I also bumped into Mad Max on the way in and he told me all about it – is that why the good doctor's here? To assist in your quest for glory?"

Eve was conscious she was losing control of the conversation. They'd been talking for less than a minute and already Cyrus was the one asking the questions. It was time to remind him just who he was dealing with so she leaned back in her chair with an air of superiority and smirked in an attempt to out-smug him.

"Maybe it would be quicker if you told me what you know, then I won't waste time going over old ground," she said evenly.

Cyrus realised he had overstepped the mark, she was the boss after all, the person who paid his wages – best to show some respect.

"I know little more than what Max told me ma'am, that you're looking to enter this year's tournament and that he's been tasked with creating the best beauty enhancing drug the world has ever seen. I assume you've brought me in to dig up some dirt, or manufacture some, on the finalists just to make sure."

Satisfied he had learned his lesson she adopted a more civil tone.

"Yes, that's it in a nutshell. First thing I need you to do is draw up a shortlist of potential finalists so we can see who we're going to be up against. Then I'll leave it to you to concoct some diabolical scheme to disgrace as many of them as you can. Should be fun for you, surrounding yourself with beautiful girls all day."

"It's a dirty job ma'am..." Cyrus joked, pleased that he would be able to employ his charm and striking looks to good effect on this one. "How's Max doing on your formula?"

"He's not been here long and so far he's not made much progress although he has asked for a team of engineers and some specialist machinery to be flown in – I've no idea what he's up to but knowing Max it will be something impressive."

"May I ask who's funding this venture ma'am?"

It was always good to know whose money he was spending and to what extent the expenses account could be abused.

"It'll be coming out of my own pocket."

Cyrus knew just how cavernous those pockets were and was relieved to know his expenses weren't going to be itemised on a daily basis by some annoying accountant type person. There was a sudden shriek of animal pain followed by cheers of triumph from outside the office window.

"What was that?" Cyrus gasped, rising from his seat.

"Oh just my security boys. They've probably just reduced the native gorilla population by one."

Cyrus shook his head.

"Why do they do that? I mean it's a bit pointless isn't it?"

"Maybe it keeps them sharp," Eve replied with a sly grin.

"Oh touché ma'am."

CHAPTER TEN

"Beware of all enterprises that require new clothes."

Henry David Thoreau

"Now, you may think of costumes as nothing more than 'packaging'," Eric explained, "but I can assure you they play a key role in the whole superhero business."

He hadn't turned the page yet and Hank was already dreading it. What horrendous ideas had he come up with? Would this be the moment his resolve crumbled and he politely excused himself from the entire affair? He was more than a little alarmed to see the beer can he held was quivering. Taking a deep breath he said:

"OK Eric, let's see 'em."

Eric flipped the page over.

Hank crumpled the beer can in his fist.

He was looking at what appeared to be a page filled with drawings by a group of five-year-old school children that had been asked to draw their favourite Halloween costumes. Whilst he was no fashion guru, Hank knew a disaster when he saw one and he was staring at a sheet *full* of them.

The problem was – what did he say to Eric?

"Obviously these are only rough sketches," Eric advised.

This came as scant relief for Hank who was pretty sure he could have made a better job armed with just a tin of paint and half a potato. He scanned the illustrations with a mixture of confusion and terror that he might one day be wearing one of these ridiculous costumes. One in particular looked like a caped banana with arms and legs wearing an old-fashioned kettle on its head. The other pictures were equally outlandish but at least he could deduce that Eric had gone for a medieval theme, in keeping with the whole 'knights' idea as there were plenty of metal looking silver patches.

"That silver stuff is chainmail, by the way," Eric said helpfully noticing Hank's furrowed brow. "As you can see they're all kinda knightish designs, I got a history book out from the library to help

60

me."

Amazingly, there was one outfit that Hank didn't find too laughable, in fact, it looked almost cool. From the bottom up it went something like this: metallic looking boots went as high as the shins, these were followed by plate armour knee pads. The tops of the thighs were protected by the tail end of a long chainmail shirt and a crimson breastplate covered the chest. Plate armour elbow pads and crimson gauntlets adorned the arms and the head was completely concealed by a helmet, the kind where the front tapers to a point as though the wearer has an unusually long nose. To finish it off a crimson cape ran from the neck down to the backs of the knees.

"This one's not too bad," Hank said thinking out loud and pointing to the picture.

"That's exactly the one I would have picked for you myself bud!" Eric exclaimed, sounding just like a used car salesman.

Hank had been so wrapped up in the gaudy designs his logic had temporarily deserted him – then it tapped him on the shoulder.

"Er...won't these be kinda heavy though?" he asked slowly.

"Not as heavy as you'd think," Eric replied cheerfully, "in fact only the helmet, boots and pads are gonna be proper metal. The chainmail will be plasti-steel, much lighter and easier to move around in."

Despite Eric's jolly reply, doubts were starting to snowball in Hank's mind but he had to tread carefully so as not to upset his friend.

"Eric I'm still interested, really I am, but I do have a few issues I'd like to discuss about these outfits," he said with the air of someone who was trying to say thank you for a birthday present they didn't really like.

"Well, that's why we're here Hank to talk it through – so fire away."

"OK, my first question is – won't these things make a bit of a racket when we walk about in them? Would make it kinda hard to creep up on people wouldn't it?"

"I was going to pad the soles of the boots with rubber to deaden the 'clang' and as for the plate armour, I figured it would be OK so long as we moved slowly."

"What if we have to run somewhere?"

"If we have to run somewhere then we've probably already

been spotted haven't we?"

"Fair enough, second question - how much protection will these things give us if we get shot?"

Eric reacted as if he'd been expecting that very question and answered with unshakable calmness.

"Depends what they shoot us with. Bullets won't usually penetrate the chainmail but they'll sting like the devil and lasers, well, they'll just rip right through it."

Not for the first time that evening Hank was speechless.

Rip right through it?

"But I don't plan on getting shot," Eric added comfortingly.

The whole costume issue was turning decidedly sour for Hank, the prospect of tiptoeing around in the hope they didn't encounter anyone armed with a laser weapon was not one he found particularly reassuring.

"Do you think we really need costumes, couldn't we just wear dark clothes, bullet proof vests and a balaclava?"

Eric flopped back in his chair and sighed.

"Where's the style in that?" he cried holding his arms out in despair.

"*Style*? I thought the plan was to apprehend hoodlums not strut down a catwalk! Or have I missed the point?"

"Remember when I told you earlier that the costumes were key? Well don't you want to know why they're so important?"

Hank cracked open another beer, maybe if he drunk himself into a stupor this would all make more sense.

"OK tell me."

"I did some research on the Captain Uno website the other night and guess what; sixty eight per cent of Cap's arrests did not involve violence – now what does that tell you?"

"It tells me that thirty two per cent of his arrests *did* involve violence!"

"Oh Hank don't you get it? In almost three quarters of his encounters the mere sight of him was enough to subdue the villains (it was actually nearer two thirds but Eric thought three quarters sounded better) If we can *scare* them into submission then we're laughing."

"That's a pretty major 'if' Eric, I mean how on earth are we gonna do that? Wear scary masks?"

Eric stiffened.

"I get the feeling you're not taking this seriously Hank!"

"Eric I *am* taking it seriously, I just don't want us to end up as chalk outlines first time out. I can see you've put a lot of time and effort into this project and I admire that but if we're gonna do this thing then let's make sure we do it right eh?"

Hank felt himself tensing up – this was it, the critical point of the whole deal, Eric would now either stomp off in a sulk or he'd agree to further discussions. As he waited for Eric to react a sudden unavoidable fact appeared out of nowhere and gave him a good slap. Recovering slightly he analysed the fact and came to the conclusion that he was in a no-win situation. The problem was this: even if he refused to go along with the plan he was certain Eric would go it alone and if he did then there was every chance he'd get his ass royally kicked sooner or later. Being a caring sort of chap Hank knew he wouldn't be able to live with his conscience if anything happened to his best friend – he couldn't just leave him to it. Therefore, it was looking more and more likely he would be one of the Avenging Knights whether he liked it or not.

They both turned as the front door slammed shut.

Sixpack wandered into the room and emptied his grocery bag on the coffee table.

"I have purchased an alternative selection of snacks, sir, crisps, peanuts and chilli crackers which included a free jar of fire sauce dip."

"Well done Six," Eric said. "Take a seat, we need to ask you something."

The droid paused for a moment.

"Which seat would you like me to take sir and where wou…"

"I meant sit down, there on the sofa."

Sixpack dutifully obeyed and sat waiting for the question.

Eric composed himself and began,

"Hank and I are embarking on a quest to bring villains in Cosmopolis to justice. We're going to become vigilantes a bit like superheroes. Are you with me so far?"

"With you sir?"

"Do you understand what I've just said?"

"Yes sir."

"Good, now we need to come up with some way of frightening the villains in an attempt to apprehend them without any violence. I've designed some fearsome looking outfits for us to wear but can you think of any other tactic we could use?"

"Is this the question?"

"Yes Sixpack – this is the question."

It didn't take long for the droid to find his answer.

"I think the key is to make your opponent think he is dealing with someone far more formidable than he actually is – a deception to trick him into submission."

"Such as?" Hank asked.

"Well, the outfits would be a good start but maybe something that altered your voice would work, something to make you sound more threatening."

Eric and Hank exchanged glances – did such a device exist? They'd never heard of anything remotely similar.

"Can you give us an example Six?" Eric asked.

"Certainly sir. Rather than walking up to them and politely asking them to drop their weapons and surrender you could try saying – what is the name of your organisation again sir?"

"The Avenging Knights," Hank answered.

"Very well, you could try something like: *IN THE NAME OF JUSTICE WE, THE AVENGING KNIGHTS OF COSMOPOLIS, ORDER YOU TO RELINQUISH YOUR FIREARMS AND SUBMIT IMMEDIATELY! FAILURE TO COMPLY WILL RESULT IN SEVERE REPERCUSSIONS!*"

The two pals nearly jumped clear out of their seats, Hank even dropped his beer can he was so startled. The sheer volume of the delivery was enough to set them shaking in their socks and the deep, menacing voice only added to the effect. One of Eric's framed photos of his mother clattered on to the carpet. Eric was the first to find his voice,

"Holy cow Sixpack! I didn't know you could do that!"

"Oh yes sir, I have a wide range of vocal facilities. I can talk in any voice you like, at any volume."

"Of course, his former owner was a language professor," Hank exclaimed turning to Eric.

"That's great, that's really great!" Eric smiled. "Oh and by the way Six, you're part of the team."

"Very well sir. Will there be anything else?"

"Yeah you can stick around while we go through the rest of the plan, you might have some useful input."

Eric selected an outfit very similar in style to Hank's crimson arrangement only his was dark blue. It transpired that the banana picture Hank had baulked at earlier was in fact Eric's design for Sixpack, a simple affair consisting of nothing more than a helmet and a cape. Plasti-steel plating would be welded on to him to provide extra protection in case the 'voice from Hell' approach didn't work. Eric flipped over to the next section – Vehicles. Again there were several diagrams and rough drawings.

"Isn't that your van Eric?" Hank asked carefully.

"Yep, with a few minor alterations of course. I'm going to call it The Silver Steed."

CHAPTER ELEVEN

"Never hate your enemies...it will cloud your thinking."

Al Pacino in Godfather III

Thanks to befriending, (maybe that should be 'manipulating') the gullible Danzo Stax, head of Perfection Island security, Cyrus had secured the most luxurious guest room in the entire facility, complete with marble floors, four poster bed, walk-in closet and...a really big telly. An office had also been made available to him and it was in here that his slur campaign would begin. Many of his existing files were being flown over but he had enough on his desk to get cracking, by using the supernet and his legion of informers, he could research the tournament to the point where an accurate prediction of the finalists could be made.

For Cyrus, this was always the boring part, deciding who his targets would be – a bit like baking a cake, no-one wants to mix the ingredients together but there's a veritable stampede when it's time to decorate the top. He much preferred to get down to the nitty-gritty of actually getting into their lives and smearing them with some horrific scandal (be it true or fabricated – usually fabricated), then watching the aftermath on TV. As a barometer for his success, Cyrus often used the ratings figures from the media. How many newspapers had been sold? How many people had tuned into the news that day? With this latest campaign being so high profile he was confident he could beat his existing record, which he had set three years ago. The Cosmopolis Prattler had quadrupled their sales on January 30th 2102 when their publication had sported the headline "Celebrity evangelist caught playing naked hopscotch with satanic cult!" One national TV station estimated they had reached over ninety per cent of the U.S. population as viewers had been glued to their screens watching the story on the evening news. The unfortunate victim, now believed to be living a life of solitude on some remote atoll in the cold, windy regions of the Bitter Isles (formerly the Outer Hebrides), had dared to question the morality of beauty products, branding them 'sinful and degrading'. Knowing the evangelist to be immensely popular and influential, Eve had given Cyrus the job of 'taking him down' and to this day, it remained his favourite all time hit.

Would he ever top it? Maybe. The Miss Cosmopolis Tournament was certainly the prefect arena in which to try, the media would be all over it like stink on dung, sniffing around for the slightest hint of impropriety.

He hoped he wouldn't disappoint them.

His thoughts on prime time scandal were interrupted as he heard a knock at the office door and Danzo Stax lumbered inside carrying a tray bearing a pitcher of pineapple juice and a glass.

"Thought you might be thirsty Mr Zifford," he said to his new best friend.

The sight of an armed Korellian performing such a refined task was almost comical, but Cyrus could hide his emotions superbly, which among other things made him an excellent poker player.

"Oh well played Danzo, yes I could do with something to wet the old whistle," he said jovially, "just set it down on the table over there will you?"

The croc seemed to take an inordinately long time to accomplish something so simple and even after he had relieved himself of the tray he loitered for a second or two, the way hotel porters do when they're expecting a tip. Cyrus read his intentions with consummate ease, but he wasn't about to make it easy and returned his attention to his computer screen. Still the croc refused to leave and began shifting uncomfortably from one foot to the other in a most un-Korellian like fashion. With preliminary screening already underway and the tournament final just over two months hence, Cyrus knew he was up against the clock and although he enjoyed toying with people's emotions he really didn't have time to waste on this imbecile.

"Need something Danzo?" he asked idly.

"Well," the croc said uneasily, "I was wondering if you'd had chance to speak to Miss Tendril about...y'know...my job?"

"Oh that!" Cyrus replied looking expertly surprised. "Yes I did manage to mention it to her and..." he adopted a pained expression, "...it doesn't look good Danz ol' buddy."

"What did she say?" Danzo gasped, hanging on every word.

"Let's just say she's not planning to change her rotation

system at the present time."

Cyrus had never seen a grown Korellian cry, few people ever had, indeed it was questionable whether they *could* cry, but he was sure if he pushed this one any further he could well have him weeping like a baby. Another waste of time. "But that doesn't mean she definitely *won't* change it," he added hastily, noticing the Korellian's bottom lip trembling. "Why don't you let me speak to her again eh?"

After clearing his throat the croc said,

"I would be most grateful Mr Zifford."

"Sure thing Danz."

The guard plodded off towards the door. "Oh and could you bring me some ice?" Cyrus shouted from his chair without looking round. He poured himself a glass and took a swig – it was delicious. But then again Eve Tendril did insist on only the finest produce.

He began leafing through a few of his files, so many phone calls to make, so many electronic messages to send before he could narrow down the field. The smearing would start with those lucky enough to make it to the interview stage; with Eve already through to the last fifteen this meant he had fourteen potential winners to spike before the final was held. If there was one thing Cyrus did suffer from it was a short attention span for the more mundane aspects of his job. Slamming the file shut he rose just in time to greet Danzo at the door who had, as requested, brought some ice.

"Thanks Danz. Can you tell me how to find Dr Ticklegrit please?"

It was 7pm, the additional files he'd requested would be here in the morning, he'd make a fresh start then, right now he wanted to see what Max was up to.

As expected the chemist was hunched over a microscope when Cyrus finally found him. Encased in four glass walls, the extensive laboratory was spotlessly clean, a large extractor fan built into the ceiling kept the air free from infection (and any unwanted bodily odours) and, much to his surprise, Max was the only person in it. Cyrus approached him from the rear, he tapped the ten digit code into the electronically sealed door and stepped inside. It slid shut behind him making barely a whisper.

"Don't you knock Zifford?" Max asked still staring down his microscope.

"Don't you say 'hello'?"

"Someone told you the code then?"

"Naturally."

"I gave express instructions for the code to be kept secret," Max said, the first hint of annoyance in his voice. "Who gave it to you?"

"Oh, just a friend," Cyrus replied unhelpfully. "What are you up to in here?"

Max didn't like uninvited guests, or being interrupted, nor did he like being questioned, in fact there wasn't much Max did like. He turned to face Cyrus with a deep sigh.

"I'm working on something to assist Miss Tendril's quest to become Miss Cosmopolis 2105 – what else would I be doing here?"

"Making any progress?" Cyrus asked, picking up a weird looking instrument and examining it casually.

"Put that down! Look I'm extremely busy Zifford, if you've got something to say then let's hear it otherwise let me get on with my work."

"Take it easy doc, I'm just wondering how you're getting on that's all. No need to be rude."

Max returned to his microscope.

"I'm not being rude, I'm just...I'm...I'm working to a strict deadline is what I'm doing, now please will you leave me alone?"

Realising he wasn't going to get anything out of the cantankerous chemist, Cyrus eyed the room and its contents carefully, there had to be something in here he could use for leverage. He spotted it partially concealed behind a microscope in the corner – sloppy, very sloppy. No wonder he wanted him out of the lab in such a hurry.

"Say doc, you're not still using that Trouble Gum[†] stuff are you?" he asked nonchalantly.

Max froze.

"Trouble Gum?"

[†] Invented by Squigleys Inc in 2102, Trouble Gum was the most addictive chewing gum ever made. People around the galaxy were admitted to hospital with frozen jaws and when supplies ran out in 2104 there were worldwide riots in the streets. Dangerous side effects were also discovered and it was swiftly banned. Manufacture and/or possession became a serious crime.

"Yeah you know, that a hundred per cent addictive chewing gum manufactured a few years ago. Weren't there rumours you used to chew it to help relieve stress? Didn't Miss Tendril threaten to sack you if you were ever caught using it?"

"Of course not, that was just vicious gossip. I'd never use it anyway, you know very well it has harmful side-effects, hallucinations, psychosis etc, not to mention being..."

"Being banned on over a hundred and thirteen planets, Earth being one of them, punishable by life imprisonment," Cyrus finished for him.

"Yes quite."

"Lord knows what she'd do if she found out you'd smuggled some on to her island. Probably feed you to the sharks."

Another thing Max disliked was being threatened and he whirled round to face the agent provocateur, his patience well and truly at an end.

"You know you ought to be careful who you threaten around here Cyrus Zifford! I'm not a man to be trifled with, I have a dozen chemicals in this lab that could turn you into a gibbering vegetable for the rest of your life. One drop in your pineapple juice and hey presto! Let's see how many women you can seduce when you're dribbling all over your fancy suits and foaming at the mouth!"

For once Cyrus found himself on the defensive and without a witty comeback.

Pineapple juice?

Had he meant that as an example or was it something more sinister? Had he already drugged him as a precaution? Perhaps he had underestimated the quirky scientist.

"OK, OK doc," he managed to say eventually, "no need to go off at the deep end. Why don't we call a truce eh? Like I said I only came up here out of idle curiosity, I'm not looking to start a fight."

The chemist glowered at him, a purple vein in his temple pulsated with rage which Cyrus found he couldn't take his eyes off. He got a grip of his temper and said,

"Alright Zifford, I'll give you a quick demonstration of my new formula and then you're going – agreed?"

"Fine by me."

"Now remember firstly, this isn't perfected yet and secondly if I find out you've told anyone then its 'gibbering time' for you, understand?"

Cyrus nodded and succeeded in wrenching his gaze from Max's throbbing forehead. "Very well then, fetch me that rat over there, the white one in the cage."

The incarcerated rodent was retrieved and placed on a shiny steel work surface as per Max's instructions. "See anything special about it?" he asked.

Leaning close, Cyrus gave the rat a swift appraisal. Furry, pointy nose, whiskers, long pink tail – yep, it was a standard rat.

"Nothing – it's just a rat. Why is it so special?"

"It isn't. I just wanted you to confirm we were dealing with a normal specimen before we got started."

Max placed a strange looking contraption about twelve inches from the cage. To Cyrus it looked like a kid's ray gun mounted on a small platform.

"What's that?"

"It's a C.D.U, chemical displacement unit. I drop the formula in here like so," Max explained, pouring a syrupy red liquid into the funnel on top of the unit. "Screw on the lid, wait a few seconds for the liquid to settle…and then voila!"

He pressed a red button on the side of the C.D.U and took a step back. Cyrus did likewise, he had no idea what was about to happen but was fairly sure he didn't want to be the one it happened to. There was a shrill whine and then a red laser burst from the muzzle of the unit, impacting on the rat inside the cage. Naturally the startled animal tried to make a run for it but could only scuttle around its cage, the laser tracked its every move.

"What's happening to it?" Cyrus said in a hushed voice.

"Ssshh! Quiet, watch carefully."

The laser beam came to an abrupt halt and the whining sound dwindled to a low hum.

Cyrus watched wide-eyed as the formula began to take effect. His face creased into a look of disgust while Max smiled appreciatively, his arms folded. After several seconds Cyrus couldn't bear to watch any more.

"Ugh good lord Ticklegrit! Is that supposed to happen?" he asked, cringing.

"Of course it is."

"Yeah but – ugh! – look at it!"

"That's precisely how it's *supposed* to look my dear boy."

CHAPTER TWELVE

"I just took a ride in a silver machine and I'm still feeling mean."

Even though Eric had the artistic flair of a labotomised slug, the images of the Silver Steed weren't too bad. He'd pinched his foreman's silver pen from work and had used it to add some much needed colour to his doodles. Hank was awash with relief after realising he and Eric would not be galloping around the city atop some monstrous metal horse.

"Fellow knights, I give you the Silver Steed," Eric announced proudly. "Comfortable, reliable and inconspicuous."

Sixpack watched on in silence, the way droids do. Eric could've been revealing his plans to start another world war or simply discussing a new recipe for scampi a la Dorfler – to Sixpack it made little difference, he was here to serve his master and it really didn't get anymore complicated than that.

"So what modifications have you made?" asked Hank.

"Er…well…none yet, I need to 'borrow' a few things from work first. I thought an external layer of armour just to be safe and maybe a turbo device in case we run into any trouble and need to haul ass."

There was that word again – trouble.

Despite having resigned himself to a new career in amateur superheroism, Hank was still extremely concerned about what would happen if they got into any *real* bother. His police training had been less than adequate, indeed, the two day course on hand-to-hand combat had consisted mainly of watching the instructor beat seven bells out of a cloth dummy, who naturally had not put up much of a fight. A professional criminal (unlikely to be made of cloth) would doubtless provide stiffer opposition and with Eric's temper as brittle as it was there was always a possibility of something kicking off. Still, they hadn't come to the Weapons section of Eric's dossier yet, so he decided to keep his fears to himself for the time being.

"We'll use the Steed to get from A to B. I'm going to install a radio in the back so we can monitor the police band. The cops don't tend to respond to emergency calls very promptly so we could be in and out before they even arrive on the scene. Plus, there's always a good chance of stumbling on to some crime as it happens, especially if we patrol the dodgier areas."

Eric was right – Hank remembered his walk home from Angelo's and the three separate incidents he had witnessed – and that had been in a half-decent neighbourhood. The truth was sad, but it was still the truth – it was actually harder to avoid crime in Cosmopolis than it was to find it, they certainly wouldn't be lounging around in the back of the van playing cards and drinking coffee waiting for something to happen.

"I was wondering about some kind of figurehead for the front, like maybe a horse's head or something, whaddya think?"

Hank found the idea utterly ridiculous.

"It's a bit obvious isn't it?" he said diplomatically, "I'd prefer to travel about incognito while we're in the va… sorry the Silver Steed."

"Yeah you're probably right, man, we don't want to advertise our presence – sorry it's just my theatrical nature getting the better of me."

Theatrical nature?

Eric you're a driller for heaven's sake, Hank thought, just how creative do you need to be to drill a hole in a rockface? The only theatre we're going to see is the inside of an operating theatre, after we get creamed trying to nab some crazed psycho.

No, wait, that wasn't fair.

Maybe he ought to wait and see the full plan before making such a negative judgement.

"So Sixpack's gonna do the driving and the scary voice stuff yeah?" he said instead.

"That's right," said Eric, "also, I've got a buddy at the mine, a guy I trust, who can help us out with the armour plating and he knows a fella who can sort us out with a turbo."

Hank grabbed a handful of chilli crackers, but gave the fire sauce a swerve, he had enough on his plate right now without having to deal with a burning throat.

Eric turned the page on to the Headquarters section.

"This is a quick section, I figured we'd use my basement as an HQ, it's secluded, spacious and I already have a computer down there – any objections?"

Sixpack raised his hand.

"You can speak freely Six, this isn't a formal board meeting or anything."

"Very well sir, it is just that if we do decide to use the basement as a headquarters for our operation then might I suggest we relocate some of the artefacts."

"Artefacts? What artefacts?" Hank asked, wondering if his pal was some closet archaeologist.

Eric made to speak but his droid beat him to it.

"The Captain Uno artefacts, photo albums, a signed picture, posters, replica outfits and at least a dozen models one of which is life sized."

"You've got one of the life sized models? The ones with the authentic Captain Uno voice?" Hank gasped. "You never told me! There were only a hundred or so ever made!"

Eric looked sheepish.

"I was gonna tell ya Hank, honest I was. But you know what it's like – I tell you, you tell someone else, before you know it everyone knows and I'm fighting off potential buyers left, right and centre!"

"Can I see it?"

"Sure, but let's finish going through this folder first eh? We're almost done."

"OK," Hank mumbled with a face like an over-eager child on Christmas Eve.

"In fact we *are* done, the last part, the Weapons section isn't until tomorrow."

"What?"

"I've arranged a meeting with Dodger Broadwinkle."

Hank was aghast;

"The mutant arms dealer?"

"He's not really an arms dealer," Eric explained, trying to dilute the situation, "he's more of a...of a..."

"Eric he's an arms dealer."

"Well so what if he is? Who else are we gonna get weapons from, a fishmonger? Look, I had a chat with a guy from work who knows him, he was the one who set up the meeting and apparently

Dodger's not as dangerous as everyone thinks. I'm told he's quite charming as it happens."

"He's done time for armed robbery Eric! He's about as charming as a Korellian with a hangover."

"You don't have to come if you don't want to. I'm taking Sixpack anyway just for peace of mind."

"No, no I'll come. I just didn't think we'd be negotiating with people like Dodger, in fact he's more likely to be the kinda guy we'd be going after."

It was a good point and Eric knew it.

"It's just a one off bud, once we're tooled up then we can get down to the serious business of fighting crime."

"What time's the meeting?"

"10am tomorrow."

Hank glanced at his watch and yawned.

"It *is* tomorrow," he said wearily.

Eric yawned back at him, Sixpack, impervious to the strange contagious effects of yawning, remained motionless on the sofa.

"Well, I'm beat," Eric said, then turning to the droid, "oh by the way Sixpack, Hank's gonna crash here tonight. Make up the spare room will you?"

"Crash sir?"

"He's staying for the night."

"Very well sir I will go and prepare the guest bedroom immediately."

He clanked off up the stairs.

Rising to his feet, Eric stretched and said;

"Y'know Hank, I'm so glad you decided to be part of this. Once we get going I really think we'll make a difference. We might even inspire other regular guys to do the same."

Dog-tired and still a little dubious Hank didn't have the energy to argue – so he didn't.

"Maybe you're right," he said yawning again. "We still need to go through a lot more things before we actually start doing any 'avenging' though."

"Sure, we'll talk more tomorrow, but like I said, it's good to have you on board."

Hank couldn't help thinking this is what the captain of the

Titanic[†] had probably said to his passengers. Eric clapped him on the shoulder and made for the door. Among his whirlwind of minor concerns Hank could feel one *big* problem looming, the trouble was he couldn't put his finger on it. He knew it was crucial to the whole operation but his brain had taken it for a walk round the block and try as he might he just couldn't pin it down. It would probably come to him in the morning. He took one last swig of beer, looked down at the folder on the table, shook his head slowly then headed for the stairs.

[†] Incredibly, still the most famous maritime disaster in living memory.

CHAPTER THIRTEEN

"Anything I've ever done that ultimately was
worthwhile initially scared me to death."

Betty Bender

Normally, Eric and Hank slept like logs on a Friday night, having had their fill of alcohol and a late night takeaway their bodies would wave the white flag long before they actually made it home.

But not this Friday night.

The excitement and trepidation of their new venture acted as a strange form of jet-lag which kept them awake almost until dawn. An ominous burning smell was enough to get them out of bed; Hank because he feared the house might be ablaze and Eric because he was hungry and knew Sixpack had started cooking.

Breakfast turned out to be a little on the crispy side and Hank chose to disregard his rule about not eating anything he could not identify. He was fairly sure the coal-like briquettes were some kind of meat-based product and the charred disc had once been a fried egg. How Sixpack would ever be able to get the frying pan clean again was beyond him. By 9am they had polished it off and were sat at the table discussing their next move over a cup of strong coffee. Much to his annoyance, Hank had still not managed to identify his big worry, which continued to nag him. As Sixpack went about the Herculean task of washing up, Eric went through the plan for the day.

"Once Six has finished the dishes we'll pay Dodger a visit as arranged, see if he's got anything interesting to offer us. Then I was gonna drive to the mine and meet up with my buddies Ralph and Helmut who should be able to fit the armour plating and the turbo by the end of the day. I thought we'd take the weapons down to the quarry while they're doing that, we can test them out and there shouldn't be anyone there at that time. If we've time after that I'll swipe a few sheets of plasti-steel and weld them on to Sixpack when we get home."

"What about the costumes?" Hank asked.

"I've already given Mum a call, she'll be making them for us."

"Your Mum?"

Though he had only met Mrs Dorfler on a couple of occasions, Hank had seen the annual Christmas gifts she had bestowed upon her son, the ill-fitting tasteless garments she'd 'created' for him. To his credit, Eric *had* worn each item at least once, usually when it was dark or he could be sure no-one he knew would see him.

"That's right, don't worry, I've told her we're going to a fancy dress party. I'll be making the armour plates, chainmail and helmets myself, she's just gonna take care of the fabricy bits."

"How are we gonna pay for all this Eric?"

"It won't be as expensive as you think, the only big outlay will be for the weapons and I've got that covered."

"I'd prefer it if we shared the cost, it's only fair."

"No need, I've still got a fair bit of dosh left over from my lottery win, there should be more than enough. Besides, you can pay me back another way."

Hank didn't like the sound of that.

"How?" he asked with a sense of unease.

"Well we're gonna need some training on firearms and hand-to-hand combat and I figured with you being an ex-cop you'd be the ideal guy to do it."

Hank sighed inwardly, during his five years on the force, he'd fired his weapon just once and that had only been a warning shot. As far as hand-to-hand combat went, he'd been involved in a bar-room brawl once but he'd been off duty at the time and after slipping on some spilled beer and bumping his head on a table he'd quietly passed out and missed the whole show. Not exactly an action man and hardly a basis for training someone else. But he didn't want to disappoint Eric, not after all the work he'd put in.

"Sure," he said, trying to sound enthusiastic.

"Great! Right I'm gonna jump in the shower and then we'll get going."

They rose from the table.

"Can I use your phone Eric? I need to call my insurance company."

"Sure go ahead, you know where it is. Sixpack – hurry up with those dishes we're gonna hit the road in about ten minutes."

Sixpack looked as confused as a droid could.

So it *was* a road-sweeping job.

Dodger Broadwinkle's 'shop' was, as you might expect, located in one of the seedier neighbourhoods of the city and not the kind of establishment you'd find listed in the Cosmopolis Business Directory. Famed for its dark alleys and broad daylight muggings it wasn't a place for the faint hearted, which is why Eric had decided to bring Sixpack along. Not because he was a particularly tough droid or had concealed weapons or anything, just because people were less likely to mess with you if you had a droid present. In 2105 people didn't buy weapons for home defence like in the old days, they just sent their droid to a specialist to have it 'beefed up'. A hidden blade here, a Shockmaster Deluxe there, perhaps the installation of a karate chip – the possibilities were endless, if you had the money. The point was you could never tell how lethal a droid was just by looking at it.

The sign above the shop read 'Dodger Broadwinkle's Gift Shop – hand crafted designs made to order'. Not an entirely truthful statement but one that would not arouse suspicion should any over-zealous cop start snooping around. Over-zealous cop? In Cosmopolis? There was more chance of Sixpack undercooking a meal. Consequently, Dodger's little enterprise in illegal weapons had blossomed and he had earned a reputation as a solid, 'no questions asked' kind of businessman. Parking the van in the spot least likely to attract vandals (not an easy task), the trio made their way into the shop. There was a soft tinkle as the door opened on to an old-fashioned brass bell suspended above it. The interior had a musty smell, as if it was rarely used, which was true – most of the trading was done elsewhere. The only action the front room ever saw was when Dodger dusted the various trinkets to make it less obvious.

There was a creaking sound from behind the bead curtain at the back of the shop, as though someone (or some*thing*) very large was getting out of a chair. After a few seconds Dodger parted the curtain and waddled into the room and yes, he was large, enormous in fact, a bizarre mutant resembling some horrific crossbreed of man and walrus. Sweating slightly and wearing a stain covered string vest he descended the few steps on to the shop floor and took his place behind the counter, already out of breath. It wasn't a particularly pleasant sight, especially so shortly after having

79

breakfast, but this was Dodger Broadwinkle, someone renowned for being far more dangerous than he looked. He regarded his customers, trying to weigh up the lethality of the droid they had brought with them.

"Help you fellas?" he gurgled.

Hank grimaced, even his voice was disturbing, accompanied by a sound similar to someone stirring a pot of thick porridge every time he spoke. Eric seemed unfazed and took a step forward.

"Morning Dodger, we're here to have a look at some of your *special* items."

Dodger flicked some food from one of his tusks and smoothed down his long white moustache – these guys certainly didn't waste any time with small talk.

"Sure, what takes your fancy? A genuine 1986 Rubik Cube? Some antique jigsaws? Over here I have an authentic game of Kerplunk, still in working order and in its original box. Or perhaps you'd like me to make you something?"

"No, I don't think you understand me Dodger," Eric said carefully, "I'm looking for some of your *special* stuff."

"Such as?"

Eric shifted his weight from one foot to the other, he didn't want to say the word 'weapons' but he was struggling to find an alternative. He tried a different approach.

"I'm a friend of Smokey Jones, the guy from Shovelbutt Mining Corporation, he was the one who arranged the meeting."

"And you are?" Dodger asked with a menacing gurgle.

"Eric, Eric Dorfler and this is my buddy Hank Halo."

Oh great, Hank thought, why not give him our phone number and home address while you're at it.

"Well if you're a friend of Smokey's then he'll have told you the password."

This stopped Eric in his tracks. Smokey hadn't mentioned any password had he? He couldn't decide what worried him most, the fact that Dodger might turn on him or that he was about to be totally humiliated in front of Hank.

"Ah yes the password," he mumbled, pretending to think hard.

Hank was getting edgy. No doubt Dodger had some hand cannon concealed under the counter to deal with unwanted customers, he found himself tensing, getting ready to bolt for the door at the first sign of trouble. Dodger suddenly burst out laughing.

"Ha-haa! I'm only foolin' with you Eric. Smokey told me to expect you, why don't we step into the back and we'll see if there's anything that floats your boat."

The two friends exhaled in unison. What a relief!

"Lead the way Dodger," Eric said triumphantly, winking at Hank.

"You'll have to leave your droid here though."

"Why?"

Dodger's smile disintegrated.

"Because I said so, that's why."

"Er, OK sure. Hang around here for a while will you Six?"

The droid looked up at the ceiling, looking for a suitable place from which to suspend himself.

"Just wait here for us Sixpack," Hank said as he made his way to the rear of the shop.

They followed Dodger through the bead curtain, down a dusty corridor that the arms dealer only just managed to squeeze through and into another, much smaller and strangely empty room. Dodger turned and faced them;

"You fellas get travel sick?"

"Travel sick?" Hank asked looking confused. "Are we going on a trip?"

"Kind of."

"What's 'kind of' a trip?"

Dodger puffed out his cheeks and released a long breath that reeked of impatience and decaying fish.

"Do you get travel sick?" he repeated, "yes or no?"

"No we don't," Eric answered for them both.

Dodger retrieved a small hand held device from within the generous folds of his fat.

"Good, then this won't bother you. Put these on."

He handed them each a pair of sunglasses and slipped on a pair himself. Hank and Eric did likewise although they had absolutely no idea why.

"What won't both..." Hank began.

A blinding flash of white light filled the room.

It took Hank and Eric several seconds to realise the floor had disappeared. They seemed to be falling through space, twisting and writhing like a couple of novice skydivers. Even with the shades on they could see nothing but white light. The ride bucked them around

81

at a dizzying pace, up and down, left and right not unlike a giant roller coaster. After roughly fifteen seconds it came to a sudden halt and the ground made a welcome (if unexpected) return. They landed in a heap and, as the brightness receded, they noticed a distinct change in their surroundings – for a start they were outdoors. Hank tried to stand up but only made it as far as the all-fours position. The insides of his stomach were kicking up a real fuss and threatening to hit the eject button.

"Good grief!" he groaned, "what the hell just happened?"

"We just teleported," Dodger explained standing over them with a big grin.

"That was excellent!" Eric enthused. "Can we do it again?"

"We'll have to if we want to get back," replied Dodger.

"You enjoyed that did you Eric?"

"Of course! Didn't you?"

Hank was about to reply but his breakfast interrupted him. Scrambling to his feet with a hand clasped over his mouth he dashed into a nearby clump of bushes and let nature take its course.

"Is he gonna be OK?" Dodger giggled.

Eric stood up, dusting himself down.

"Yeah he'll be fine, weak stomach."

He took in the surroundings. They were in the middle of what appeared to be a forest clearing. Gigantic trees bordered the clearing and there was an acute smell of what Eric mistakenly took for pine air freshener. Birds flitted between the branches and the occasional insect scuttled among the dead leaves that covered the forest floor. Some blue coloured frog-type creature, with eyes on stalks, hopped on to a tree stump and regarded the newcomers intensely. Timing his words between Hank's retching sounds Eric eventually asked the obvious question;

"Where are we Dodger?"

"That's not important."

"Er...OK...why are we here then?"

"To do some business of course. I teleport here to conduct my arms dealing – it's far safer. No surveillance devices or bugs to worry about."

Hank emerged from the bushes clutching his stomach and looking much paler.

"Where are we?"

"That's not important," Eric said officiously. "Dodger always teleports here to conduct his arms dealing – it's far safer. No surveillance devices or bugs to worry about."

"Oh I see, so where are…whoa!…what the hell is *that*?"

The blue frog-type creature flicked out its tongue, plucking an unfortunate insect from the air. It hopped off into the undergrowth, blissfully unaware it would play no further role in this entire story.

"That's not important either," Dodger grumbled, "now if you'll follow me."

He shuffled off into the undergrowth leaving the chums gawping at each other in silence. They decided to follow him before he disappeared into the forest.

A short walk brought them to a large log cabin in another clearing. Dodger tapped some numbers into the keypad by the door and it swung open. "After you chaps," he smiled extending a chubby arm. Hank and Eric stepped inside to find the place was jam-packed with rack upon rack of gleaming weapons. Handguns, carbines, grenades, blades, rocket launchers, things with backpacks attached – he had the lot.

"See anything ya like?" Dodger asked proudly.

CHAPTER FOURTEEN

"Anger is a wind which blows out the lamp of the mind."

Robert Ingersoll

Had it been left to Eric, Dodger Broadwinkle's Gift Shop would have closed early that day, but Hank had shown great diplomacy and had persuaded his colleague not to buy every weapon on display. After all, there were only three Avenging Knights, how many weapons did they need?

Having made their choice and endured another stomach-churning return teleport, Eric had driven them to the mine where, as planned, they had hooked up with his workmates Ralph and Helmut. Eric's story about entering the van for a stock-car race hadn't raised any suspicion so leaving the van with them, the trio had made its way down to the secluded quarry to give their recently purchased firearms a road test. At least they *hoped* it would be secluded – quite what they would say to anyone who happened to stroll past had not even been discussed. Needless to say Sixpack had been given the job of carrying the weapons, which were stuffed inside a large sack. He hadn't seen them yet and assumed he was carrying specialist cleaning tools for the imminent road sweeping task, although why they were going to test them in an environment such as this remained a mystery to him.

As they descended into the quarry, it came as a welcome relief to both Eric and Hank to see there was no-one about.

"Keep your eyes peeled Six," Eric said, "we don't want any gatecrashers."

"Sir?"

"He means keep a lookout for anybody heading this way. If you see someone, give us a shout," Hank explained. "You'll probably be able to see more if you go back up to the top."

"Very good sir," Sixpack replied, climbing the steps they had just come down.

"Oh Sixpack – we'll be needing that sack please."

He handed the sack to Hank and made off up the steps. "Y'know Eric, you really must try and ease up on the slang if Sixpack's gonna be coming with us. If we get into a tight spot it could be crucial that he understands you immediately."

"He'll be OK," Eric said casually, eager to start testing the guns.

"I'm serious Eric!"

"Alright, alright, I'll make an effort. Maybe we can pick up a 'slang' chip from somewhere. Dodger's bound to know where we can find one."

"I'd rather not do any more business with Dodger if that's alright with you?"

"Why not?"

"Eric! He deals in illegal weapons! I don't fancy getting chummy with him, next thing we'll be inviting him to come bowling with us! That reminds me, have we got a league game this Wednesday?"

Then it hit him.

That nagging doubt he had been trying so hard to identify. He swallowed hard. It was a pretty heavy-duty doubt, one that could jeopardise the whole deal. Nor was it something he could just sweep under the carpet, it wouldn't wait until the 'right time'. He had to mention it now – right now. The essential problem was this – for as long as he could remember he and Eric had stuck to the same old weekly routine. They worked Monday through to Friday and had the weekends to themselves but their evening activities were virtually etched in stone and went something like this;

- Monday – smashbowling at Smiling Larry's (practice).
- Tuesday – Moonraker Stadium to watch a ball game.
- Wednesday – smashbowling at Smiling Larry's (practice unless playing a league game).
- Thursday – Captain Uno Fan Club meeting.
- Friday – drinking at Angelo's.
- Sunday (day) – Eric visits his Mum
- Sunday (evening) – poker with colleagues from the mine.

As you can see, Saturday was the only day they didn't indulge in some form of regular social activity.

"No, the league game's *next* Wednesday, come on pass me the sack let's test these babies out."

Hank moved the sack away from Eric's reach.

"Um, Eric," he said, his throat drying up.

"*Now* what?"

"Has it crossed your mind exactly *when* we're gonna be going out and doing all the avenging?"

The driller's patience was wearing thin, he blew out his cheeks and put his hands on his hips.

"Meaning?"

"Meaning, well, we're usually busy almost every night of the week doing one thing or another and if we just like stop all that then it would be kinda obvious that we're up to something wouldn't it? But if we keep up our regular social activities then we're hardly gonna have any time left for crimefighting are we?"

There – he'd said it.

Now he had to deal with the aftermath.

Eric paused, but only for a second – it seemed he'd already given this problem some thought.

"I agree. We're bound to hit the headlines at some point once we get started and if we suddenly vanish from poker and bowling and stuff then yes, questions will be asked. As I see it we only have Saturdays free for any avenging."

"So?" Hank asked, relieved that it hadn't come as some great surprise.

"So we limit our superhero activities to Saturdays, any other free time we get I figured we'd use for reviewing and planning."

"And you're cool with that? Just going out on Saturdays I mean?"

Hank was astounded, he'd fully expected Eric to want to go out every single night of the week. He felt like a schoolboy who'd just been let off with a mild warning from the headmaster after burning the school down. But it reassured him a little too in that he'd only be risking his life one day a week out of a possible seven.

"Groovy – we have to be realistic about it Hank."

Realistic? Two grown men about to go running round the most dangerous city in America dressed as medieval knights was hardly realistic. The only realistic thing about the whole caper was just how absurd it sounded. "So are we gonna test the weapons or what?"

"Hmm?" Hank was momentarily lost in thought.

"The weapons – are we gonna give them a try?"

"Sure, sure!" he said, snapping back to the present and handing the bag to Eric. "Which one you wanna try first?"

As Eric rummaged through the sack, Hank withdrew several pieces of paper from his pocket. Dodger had been good enough to provide them with instructions for each weapon, which was a real bonus as Eric often dismissed manuals and handbooks as irrelevant complications.

"How about this one," Eric smiled, pulling the biggest gun out of the bag.

He hefted it into his hands, a monstrous two-handed carbine with several barrels that tapered into one long, thick muzzle. A large oval canister, gleaming silver in the sunlight, sat atop the gun. Hank sifted through his papers until he found the right one.

"OK, the Garbage Shoot," he read aloud. "An effective non-lethal weapon ideal for today's urban warrior. By utilising the revolutionary Trash Compacting Putrifier, this weapon requires minimal ammunition and can be reloaded using simple everyday waste. With a range well in excess of one hundred feet it will render an enemy immobile within seconds enabling the user to close in for the kill or beat a hasty retreat."

Eric swung round to face him, the unmistakable grin of an excited kid on his face, the gun swung around with him. "Eric!" Hank cried, pushing the barrel away from him. "Dodger loaded that thing for us before we left remember?"

"Oh yeah sorry, " Eric replied humbly. "So what are we gonna test it on?"

The quarry was, not surprisingly, just a huge pit strewn with rocks of varying sizes. Hank looked around frowning.

"I could pile up some stones if you like, same kinda size as a human?"

"Let's try it on Sixpack," Eric suggested.

"Sixpack? Are you nuts? Anyway he's keeping guard up at the top."

"Just a thought."

"Wait here while I gather up some rocks," Hank instructed.

While his friend went rock hunting Eric wheeled the gun round, left to right, testing the weight and manoeuvrability. For such a sizeable weapon it was incredibly light. He continued to play around with it, pulling it into his shoulder, going down on one knee, laying flat, making childish gun sounds as he did so.

Meanwhile Hank had begun piling up the stones he had collected, arranging them into a vertical pillar about six feet high and two feet wide. It was slow going and Eric's eagerness was beginning to overflow.

"Come on Hank, get outta the way!"

"Just a second bud, I need to find a stone for the head!" he bawled back.

Eric was back on his feet some forty feet away, the gun hefted against his shoulder, his finger already on the trigger.

"Villains of Cosmopolis!" he boomed, trying to mimic Sixpack's menacing delivery, "we the Avenging Knights find you guilty of illegal activity, prepare to meet with justice!"

Hank rolled his eyes and shook his head as he gingerly placed the final stone on his pillar. Why did everything have to be so dramatic? They'd come to the secluded quarry to practice without making too much noise and here was Eric shouting at a pile of rocks. He was obviously going to have to introduce his pal to the art of self-control before they hit the streets. Satisfied the 'head' would not keel over, Hank took a step back to admire his creation. Not bad – roughly the same height and girth of a regular humanoid.

"OK Eric," he said turning to face his gung-ho partner, "give it a…"

Eric hadn't meant to pull the trigger so soon, really he hadn't. The manual *did* have a section of small print regarding the sensitivity of the trigger but they hadn't read that far. There was a sound similar to that of someone stepping on a rotten apple and then a thin jet of dirty-green liquid spewed forth from the gun. The only good news for Hank was that Eric's aim had been a little off – had he hit him in the head (the height at which he'd been aiming) then things would have been a lot worse. As it happened, the sticky goo impacted on his chest, but the reaction was still significant. As a rule Hank rarely lost his temper, he was a laid back kind of chap and it took something pretty serious to upset him.

Being shot in the chest by Eric was more than enough.

He looked down at the offensive green stain on his shirt, which was beginning to dribble down towards his waist and then lifted his gaze towards Eric, who was rooted to the spot, the weapon still at his shoulder.

"Uh-oh," Eric murmured to himself.

Without a word Hank marched in the direction of the dumbfounded driller, his face stern and getting redder by the second. He had only managed a few steps when the pong hit him. It was quite possibly the most disgusting thing he had ever smelled, a combination of the stinkiest things he could imagine all rolled into one. It was enough to halt him in his stride. His eyes began to water involuntarily and he gagged, doing his best to breathe through his mouth.

It was *awful*!

Even though he was a good thirty feet away Eric was facing downwind and could smell it too. He wrinkled his nose at the foul stench and looked down at the weapon in amazement. How could it make such a hideous smell? His attention was drawn away from the gun as he heard Hank starting to run – towards him. One look at his pal's face told Eric a polite apology would probably not be adequate so he took more drastic action.

He dropped the weapon and fled.

This wasn't the first time the two friends had had a dust-up, although it was usually Eric that flipped. Everyone knew that you had to be wary of the 'quiet ones' as they tended to go completely berserk when their temper snapped. This thought only served to hasten Eric's rapid exit and he bounded back up the steps two at a time, Hank in hot pursuit. He was about halfway up when he saw Sixpack making his way down.

"Sir there are two gentlemen approaching from the south-west," he said calmly. "Sir? Are you alright?"

Eric's mind was a blur – whoever was about to interrupt them would be highly suspicious if they saw him fleeing from the quarry in such a state. But at the same time he wasn't exactly thrilled at the prospect of going back down the steps to face his irate chum. He managed to arrest his flight before he slammed into the droid.

"Stall them Sixpack…er…don't let them come down here!" he blustered and then turning on his heel he charged back down the way he had come. As expected, Hank was sprinting *up* the steps. Eric skidded to a halt and raised his hands in submission. "Someone's coming Hank! We have to hide!"

Unfortunately Hank wasn't listening, a combination of rage and the unholy stench that clung to him had totally unhinged him. His flying tackle caught Eric about waist height and knocked them both off the rough stairs and on to the adjacent slope. Locked in a bear-hugging embrace the two of them rolled down the hill, dislodging stones and pebbles as they went, causing a mini-avalanche. They crunched down into the base of the quarry, a cloud of dust enveloping them as they tried to get to their feet. Eric was up first, grimacing at the horrible green gunk that had rubbed off on his clothes. Wincing at the terrible pong but suspecting Hank's tantrum was far from over he hot-footed it towards the middle of the quarry. It didn't take long for Hank to stagger to his feet and, still consumed with anger, he raced after his trigger-happy partner. The only cover Eric could use was, ironically, the pillar of stones he had so spectacularly failed to hit a few seconds ago. He ran behind it and, clutching it at the sides, peeked out from the side to face the incoming Hank.

"Come out you coward!" Hank snarled, slowing to a walking pace.

Eric leaned out further from behind his makeshift shield so Hank could see his face, so he could see how sorry he was.

"Hank buddy, I'm so sorry, I didn't mean to hit you, you know I didn't!"

"*Come out!*"

Things were going from a small problem to a medium–sized nightmare for Eric, not only was Hank in a seemingly uncontrollable fury, but he could now see Sixpack leading two men down the steps towards them. He whimpered pathetically – the whole superhero thing was crumbling around his ears.

"Hank someone's coming look!" he pointed to the advancing party.

Convinced this was just some trick to divert his attention Hank didn't turn to investigate straight away, but the look on Eric's face suggested there really was something amiss behind him. He glanced over his shoulder – Sixpack and two other guys were making their way down the steps. He whirled round to face Eric again.

"Alright Eric, we'll deal with these fellas first, but then you and I need a *serious* talk!"

CHAPTER FIFTEEN

*"It has become appallingly obvious that
our technology has exceeded our humanity."*

Albert Einstein

Sunday morning arrived on Perfection Island in typically breathtaking fashion. The rising sun (who enjoyed showing off in a morning) bathed the east side of the island in a tropical glow, a warm breeze drifted through the trees and from somewhere in the jungle a gorilla yelped in pain as his behind was singed by a Korellian laser bolt.

Eve Tendril was out early, sunning herself on the balcony of her bedroom, sipping a glass of high quality orange juice and leafing through yet another beauty magazine. She was excited, today was going to be an interesting one. The special equipment and team of engineers Max had requested would be flying in at any moment, Cyrus's files would arrive about 10am, then Max had promised her a demonstration of his new formula after lunch. This was due to be followed by a progress report from Cyrus mid afternoon. With manicures, facial cleanses and massages to squeeze in somewhere she was going to be busy. But this didn't bother her, victory came at a price and if all she had to worry about were missing the occasional beauty treatment she would be more than happy.

She grinned maliciously beneath her enormous sunhat, wondering what futile activities the other contestants were currently engaged in. As her daydreaming continued, she even allowed herself a chuckle of satisfaction – oh to be crowned Miss Cosmopolis one more time – what a feeling it would be, what a triumph! Her name would go down in tournament history, the woman who had defied the odds and snatched victory from...

"*Help!*"

The cry had come from the beach under her balcony and, more annoyed than curious, she rose from the sun lounger to see what the fuss was all about. She didn't have to look far – sprinting along the sand (or as close to a sprint as he could get) was Ernest, her elderly head gardener in his customary grass-stained dungarees and cap. Hot on his heels, galloping along on all fours was an enraged gorilla, well over twice the size of the terrified gardener. Ernest was a meticulous worker, always checking and double-checking the shrubs were cut to the correct height, scouring the earth on hands and knees searching for weeds, never rushed, always patient and the sight of him in such a flap was quite hilarious.

"Run into the sea!" Eve yelled between laughs, from her vantage point. "Gorillas can't swim!"

She didn't really know if they could or not, she just wanted to see if he'd do it. Ernest glanced up at her and immediately changed direction, heading for the surf, the snarling gorilla continued to pound after him. Regardless of the fact the island was situated in a tropical region, where sharks, jellyfish and other marine unpleasantries lurked beneath the water, Ernest charged headlong into the sea, trying to lift his legs as high as he could to maintain his speed. After a few frantic seconds he was up to his waist but he didn't let up and 'front crawled' for his life, putting as much distance between himself and the shore as he could – just in case the gorilla had a merit badge for long-distance swimming. Only when he was fully fifty feet from the beach did he stop, turning to face back the way he had come, treading water nervously.

With a grand total of just two merit badges (one for chest-beating and the other for making scary faces), the gorilla stood on the shoreline, the waves just reaching his toes before they retreated back into the ocean. He watched his adversary through wide, angry eyes and then with a beat of his chest, a *very* scary face and a howl of frustration he lumbered off back towards the undergrowth.

As Ernest began swimming back to shore Eve suddenly wondered where her security guards were. There had certainly been enough commotion to alert them – so where were they? What if the gorilla had been chasing *her*? Furthermore, it was probably their relentless target practise that had sent the ape bananas in the first place. But what was the point of practicing if they didn't show up when it really mattered? It simply wouldn't do. She stormed into her bedroom and began to get changed, irritated at the incompetence of her guards. Down on the beach, an exhausted Ernest collapsed face first into the sand.

Max supervised the unloading of his specialist equipment and staff personally, making sure each crate was taken to the correct location and keeping the Korellians at bay as best he could. The entire croc security team had been on the end of a scorching rollocking from Miss Tendril who had made it clear that any further lapses of concentration would result in immediate dismissal. In an effort to make up for their sloppiness they were overseeing the arrival of Max's apparatus with a little too much zeal for the chemist's liking.

"No you can't search through it all!" he fumed, "I've got deadlines to meet, I haven't time for your petty rules."

Danzo Stax watched as crate after crate was unloaded, there were literally hundreds of them and he was dying to know what was in them. Being head of security he felt it incumbent on him to set an example to his colleagues, he was also terrified he might lose his job.

"Look Mr Ticklegrit, I must inspect all deliveries to the island – now will you co-operate or do I have to get rough?"

He wasn't threatening to push Max around or anything like that, 'getting rough' to a Korellian meant removing limbs. Max tried to keep hold of his temper but it was like trying to keep hold of an enthusiastic eel.

"Don't threaten me you oversized bullfrog! If Miss Tendril finds out you're hampering me she'll have you on the first transport out of here – and it's *Doctor* Ticklegrit!"

"At ease gentlemen."

Cyrus had appeared on the scene, dressed in a casual white linen shirt, his hands in the pockets of a pair of khaki shorts, the very picture of a rich man on holiday (which was fifty per cent true).

"Oh great, that's all I need," Max huffed, "perhaps we could get the entire island to come and interrupt me?"

Ignoring the jibe Cyrus turned to Danzo:

"I wouldn't worry about checking all this gear Danz, I can vouch for the doc. It's probably nothing but harmless chemical nonsense anyway, I doubt he's smuggling in a team of ninja assassins. I've got a delivery coming in this morning myself as it happens, just files and paperwork and stuff, you won't be wanting to check it through will you?"

"Of course not Mr Zifford, you'll be able to take delivery

personally, in fact, I'll contact you once it gets here. As for you doctor, I'll let you unpack in peace."

Cyrus beamed:

"Thanks Danz. Well, keep up the good work chaps," he said cheerfully and dawdled off in the direction of the beach, whistling a happy tune.

Max watched him go through narrowed eyes, he hated being indebted to someone that annoyingly smug. Maybe he'd slip something nasty into his drink after this project was finished, teach him a lesson. He noticed the Korellian was still watching him.

"Well go on then – clear off!" he snapped.

Cyrus's files arrived bang on time and he took great pleasure in watching Danzo and his fellow guards lug them all into his office, while he himself did very little. After that he settled down to the serious business of predicting the finalists. It was slow going at first but once he got into his rhythm he made real progress and by lunchtime had drawn up a preliminary list of twenty potential targets. He knew Max was due to unveil his new formula in about an hour but he had better things to do than watch the chemist faff about with his fancy potions. Deep down he really wanted to outdo him, to make more of an impact on Miss Tendril's project than he did. Obviously, he would stop short of sabotage but it would be immensely satisfying to emerge with more credit once it was all over. The only thing that bothered Cyrus was that Max was one of those rare people who seemed impervious to his manipulative techniques. He'd even threatened him when Cyrus had mentioned the Trouble Gum, which he suspected the doctor was still using. No – he'd just have to out perform him, beat him fair and square – something of a novel experience for someone like Cyrus.

Eve was confused.

She had just witnessed the effects of Max's new formula, on a fresh (but similarly luckless) rat this time. It had turned a normal looking rodent into something so utterly grotesque it defied description.

"I thought you were going to come up with a formula that would enhance my beauty...not reverse it?"

Max had expected he'd have to win her over and did so with great patience.

"Ma'am, the beauty enhancement market is exhausted, it plateaued over twelve months ago. There *was* talk earlier this year of Med USA coming up with some miracle formula that could halt the ageing process but it turned out to be nothing more than a rumour. It's simply impossible to improve on the existing products without some major technological breakthrough."

"Max I pay you to create the impossible."

"Yes but don't you see? It's far easier to make someone uglier than it is to make them more attractive (it was also a lot more fun but he decided not to mention that). Rather than enhance your own beauty I decided to target your opponents. It's so much simpler and yet we get the same result, which is complete victory."

Eve thought about it. He was probably right, it would be better to spike the opposition in this manner. It also provided an excellent back-up in case Cyrus failed to discredit them.

"Does this contraption have a name?" she asked.

Max stroked the device as if it were a pet.

"I call it The Uglifier," he said proudly.

"And how do you plan to target specific people with it? I mean, you can't possibly expect to take this thing to Cosmopolis and walk around with it."

"Well I have thought of a way around that problem," Max said carefully as though he were building up to a 'but'.

"Which is?"

"Which is…going to need a bit of help from you ma'am."

"What do you need Max?" Eve asked growing impatient.

He took a deep breath before answering.

"I'm going to need to use the company satellite."

"The satellite! Why on earth do you need that? Do you know how hard that's going to be?"

Eve was no satellite technician, but whatever he planned to do with it was bound to be extremely difficult – or at best a bit tricky.

"Very difficult ma'am – but not impossible and it *will* virtually guarantee your victory. You see I plan to build a much larger version of the Uglifier, which is why I asked for those engineers and equipment. Then I'll be able to bounce the laser off the satellite to any given co-ordinates. There are a few more tests to run but I'm fairly confident I'll be able to target individuals. Heck, with the satellite I could target anything you want, a whole city, *the entire planet!*"

Eve flicked her mane of jet black hair to one side, a gesture which suggested she was quietly impressed with the plan even though she didn't fully understand the 'in's and out's' of it.

"It certainly *sounds* impressive Max, will you be able to build the larger version in time?"

"My men are working on it now ma'am. I'll also need Mike Snapstick from Satellite Control working for me for the duration of the operation."

"No problem – I'll call him."

"The last thing I'll need after that is a surveillance team in Cosmopolis to shadow the finalists so I can input their co-ordinates into the satellite."

"I'm sure we'll be able to manage that without too much trouble."

Max nodded his thanks and began to pack his equipment away. "Er, just before you go Max I'd like another demonstration."

"Ma'am?"

"I want to see the effects on a human."

"Do you have anyone in mind?" he asked, somehow resisting the urge to propose Cyrus Zifford as a candidate.

When it came to recruiting her island staff, Eve made a point of choosing people that were below par in the good looks department – it was vital she was by far the most beautiful person on the island. She racked her brains to think of the least offensive looking employee, then flicked the switch on her comm unit. A static laden voice answered.

"Danzo, can you send Doris the maid up to my private office please?"

CHAPTER SIXTEEN

*"How many a man has thrown up his hands at a
time when a little more effort, a little more
patience would have achieved success?"*

Elbert Hubbard

It's easy to overlook minor details whilst in the grip of high spirits –
and this is exactly what Eric had done when they'd arrived at the
mine. In all the excitement he'd completely forgotten to hand over
the van keys to Ralph and Helmut, which is why they'd come
looking for him. Sixpack had done his best to hold them up but, like
many service droids (and the odd nun), he was singularly inept at
anything that involved deceit. The circumstances had not been easy
to explain and, after handing over the keys, Eric had spun them a
line about coming down to the quarry for a picnic (which explained
the sack) and how Hank had been violently sick (which explained
the stain on his shirt). He was however, quite at a loss to explain the
strange stone pillar in the centre of the pit and had mumbled
something about 'pagan religions being more common than they
used to be'. Eager to get on with the job of modifying the van his
colleagues had parted with nothing more sinister than a couple of
shrugs.

Then the real grilling had begun.

With absolutely no scope for blaming anyone else, Eric had sat
through the lecture in subservient silence. The interruption provided
by Ralph and Helmut had given Hank enough time to calm down
and the red mist had lifted to be replaced by cold, hard logic –
which didn't represent much of an improvement from Eric's
perspective and was a completely different colour. Words such as
'self-control', 'patience' and 'common sense' were used extensively
throughout the one-way conversation. It went on for nearly ten
minutes, Hank talking in a slow calculated voice, Eric nodding
when he felt it appropriate. Finally Hank wrapped it up;

"So are we clear?"

Eric nodded for what felt like the hundredth time. "Good, then let's get back to testing these weapons. Sixpack would you please go back up to the top and keep a lookout?"

"Very well sir," the droid replied and scampered back up the steps.

"Now," Hank said calmly, "it's quite clear the Garbage Shoot is in working order so let's give this one a try."

He reached into the sack and withdrew a much smaller weapon, a battered looking handgun. One of the new rules following Eric's reprimand was that Hank would be handling all the firearms during the testing phase. Eric had been demoted to reading the instructions.

"You know I wasn't overly keen on this one," he frowned, "but Dodger said it was far more effective than it looked."

Hank had to agree – it didn't look like much and the fact that Dodger had flatly refused to go into any detail had only heightened his doubts.

"What's it called again?"

Eric shuffled through the papers.

"Ah here it is. The Dissolver Revolver – a weapon of incredible power and not to be used in enclosed spaces. No danger of that here is there?"

"Anything else?"

"Yeah hang on," Eric said squinting at the page, "it says here that the due to its massive energy release the gun needs ten minutes to recharge between shots. Apparently the 'matter evaporator' will disintegrate *anything,* organic or otherwise, up to a maximum of thirty thousand cubic feet."

"Holy smoke! This little thing?"

"That's what it says bud. But remember there are twenty-seven cubic feet in just one cubic yard."

"Thanks for the maths lesson dude. Well, I guess there's only one way to find out," Hank said, a little unnerved about being in possession of something so potentially destructive.

"Take a shot at that pile of rocks you made," Eric suggested.

The column was less than twelve feet away, an easy shot even for someone as rusty as Hank.

"OK stand clear Eric," he said warily, hoping the gun wouldn't blow up in his hands and dissolve *him.*

Taking careful aim Hank depressed the trigger, almost closing his eyes and turning away as he did so. The gun emitted a swift zapping sound and then there was silence.

"Oh my g…!" Eric blurted out.

Hank opened his eyes – the column had disappeared.

"What happened?" he gasped.

"It just…it just…"

"It just *what*?"

"It just turned bright green and then vanished! Oh Hank that is one excellent weapon!"

"Excellent?" Hank exclaimed, "Eric it's freekin' *lethal*!"

Having seen the awesome power of this weapon Eric was determined to hang on to it – Hank's one-to-one had, it appeared, gone in one ear and straight out the other. He went for the responsible approach to try and win him over.

"I'm not talking about using it on *people*. But what if some armed robber is running towards a car, trying to make a quick getaway, we could fry the car in one hit!"

"And suppose there's someone behind the car that we can't see? Suppose some kid's asleep in the back seat? – then what eh? Sorry Eric, this one's going straight back to Dodger."

He stuffed it back inside the sack to show he was serious.

"I don't think Dodger does refunds."

"We'll cross that bridge if or rather 'when' we come to it," Hank said assertively.

"Okaaay," Eric said despondently, "I'll take it back tomorrow."

"No Eric, *I'll* take it back!"

"I thought you didn't want to see Dodger again, what's wrong? Don't you trust me?"

Hank gave him one of those looks which had featured so prominently in his recent lecture.

"Eric you've just *shot* me, what do you think?"

Sensing Hank could well be on the way to losing his temper again Eric decided to change the subject – kind of.

"Let's try another one instead."

This time Hank retrieved a much larger weapon, not as big as the Garbage Shoot but still a two-hander. "I think we're gonna struggle to test that one bud," said Eric.

"Which one is it?"

"It's the sleepy one," more paper sifting, "the Slumberjack.

The one that sends people to sleep."

"Hmm, you're right," Hank mumbled putting it back in the bag. "I suppose the same goes for the Inebriator too."

Eric grinned mischievously.

"Pity, I kinda liked the sound of that one. Transforming people into drunken idiots and all that."

"Guess that just leaves this one."

The last weapon resembled an old-fashioned Tommy gun, the type used by gangsters in the 1920s except the circular magazine was laid flat across the top. Eric read from his sheet;

"Trap your enemies like a spider with the brand new Web-o-matic Deluxe. Using specially modified spider's silk, the Web-o-matic will coat your adversary in a glutinous net, just like a fly. The more they struggle, the tighter the net becomes. Not for use by children under six years."

"Not really much we could try it on is there?" Hank said, looking around the desolate quarry.

"Let's bring Sixpack down," Eric suggested.

"What is this morbid fascination with wanting to try everything out on Sixpack?"

"Well there's no-one else is there? Besides it's only spider's web, it'll wash off easily."

Hank was already starting to feel guilty about his earlier outburst, it really wasn't like him to throw a wobbler like that and he *had* given Eric both barrels. Maybe he should cut him some slack.

"Alright," he sighed, "bring him down."

Sixpack was duly summoned and asked if he wouldn't mind being used for target practice – naturally he agreed without hesitation. Standing about twenty feet away with a tinge of sympathy for the poor droid, Hank hefted the Web-o-matic to his shoulder.

He took careful aim and then fired.

A strand of silver-white web flew from the gun and immediately enveloped the robot's head and upper torso, sending him into something of a panic. His arms flailed wildly but, as per the manual, he only succeeded in entangling himself further. The strand was unbroken, leading back into the gun's muzzle.

"Help! I am unable to move!" the droid spluttered.

"Well that seems to work OK," Eric summed up.

Sixpack stumbled over a loose rock and went crashing to the deck.

"Hold on Six, we're coming," Hank cried, dropping the weapon and running over to him.

Eric suddenly noticed there was more to the Web-o-matic instructions and began reading through it. Apparently, there was a 'reel-in' function, which allowed you to...well yes, 'reel in' your victim, like a fish on a line. Hank grabbed Sixpack by the shoulders and hauled him to his feet.

"Are you OK Six?" he asked.

Before he could answer Hank realised his hands were stuck to the service droid. Try as he might he simply could not let go of him. Eric, oblivious to their plight was busy reading. Without looking up he said,

"It says here that you need to coat your hands with a special solution before touching the web, apparently it's very similar to Mega-Glu[†]."

Hank hung his head – why had he agreed to using Sixpack? Would he ever learn?

Meanwhile Eric had looked up to see the strange embrace between man and machine.

"Hank what are you? ...oh."

"A little late with your advice there Eric!"

He was getting angry again.

Eager to help but, but not really sure how, Eric jogged over to them.

"No wait! Get back!" Hank warned. "If you get caught up in this then we've had it. Go find a cleaning solution or something, there must be industrial chemicals around here somewhere."

Not wanting to appear uncooperative, Eric raced back up the steps with absolutely no idea where to start looking. As he disappeared from sight over the lip of the quarry Hank turned back to Sixpack, their faces only inches apart.

"Do you know if Eric's life insurance is paid up Six?" he asked casually.

[†] Multiply Super Glue by a factor of ten and you're there.

CHAPTER SEVENTEEN

"It is better to be defeated on principle than to win on lies."

Arthur Calwell

When it came to giving presentations Cyrus was something of an artist. He used only state of the art technology to 'wow' his superiors, all singing all dancing graphics, extra large display monitors, surround-sound and often some stirring music to accompany his commentary (which he could deliver without an 'erm', 'obviously' or 'basically' in sight). In an attempt to outdo Max, he had pulled out all the stops for his first progress meeting with Eve and had been rehearsing solidly for the last hour. It was late afternoon and Cyrus knew Max had already given his demonstration, just after lunch.

A hand held device that turned people ugly.

Feeble.

He was convinced his own tactics were both superior and far more entertaining. Where was she? he thought, glancing at his watch, she wasn't usually la...

The door to the conference room opened and Eve strolled inside.

"Looks like you've been busy Cyrus, " she remarked, looking at all the visual aid hardware on display.

It had the air of NASA mission control rather than a conference room, she couldn't recall the last time she'd seen so many screens.

"Busier than you might think ma'am," he replied smugly, "in fact I've already drawn up a very reliable list of whom I believe will make up the other fourteen ladies for the interview stage."

"So quickly?" Eve asked, genuinely astonished.

"It's been quite easy actually, please, take a seat and all will be explained."

Eve sat opposite the huge screen (surrounded by smaller peripheral screens) in the far wall, she'd seen Cyrus do presentations before, they were usually stunning if a little lengthy but she was looking forward to seeing what he'd been up to. Cyrus's wheeled chair glided over to his control panel and he got the show on the road. The lights dimmed until they were shrouded in gloom and Eve half expected a droid selling ice-cream and choc ices to come wandering down the aisles.

The screen flickered into life and began showing old footage of previous Miss Cosmopolis tournaments, Eve noticed they were the three tournaments she had won back in the sixties.

"Glorious times eh ma'am?" Cyrus reminisced.

She had to agree and it almost brought a tear to her eye to see herself being crowned Miss Cosmo 2067, her final victory. "And with my help, you will be able to relive them," he said dramatically.

The film then showed her being crowned Miss Cosmo 2105! Obviously some kind of computer graphics trickery she mused, but the impact was amazing, as though she were being a shown a slice of the future. "The reason it's been so easy to predict the finalists is this," Cyrus began, "amid the avalanche of applications following the abolition of the age restrictions, several other former winners have decided to enter. As you know the rules of the tournament *specifically* state that any previous winners are automatically permitted to progress straight to the interview stage. Then, once all the bribes have been submitted, they are whittled down to ten and the televised final is held."

"I do hope you're not suggesting that I bribed my way to three titles Cyrus," Eve interjected.

"Not at all ma'am, I'm sure in your case it was a matter of pure beauty and nothing else."

And the award for Best Liar goes to...

"Now, since the tournament began in 2062 there have been twenty-five different winners, several of which went on to win a second time but only your good self managed to achieve the magic 'three' titles, consecutively I might add."

Images of former winners rolled across the screen, with their names and triumphant years underneath and soft classical music drifted from the surround-sound speakers. "Of those twenty-five, only thirteen, yourself included, have entered this year's tournament. So you see, you and the other former winners will make up the majority of the fifteen interviewees, I only had to look for another two."

He reeled off the names of the appropriate former winners, most of whom were familiar to Eve for one reason or another. The screen split up into a five by three grid with thirteen spaces already filled with beautiful faces, two spaces were left blank, a big question mark where their faces should have been. "So who are our two mystery finalists? Well, in my considered opinion, after much research and investigation the first will be Lola Lascala."

An image of Lola popped up on the screen and Eve's eyes narrowed in envy. She was jaw-droppingly attractive.

"Who is she?" she said through clenched teeth.

Cyrus wheeled over to another monitor and consulted his data file as though he'd anticipated her question – which of course he had.

"Eighteen years old, born in Cosmo – naturally. Winner of the 2103 New Faces Contest and runner up in last year's Babes of the U.S.A Competition. Still lives in Cosmo and works as a model for Elegance Quarterly magazine."

This was exactly why she needed Max and Cyrus, head to head she'd never be able to compete with the likes of Lola. Cyrus could sense his boss's angst – which was good, it was just the response he had been hoping for.

"But she's vulnerable," he said quietly.

Eve was all ears and anticipation;

"Go on."

"I did some digging on her background and it appears she once dated Hip-Hopster Dredz."

"The rapper?"

"That's right, but as we all know not *just* a rapper. A major player in the Cosmopolis Trouble Gum trade and due to spend the rest of his tone-deaf life behind bars at The Joint. I think a pack of Trouble Gum planted in Lola's apartment and an anonymous phone call to the cops should do the trick. Even the Cosmopolis police couldn't muck that one up."

"Yes but Trouble Gum? It's doesn't exactly grow on trees, where on earth would you find some."

Cyrus smiled.

"I think you'll find it's easier to locate than you think."

The fact that he planned to swipe some from Max's lab wasn't something he felt Eve needed to know, although the temptation to drop the chemist into the meat grinder was delicious. Now it was

Eve's turn to smile, Cyrus really was a smooth operator, cunning and lethal.

"Who's the second one?"

It came as a welcome relief for Eve to see Lola's face wiped from the monitor, but her respite was short lived when the next image dissolved into view. This girl made Lola look positively average. Eve gripped the arms of her chair, her manicured nails digging into the leather.

"Anette Kurtin," Cyrus announced, "nineteen years old, currently living in Scando 2 (formerly Finland) and heiress to her father's sausage empire. She's a director of Kurtin Enterprises and spends her time engrossed in the business twenty-four seven. But she's clean, not a trace of scandal anywhere."

"So how are you going to discredit her?" Eve asked, a trace of panic in her voice.

"Good question ma'am. There's the sausage angle of course, I think she'd do anything to protect the business, so some kind of industrial sabotage could be an option. Failing that I've plenty of pre-packaged stings I could use – don't worry ma'am, I'll make sure she doesn't make the final."

"Make sure you do," Eve said menacingly, she hated to admit it but Anette was quite possibly the most beautiful girl she had ever seen. "I want her packing frankfurters for the rest of her life!"

"I've still got some research to do on the former winners but there's no shortage of material on them, it's only a matter of time before I find their weaknesses."

The screen had gone back to the image of Eve being crowned this year's winner. "Just leave it to me ma'am," Cyrus beamed as the music went into a dramatic finale, "I'll nobble the competitors for you." The presentation reached it's climax with the old rotating newspaper trick, Cosmopolis tabloids spun their way on to the screen bearing headlines such as "Unprecedented 4th title for the undisputed Beauty Queen of Cosmo!" and "Tendril takes the title!" and finally "Eve storms to glory in Tendril-tastic final!"

The screen faded to black and the lights came back on.

Eve could still feel the adrenaline rushing through her body, the newspaper headlines especially, had worked her up in to a real state. She applauded enthusiastically.

"Excellent work Cyrus, if you pull this off we may not even need Max's ugly machine."

"Ugly machine ma'am?" Cyrus said playing dumb, "whatever do you mean?"

"Oh Dr Ticklegrit has come up with a device that turns people ugly – he's planning to use it on the finalists."

Cyrus began packing his equipment away looking thoroughly disinterested.

"Sounds a little basic to me ma'am."

The professional rivalry between Max and Cyrus was something Eve knew all about and she allowed herself a chuckle.

"It's very effective Cyrus, maybe you should ask him for a demo."

"I've more important things to do than waste my time with that far-fetched chemical mumbo-jumbo. I prefer to rely on more down to earth methods, like good old-fashioned scandal."

"Well, I'm sure between you, you'll get the job done."

She rose and made for the door, unaware Cyrus was mumbling something about irresponsible, mad scientists.

"I'll have another progress report ready for you in a week ma'am."

"Good, I look forward to it. Anything else you need while you're on the island?"

Cyrus thought about it. With Danzo Stax eating out of his hand he was pretty much catered for, although he did miss the comforts of his own office back in the city.

"No, not really," he replied coolly.

"Fine, I'll catch up with you next week then."

Eve wandered back to her bedroom oozing confidence, a broad smile on her face. With Max and Cyrus on the case she surely couldn't fail. Cyrus meanwhile was replaying his presentation for analysis purposes – no 'erms', no 'basicallys' and no 'obviouslys' – a textbook performance.

CHAPTER EIGHTEEN

"Forgiveness is a funny thing.
It warms the heart and cools the sting."

William Arthur Ward

It took over three hours for Eric to separate his droid from what he hoped was still his best friend. In the grand scheme of things this was probably not a bad result as it gave Hank plenty of time to calm down, like most people he was incapable of maintaining a foul mood for more than thirty minutes.

Glue-dissolver is not easy to find at a mine, after all the idea of a mine is to break things apart not glue them together. Consequently Eric failed to locate any by himself and had been forced to ask Ralph and Helmut for help. Naturally this raised more questions than Eric wanted to answer and again he struggled to come up with a convincing explanation. Luckily, his workmates weren't the suspicious type and they pointed him in the right direction. Armed with two canisters of anti-adhesive, a bucket of warm water and a handful of cloths Eric had made a hasty return to the scene of the crime.

The process was a slow and (for Hank) painful one. By the time they had been prised apart, he was considerably lower down the anger scale than he had been – which meant he was intensely annoyed rather than hopping mad. The entire operation was accompanied by a string of apologies from Eric, as though his monumental gaff would seem less serious the more times he said it. But Hank showed great self-control and a degree of empathy by resisting the urge to plant his boot in Eric's backside. Another lecture seemed the appropriate thing to do but if Eric hadn't listened to the first one what was the point of wasting time on another?

Sixpack meanwhile was so confused he nearly blew a fuse. He didn't have a clue what was going on but had finally come round to accepting this *wasn't* some form of road sweeping enterprise – for a start there were no roads involved. His paint had been stripped in several places, most of which was stuck to Hank's clothes and he looked as if he'd just been through a high-powered car wash.

"So," Hank said gruffly, washing off the last remains of Web-o-matic webbing with a damp cloth, "any more weapons you'd like to test buddy?"

Eric knew this was just a sarcastic jibe but he played the role of 'the reprimandee' anyway. Looking down at his feet he mumbled:

"Er...no thanks, I think we've had quite enough testing for one afternoon. Let's call it a day."

"Positive? You don't fancy taking a pop at me with the dissolver gun or perhaps giving me a second coat of puke from the Garbage Shoot?"

"Look Hank, I said I was sorry, I must've said it fifty times!" he pleaded.

"Well, I guess that makes everything alright then doesn't it?"

Eric was in no doubt he'd really fouled things up this time. Putting Hank into a mood like this was not easy to do – thankfully it was a lot easier to *un*do. This was a debate he couldn't win so he did what he usually did in such situations and changed the topic.

"I think the lads will have nearly finished on the van, shall we pack up and go up top?"

Hank sighed heavily. He wasn't very good at bearing grudges, not nearly as accomplished as Eric, he always adopted a far more 'water-under-the-bridge' approach.

"Come on then," he groaned, coming round.

"Get the bag Six," Eric said cheerfully, sensing his companion's mood was already on the mend.

They climbed the steps in silence, neither chum wanting to say anything that might jeopardise the uneasy truce they appeared to have reached.

Eric drove them home with mixed feelings, the weapons testing could have been better but at least they knew most of them worked and that Dodger hadn't taken advantage of their naivety by trying to palm them off with some junk. The other news on the plus side was that Helmut and Ralph had done a good job on the van, the armour looked solid enough and the turbo they'd installed was exactly what Eric had asked for – a terrific burst of speed at the touch of a button. He'd given it a quick test at the mine and hadn't asked twice when Hank had declined to ride with him. Then he'd paid them and after swiping a few sheets of plasti-steel they'd made tracks.

They still hadn't really engaged in any meaningful conversation since they'd set off for home and it was starting to represent a sulky silence.

And no-one likes a sulky silence.

Eric figured enough time had elapsed since the farce in the quarry so choosing his words carefully he said:

"There's bound to be teething problems I guess. But at least we know the weapons work now."

"Oh they work alright Eric, no doubt about that."

Maybe he hadn't left enough time after all.

"Can I offer you another room for the night?" he asked, going for the peace offering.

Hank had to smile – his friend had about as much tact as a bulldozer. But he had to admit he didn't feel like going back to his apartment, which was still in a real mess, so he accepted the olive branch.

"Yeah, thanks I will."

"Great! I'll give Sixpack a night off from cooking and we'll get some take-out food eh? Whatever you like, it's on me – and beer, lots of beer!"

Eric's olive branch was swiftly developing into an entire grove.

"Alright bud, no need to go overboard, let's just put the whole thing behind us shall we?"

"You know how sorry I was – *still am* don't you?"

"I know Eric, you've probably set a new record for consecutive apologies. Let's just get back to your place so we can relax."

"OK mate...we are still mates right?"

"Don't be daft! Of course we are, it'll take something a lot more serious than you shooting me to ruin this friendship."

"Groovy."

In spite of the obvious warning signals the quarry episode represented and the inevitable danger that lay ahead, Hank found himself laughing and it wasn't long before Eric joined in.

After a hot shower to ensure he was completely 'de-glued'

Hank joined Eric in the sitting room.

"Yep, that's right," Eric said down the comm unit, "and no pineapple and I mean *no pineapple*, pineapple belongs in a fruit salad, not on top of a pizza. Yes. And extra mayonnaise on those fries."

Hank beamed – he loved mayo on his fries, Eric really was giving him the cordon-bleu treatment. "How long? Thirty minutes? Are you walking it round? OK, alright I apologise, see you in thirty minutes."

"Top Toppers?" Hank asked.

Eric nodded, disconnecting the comm unit.

"Not as fast as they used to be."

Hank eased himself into an armchair as Sixpack walked in carrying a full crate of beer.

"Cripes, you really did mean a lot of beer didn't you?" Hank remarked, reaching for a bottle.

"Least I can do after today's cock-up," Eric sighed, catching the bottle Hank tossed him.

"You just need to be a little less impulsive bud. I don't want you going charging into anything until we're both ready, know what I mean?"

Eric tilted his bottle and drank deeply, guzzling like a true professional.

"Yeah I understand Hank, it won't happen again."

"I'm still game for this idea but I have to be able to trust you, I can't afford to be checking on you all the time." He was aware this was bordering on another lecture and decided to finish it. "Today was an example of what *not* to do, so let's hear no more about it eh?"

Eric leaned forward, offering his bottle.

"To the knights!" he said.

Hank clinked his bottle against Eric's.

"To the knights."

The remainder of the evening followed a fairly predictable course. They drank their beer, ate their pizza and fries, drank more beer, told some old stories, burped a lot, drank more beer and then finally, at about 2am fell asleep where they sat.

CHAPTER NINETEEN

"When you discover your mission, you will feel its demand.
It will fill you with enthusiasm
and a burning desire to get to work on it."

W Clement Stone

Once again it was the smell of burnt food working its magic that roused the slumbering friends. Eric was first to come round and surveyed the room through bleary eyes. An empty pizza box, a mountain of empty beer bottles and enough empty crisp packets to wallpaper the room.

It'd been a good night.

As his senses began to return he noticed there was another lingering odour in the air, the kind of odour that suggested they had been playing some mean tunes on their bottom trumpets during the night. Sixpack wandered in;

"Breakfast will be ready in approximately eight minutes sir."

"Smells like it was ready half an hour ago," Eric teased.

"Sir?"

"Oh nothing, can you get me a coffee? I need to feel human again."

"Very well sir," the droid replied, wondering what it must be like to feel human and deciding it was probably not as good as it sounded.

Hank too was beginning to stir.

"No! No...get it off me, I can't stand it...it stinks!" he gibbered, coming out of his nightmare.

He snapped awake, staring around him with wide fearful eyes.

"You OK bud?" Eric asked.

Hank rubbed his temples and took a while to answer;

"Yeah fine, just bad dreams. I trust that's breakfast I can smell and not a house fire."

"Sure is. Six! Make that two coffees will ya?"

They sat where they were for the moment, neither wishing to

engage the vertical too soon.

"So what's the plan for today?" Hank said through a yawn.

"Well, I'm gonna make a start on the armour for Six and also the chainmail shirts, helmets etc, then I'll pay a visit to Mum, see how she's doing with the costumes. I could drop that dissolver gun off to Dodger on my way if you like and then I'll be back around 6 pm 'ish'. I guess you'll be spending the day sorting out your place right?"

"Yeah, I can't stay here forever, gotta face the music sometime."

"You know you can stay here for as long as you like don't you?"

Hank smiled. It was a kind gesture and just the sort of thing friends did for each other, but he needed his own space and the thought of forcing down chunks of blackened food every mealtime held scant appeal.

"Thanks bud, but I'll probably be alright at my pad. Just needs tidying up a bit."

Sixpack breezed in with two cups of steaming coffee. He gave them both to Eric.

"No. The other one's for Hank," he said patiently.

Sixpack handed Hank his drink and reminded them about breakfast.

As usual the meal gave their jaws and their cutlery a strenuous workout. They ate in silence, which was especially strange behaviour for Eric and Hank wondered what could have sent him into such a state – was he on edge about something? Maybe it was the fact they were about to embark on a life-threatening adventure – or it could be the fact his bowling averages were tailing off. The cloying aftertaste of charcoal was alleviated by a few more cups of coffee and just as Sixpack was about to start the washing up Eric said; "Hold it Six, sit down will you? I need you to hear this."

So this was it. There was clearly some big announcement on the horizon. Hank hoped it wouldn't be another, more formal apology for yesterday's debacle at the quarry, although afterwards he wished it had been.

"Fellow knights, I've been thinking about the timeframe for our project. Costumes should be ready in a few days, we still need a radio for the Silver Steed, which I can procure and install this week by which time Sixpack will have prepared the basement for our headquarters. After that we'll be pretty much tooled up and ready. Therefore…"

He took a deep breath and made a point of avoiding eye contact with Hank. "…I propose we hit the streets next Saturday, August 13th, exactly six days from today."

He braced himself for the inevitable.

"*What*?" Hank cried, nearly spilling his coffee. "Eric, that's a bit early isn't it? What about the training, I thought you wanted me to school you in firearms and hand-to-hand combat?"

He declined to admit that, with his limited knowledge and ability, this would take no more than a couple of hours, even with a session for questions at the end.

"I figured we'd learn as we go. Besides, every day we delay is another day for the criminals to wreak havoc. Time is of the essence Hank."

"We can't possibly be ready in six days! Eric, mate, it's too soon."

Hank's protest had come as no shock to Eric and he was ready for it.

"Remember how you felt on Friday night when you got back home to find you'd been burgled? Remember that? Wasn't very pleasant was it? Well that's *exactly* how hundreds of other innocent people are gonna feel if we don't act. We can spare them that misery, you and me…and Sixpack."

The droid raised a hand.

"Six, for goodness sake, you don't need to do that, just chime in whenever you like."

He was annoyed that the impact of his inspirational speech hadn't had enough time to sink in.

"Sir, I have yet to be properly briefed on this new venture. May I ask exactly what is it we are supposed to be doing?"

For the next ten minutes Eric explained all about the Avenging Knights and how they would go some way to reducing the escalating crime wave – it should have taken five minutes but Eric's constant slang slowed things down considerably. It still didn't get him over his current obstacle though, which was talking Hank into a quicker than expected start.

"So whaddya say Hank? Let's get out there and start doing some good eh?"

Hank sighed, this is exactly what he was worried about – not rushing into things before they were ready. Most people cut corners, but sometimes Eric forgot the corners were there altogether, he seemed obsessed, like a racing car permanently stuck in high gear. Somehow he had to slow him down and get him into the pit lane.

"Let me sleep on it Eric, but I gotta tell ya, I'm not keen."

"OK, think it over and let me know later."

Not a bad result Eric thought. A solid 'yes' would have been too good to be true but at least he hadn't given him a solid 'no' either. He'd grind him down in the next few days.

It was actually Thursday (four days later) when Hank cracked.

Eric had been pestering him all week but Hank had stood firm and demanded more time, much the same way as a hostage negotiator. They had just left their regular Captain Uno Fan Club meeting (which had been more like a wake than a meeting) and were driving to Hank's apartment in the newly modified van. After a period of prolonged silence Hank finally said;

"Eric I have to tell you something."

Eric's heart leapt – this was it, he was going to crack.

"What is it?"

"You're never gonna get up this hill in third gear."

Cursing under his breath Eric changed gear.

"And you've even less chance in fourth."

Cursing out loud this time Eric made another adjustment. Hank was clearly not ready to capitulate just yet, but he was determined to keep chipping away at him.

"So you got your apartment cleaned up yet?" he asked casually.

"Yeah, it's not looking too bad, would have been easier if I'd had my Dust-Zucker though."

"Makes your blood boil doesn't it?"

"Yeah, but the insurance cheque should be here soon."

"I mean it really does make your blood *boil*!" Eric said passionately, ignoring Hank's last sentence. "That girl for example… such a shame."

"What girl?"

"I keep telling you Hank, you've got to keep abreast of current affairs. Didn't you hear about that nine year old girl who got injured yesterday?" He wrenched the van to the right. "*Oh nice one! You never heard of signalling scumbag?*"

114

Hank had never had any kids of his own (or anyone else's for that matter), he'd never even been close to getting married, but he liked kids and to hear about one getting hurt always saddened or maddened him.

"No, what happened?"

"Well you *did* hear about that bank raid?"

"Uh-hmm."

"Well, she got in the way of the getaway car, mindless thugs just kept on driving, she could've been killed."

"What happened to her? Is she OK?"

"Broken leg, she'll be able to walk again in a few months. Poor kid," Eric said shaking his head.

As you may already have guessed, Eric was being slightly economical with the truth. But, then again he wasn't lying through his teeth either. There *had* been a bank robbery yesterday and it *had* led to the injury of a young girl. That much was true. But she'd suffered nothing more than a twisted ankle and had been nowhere near the getaway car. No sir. Having heard the bank's whining alarm and seen the small crowd of onlookers gathered around the entrance she had simply been trying to get a better viewpoint by standing on a trash can. As the armed gang had burst from the bank, the onlookers had suddenly dispersed and in the resulting commotion she had fallen off.

Hank seethed in silence for the rest of the trip and eventually, they drew up outside his apartment building.

"See you tomorrow, " Eric said, as Hank disembarked.

"Yeah, seeya."

Eric watched him go, knowing his 'injured girl' story had hit the target but not sure if it had been close enough to the bullseye. He was about to pull away when he saw Hank walking back to the van.

"Forgotten something bud?" he asked, through the open window.

Hank still had a face like thunder.

"No. I just wanted to tell you that I've been thinking about your suggestion."

"And?"

"And we go on Saturday!"

With that he turned on his heel and disappeared inside the building. Eric beat the steering wheel with his fists then tore off into the traffic, somehow resisting the urge to engage the turbo – just.

CHAPTER TWENTY

"Don't worry about the world ending today.
It's already tomorrow in Australia."

Charles M Shultz

For now, events on Perfection Island are more than capable of looking after themselves. Max is fussing over his formula and overseeing construction of the full size Uglifier and Cyrus is knee deep in scandal as he prepares to launch his offensive on the unsuspecting Miss Cosmo finalists. Eve is having a much easier time of it, pampering herself (or rather getting others to pamper her) and generally making sure Max and Cyrus do what they're supposed to. You know how they feel about interruptions, so we'll concentrate on our two unlikely heroes for the time being.

Friday 12th August, 9pm – sat outside Angelo's.
Maria Valentino was perplexed which wasn't something she enjoyed, she was far happier being happy. Her two favourite customers had been in at 6pm as usual yet now, three hours later, they had still not finished their first beer – a landmark event in the history of Hank and Eric beer consumption. She knew they prided themselves on getting into double figures, sometimes they even ordered Mindscrew chasers and were often the last to leave.

But not tonight.

Tonight they had been in whispered discussion since they'd arrived and nothing, not even her best dazzling smile could snap them out of it – and let's not forget a smile from Maria is the equivalent of a slap in the face (a really hard one) followed by a shot of neat adrenaline. Eric hadn't even tried to chat her up, another first. Something was definitely amiss and despite having to help serve the two hundred or so other revellers, she was determined to find out what it was. Her fellow bar staff seemed to be keeping the horde suitably fed and watered so she sauntered over to them. Just as they had done on her two previous visits, the two friends leaned away from each other and the secret whispering came to an abrupt halt as she approached. She gave them a real belter of a smile, the type of smile that could make a man forget he was married.

"My, my you two certainly have something on your minds tonight," she said cheerfully.

Hank and Eric just smiled pleasantly giving nothing away. "So c'mon guys, what gives? You're normally on your seventh or eighth by now. You dieting?"

She knew this was highly unlikely, but she had to try and oyster-fork the big secret out of them somehow. At Hank's insistence, they had rehearsed a feasible story for any busybodies – nothing too detailed just enough to deter people from asking too many questions.

"It's kinda private Maria," Eric said, sticking to the script.

Hank said nothing, again all part of the charade.

"Aw, come on now, too personal to tell little old Maria?"

She ruffled her hand through Eric's close shaven hair, a technique few men could resist – including Eric Dorfler.

"Er...OK, well y'see Hank here has this rather embarrassing medical problem."

Hank nearly choked on his ale. *What was he doing?* This wasn't part of the plan at all! "And I don't think he'd thank me for giving you all the nasty details."

Maria looked at him with a sympathetic smirk, her way of telling him she was sorry to hear about his 'problem'. "Unless you *really* wanna know, in which case we could discuss it over dinner at...ow!"

Hank kicked him under the table.

"Not really my idea of a romantic evening honey," Maria giggled, then turned to Hank. "But I wouldn't worry Hank, they can do amazing things nowadays, medical science is so sophisticated."

So this is what it was all about, she surmised, Hank's malfunctioning plumbing.

"I'm sure they'll be able to help you, y'know, if you're having trouble getting it u..."

"I'm perfectly fine thanks Maria," Hank put in hastily, "I'm afraid Eric tends to embellish things a bit. *Don't you Eric?*"

The last part didn't come across as a question, it was much closer to a threat and (for once) Eric took the hint.

"Yeah, sorry Maria, Hank's right, I can get carried away now and then. But my offer for dinner still stands, with a different topic of conversation."

"Sorry Eric, you're going to have to do better than that. In a few months you could be trying to seduce a beauty queen rather than a barmaid."

She gave them a twirl, finishing with her hands on her hips accompanied by another humdinger of a smile.

"What do you mean?" Hank asked.

"I'm entering this year's Miss Cosmopolis Tournament."

"You're *what*?" Eric laughed, oblivious to the offence he was causing.

"That's right you heard me," Maria said indignantly, "I'm gonna chance my arm at Miss Cosmo, see how far I get."

"But aren't you a bit, well, you know...*old* for that?" Eric asked, unwittingly digging his hole even deeper.

"They've abolished the age restrictions this year honey, any girl born in Cosmo can enter, don't you read the papers? Besides, I'm only twenty-nine."

Hank saw his chance and dived in:

"Yeah, it's important to *keep abreast of current affairs* Eric," he said grinning from ear to ear. "I think you'll do us proud Maria."

"Why thank you Hank," she beamed, "nice to have some encouragement. Now are you two gonna start knocking this beer back or do I have to pour it down you?"

They both drank deeply, draining their bottles. "That's more like it, same again?"

They nodded and watched her mingle back into the crowd.

"You smoothy!" Eric laughed.

"I think she's got a good chance, I can't think of *anyone* I know who's better qualified."

This was very true. It was easy to forget that behind the bland waitress guise Maria was incredibly attractive. "Anyway, back to business, where were we?"

They were leaning toward the middle of the table again, their voices low, keeping one eye out for Maria returning with their beers.

"OK," Eric began, "Six is all armoured up and should have already picked up the costumes from Mum, we can try them on when we get back. The radio's installed in The Steed, the basement is now fully converted into our HQ and the weapons have been cleaned and checked as much as possible. We're ready bud!"

'Ready' was hardly the word Hank would've used – 'woefully unprepared' would've been more appropriate. But even if they stopped just *one* crime tomorrow it would be worth it, if they spared just *one* person the agony of becoming yet another victim. His hopes still rested largely on the premise that most crooks would be too dumbfounded to move when confronted by two medieval knights and a droid (complete with terrifying voice) brandishing fearsome looking weapons. They planned to use the Web-o-matic the most, it was an excellent immobiliser and had a decent range. Needless to say Hank had laid claim to it with Eric settling for the as yet untested Slumberjack, another non-lethal weapon with the capacity to put opponents down (assuming it worked). Communication between all three of them would be achieved via the headsets they would be wearing inside their helmets.

The names had also been finalised, Eric had stuck with Sir Prize, Hank with Rough Knight and Sixpack had been told he would be known as Excalibot. He hadn't questioned this, much the same way a four year old child wouldn't question $E = MC^2$.

"I think it's best that you crash at my place tonight," Eric whispered, "We should be able to hit the streets at about midday all being well."

Hank found himself nodding but it all still seemed a bit surreal. He really *was* going to be running round the city dressed as a knight tomorrow. He wondered if his anxiety was too obvious. Eric took another slug of what was left of his beer. "I gotta tell ya man, I can't wait to get out there and kick some criminal butt!"

Nope.

"Just promise me one thing tomorrow Eric."

"Name it."

"Let's be careful OK? For all we know we could run into the Ravanelli Gang[†] on our first day. We need to start off dealing with minor crimes and work our way up to the more demanding stuff. Let's learn to walk before we can run yeah?"

"No problem Hank, we'll watch our backs and each others',

[†] The meanest, baddest gang in the U.S. Originally from Mafio (formerly Italy) they have a reputation for ruthlessness, flashy suits and outstanding pizza making abilities.

take things one step at a time."

Hank dearly wanted to believe him. He certainly sounded sincere, but he knew Eric of old and how headstrong he could be.

"Alright, one more beer then we'll hit the road eh? We need to be sharp tomorrow."

"Sure."

Maria duly returned with two more bottles of ale and, as she meandered back into the bar, Hank couldn't help wondering if he'd ever see her again.

CHAPTER TWENTY-ONE

*"My philosophy has always been to help women and men feel
comfortable and confident through the clothes they wear."*

Georgio Armani

Friday 12th August, 11pm – Eric's place.

Hank looked at Hank in the full-length reflectogram.

His feelings were split roughly fifty-fifty. On the one hand he
felt rather cool, suave and a tad macho, there was just something
about being dressed as a medieval knight that sent his nerves
tingling. The cold metal of the chainmail shirt against his skin, the
way the breastplate caught the light and shone with a dull radiance.
He'd once seen a documentary on TV about noblemen of the middle
ages, how they championed causes, fought against tyranny and
oppression, how they had been revered by the common folk – true
guardians of justice.

Then there was the other half.

And this half made him feel utterly ridiculous.

It was a sensation akin to being dressed as a member of the
opposite sex. That self-consciousness that eats away at your dignity
(especially for men dressed as women) until you are forced to
accept the fact you look completely laughable. You could rescue a
child from a burning building in front of a horde of appreciative
onlookers and still feel stupid. There was no getting away from it –
he *did* look a bit daft.

He turned sideways to check out his profile. The beer belly
was still there, just as it had been for the last fifteen years. He really
needed to shed a few pounds, there probably hadn't been too many
podgy knights running around in medieval times. Reaching forward
he adjusted the dial on the side of the reflectogram to project a
slimmer image. That was more like it. Perhaps he ought to join the
local gym or lay off the beer for a few weeks – now that *would* be a
sacrifice.

"Pretty snazzy huh?"

Eric was stood in the doorway also in full costume, his helmet tucked under his arm and a big grin on his face. The kind of grin that said 'I told ya so!'

"Er...yeah," Hank replied, trying to sound keen.

"Try the helmet on for size."

For a moment Hank's world went dark as he slipped the helmet over his head, then the light made a welcome return via the narrow slit of his visor.

"It's a bit loose isn't it?" he said, his voice echoing around the inside of his helmet.

"Yeah well I didn't want to make them too tight in case we need to take them off in an emergency. As you can probably tell I've installed a receiver and transmitter so we can communicate effectively. Now wait here while I nip downstairs to give it a try."

Hank turned back to the reflectogram as Eric thundered down the stairs. He frowned inside his helmet as he took another look at his overhanging belly. Yes, he would definitely have to do something about it – but what? Slimming pills? Or just regular exercise? He could always...

"CAN YOU HEAR ME?"

Ever put on a pair of headphones without realising you'd left the volume on full?

"*Argh*! Yes, I can hear you Eric but drop the volume a few notches will you?"

"OH SORRY BUD (crackly static) is that better?"

"Yeah much better, I take it you can hear me OK?"

"Clear as a bell. Alright, I'm coming back up."

With his ears still ringing Hank removed his helmet and replaced it gingerly on the bedside table as though it might turn round and bite him. Eric reappeared in the doorway, he too had 'de-helmeted'.

"Right then, successful test completed. It's cracking on for eleven-fifteen so I recommend we hit the sack, tomorrow's gonna be a big day. You alright bud? You look a bit distant."

Distant wasn't the right word, Hank was positively light years away. He had no idea if tomorrow would be the last day of his life, the greatest thrill he had ever known or a massive anti-climax. Whatever lay in store the chances of a good night's kip were looking distinctly remote.

"Hank?"

"Hmm?"

"I said are you OK?"

"Oh yeah, yeah, no problem."

The problem was going to be sleeping.

"Right-o, I'll catch you on the sunny side then. G'night"

"Yeah night Eric," Hank mumbled and began to get ready for bed.

Further down the hall, in his own room, Eric was also disrobing – with a troubled mind. What was wrong with Hank? Why did he seem so unenthusiastic? Didn't he realise they were on the verge of something incredible? Then the doubts started creeping in, like the first droplets of water leaking through the cracks of a dam. Had he *really* thought this through properly? Maybe he was about to plunge himself (and Hank) into a world of trouble with terrible consequences. Eric knew if he allowed these doubts to cloud his mind then the dam could well burst. No! They'd be fine, they had the weapons, they had the determination and they had the force of 'good' on their side which had to count for *something* – 'good' usually did pretty well in the grand scheme of things. The only real wild card was Sixpack, if only he could make sure he didn't do anything daft they'd be OK. Eric had haphazardly welded some plates of plasti-steel to the droid to try and give him extra protection, these had then been painted yellow to match the droid's original colour. All a bit rushed and not the slickest job he'd ever done, but time was short.

Earlier that evening he'd given the droid another detailed (and slang-free) explanation of exactly what it was they were hoping to achieve. In true droid fashion, Sixpack had sat patiently and listened without interruption. Afterwards he had voiced his one and only question; wouldn't this form of activity be deemed illegal? In true human fashion, Eric had made up a hasty lie. He'd told Sixpack that since the retirement of Captain Uno, the Cosmopolis Police Dept was now *encouraging* the help of vigilantes although to admit as much in public would be a gross breach of policy. The 'soon to be famous' Avenging Knights would actually be doing the city a great service. This also explained (rather fortuitously) why it all had to be so hush-hush. Eric's sales pitch had worked like a dream and Sixpack had been much happier about the whole thing once he'd ascertained no laws were being broken – such was the universal droid philosophy of believing everything their master told them. Marvelling at the droid's gullibility and feeling a teeny bit guilty, Eric had briefed him on his specific functions and then called the meeting to a close.

As he snuggled under the covers, Eric concentrated hard on trying to go to sleep – which wasn't easy. He was right about one thing though – the Avenging Knights *would* soon be famous, but not in a way even he could have imagined.

CHAPTER TWENTY-TWO

"Failure to prepare is preparing to fail."

Mike Murdock

Both friends did eventually manage to hop aboard the Slumber Bus, but their journeys were brief and riddled with freakish dreams. This was especially the case with Hank, who found himself sitting bolt upright in bed on more than one occasion with images of giant spider-webs and squashed helmets racing through his mind.

Day One of their crime fighting careers began innocuously enough. The now familiar smell of Sixpack's over-zealous cooking drifted its way into their rooms and was enough to rouse them. Hank dressed 'normally' for breakfast and as he padded out of his room he prayed he wouldn't meet Sir Prize in full costume on the landing.

He didn't.

In fact when Eric did surface he was still wearing his Captain Uno pyjamas and slippers, shuffling along like a zombie, his eyes barely open.

"Sleep much?" Hank asked as he approached the top of the staircase.

Eric's yawn threatened to unhinge his jaw and he shook his head – it was far too early to engage his vocal cords. He waved his arm, encouraging Hank to go downstairs first, bracing himself for yet another gargantuan intake of oxygen. This is how Eric looked every Saturday morning, yet ironically this time it had nothing to do with alcohol – he wasn't hung-over, just dog-tired. Not sure if he could face one of Sixpack's death-by-fire breakfasts, Hank poured himself a glass of Supa-Slurp[†] and gulped it down greedily. He

---

[†] The most popular breakfast beverage of 2105. A highly refreshing drink made from the juices of the Bumba, a fruit with incredible powers of rejuvenation which grows only on the planet Moonashi (home to quite possibly the most energetic population in the universe).

glanced at the clock – 9.06am. They hadn't discussed exactly what time they would hit the streets, yet Hank's stomach was already tying itself in knots – the really complicated kind that only sailors could do. Eric on the other hand, seemed the very model of calmness – perhaps he was too tired to get agitated, Hank thought. Sixpack served up what could only be described as a 'soot special' and the two chums set about devouring it with little relish (but plenty of sauce). Not for the first time Hank wondered just how his pal could eat this stuff day in day out, maybe he had an unconscious hostility towards his stomach. With 'food' in his belly Eric suddenly perked up.

"How you feelin' bud?" he asked.

Terrified – was the honest answer, but Hank didn't want to dampen their spirits.

"A bit nervous," he admitted, forcing down a lump of charcoal that had probably been a mushroom in a previous life.

"Yeah me too. Still, it's perfectly normal I suppose, I mean, we *are* about to risk our necks."

Hank swallowed hard. If this was Eric's idea of motivation he'd hate to see him trying to put the downers on something.

"If we come across any suicidal jumpers during our exploits, let me do the talking will ya?"

He took another swig of his juice to wash down the black grit that clung to the inside of his throat. "So, what time are we gonna, y'know...start?" he asked tentatively.

"Well, I wanna give the Silver Steed one last check, make sure everything's working properly and I'd really like to try the Slumberjack and the Inebriator, they're the only things we haven't tested."

"On who?"

"My neighbour Cunningham usually goes jogging around this time, thought we could get him when he comes back, in about half an hour."

"I'm not sure Eric, what if these weapons really do some damage? It might even kill him!"

"It won't kill him! They're designed to be non-lethal remember?"

"For the record, I think it's a risk we don't need to take."

"I agree with Mr Halo sir," Sixpack piped up, "we know very little about the power of these weapons."

126

"Everything will be alright," Eric reassured them, apparently happy to throw caution to the wind along with commonsense.

"Well, you can't try both of them at the same time though can you?" Hank said.

"That's true. I thought we'd hit Cunningham with the Inebriator and use the Slumberjack on Shambles."

"Who's Shambles?"

"His dog."

"Not exactly a neighbourly thing to do is it mate?"

"Don't worry about it, I've never really liked him anyway. Not since he reported me to the cops for that Captain Uno twentieth anniversary party I threw."

"Yeah but you *did* almost burn his house down, Eric."

"Aw come on, it was just high spirits that's all. But I'm not going to go into that again, besides, it's only gonna make him drunk isn't it? He's tee-total as I understand it, so it'd be nice to let him know what it feels like to be worse for wear and Shambles has fouled my back yard more times than you've had hot dinners so he's due for some payback too. As far as kick-off time is concerned, I reckon we should start cruising about 1pm."

Hank's conscience was still gnawing away at him. He knew they weren't properly prepared, they hadn't discussed tactics in any great detail, hadn't trained, hadn't planned contingencies if things did go askew, but every day they delayed was another day for the criminal fraternity to run riot virtually unopposed.

"What about tactics?" he asked, desperately hoping Eric had given it at least *some* thought.

"You'll be pleased to know I have actually given this some thought," Eric replied. "As I see it we have three main objectives every time we hit the streets. Catch the criminals in the act, subdue them, then alert the police so they can arrest them. The first objective will be achieved by eavesdropping on the police band using the radio in the Silver Steed. Then we have to catch them in the act so I've equipped Sixpack's helmet with a tiny video device located on top of his head, whatever he's looking at gets recorded, I figured we'd send discs with video footage of the crimes being committed to the police – we don't want any of our victims being released due to lack of evidence."

Hank glanced at Sixpack's helmet on the kitchen worktop, sure enough there was a recent attachment on the top, nothing more than a small black tube to the casual observer.

"Nice one," he said, genuinely impressed. "But I was thinking more about how we'd achieve objective number two, the subduing part."

"That's obviously gonna be the trickiest bit, but you're right, we do need some kinda procedure. I reckon once we've established how many we're up against we go in and issue the challenge. If they resist then we use our weapons to 'pacify' them. I think we should *all* be armed, Sixpack included. As discussed, you take the Web-o-matic and I'll have the Inebriator, Six can take the Garbage Shoot."

The idea of giving the droid a weapon did not sit well with Hank, Sixpack couldn't even rustle up a decent breakfast let alone handle a weapon.

"Will he be OK with that?" Hank whispered.

"What do you mean?"

"I mean can he operate it?"

"Of course! It's not difficult Hank, you just aim at the bad guy and pull the trigger."

"C'mon Eric! There's more to it than that and you know it. Your debut wasn't exactly a monumental success was it?"

"I just got over-excited that's all, but Sixpack won't. He's a droid he can't get excited about anything."

It was a fair point but Hank still wasn't happy, he was about to tell Eric that if anything went wrong *he* would be to blame when Sixpack (who had been preoccupied with the washing up) chimed in:

"Sir, I can assure you I am more than capable of operating most mechanical devices to a satisfactory standard."

"See?" Eric said encouragingly.

"Six, have you ever handled a weapon before?" Hank asked.

"No sir I have not. Unless frying pans can be classed as weapons."

Hank spread his arms towards Eric, palms up in a clear 'see my point?' manner. Sixpack continued to scrub the blackened pan furiously.

"OK," Eric conceded, "we use him as back-up then. If we're in the mire he can help us out. Deal?"

"Deal."

"Alright, we'll finish breakfast then I'm going to set up my ambush for Cunningham and his mutt. In fact, maybe we should let

Sixpack do it? Y'know, give him some practise?"

There was a loud clatter as the frying pan slipped from the droid's grip and hit the kitchen floor. "Er... maybe not."

As Sixpack retrieved the pan from the floor there came a knock at the front door. Three soft, tentative knocks, like an office junior about to enter the boss's office for the first time.

"Expecting someone?" Hank asked.

"Nope, probably another one of those infernal door to door salesmen, we've been getting a few lately."

Eric made for the door.

"Maybe you should take the Inebriator," Hank grinned, "it could be Cunningham."

Wearing his best 'whatever you're selling I've already got one' face Eric swung the door open. The man stood on his doorstep had everything but the word 'salesman' tattooed on his forehead. He looked like a throwback to the vacuum cleaner salesmen of the 1950s. Ill fitting grey suit, crumpled tie, trilby hat, he had the lot, including the fake smile, all that was missing was the enormous sample case although he did have a thin briefcase under one arm.

"Oh...er...nice pyjamas sir...er...Eric Dorfler is it?" he stammered.

"No sorry pal, you've got the wrong house."

Eric could lie to most people (even good friends) without too much trouble so fibbing to this complete unknown was a walk in the park. The stranger frowned, clearly confused and checked the number on the front door one more time.

"This is ninety-nine Fargo Drive isn't it?"

There wasn't much point in trying to deny that, the number was there for all to see and the street sign at the end of the drive made it doubly obvious.

"That's right," Eric said innocently.

"And you're *definitely* not Eric Dorfler?"

"Look pal, Eric Dorfler *used* to live here but he moved about a year ago OK? Are we done?"

He began to close the door. The man's confusion level went up a notch.

"Er...in that case I suppose we are."

"Bye then!"

"But you look so much like his statue!"

SLAM!

Eric huffed and grumbled to himself as he padded back towards the kitchen – bloody salesmen, had they nothing better to do than...wait a minute? *Statue?* He ran back to the door and flung it open but the stranger was nowhere to be seen.

CHAPTER TWENTY-THREE

"We're eyeball to eyeball, and I think the
other fellow just blinked."

Dean Rusk

It was actually 1.30pm when the Silver Steed rumbled out of the driveway. The Cunningham hit had gone as well as could be expected even though Eric had missed with his first shot. But, after a quick curse and slight aim adjustment, he'd made no mistake with his second. The Inebriator had three settings: Tipsy, Well-oiled and Banjaxed. Cunningham had taken a direct hit of Well-oiled and was, much to Eric's delight, staggering around the garden burbling incoherent nonsense. His dog Shambles was snoring by the doorstep having been soundly Slumberjacked. Eric had taken full advantage of the 'I told you it would be alright' situation and had demanded apologies and beer kegs from both Hank and Sixpack. This had lifted their spirits, now they had tested *all* their weapons and all were in working order. However, as they cruised into the seedier neighbourhoods of the city, their nerves began to show.

They were in full costume, except for their helmets which, for the time being, resided in the back of the van along with Sixpack and the weapons. Hank massaged his gloved hands together anxiously,

"When are we gonna turn the radio on?"

"Just a little further bud," Eric said as calmly as he could, steering the van into the notorious borough of Mawldeath.

"Eric, Mawldeath is more than adequately crime-infested, if we go any further we'll be in 'Crime Central'. We won't even need the radio, there'll be villains on every corner."

Eric turned into a deserted side street, brought them to a halt and cut the engine – it was 2.04pm and the Avenging Knights were about to go 'live'.

"OK, we'll park up here til we pick up something worth tackling. Six, get the map out and crank up the airwaves will ya?"

Hank shot him a look. "Er... I mean, turn the radio on please."

Now before we go any further you need to know about Mawldeath – you need to know just how unpleasant and dangerous it really is. Imagine the worst neighbourhood in your city, the most crime-ridden ghetto you've ever heard about. The one place you wouldn't want to run out of gas. Take that fear factor, that awful sense of trepidation and multiply it by ten – then you'd be close to a place like Mawldeath. Walls are tagged with provocative graffiti, litter adorns the streets...and the alleys – you don't even want to know what goes on in the alleys – just conjure up some form of unbelievably brutal illegal activity and you'll probably be closer to the truth than you thought. In Mawldeath your knuckles go beyond white, your breath goes beyond heavy and your emotions go way beyond panic. If you can avoid the purse snatchers then you've done alright for yourself, it gives you a better than average chance of evading the knife-wielding muggers which means you might just escape the vicious tribal gang element leaving only the psychotic murderers to worry about. Even the dogs carry switchblades. Walk away unscathed and you've become one of the lucky one per cent to leave Mawldeath in one piece.

There was a burst of static followed by the disorganised dialogue of the Cosmopolis Police Dept dispatch team. At first it was like listening to a three year old talking through a faulty microphone. They listened in silence for a few minutes until they got the gist of what was happening. The main issue seemed to be a huge traffic jam on the Excalibur Zoomway following a collision involving two transporter vehicles, one laden with a cargo of live chickens the other carrying large vats of treacle – it was messy and the cops had their hands full.

"Could be a diversion," Eric suggested. "Something to keep the cops busy."

"Unlikely, these things happen all the time," Hank replied.

He hoped this was just Eric's way of dealing with the initial tension, they wouldn't get very far if they automatically assumed every little event was crime related. 'Hey that old lady crossing the road might actually be a mass murderer with a blitzer pistol built into her walking stick! Let's take her out!' No, they would have to be a little more level-headed if they were to make any progress.

"Hank can you stop that please? It's making me really nervous."

"Stop what?"

"*That!*" Eric exclaimed nodding towards Hank's frantic hand rubbing.

"Oh sorry, I didn't even know I was do…"

The conversation froze as the following announcement came crackling over the radio:

"All units, all units we have a report of possible mugging at the corner of…no wait that could be a kidnapping, hang on…OK now someone's telling me it's a robbery. Aw heck – there's definitely something going on at the corner of Casino Boulevard and Westworld Plaza, please respond."

For a moment no-one spoke, then Eric fired up the van.

"That's it," he said grimly, "time to get this show on the road. Six, I need you to direct me to the corner of Casino Boulevard and Westworld Plaza."

Sixpack spread the map out and began to relay directions. Hank would've preferred to know more about the crime they were about to try and tackle but it seemed not even the police had much idea what the problem was – no change there. They'd just have to deal with it once they arrived, assuming of course the cops had managed to get the address right.

2.23pm – the corner of Casino Boulevard and Westworld Plaza.

In the old days it used to be the aliens that did all the abducting but in 2105 the tables had turned, now it was the aliens who were in danger. Kidnapping aliens to sell them on as slaves was a nasty business, especially if you were an alien. But it was also a thriving business. Aliens came in all kinds of shapes and sizes and could be used to perform a variety of different tasks.

'Shulkers' for example were incredibly powerful creatures, bristling with muscle and almost impenetrable rock-like skin, yet they were extremely placid making them ideal for slave labour in mining colonies. No-one was going to file a lawsuit if a shulker got crushed in a cave-in, you just sent in more shulkers to clear up the mess. Another favourite was the 'doberfurt', a long, tubular canine type animal with luxurious thick fur, razor sharp teeth and a serious lack of social warmth. They were ideal guard dogs and the unfortunate beasts often spent their days chained to posts outside some celebrity's mansion to ward off unwanted visitors, they also

133

doubled up as superb draft excluders when sufficiently sedated.

But on this occasion the brand of alien in peril was the 'skoob' – a trio of skoobs to be exact. Predominantly humanoid in appearance with an average height of only five feet, these spindly creatures were usually sold into service as servants due to their subservient nature. Their obedience could be further enhanced by getting them hooked on waffles, their favourite food. After that you had them in your pocket. These particular skoobs (who were new in town) had been on their way to the hyper-market and had taken a wrong turn. That's when they had encountered the five unsavoury individuals who now had them cornered in an alleyway just off Westworld Plaza.

The hoodlums had initially intended to rob them, but skoobs weren't renowned for their wealth, indeed their idea of a well paid job was serving popcorn at the ball game. So the thugs had decided to go for the next best thing – abduction. It would be a little trickier to accomplish but infinitely more lucrative. They had chased the terrified skoobs for several minutes until the pursuit had led into the alleyway – now the skoobs had nowhere to run and the thugs were closing in.

Their leader was a seasoned villain by the name of Skip Bridges. Neither he nor any of his crew was armed, but he wasn't worried, he'd abducted skoobs once before and knew they were poor fighters – he also knew their weakness.

"Hey Benny," he hissed to one of his mates, "why don't you nip round the corner to Oswald's bakery and get us some waffles."

"Waffles? Is this really the time for a snack break Skip?"

"Just do as I say Benny! A nice tasty pack of waffles and these losers will do whatever we tell 'em."

"Er…OK boss. You got any money?"

"Oh for cryin' out loud, why do you *never* have any dough Benny?" Skip groaned digging into his pocket.

"Cos I don't have a job boss."

"*This* is your job bozo – doing illegal stuff like this! Here, there's five bucks now get movin'. We'll keep our friends here entertained until you get back."

The skoobs huddled together in a quaking mass, trying their best to merge into the brick wall behind them.

"Any particular flavour waffles?"

"No just regular, we'll move on to the more exotic flavours

once we've..."

"*IN THE NAME OF JUSTICE WE, THE AVENGING KNIGHTS OF COSMOPOLIS, ORDER YOU TO SUBMIT IMMEDIATELY! FAILURE TO COMPLY WILL RESULT IN SEVERE REPERCUSSIONS! YOU HAVE TEN SECONDS!*"

The deafening voice echoed around the confines of the alleyway and all five crooks spun around to see what had just caused their collective hearts to miss a beat. Three figures were stood facing them about thirty feet away, another twenty feet behind them was a silver van which had clearly seen better days. The enigmatic trio was dressed in medieval attire and the figure in the middle appeared to be a droid, even though he too wore a cape and a helmet.

They were all armed with bizarre looking guns.

"Holy cremola!" Skip murmured, "who the hell are these guys?"

"They sure ain't cops, boss."

"Oh well spotted Benny, there's no foolin' you is there?"

"What are we gonna do?"

Skip opted not to answer straight away, partly because he was a little confused but mainly because he didn't know what to say. He'd had plenty of run-ins with the law in his time although he had never come up against anything quite like this. Being the leader of his gang meant the decision was his and at the end of the day it was five against three. But their opponents were armed and he had no idea if their guns were fake toys or state of the art weapons capable of blasting them all to kingdom come. Plus there was the droid issue. Was it a standard service droid, more likely to try and polish them to death or could it be something more sinister? It was impossible to tell.

Brick by brick, layer on layer an invisible wall of tension had formed between the protagonists and the situation had developed into a good old-fashioned Mexican stand off[†]. On the Knights' side of the wall doubts were beginning to creep in. Hank felt a bead of sweat running down his temple, it was either that or a bug had flown into his helmet and was crawling down the side of his head. In the 'not so good' department they were outnumbered which wasn't great but they *did* have weapons and despite this being their first 'live' test he drew a smidgen of comfort from the fact they were tooled up. He erected mental blinkers to deflect the doubts, he had to stay positive or it was curtains. At the other end of the confidence scale Eric was desperate to fire his Inebriator. He didn't really care about the ten second warning, as far as he was concerned 'rules of engagement' were something to do with who chose the ring before getting married. Luckily for him the Inebriator's trigger wasn't particularly sensitive, otherwise he would have gotten the ball rolling a lot earlier. As for Sixpack, well, being a droid he was pretty indifferent to the whole scenario and quite unaware it was one big stress-fest. He was fairly sure the five ruffians before him were the enemy and if things did go sour he would be forced to shoot one of them. Being devoid of emotion did have its benefits – things were so much simpler, although appreciating jokes, even really funny ones, was a real challenge.

Just as things were on the verge of becoming unbearably tense Skip made his move.

"I know one thing Benny, I'm not about to surrender to some fancy dressed freaks just cos they've got loud voices. Come on boys, let's take 'em."

Not the most intricate of offensive manoeuvres, but Skip wasn't on the shortlist for the Cosmopolis Award for Forward

---

[†] Quite why Mexicans are accredited with inventing the stand off remains a mystery. Surely the ancient Greeks or even prehistoric Neanderthals must've had the odd stand off here and there – caveman vs dinosaur, Greek vs mythological creature. However, to give the Mexicans their due they are very good at organising sweeping waves among spectators during high-profile sporting events and tortilla chips are simply divine.

Thinking[†]. He just assumed the tried and tested formula of numerical superiority would win the day.

"They're not buying it Hank, let's blast 'em," Eric whispered.

"Wait! Their ten seconds isn't up yet."

"Who cares?"

"We can't just go around shooting people willy-nilly, Eric, we're here to prevent violence not encourage it!"

"Yeah but look at 'em man, they clearly have no intention of surrendering to us. In fact, they look as if they're getting ready to... too late! Here they come!"

Eric brought the Inebriator up to his shoulder. All five hoodlums were rushing towards them, unarmed but still looking very frightening. Hank decided this was clearly not the time or the place for the 'be responsible' speech, it would have to wait. "Open fire Six! Shoot! Shoot!" Eric yelled as his comrades raised their weapons simultaneously.

Skip and co were a good twenty feet away but closing rapidly, they obviously weren't going to go down without a fight and were quite willing to risk the 'severe repercussions'.

Eric fired, with the Inebriator set to 'Banjaxed', and watched with great delight as his target slumped to the floor.

Sixpack fired and missed, the Garbage Shoot's vile-smelling green jet impacting on the wall close to the bewildered skoobs.

Hank fired and scored a direct hit, stopping one of the advancing thugs in his tracks as the Web-o-matic's sticky web did its thing.

It was now three against three but there was no time for a second shot, the gang was upon them. Skip Bridges, eager to avoid the droid, lunged for Hank, who just managed to pull his weapon up in time to meet the charge. The gluey strand still hung from the muzzle and Skip ran straight into it, knocking Hank off his feet in the process. They crashed to the floor, rolling over several times in a proper tangle, the Web-o-matic's webbing wrapping around them as they struggled with each other.

[†] The hot favourite for this year's award is social behaviour research scientist Bendo Wangleton, who suggests a mobile, multi-functional facility to be deployed outside every bar and nightclub. The facility comprises a pharmacy, bathroom, fast food service, launderette, and taxi service – it also sells more booze.

The second hoodlum, known affectionately to his friends as 'Worm' also chose to give Sixpack a wide berth and directed his attentions towards Eric. They too went down in a heap, the Inebriator flying from Eric's grasp, coming to rest against the wall of the alleyway.

Realising he had drawn the short straw, Benny skidded to a halt a few yards short of Sixpack. Like most people he had no wish to get involved with a droid he knew absolutely nothing about. The other big problem with droids was they were made of metal; you couldn't punch them without breaking most of the bones in your hand. However, the one thing nearly all droids were notorious for (military and insurance company droids excepted) was their gullibility. Holding up his hands in a peace gesture Benny said:

"OK rustbucket, no-one needs to get hurt here. Just gimme the gun and…er…everything will be alright."

He breathed a sigh of relief as Sixpack, mightily confused, lowered his weapon.

Meanwhile Hank and Skip had become so badly entangled in web strands they could hardly move. For Hank it was a case of deja-vu, this is exactly what had happened the last time the weapon had been used and he was beginning to think it had some kind of grudge against him.

Eric was faring slightly better and had somehow managed to get to his feet and wrap his opponent up in a vice-like bear hug from behind. He glanced across at Sixpack. What was he doing? Why didn't he just blast the guy?

"Whaddya waitin' for Six?" he bawled. "Let him have it!"

Sixpack didn't hesitate.

He handed the gun over to Benny.

Had his hands been free, Eric would have swung a punch at Sixpack himself, instead he just groaned inwardly and focused his attentions on subduing Worm, who was struggling in his arms like a mad thing. Benny, on the other hand, couldn't believe his luck. Even though he'd never seen a weapon like this before he was fairly sure it was designed to do something unpleasant (as most guns are). In a flash he levelled it at Sixpack and squeezed the trigger. Being fairly heavy and quite sturdy, the droid weathered the impact well, staggering back a pace or two as the gunk from the Garbage Shoot exploded against his chest. Benny was not so lucky and (standing so close) took a significant amount of splashback. The foul liquid splattered across his face, some of it even going into his laughing mouth.

He didn't laugh for long.

Instead he dropped the weapon and clutched his throat with both hands, making an awful sound like someone gargling with a mouthful of thick custard. Eric now had a firm grip around his assailant's neck and was squeezing hard, waiting for him to pass out. He looked over at Sixpack again:

"Hit him Six! Knock him out!"

Benny was so preoccupied with trying not to puke he never saw the punch coming, which was fortunate for Sixpack as he delivered it with such obvious exaggeration a blind man could have dodged it. He drew his arm back slowly, lifted one leg from the ground, curled his hand into a fist and clouted Benny as hard as he could. After travelling roughly ten feet in mid air, Benny landed heavily on the tarmac floor, bruised, unconscious and starting to smell very nasty indeed. Eric's struggle finally came to an end when, much to his relief, he felt Worm go limp in his arms. He laid the insensible thug on the ground and trotted over to Hank and Skip, who had now been rendered virtually immobile by the Web-o-matic's adhesive grip.

"Get him off me!" Hank wailed from inside his helmet.

The two-man cocoon rolled around lazily, neither man capable of anything much.

"Who the hell are you freaks?" Skip blurted out.

"My name is Sir Prize," Eric said proudly, standing over them. "This is Excalibot and the man with whom you are currently ensnared is Rough Knight. Together we form the Avenging Knights of Cosmopolis, scourge of every street criminal in the city!"

"Great speech mate," Hank puffed, "but if you could knock this fella out then we might be able to make some progress."

"Oh yeah, sorry dude."

Eric stepped forward and bopped Skip on the head, snuffing his lights out completely. He was careful not to get too close, both men were still covered in sticky webbing and he knew only too well how difficult it was to get off. With this in mind Eric had, in a superb display of forward thinking (not quite worthy of an award but still very pro-active), brought along an anti-adhesive solution. He turned to Sixpack:

"Six, go into the back of the van and fetch me the plastic red container will you? The red one with the skull and crossbones picture on it."

The droid scuttled off towards the van but returned only a couple of seconds later.

"Sir?"

"It's in the back Six, red container."

"But sir…"

"For heaven's sake Six," Eric blustered, "there's only one red container in the van it can't be that difficult!"

"Yes sir, I understand your request but I feel we have a more urgent problem to resolve."

"What do you mean?"

Rather than explain Sixpack just pointed.

Eric followed the droid's finger to see the three skoobs (who had been completely forgotten in all the confusion) clambering into the van. One of them slid behind the wheel and switched on the engine. "I don't believe it!" he squealed. "They're hijacking our van!"

CHAPTER TWENTY-FOUR

*"We can never be certain of our courage until
we have faced danger."*

Francois Duc de la Rochefoucauld

For a man with a reputation for haphazard organisation it came as a pleasant surprise to Hank that Eric had thought to bring along a canister of anti-adhesive solution. He had amazed him further still by insisting they log all their activities in a notebook he had purchased specifically for this purpose. Everyone knew Eric hated paperwork, so to see him scribbling away with such fervour was indeed a rare sight. Then again, this wasn't some banal tax return or tedious expenses claim – this was a record of the Avenging Knights' exploits – something to be treasured for years to come. By 6pm the list of events read as follows:

2.25pm: Alien abduction – all five perpetrators subdued. Had to de-glue Rough Knight after Web-o-matic complication and victims (skoobs) nearly made off with the Silver Steed but Inebriator came in handy. Drunken skoobs are hilarious by the way.

3.02pm: Mugging – both perpetrators fled (empty-handed) following vocal challenge from Excalibot. Knights gave chase but were forced to abandon pursuit to disentangle Rough Knight when cape got caught on razor-wire fence. Victim (elderly woman with awful teeth) unharmed and very grateful.

3.19pm: Assault – perpetrators escaped. Took a wrong turn on Vertigo Drive and arrived too late. Will look into possibility of installing Excalibot with city map data chip to avoid further navigational problems.

3.55pm: Auto-theft – lone perpetrator escaped after short vehicle chase through back streets. Accidentally reversed into

Rough Knight while he was checking rear tyres afterwards but he seems OK now. Breastplate withstood impact extremely well!

4.32.pm: Mugging – both perpetrators subdued. Cops turned up just as we were leaving. Had to make a hasty exit. Fake plates should thwart any attempts to trace.

4.50pm: Assault – Arrived to find female pensioner battering young man who had tried to steal her purse. Figured he deserved it so decided not to intervene.

5.12pm: Vandalism – all four juvenile perpetrators subdued. Our first surrender! A well-planned flanking manoeuvre prevented any escape and we also drew a small crowd of onlookers. Introduced ourselves to the public then left.

5.33pm: Mugging – three perpetrators subdued, one escaped. Toughest challenge so far as all criminals were armed with hand weapons (knives, bike chains etc). Excalibot shot Rough Knight with Garbage Shoot by mistake which allowed one mugger to get away, but other than that a successful encounter. Victim (youth of questionable moral fibre) quite grateful.

6pm – back at Eric's place.
Between them they had done their best to clean up the foul-smelling gunk that had attached itself to Hank following the unfortunate Garbage Shoot incident. But the soap and water Eric had brought along had been woefully insufficient and after sitting in the van for roughly five minutes they had (through streaming eyes) come to the conclusion that a full scale scrubbing was required. It was either that or sit in the van wearing pegs on their noses for the remainder of the evening. Also, creeping up on anyone was going to be tough, especially if they were facing upwind.

For the first time that day Hank felt himself starting to relax. He leaned forward in the shower, his palms flat against the tile wall in front of him letting the hot water gush down on top of his head. From a personal point of view things hadn't gone particularly well, he'd been hit by the van, ensnared in the Web-o-matic's web (again!), shot by Sixpack and had ripped a big hole in his cloak. But – he was alive and that was a *big* plus.

Not for the first time his thoughts were cut short by Eric who was thumping impatiently on the bathroom door.

"C'mon dude, we need to get back out there!"

Hank rested his forehead against the wall – good lord, would his appetite for adventure ever be sated? He was like a dog with a bone, the whole crimefighting thing was acting like neat adrenaline. Sure it was exciting but it was more of a 'scary' excitement than a 'fun' excitement.

"Alright Eric, I'll be done in a minute!" he bawled above the hiss of the shower.

So far they'd been lucky, none of their adversaries had been packing any serious heat but now they were about to embark on the really tricky part – the night shift. A time when more hardened criminals would put in an appearance, and this meant guns, maybe even laser weapons, something he had been dreading since he'd learned of the chainmail's less than considerable stopping power. Then again, no-one ever said this would be easy.

6.59pm: Corner of Ronin Avenue and Wolf Street.

After recent events Hank was (quite understandably) a touch apprehensive.

"OK Eric, let's just creep around the corner this time instead of charging in. Lets try and see what we're up against eh?"

"Understood, we'll send Six in first."

"No that's not what I meant, let's just exercise a little caution, the radio said these guys were packing remember? And we're not sure how many there are."

"Yeah I remember!"

Despite his face being hidden, Hank suspected Eric was grinning broadly inside his helmet as if this were just the type of situation he'd been waiting for. Conversely, Hank was thinking of all the places he'd rather be right now, which was pretty much *anywhere*. "Ready?" Eric hissed.

"No wait we need a plan first!"

"Come on Six, follow me!"

And with that he darted around the corner, Sixpack at his heels, leaving an exasperated Hank Halo leaning against the wall and doing a good deal of mental cursing. Why wouldn't Eric listen to him? He'd used plain English hadn't he? Did he have some sort of death wish? With a sigh of frustration Hank levered himself away from the wall and prepared to follow his impetuous chum. Bracing himself for whatever lay round the corner he readied his weapon and took a step forward.

That was as far as he got.

Eric and Sixpack came hurtling back the way they had come and collided with him.

"There's dozens of 'em!" Eric screamed. "Get back to the van!"

Hank didn't need to take a peek to verify the claim, the corner of the wall exploded in a hail of bullets which suggested there really *was* a significant gathering of perps on the other side. The Avenging Knights ran for their lives, not exactly a dignified sight but one that gave them a fair chance of escaping with the skin on their behinds. Mercifully, Eric had parked the van fairly close and they were already clambering inside when twenty-seven angry members of the Wingnut Gang came steaming into view, every one of them armed to the teeth with weapons of varying lethality.

Following the attempted hijacking of their van by the skoobs earlier that day, the Knights had decided not to leave the keys in the ignition anymore. Eric fumbled around for them, not an easy task with a knee length cloak doing its best to hinder his efforts. Hank glanced in the wing mirror, which was rapidly filling with irate gang members.

"Come on man!" he whimpered.

Finally Eric plucked the keys from his cloak and tried to find the right one for the van.

"It's OK, I've got 'em, we're OK!" Eric gasped, ramming the key into the ignition.

A deadly combination of laser bolts and bullets tore into the back of the van, puncturing both rear tyres and reducing the back doors to something resembling Swiss cheese.

"Sir may I suggest we exit the vehicle and proceed on foot?" Sixpack asked without a trace of emotion.

"He's right," Hank yelled, "we're gonna have to leg it! Come on!"

They leapt from the van as more bad news ripped into it from behind. Eric and Sixpack, who had exited on the driver's side, fled down a grubby looking alleyway to their left while Hank chose a similarly unkempt side street to his right. It was a bit late to be coming up with a plan but all the same Eric had the presence of mind to try and co-ordinate things as best he could.

"So much for the armour! The van's toast!" he shouted into his mike, "we'll meet up back at my place!"

"Copy that!" Hank replied.

As if things weren't bad enough the Wingnut Gang decided to give chase. They didn't take kindly to be interrupted just before a robbery. Being a fairly organised kind of outfit, they left one third of their group with the van, another third pursued Hank and the remaining nine went after Eric and his droid.

Hank's lungs were on the verge of collapse – remember cross-country running at school? He'd been running for what felt like an hour (it was more like seven minutes) and knew if he kept going any further he'd be seeing Sixpack's burnt breakfast again. Because he was in an unfamiliar part of town he had absolutely no idea where he was, he'd made lefts and rights at random hoping to throw off any would be pursuers, his survival instincts overriding any sense of navigation. For all he knew he could take the next turn and end up back at the van – or what was left of it. Fatigue got the better of him and he jogged to a standstill, clutched his knees and gulped down some much needed oxygen. He didn't know if Eric would be able to hear him or not but he tried anyway.

"Eric? (gasp) Eric are you there?"

Nothing – just static interference.

Was there a range to these headsets? He couldn't remember, he just prayed Eric and Sixpack had managed to escape unharmed. A couple of minutes passed as the Rough Knight got his wind back, then with a deep breath he considered his next move. Ahead of him the alley reached a T-junction and although he usually had a pretty good sense of direction he had to admit he hadn't a clue which way led out of this labyrinth of back streets. To the left he could hear the far away drone of traffic, which was surely the Multiplicity Mega-drag, one of the main roads into the city centre and the same route they had used to get here. Setting off at a jog he rounded the corner, heading for the sound of civilisation. He stopped dead in his tracks as he almost ran into a small black girl of perhaps five or six years. She was scruffy and a bit dishevelled, wearing clothes that looked as if they hadn't been cleaned for a month (a bit like Eric's lucky bowling shirt which he refused to wash). Her eyes widened in surprise, after all it wasn't every day you ran into a medieval knight in the middle of Cosmopolis and Hank braced himself for the inevitable scream.

But the little urchin did not scream, in fact she looked up and gave him a broad smile.

"Which one are you?" she squeaked, "Hank or Eric?"

CHAPTER TWENTY-FIVE

*"To err is human, but to persevere in error is only
the act of a fool."*

Cicero

Things were less complicated for Eric and his mechanical companion, all they had to worry about was running as fast as they could. Sixpack's power cells had been recharged back at the house so the only one in danger of running out of juice was Eric – and he was starting to feel the pace.

"Six!" he gasped. "Six, wait a minute, I need to catch my breath."

The droid slid to a standstill.

"Do you need medical attention sir?"

"No, no. I'm just knackered."

"Knackered sir?"

"Yes knackered! Tired! Fatigued! Exhausted!"

"I understand."

Eric leaned against the wall of the alley, his chest rising and falling rapidly. He took off his helmet to increase his air intake, then looked back the way they had come.

"I'm sure we're being chased. Do you hear anyone?"

Sixpack was a standard service droid, his hearing was no better than that of a human but Eric assumed, like most people, that all droids had heightened senses.

"I can hear the sound of traffic in the distance sir, nothing else."

"Yeah me too. Even if we are being followed, we'd never hold 'em off with these weapons, which way do you reckon leads out of here?"

He also assumed it was impossible for Sixpack to get lost.

"I am unsure sir, but we could head towards the sound of the traffic."

"You mean you don't *know*? I thought all droids could ...oh never mind. God I hope Hank's alright. Although he's probably gonna kill me if we make it outta this alive."

Hank was so dumbfounded by the question that for a second or two he couldn't reply, even though he knew the answer.

"How can you – I mean who – what are you doing out here by yourself? Don't you know this place is dangerous at night?"

It was no picnic during the *day* but he wasn't going to get pedantic.

"I'm looking for *you*!"

"But how do you know my name? I've never met you before!"

The girl suddenly put her hands to her temples and closed her eyes. "Are you alright?" Hank asked, removing his helmet.

Her eyes flicked open, wide and fearful.

"They're coming! Quick let's hide in there!" she shrieked pointing to a nearby dumpster.

Hank didn't hesitate, if this girl was clever enough to know his name he was more than willing to follow her advice. Dropping his weapon he opened the dumpster, scooped up the urchin, placed her inside then jumped in after her, closing the lid after them. For a moment there was nothing but silence, darkness and a terrible stench of rotting food. Having been hit with the Garbage Shoot (twice) Hank was becoming accustomed to bad smells so it didn't bother him too much. His new friend on the other hand was far less impressed.

"Ugh – it's stinky in here!"

"Ssshhh!"

He would have reached out to cover her mouth but in the gloom he couldn't see a thing and didn't want to poke her in the eye. The sound of approaching footsteps shut her up. Then they heard voices, unfriendly voices.

"Look! They must've come this way!"

Hank cursed himself for leaving his gun behind. Not only did it serve as a clue to his pursuers but it also left him completely unarmed.

"Who were they anyway?"

"Beats me man, but they sure put the willies up me when I first saw 'em. Dressed in those weird outfits and 'all."

"Maybe they went in there!"

"Where?"

"*There!*"

Hank felt his blood run cold, they were surely talking about the dumpster. But it wasn't his own welfare that concerned him, what really bothered him was how he was going to be able to protect the girl. He knew the perps would be armed and without a weapon he wouldn't last long in a stand-up fight. And who did he have to thank for all this? His best friend Eric Dorfler, that's who. The one who had talked him into this insane venture in the first place, the one who seemed incapable of self-control, the one he would probably kill if he ever got out of this dumpster alive.

"It's not his fault," said a tiny voice from the darkness.

Hank put his fingers to his lips to silence her but then realised she wouldn't be able to see him so said:

"Ssshh," again, very quietly.

It took him a while to cotton on to the fact she had just read his mind. "Wait a minute. How did you know what I was…"

His stomach churned as he heard one of the voices from outside say, "alright open it up and let's take a look!."

Panic began to consume him, what the hell was he going to do? Surrender? Fight? Flee? Try and hide? Neither option was particularly palatable and he had about five seconds to pick one. Still, amid the chaos, his overriding concern was for the girl. Whoever was outside (and he had no doubt they were members of the gang they had so rashly interrupted) was looking for a man dressed as a knight. They weren't expecting to find a child. Hank made his decision and slipping his helmet on whispered to the girl:

"Listen, I'm getting out, cover yourself up with this rubbish and don't make a sound!"

His instructions had obviously been understood as a frantic rustling ensued. Then with a deep breath and quick prayer he lifted the lid of the dumpster and stood up, making sure he got his hands in the air nice and early. It wasn't exactly a shock to find two armed ruffians waiting outside but it unnerved him all the same. Instinctively they raised their laser rifles to meet his sudden appearance.

"Don't shoot, I give up!" Hank pleaded.

The two gangsters exchanged grins, the way school bullies do when they've got the nerdy kid trapped in the toilets.

"Who are you?" one of them snapped.

Not a bad question really.

What did he say?

Did he come clean and give them his real name or should he continue the charade and tell them his name was Rough Knight? He could always make one up. An evil thought flashed through his mind and he considered giving them Eric's name, complete with home address, contact number, place of work, vehicle registration number, favourite colour, etc. But not even Hank, who was fairly confident the end was nigh, could find it in his heart to betray his pal.

"I am the Rough Knight," he said eventually, "a member of the Avenging Knights of Cosmopolis, scourge of..."

His speech was cut short by the thugs, who were chuckling heartily.

"Well rough boy, we don't take kindly to vigilantes around here, 'specially when we're in the middle of a robbery. So we're gonna have to teach you a lesson."

Hank noted for the first time the guns pointing his way were actually laser rifles.

Lasers.

Guaranteed to cut through chainmail like a knife through butter. They saw his eyes widen through his visor, which was just the reaction they had hoped for. What a way to go, Hank mused – stood in a dumpster, knee deep in garbage dressed as a knight. There was so much he still wanted to do with in life, win the State Smashbowl finals, visit the Hula Archipelago, give Eric a good hiding. But what the hell, if he was going to meet his maker, he refused to do so begging for his life and taking himself a bit by surprise he removed his helmet, tossed it in the dumpster, put his hands on his hips and said:

"Go ahead scuzzbucket, I'm not afraid of you. Other vigilantes will take my place and your pathetic gang will be crushed along with every other lawless rabble in the city."

Wow! Not bad to say he hadn't rehearsed it.

Wingnut Gang members weren't accustomed to provocation, usually their victims would collapse in a quivering heap and plead for mercy.

"You got guts rough boy, I'll give you that," one of them snarled. "But no-one talks to us that way and gets away with it, so say your prayers and when you meet the devil, tell him the Wingnut Gang sent ya!"

Hank squeezed his eyes shut and braced himself for the inevitable. There really was nothing else to do, he couldn't run anywhere and if he tried to rush them they'd waste him before he got one foot out of the dumpster. Selfless to the end, his last thought was of the girl who lay hidden among the trash.

Or at least it *would* have been his last thought had Fate not intervened.

Several agonising seconds limped by – but the shots never came, there was just a dreadful silence. 'What were they waiting for?' Hank thought, he was an easy enough target wasn't he? Even Sixpack could've hit him from this range. Cautiously, he opened one eye. The two thugs were still there, but they had lowered their weapons and were facing each other looking very puzzled. Thug No.1 looked down at his weapon, frowning.

"Y'know I never wanted to be…a…criminal," he said with an effort, "I always…wanted to be a brofessional Ploodball player."

Thug No.2 blinked back at him.

" A…what?"

"I mean a professshhhional Bloodball playyyer…"

"So why'd you choose a crime of life? Er…a life of crime."

Thug No.1 staggered forward a pace unsteadily, he appeared close to tears and his voice trembled with emotion.

"I fell in with…the…wrong crowd when I was younger."

Thug No.2 swayed on his feet and nearly keeled over but used his rifle to prop himself up.

"Well, it's never too mate late, I think you'd be a tanfastic player."

It was all too much for Thug No.1 and he broke down in a flood of tears, casting his weapon aside and hugging Thug No.2.

"I never told you this, but…you're my best friend," he sobbed.

"And you're mine, in fact…I luurrv you man."

Thug No.2 was now weeping too. Hank watched the exchange spellbound – what the hell were they doing? The ruffians continued hugging and blubbering until they noticed him stood in the dumpster. Drying their eyes they broke up the embrace and turned to face him, wobbling on shaky legs.

"Hey man," Thug No.2 began, "who the hell are….?"

Before he could finish the question his eyes rolled back into his head and he keeled over. Thug No.1 looked at Hank through bleary eyes.

"If you don't mind, I think I'm gonna...yes...I'm definitely gonna join my buddy here."

His legs buckled and he too slumped to the ground. Hank just stood there, quite unable to explain the bizarre spectacle. A movement at the end of the alleyway caught his eye and he had to blink twice before he could believe the evidence of his own eyes.

Eric and Sixpack were running towards him.

Now here's a dilemma. How grateful should you be to someone who has just saved your life but is also responsible for putting you in that life-threatening position to start with? It wasn't that much of a struggle for Hank who retrieved his helmet and hurled it at Eric as hard as he could. He ducked and it hit Sixpack.

Eric ground to a halt as he reached the dumpster, removed his own helmet and said;

"Hey! Is that any way to greet your saviour?"

He seemed genuinely startled.

Hank seemed genuinely incensed.

"Saviour? *Saviour*? We wouldn't be in this pickle if you hadn't gone charging in guns blazing!"

"I never fired a shot!"

Gripping the edge of the dumpster to try and keep control of his temper Hank looked to the heavens.

"That's not the point Eric! We could've been killed! Anyway, it makes no difference, I quit, you can go and avenge til your heart's content, I'm through."

Eric had expected a bad reaction, but he hadn't expected a resignation, he tried to rescue things.

"OK, I'm sorry Hank. You're right, I was rash, I should've waited, it won't happen aga…"

"English *is* your first language isn't it? Forget it, I gave you an opportunity to mend your ways and you blew it. No more second chances. I'm serious man, I quit. I'm not joking Eric."

"I'm not laughing! But Hank you *can't* quit!"

"Watch me!"

"What about all the crimes we prevented today, the innocent victims we saved?"

"Oh wake up and smell the Garbage Shoot will ya? I don't mind taking a risk here and there to help the cops keep the crime level down, but you're a 'logic-free' zone Eric, you don't know when to quit! You're like a runaway freight train! Yes, that's it –

you're the Gung-ho Express, hurtling down the track completely outta control, flying right past the platform at Common Sense, giving the vital town of Reason a miss and heading directly for the terminus at Oblivion. Well I'm sorry pal, I am *not* prepared to risk my neck because my shoot-first-ask-questions-later partner needs to keep his adrenaline levels topped up!"

He was about to climb out of the dumpster when he felt something move by his feet. In the commotion he had forgotten all about the girl. She extracted herself from the refuse and looked up at him, a little bewildered.

"Are you OK?" he asked, reaching down to remove a piece of spaghetti that had attached itself to her hair.

She nodded.

He clambered out, then lifted her out and placed her gingerly on the floor of the alley.

"Who's this?" Eric asked.

Hank frowned.

"I don't know, we just kinda bumped into each other."

"My name's Dolores and Eric's right, you mustn't quit. The Avenging Knights must stay together."

"Why?"

"Because something terrible is going to happen and you're the only ones who can stop it."

"See?" Eric said. "We're the only ones who can stop it."

"Eric this girl can't be more than six years old, you don't even know what she's talking about. Er…just what *are* you talking about Dolores?"

She was about to reply when they all heard the sound of distant footsteps – lots of footsteps. "Come on we have to get outta here!" Hank said taking Dolores's hand.

"We've found a way back to the Multiplicity Mega-drag," Eric smiled, "follow us!"

At first Hank was reluctant to tag along. The last time he'd followed Eric's lead had almost been his undoing, but the footsteps were growing louder and he had no wish to hang around, especially with Dolores in his charge. He grabbed his Web-o-matic and helmet and the four of them ran off into the darkness, towards the sound of the traffic.

153

CHAPTER TWENTY-SIX

*"How come you never see a headline like
'Psychic Wins Lottery'?"*

Jay Leno

Hailing a cab proved to be a lengthy process, which was most likely due to the way they looked. But it was *staying* in the cab that turned out to be the real challenge due to the way they smelled. Eric had to dig deep into his library of plausible lies to pacify the driver and settled for a less than convincing story about taking Dolores to a fancy dress party but...er...it was one of those parties where the parent (foster parent of course) had to dress up instead...and the droid well he was here for security...and...er...Hank was her friend who had also been invited. And the smell? Oh yes, the smell was from the capes they wore, which had been used to...er...block a sewage pipe at home which had burst only moments before they had been due to depart.

Of all the rotten luck eh?

The cabbie was either incredibly stupid or incredibly desperate but eventually agreed to take them and it wasn't long before they were back in the safety of Eric's house. After getting cleaned up they ordered in some pizza, which was eaten in relative silence, then with the time approaching 10.20pm they reassembled in the lounge. Hank and Eric were back in normal clothes while Dolores was dressed in Eric's bathrobe, which was rather like wrapping a doll in a beach towel, indeed only her head was visible.

"So how did you find me?" Hank asked.

"Quite by accident," Eric replied. "We'd gotten lost and were trying to get back to the Multi. Luckily I'd kept my helmet on and picked up your voice when you were talking to those hoodlums. I followed the sound and then hey presto there you were right around the next corner. I took out the scumbags with the Inebriator, got them both with one shot I might add."

"I was talking to Dolores."

"Oh sorry."

For a moment she said nothing and the only sound was that of Sixpack trying to hand wash the dirty clothes/armour in the kitchen.

"The voice told me to find you," she said at last.

Eric and Hank swapped glances.

"The voice?"

She nodded.

"What voice?"

"The one in my head."

Eric looked at Hank again, the unmistakable look of scepticism. He drew breath to say something but Hank cut him off, he didn't want Eric using words like 'crazy' or 'nutcase' until they'd got to the bottom of this.

"You hear voices in your head Dolores?"

"It's only one voice. Why?"

"Because Dolores, it's quite unusual for people to hear voices in their heads," Hank said carefully.

"Is it?"

"Well...yeah," was all he could say.

"But it's only *one* voice," she insisted.

He tried another approach.

"Was it the voice that told you my name?"

"Yeah it told me you were Hank Angel."

"Hank *Angel*?"

"Yeah and your friend is Eric Duffer."

Hank couldn't suppress a smile.

"Pretty close. I'm actually Hank *Halo* and Eric's other name is Dorfler not Duffer."

Actually, Duffer was probably nearer the mark now he thought about it. He glanced at his watch. "We should call your folks, they must be worried sick about you."

"Don't have any folks."

"Well who looks after you?"

"The church ladies."

Hank's face creased in confusion.

"She probably means the nuns," Eric piped up, "at the orphanage on Spiceworld Drive."

Hank rose from his seat.

"I'll give them a call."

This put Dolores into a real flap.

"No don't!" she wailed.

"What's wrong?"

"I don't like it there!"

"Why not?"

"I don't like the church ladies, they're mean to me."

"Mean how?" Hank asked, his anger rising.

"They make me talk to the voice."

It was slow going but Hank persisted.

"Why?"

"They want the voice to tell them the lucky numbers."

"The lucky numbers?"

"Yeah, for something called the lottery."

The penny dropped and Hank understood the nuns were exploiting Dolores' innocence. But was she really psychic? Could she really read people's minds? Eric hadn't said much during the conversation, he wasn't as good with kids as Hank, in fact they tended to get on his nerves. In his experience they were either causing mischief or asking for sweets – but then again his experience was very limited. He knew Hank was fond of kids and could see he was already warming to this one, which gave him the gnawing feeling she might be around longer than he would have preferred.

"Well nasty nuns or not, we have to take her back," he said.

"Not so fast Eric, I'd like to know what this terrible disaster is all about first."

They both looked back to Dolores who was snuggling up inside the capacious bathrobe and looking far too comfortable in Eric's armchair for his liking. "So what's it all about Dolores? What horrendous thing is going to happen and why did you come to find us? Why didn't you just go to the police?"

"I don't really know what's going to happen, the voice just told me it was going to be very terrible. It's all a bit mucked up but I remember it said about broken reflectograms and scary faces. The policemen wouldn't believe me if I went to them and anyway the voice told me to find the men in the metal suits. It sent me to that alley and that's where I found you."

Hank nodded slowly, he was still undecided as to whether she was a raving lunatic or had a genuine gift that could be used to avert some great danger.

"Can you be any more specific?" he asked.

"Any more *what*?"

"Can you give us some more details? Like for example when this might be due to happen?"

"It didn't say."

She yawned and cuddled into the robe again, looking sleepy.

Hank glanced at Eric, who didn't need to read his mind.

"No!" Eric cried, pointing at Hank and shaking his head.

"Come on bud, it's only for one night. I'll take the sofa and Dolores can have the spare room."

"She'll make a mess Hank, kids always make a mess, and they break things!"

Dolores yawned a second time, on the verge of sleep.

"No she won't! Look, I'll take personal responsibility for her while she's here, alright?"

Eric was about to deliver another round of protests but paused. Maybe he should cut Hank some slack, he had after all almost gotten him killed today.

"We'll discuss it later, look she's obviously tired and I don't want her falling asleep in the armchair. Take her upstairs and put her to bed will you?"

Hank took full advantage of the ceasefire. He scooped up the snoozing bundle and carried her up the stairs, after a few minutes he returned to find his chum deep in thought.

Events were moving along at a frantic pace and Eric was finding it hard to keep up. They still hadn't really talked about Hank's decision to quit and now this strange urchin had turned up things had become even more complicated. They were at something of a crossroads and he had to weigh up the pros and cons. He was certain that Hank would stick around if he agreed to investigate Dolores's forecast of calamity and it did sound tempting, after all this is exactly why he had formed the Avenging Knights in the first place – to protect people. But on the down side it would mean having the kid around for the foreseeable future. He knew there was no spare room at Hank's place, which meant he would be burdened with housing the little mite until alternative arrangements could be made; assuming of course that she was telling the truth.

Decisions, decisions.

Hank flopped down in the armchair Dolores had just vacated and said:

"So whaddya think bud?"

"I dunno, everything's happening too fast."

"Do you think Dolores is for real?"

"Do you?"

"Well, she found *us* didn't she? And she knew our names."

"Mate, for all we know it could just be a clever ploy to get a free bed for the night."

"Oh come on Eric, she's too young for a scam like that."

To Eric's delight Hank appeared to have forgotten all about quitting. A plan began to form in his mind. He knew Hank would be unable to leave Dolores to the mercy of the scheming nuns.

"I'm not convinced, " he said dismissively, "maybe she just had a nightmare and then went AWOL from the orphanage."

"No I think there's more to it than that."

"I doubt it. I mean really – broken reflectograms and scary faces? Kid's probably been watching too many horror movies. Besides, you quit remember?"

"Yeah but that was before we knew about *this*."

"Does this mean you'll carry on as one of the Avenging Knights?"

" I certainly think this warrants further investigation."

"Is that a 'yes' then?"

"It's a 'yes' on one condition."

"Name it."

"I run things from now on."

"OK."

To be honest, Eric didn't really care about who was in charge, he just wanted to keep the Knights project alive.

"I mean it Eric, you have to do as I say."

"No problem."

"Right then, we'll talk to Dolores in the morning, see what else we can find out."

Now that he had Hank back on board Eric changed his tune a little.

"It's kinda creepy though don't ya think? All this impending disaster stuff, it's like she's giving us a…oh…a…what do you call it?" He clicked his fingers rapidly. "It's a 'P' word."

Hank thought for a moment.

"Prophecy?"

"That's it! Yeah, a prophecy of *doom*!"

"Don't let your theatrical nature get the better of you bud, we don't know what she's talking about yet."

Eric changed the subject; he wanted to close the book on the Wingnut Gang episode while still focusing on the positive – if that were possible.

"Not a bad day's work all told," he summarised, "we sent the video footage showing all our successful encounters which should enable the cops to charge them. I think it's fair to say we've made a small dent in the criminal fraternity today."

'Not a bad day?' Hank thought – who was he kidding? They'd almost been killed back at Ronin Avenue. True, they'd prevented a few minor crimes but it was hardly cause to break out the bubbly.

"Yeah," he mumbled.

An idea suddenly struck Eric, a well aimed idea which hit him right between the eyes.

"You know Dolores might be of some use after all. I mean if she *can* see into the future then she might be able to predict crimes before they happen or at least point us in the right direction. Sure would be an improvement on our existing method."

He had a point but Hank didn't want Dolores anywhere near the danger zone, he wasn't over the moon about being there *himself*. The other problem was that her psychic ability didn't seem fully developed yet, her predictions were close but not a hundred per cent accurate and he was going to have enough on his plate trying to control Eric without having to try and decipher her clues as well.

"That's not a bad idea," he replied, "we'd need to talk it over with Dolores first obviously."

"So are we gonna get back out there? The night is young and there are more crimes for us to tackle."

"We can't, who's gonna look after Dolores?"

"I'll leave Sixpack here."

"You can't leave a *droid* to take care of a child, especially not Sixpack – can you imagine the complications when she wakes up and tells him she needs to 'go tinkle'? Besides, we need Six for his booming voice thing. No, I think we should call it a night Eric. We've had enough excitement for one day, let's get some kip and regroup in the morning."

"OK mate, you're the boss."

A weary Hank Halo tramped up the stairs, leaving Eric in the lounge. He was too tired to think and just wanted some sleep. Still, he allowed himself a brief moment of levity and chuckled as he heard Eric talking to Sixpack downstairs.

"Six! When I said I wanted that breastplate clean enough to eat my dinner off I didn't mean...."

ONE MONTH LATER

CHAPTER TWENTY-SEVEN

*"Scandal is what one half of the world takes
pleasure inventing, and the other half in believing."*

Paul Chatfield

Front page of the Cosmopolis Prattler.
  Monday September 12th 2105
  "SATURDAY KNIGHTS FOIL ARMED ROBBERY!"
  By Zac Puddlejump
  Is it me or are these guys starting to get a reputation? I
remember when they first showed up on the scene some four weeks
ago. I, like my fellow reporters, initially dismissed them as
costumed freaks with some loose wiring, this is Cosmopolis after
all, where costumed freaks rub shoulders with the likes of you and
me on a daily basis.

But (yes I admit it) I was wrong and it looks like they could be
here to stay. Dubbed the Saturday Knights by the public – as they're
dressed as knights and have only ever been seen on, you guessed it,
Saturdays, this trio of do-gooders has been spotted on no fewer than
fourteen occasions. Specific details are still sketchy at this stage but
it looks like our armoured saviours comprise two humans and a
droid. Like a gleaming machete of freedom they seem intent on
slashing their way through the jungle of crime that threatens to
suffocate our once great city.

So who are these helmeted heroes? So far we have only
managed to ascertain their 'stage' names; Surprise (or should that be
Sir Prize?), Rough Knight and Excalibot (the droid) form the
Avenging Knights of Cosmopolis – a tad cheesy perhaps but a
welcome sight in the wake of Captain Uno's recent retirement.
Their true identities are unknown, but rest assured, it won't be long
before your roving reporter Zac Puddlejump uses his unique blend
of tenacity and charm to discover the names behind the capes.

After interviewing several eye-witnesses, it would seem the
enigmatic vigilantes possess no super powers whatsoever and rely

instead on a dazzling array of weaponry, which appears to be non-lethal. Just how they manage to turn up in the nick of time is still a mystery, but they are usually one step ahead of the police (not difficult I know) and are developing an uncanny knack of arriving just in time to catch the crooks in the act. Perhaps they do have special powers after all – perhaps they're psychic? This time the Knights were spotted just off Gunsmoke Street in downtown Cosmo at approximately 11.15pm on Saturday 10th Sept by local resident Wilma Clorette. She told us:

"I was on my way back from the mutant wrestling when I heard the sound of an alarm or somethin' just up ahead. Ordinarily I woulda just run, I mean this being Cosmopolis and all you don't tend to stick around when you hear bells ringin' but I decided to wait and see what was occurin'. As I got closer I saw four or five thieving low-life scum – I mean – four or five men running from the Dangling Carat jewellery store, they were all carrying bags, which must've been filled with stolen loot – I mean come on, why else would you be runnin' from a jewellery store after 11pm? They'd gone no more than a few steps when the Saturday Knights appeared as if out of nowhere. I mean I don't know where they'd been hidin' but they sure as hell gave me a fright, I nearly dropped my...anyway...they threw down a challenge...and that voice...heck I almost filled my...anyway...it was a real loud, scary voice. The scumbags, I mean the guys carrying the bags ignored it and went for their guns. I don't know what happened next, I was too busy cowering behind a garbage can, but I think there was a brief firefight and the next time I looked the robbers had been subdued, although I think one of the Knights got hit too, the taller one, by some kind of freaky gun that seemed to fire vomit."

A strange encounter to be sure but eye-witnesses like Wilma Clorette are becoming more and more commonplace, which suggests that our newfound guardians are not just a flash in the pan. No sir, it would appear the Knights are hell bent on finally ridding this city of its criminal element. Like medieval knights of old they patrol the streets, administering justice as they see fit, choking the life from the lawless with a gauntleted fist. Let us hope Mayor Strada and Police Commissioner Spencer Arkwright see them as nothing more than a band of willing volunteers happy to assist an already overstretched and under-equipped police force. Like Captain Uno before them, they should be welcomed with open arms and warm hearts.

And finally, a message to the Knights themselves – if you're reading this fellas, give me a call at the Prattler for an exclusive interview.

From page 3 of the Cosmopolis Prattler.
Tuesday September 13th 2105
"IT'S CURTAINS FOR THE SAUSAGE PRINCESS!"
By Natasha Slight

With the list of this year's lucky ten Miss Cosmo finalists only forty-eight hours old we've already got our first scandal. Confirmed in the last ten and one of the tournament's hot favourites, 19 year old Anette Kurtin has announced she will be withdrawing from the competition. Heir to her father's sausage empire based in the town of Vammaberg in Scando 2, the teenage beauty claims the contest will distract her from the important role she plays in her father's business, which until recently had been flourishing. Disaster struck at Kurtin Enterprises last week when a consignment of raw meat from one of their farms became contaminated with a mysterious chemical. Unsightly hair and gristle began sprouting from the meat and the entire batch had to be disposed of. Naturally, this has sent shock waves through the sausage industry and long-standing customers of Kurtin Enterprises are believed to be looking for alternative suppliers. At a press conference yesterday a despondent Anette Kurtin told reporters;

"This couldn't have happened at a worse time – well OK if it had happened on my wedding day then I guess it could've been worse, but I'm not even seeing anyone right now so that's not really very likely, although Shifty Tattler at the processing plant is kinda cute. Obviously I was looking forward to competing for the Miss Cosmopolis title (deep sigh), it sure beats the hell out of watching a conveyor belt full of endless sausages, but I feel it would be inappropriate to allow myself to get distracted from my duties as a director of Kurtin Enterprises. With the company facing a difficult time I have to believe – or rather my father would have me believe – that withdrawing from the tournament is the right thing to do. And he's the guy who controls my allowance so who am I to argue? No allowance means no tennis lessons, no horse-riding and I've got my eye on a new Superfloot Deluxe Hovercar so at the end of the day it's a small price to pay. "

Not surprisingly the gossip machine has swung into action and accusations are rife, ranging from coercion to bribery. Three time former winner and fellow finalist Eve Tendril expressed her sympathy for the teenager during a recent radio interview saying "it's a real blow for the tournament as a whole but these things will happen." Whatever happens we are now down to nine finalists (see page 18 for full details) and with a little less than a month to go before the televised final it's anyone's guess as to how many will actually be on stage for the big night.

Front page of the Cosmopolis Prattler.
Monday September 19th 2105
"SATURDAY KNIGHT FEVER GROWS!"
By Zac Puddlejump

Gadzooks and forsooth gentle folk of Cosmopolis! Another weekend and another busy day for our favourite crimebusters. It seems the Knights were *everywhere* on Saturday, confronting do-badders in every back-alley and stamping out crime in their own inimitable style. Again they were appearing from the shadows at just the right time and rumours persist concerning the possibility of psychic abilities. However they're doing it, it's working like a dream with Cosmo police cells bulging with villainous scum.

While the public is firmly behind the Knights, the police have given them a lukewarm reception – presumably because it only highlights their own inadequacies. In a guarded statement Police Commissioner Spencer Arkwright admitted the police were 'reluctantly tolerating' the activities of the three vigilantes but would not hesitate to apprehend them should they 'overstep the mark'. He made no effort to clarify exactly what sort of thing might warrant 'overstepping the mark' and then went on to make a clear distinction between the now retired Captain Uno and our most recent crime-fighters, describing the Captain as a 'never to be repeated legend' and labelling the Knights as part-time amateurs. After canvassing the public myself, I found the feedback to be a little more upbeat.

Lucille Schwarzer, a housewife, described them as: "a breath of fresh air for the city." Gus Galavant, a surgeon, said: "it's nice to know they're watching over us, they certainly get my vote!" And finally, retired bodybuilder Jessica Defanto told me: "three cheers for the caped crusaders, they're great and if they need a fourth member I'm ready, willing and able."

So it looks as if the Knights are winning the hearts and minds of the people, it's just a pity the Cosmopolis Police Dept can't show as much enthusiasm. As for me, I'll raise a tankard of mead and wish them well in their crusade against crime and don't forget guys; my offer of an exclusive interview still stands.

Cover story from Looking Guuurd Weekly.
"BUBBLE BURSTS FOR LOLA!"
By Olivia Garlando.

And then there were eight! In the wake of Anette Kurtin's unprecedented withdrawal from the Miss Cosmopolis Tournament last month the smart money was on Lola Lascala to clinch the title. For those not in the know, Lola burst on to the scene in 2103, winning the New Faces Contest aged just 16, which she followed up with an impressive runners-up place in last year's Babes of the U.S.A Competition. Now 18, she earns her living as a model for that low-budget rag Elegance Quarterly.

Not any more.

Unfortunately for Lola, her shady past has caught up with her in the shape of former boyfriend Hip-Hopster Dredz, the rapper. Many of you may remember the utterly tuneless and mercifully short career of the Dredzter which came to a sudden end when he was exposed as a significant figure in the Cosmopolis Trouble Gum trade in 2104. He was subsequently arrested and tossed into a (hopefully soundproof) cell in The Joint. Lola has always claimed she was totally unaware of his seedy dealings but recent evidence would appear to contradict this. Her world fell apart at roughly 11.55pm on Tuesday 20th September. It would have been earlier were it not for our intrepid boys in blue raiding the wrong residence at first. But after apologising to the indignant tenant and double checking their information (received from an anonymous source) the pinnacle of Cosmopolis law enforcement finally hit the jackpot and raided Lola's apartment on Commando Way. After an extensive search they found a sizeable stash of Trouble Gum (hidden under the floorboards of all places) and carted a disgruntled Lola off to Police Dept Headquarters where a series of uncomfortable questions were asked.

For some reason, this year's tournament seems to be attracting more scandal than a presidential election and bookmakers have already laid odds on how many finalists we'll be left with on October 8th. With Anette Kurtin and Lola Lascala out of the running the last eight consist of seven former winners and this year's surprise finalist, a complete unknown by the name of Maria Valentino, a waitress at Angelo's Bar on Yentil Street. So roll the dice and place your bets folks, will the judges still have eight to choose from in thirteen days time?

CHAPTER TWENTY-EIGHT

"Beauty is a short-lived tyranny."

Socrates

Wednesday 28th September – 10 days til the final.

"Disqualified!" Eve screamed at the letter in her hand and once more, *"disqualified!"* in case the letter had hearing trouble. With trembling hands and a face that was reddening by the second she read through it again:

Dear Miss Tendril,
It is our solemn duty to inform you that, after careful consideration, we have decided to disqualify you from this year's Miss Cosmopolis Tournament. You'll probably be wanting some kind of explanation so here it is.

Firstly, you've already won it three times and that really should be enough shouldn't it? I mean come on, there are literally thousands of young girls who dream of being crowned Miss Cosmo just once! Three times is enough for anyone and to be honest we feel you're being a bit greedy going for a fourth.

Secondly, you're not really in with much of a shout are you? According to our records you'll be celebrating your sixtieth birthday in a couple of months. Most of our other finalists are young enough to be your daughter and whilst we agreed to abolish the age restrictions this year to add a bit more spice we didn't expect applications from senior citizens. You're bound to get whipped by one of the younger girls.

Which brings me on to my final point.

Here at *Out for the Lads & Co Ltd* we pride ourselves on showcasing only the most glamorous, attractive *young* girls. Quite frankly you don't even come close to fitting our portfolio. Maybe you should contact other organizations. I am a personal friend of Mandy Barkwright, editor of the tasteful Glamorous Grans magazine and could arrange an interview should you so wish. With our two youngest contestants out of the tournament we are already facing a rather more mature looking final than we would wish.

The bottom line is you're just too damn old, lady, so we recommend you polish your three trophies, sit back and watch the final on TV and leave the glamour business to us professionals.

Wishing you all the best for the future,

Emma Beastly

Tournament Organiser

Upon reading the letter the first time Eve had gone for the rational approach. Was this a joke? A malicious prank from a corporate rival? If not, then how could she get herself reinstated into the tournament? Was there an appeals process? Or would she have to employ Cyrus to give Emma Beastly a change of heart? After roughly twenty seconds she had abandoned the rational approach and relied on good old fashioned rage. Tearing the letter in two she looked round for something heavy to throw through the window.

Cyrus gave the vending machine another kick, like many people he was a firm believer in the 'if it doesn't work – hit it' theory. The machine grumbled but still refused to cough up the can of Supa-Slurp he had asked for – it seemed even Cyrus Zifford's powers of persuasion had their limits. Ever since Max had threatened to spike his pineapple juice with some nasty chemical, Cyrus had made a point of drinking from cans only, he'd even taken to preparing his own meals. He gave a sigh of annoyance and stared at the floor. He wasn't short of money – far from it – but he'd be damned if he was going to keep shovelling coins into this machine until it decided to deliver. Salvation arrived in the hulking form of Danzo Stax, the Korellian security guard who was now well and truly in Cyrus's hip pocket. He plodded over and (being a good foot taller than Cyrus) was able to give the top of the machine a whack with the flat of his claw. The can rumbled its way through the internal workings and finally clattered into the tray at the bottom.

"It's all about knowing *where* to hit it Mr Zifford."

"Thanks Danz, any more news on Dr Ticklegrit?"

In an effort to keep a sneaky eye on Max's progress, Cyrus had inflated Danzo's ego by appointing him 'head spy'. Not only did it keep him informed on his rival's movements but he knew it would

169

annoy the hell out of him having a Korellian snooping around his lab all the time. On the down side Danzo was not exactly James Bond and often his information was (like his spying abilities) quite limited. Still, it hindered Max and allowed Cyrus to get on with his work without having to waste time doing any snooping of his own which was a bonus.

"I think he's finished building his big machine."

As usual Cyrus already knew this, but he didn't want to disappoint the croc.

"Really? Well that's excellent news! Are you positive you haven't done this kind of thing before? Seems to me you're a natural."

Danzo swelled with pride and smiled, not a particularly pleasant thing to behold but crocs had never been designed with smiling in mind.

"Thank you Mr Zifford. I also know that most of his engineers are flying back to Cosmopolis tonight, only a few are staying here."

"Good, good," Cyrus murmured, nodding slowly.

It was pretty useless information but keeping Danzo keen was crucial. He retrieved his can from the vending machine. "Well Danz, no rest for the wicked, I've got important business to attend to. Keep up the good work eh?"

Speaking of good work, Cyrus was excelling himself and beginning to justify his extortionate salary. So far he had managed to discredit Anette Kurtin and Lola Lascala without even breaking a sweat. For the Kurtin hit he had swiped some of Max's chemicals which had in turn been used to contaminate the consignment of raw meat at the Kurtin factory. That had been a nice touch, the fact that Max had unwittingly assisted him. He'd taken yet more enjoyment from the Lascala job by bringing the subject of Trouble Gum back into the headlines. He knew Max was a 'user' and just wished he could've been there to see his face when the news had reached him. So with the score poised at Cyrus 2 – Max 0 the scandalmonger was feeling extremely smug. If only he could discredit the remaining finalists before Max's 'ugly machine' was operational, that really would be satisfying. The temptation to sabotage the chemist's hellish contraption was becoming increasingly difficult to ignore, but Cyrus was no fool. He knew if Eve Tendril found out he'd be fired in a heartbeat and would probably never find work again, it was one of the golden rules and – for a man whose career depended on dishonesty – a somewhat ironic one, you didn't betray your employer.

Back in his office, Cyrus settled down at his desk and analysed his results using the 'media coverage' method. Not a bad performance, page three of the Cosmo Prattler and a cover story for Looking Guuurd Weekly. The Lascala hit had also made the second item on the evening news, pipped only by a story regarding the break-up of The Splice Girls, the latest mutant girl band to take the world by storm. Flipping on his computer he got his brain in gear and prepared to do what he did best – invent some scandal. He scanned down the list of finalists, most of whom were former winners, until he reached a name he didn't recognise. His brow furrowed as he read the brief information on Maria Valentino. Whoever she was, he hadn't predicted she'd make it to the final and to add to his unease there was virtually no data on her (or at least nothing he could use).

He'd have to do some digging.

After a quick swig from his can he dialled a number into his comm unit.

"Information? Yes hello, I'd like the number for Angelo's Bar in Cosmopolis please."

Had Danzo done a better job with his spying he would have learned that not only was Max Ticklegrit's Uglifier now complete, it was also fully operational. Assembly had taken place in a gigantic hangar which adjoined the main lab complex and had, to everyone's surprise, been finished ahead of schedule. But the engineers had been well aware of Max's reputation as a hard taskmaster as well as his short temper and they had worked day and night to get the job done. No-one wanted to return to Cosmopolis with a bald head or a face full of warts. For maximum impact, Max had purposely kept Eve away from the hangar, he wanted her to see his full size Uglifier in all its glory, as the finished article.

It was indeed an awesome sight and was situated dead centre of the hangar. Standing roughly ninety feet high the Uglifier consisted of a humungous satellite dish supported by a mish-mash of steel girders. Halfway up one wall a railed walkway extended to the machine. At the end of the walkway was a three feet tall control panel, linked to the Uglifier by a mass of snaking cables. The walkway was railed for good reason, directly beneath it was a massive vat of repullium, Max's custom-made uglifying chemical. One slip on an *unrailed* walkway and you were straight in. Not the safest of locations for a giant tub of toxic sludge but then again safety hadn't been their highest priority.

A progress meeting had been arranged and the chemist was busy fussing around the hangar, making sure everything was just right.

"Charlie! What's that piece of cable doing over there? Get rid of it, I want this place like a new pin!"

"Yes doctor!"

Charlie scurried off to dispose of the offending item.

Max organized his team of engineers into a line, like a sergeant major conducting an inspection.

"Alright you lot, listen to me very carefully. Miss Tendril will be here in a few minutes and we need to impress her. That slimy creep Cyrus Zifford is already off to a good start and it is vital we...Victor! What's that on your lab coat? Is that an oil smear? Heavens man we're supposed to be trying to make a good impression!"

The engineer withdrew a handkerchief, spat on it, then rubbed the stain as if his life depended on it. Even Max had replaced his own dilapidated lab coat with a fresh one. It was *that* important. "That's more like it, now as I was saying we need to knock Miss Tendril's socks off with this presentation, which means you do exactly what I say when I say. Understood?"

The engineers nodded enthusiastically. "We've rehearsed this a dozen times so I don't want any mistakes. As you know we've only enough repullium on the island for one demonstration, so it's a one shot deal. Now, you all know where you're supposed to be and what function you're supposed to be performing?"

Even if they didn't know none of them dared admit as much, it was simply too late and again the team answered with nods. "Juliet, you arranged for the refreshments didn't you?"

"Yes, doctor they should be here any time."

"Good, well I guess we just need to wait for Miss Tendril now, oh and Charlie, you've got something in your teeth."

Being inactive didn't agree with Max, he liked to keep busy and having to wait around, even for a few minutes almost caused him physical pain. He stomped around the vast hangar, checking his watch every twenty seconds.

Finally there was a knock at the main doors.

"Alright this is it! Get ready! Get ready!" Max spluttered, making for the entrance.

His team, comprising two men and one woman stood to attention as if they were on parade. Max reached the doors and slid them open, delivering a deep bow as he did so. "Ma'am, so good of you to spare us the time. May I present the instrument of doom for your so-called rivals, – the one, the only...*Uglifier!*"

He turned to face his mechanical monstrosity and spread his arms dramatically. "Behold my greatest creation!" he shrieked.

"Yeah not bad baldy. Now where do you want the tea and biscuits?"

Max whirled round to find himself face to face with Wayne, one of Eve's many servants – he was holding a silver tray laden with refreshments.

"Over there on the table and be quick about it!" Max snarled, trying to hide his embarrassment.

Smirking to himself Wayne deposited the tray and beat a hasty retreat, closing the doors behind him. Max resumed his pacing, looking over his glasses at the engineers, daring one of them to so much as smile. His torture lasted only a few more seconds, then Eve made her entrance sliding the doors open and stepping inside. She was dressed in one of her notorious 'power outfits', as though she were attending a high-level board meeting and Max knew straight away she was asking to be impressed. He hurried over to her and gave another bow, wondering why she looked so angry.

"Ma'am, so good of you to spare us the..."

"Yes I heard it the first time Max, now sit down and listen carefully, we're changing the plan - *significantly.*"

CHAPTER TWENTY-NINE

"I'm so gullible. I'm so damn gullible.
And I am so sick of me being gullible."

Lana Turner

Thursday 29th September - 9 days til the final.
11.48am – The Pitz Hotel, Cosmopolis.

"This is operative number forty...I mean..."
Frantic rustling of creased paper.
"...this is *agent* forty-seven reporting in. Security clearance level fifteen, code number eight...no wait..."
Frantic straightening out of creased paper.
"... that should be *six*, five, zero, nine..."
"Alright you can cut the secret agent crap Frank, I know it's you."
"Oh...hello sir."
"Where the hell have you been? We've been worried sick about you back here – you've been gone nearly seven weeks!"
"It took me a while to find him sir."
"Yeah but Frank – seven weeks?"
"I did say before you sent me that I wasn't exactly familiar with all this espionage stuff."
"It's not espionage Frank, it's simple data retrieval – except you're in the field. So how did it go?"
"I regret to announce I have failed to locate target."
"*What*?"
"I have failed to locate the target sir."
"Frank what the hell are you talking about?"
"Well sir, I went to his house, just as instructed but he wasn't there. The current owner told me our target relocated approximately twelve months ago."
"We have no record of a relocation! Are you sure you got the right address?"

174

"Yes sir, no question – ninety-nine Fargo Drive. I checked the street sign and the door number and everything."

"And you're in the right year?"

"Yes sir, I checked the newspapers as soon as I arrived, it's September 2105 as planned."

"Well either our data is inaccurate, which is highly unlikely, we are after all the data specialists, or the current owner is lying to you."

"I must say sir he did bear an uncanny resemblance to the statue."

"Then he's lying to you Frank!"

"I thought that too sir."

"Then why the hell didn't you press him further?"

"Er...well...as you know sir I am descended from English parentage and...well...conflict isn't in our nature, it's just not the done thing to provoke people. It's as they used to say... 'just not cricket'."

"Cricket? What the hell is cricket?"

"I'm not entirely sure sir."

"Look - I don't give a damn about cricket, go back there and get the information we need. We've got exactly nine days before we unveil the statue and I'm not going to be the one who stands before the president and says 'oh I'm sorry Mr President we didn't get the name quite right!"

"I fully understand sir."

"Good! Then get your ass back to his house and get the data we need!"

"Absolutely sir. But…"

"But *what*?"

"But what if he gives me the same story?"

"Challenge him for goodness sake! What is it about you English?"

"I'm only *descended* from English ancestors, as you know I was born back there in Vestra-Majora. I still don't like to muddy the water though sir."

"Frank, you'll be muddying your entire career at Historical Data Retrieval if you don't!"

"Very well sir, leave it to me I'll get it done."

"Glad to hear it Frank – let me know when you have the information. One last thing."

"Sir?"

"What's Earth like?"

"Not that impressive to be honest sir – a bit grubby. Shame really, this would all seem much more worthwhile if it had actually been worth saving."

"It wasn't saved Frank. It was *almost* saved."

"Yes, but I meant…"

"Never mind that, it's all in the past now and let's be honest no-one misses it that much these days. But I'm afraid you're gonna have to stay there until you get the job done."

"Worry not sir, I'm on it. Operat…er…agent forty-seven signing off."

Frank Bazonka snapped shut the inter-planetary, time-splitting communicator, shoved it back into the inside pocket of his jacket and let out a long sigh. Sat on the edge of the bed in his low-budget hotel he put his head into his hands and made an excellent job of looking thoroughly pathetic. Surely there were other people more suited to this kind of work, people with more self-confidence and trendier suits.

He'd volunteered for this assignment quite by accident.

A new position had been advertised on the office notice-board, a job which offered the chance to travel and boasted 'great historical significance'. Whilst he enjoyed his one-paced, routine job at Historical Data Retrieval he had been looking around for something a little more engaging. This new position sounded just the ticket, it would undoubtedly take him to other parts of the city, maybe to the odd museum or two. And that had been his big mistake. The other real kick in the teeth had been that no-one else had applied for the job. So when he had eventually learned the true nature of the advertisement (and been hastily brought back to consciousness by the office nurse) they had been unable to give it another applicant. Travelling back in time to a planet that didn't exist anymore had definitely not been on his 'to do' list in fact it was more likely to feature on his 'would rather die than do' list. What if there was some mix up and he got stuck there? It would be the equivalent of booking a fishing trip and finding yourself aboard the Titanic. But rules were rules and at the end of the day he *had* put his name forward. So, hampered by his natural aversion to conflict, he had reluctantly agreed to take the assignment on the understanding it would be a one-off and that afterwards he could return to his data input job which now looked more beautifully mundane than ever.

It had been three days since his encounter with the man who claimed not to be Eric Dorfler but looked exactly like him and Frank was struggling to come up with an alternative plan of attack. The prospect of further confrontation only made it harder to think clearly and he resolved to make a fresh start in the morning after a nice cup of tea.

CHAPTER THIRTY

"Anger is a momentary madness,
so control your passion or it will control you."

Horace

Thursday 29th September – 9 days til the final.
    9.28pm – Cyrus Zifford's office, Perfection Island.

Controlling his emotions was one of Cyrus's talents but he always struggled to suppress his anger, probably because he rarely had anything to be mad about. He was good looking, successful and very gifted in his particular field of endeavour – there weren't many things that bent him out of shape.

But today was different.

Today Eve Tendril had called him to a meeting where she had explained her change of plan. It had been a short meeting and Eve had been blunt. Her opening line of: "there's been a change of plan Cyrus and your services are no longer required," hadn't left much room for misinterpretation. Yes, she had told him, he'd done a great job so far, but there were still a handful of finalists he had failed to discredit and after learning of her disqualification she had decided to take matters a step further. A more radical plan that needed just one thing to succeed – the Uglifier.

Max Ticklegrit's Uglifier.

Cyrus hadn't questioned his employer, hadn't begged her to reconsider, he'd accepted the decision quite calmly in fact. But inside he was seething. How could she reject him in favour of that psychotic scientist? It was easily the worst thing she could've done as far as he was concerned. Had she ditched them *both* then he could have lived with it, but now Max would be getting all the glory, he'd be the one taking all the 'thank yous' and 'well dones'. And knowing Max he'd take every opportunity to rub Cyrus's nose in it.

No matter which way he twisted it around, Cyrus simply

couldn't find a positive angle. Max was going to win – and there was nothing he could do about it. That made him mad. After nearly two hours of intense, red-faced pacing (during which time he'd worn a neat furrow in the office carpet) he finally made a decision. It was a risky one, one that could terminate his employment at You Beauty, one that may have even more serious consequences. But, as with most plans, he'd only be in trouble if he got caught and when it came to covering your tracks there were few people better than Cyrus Zifford. He stopped pacing and turned the plan over in his mind. If it worked then he would be spared the indignity of Max's gloating, but it would also wreck Eve's new plan and that was the part that concerned him. Whatever happened he could not allow any of it to be traced back to *him*. He'd need a fall guy, someone foolish enough to go through with it on a 'no questions asked' basis. Someone who wouldn't betray him, but also someone Cyrus could quite happily feed to the wolves if the occasion demanded it. For the first time that day Cyrus found himself grinning as his plan began to take shape. It was a dark, swirling, nasty plan with sharp edges. Yes! That would be perfect! He could even make it look like Max was to blame! His face lost some of its redness and he strolled over to the desk. As he was about to hit the call button on his intercom there was a knock at the door.

"Enter," Cyrus cried and then smiled as Danzo Stax plodded into the room carrying a plate of sandwiches and a can of beer.

"Thought you might like some supper Mr Zifford."

Cyrus smirked to himself. Since his arrival on Perfection Island he'd reduced this Korellian, this hulking lump of violence, into his personal butler. The fact that Danzo was *thinking* was substantial progress in itself, the fact he was thinking of someone other than himself was close to a miracle.

"Ah, hi there Danzo," Cyrus beamed, "I was just about to call you. I've got a little job for you."

Danzo did his best to beam back, which ended up looking pretty awful.

"Certainly sir, what can I do for you?"

It was so nice to be wanted.

CHAPTER THIRTY-ONE

"The art of simplicity is a puzzle of complexity."

Doug Horton

Friday 30th September - 8 days til the final.
    8pm - sat outside at Angelo's.

"I don't like it Hank, something's not right."
"Knock it off man, she's probably on vacation or something."
"This close to the final? Come on – she's in the last ten! There's no way, anyway if she's on holiday then why didn't she tell her boss eh? Why didn't she tell *us*?"
"You know what Maria's like, it must've slipped her mind."
Eric gave his beer the guzzle treatment, then shook his head.
"I'm not buyin' it dude."
"What do you think Dolores?"
Dolores sat between the two friends, drinking her chocolate milkshake through a straw.
"About what?"
"About Maria not being here," Hank answered, using his sleeve to dab some milk from her chin.
"Dunno."
"What does the voice think?" Eric asked.
Dolores returned her attention to her shake, had a good slurp then said:
"She's somewhere warm and sunny with palm trees."
"See?" Hank said, leaning back in his seat and clasping his hands behind his head, "she's on holiday."
'Same old Eric' he thought to himself, always assuming there's some big conspiracy.
But Eric still wasn't convinced. Over the last six and half weeks they had come to realise the voice wasn't infallible, it was *usually* correct, but not always. He drained his bottle.
"Hmm, well maybe."

"Relax will ya? And ease up on that beer, remember four bottles maximum now."

"Yeah, yeah I remember."

The four bottle rule was just *one* of the changes Hank had made since assuming control of the Avenging Knights and they had, under his rather more restrained leadership, made excellent progress. A key factor had been the decision to stick to preventing relatively minor crimes *and* knowing when to walk away – something Eric found very difficult. But Hank had gone on to explain that laying in a hospital bed, or six feet under, wouldn't help the public at all and until they got some experience under their belts it was vital they worked within their limitations. One thing he had been powerless to stop (and it irked him terribly) had been the number of times he'd been accidentally hit with the Garbage Shoot. Sixpack's aim was on a par with his cooking skills and his hit ratio (even including those on Hank) was abysmal. They had considered rotating the weapons, giving everyone a chance to become familiar with each one but the Garbage Shoot was the least lethal and if the droid were to have a weapon this one was the obvious choice. A poorly directed shot from the Web-o-matic or the Slumberjack could have devastating consequences. The other option was to go out and buy a military chip which, once installed would increase Sixpack's weapon handling capabilities immeasurably. Unfortunately they were expensive – real expensive – and no-one was particularly keen on parting with any more dosh just yet (the new van had not been cheap). Hank had also introduced a fitness regime (more for his own benefit than anyone else) and through a painful process of careful eating and some limited exercise they were both beginning to lose weight, albeit gradually.

But their success hadn't just been down to Hank; Dolores had made a significant contribution too. Her 'voice' had been able to predict a large amount of crimes, enabling the Knights to become proactive rather than reactive. During the week she would drop out clues, the Knights would write them down, decipher them, then act on them every Saturday. Not having to rely on imprecise police information – which was at times relayed too late to act upon and was something of a 'lucky dip' – had proved to be a real bonus. The inaccuracy she had displayed when revealing their names had been a warning that the voice was perhaps prone to error now and then and this had persisted during their Saturday activities. On a couple of occasions she had led them on wild goose chases but Hank and Eric had tolerated it, after all, her mistakes hadn't resulted in anything catastrophic.

Yet.

Nor had there been any further information regarding the impending disaster. 'Broken reflectograms' and 'scary faces' were still the only clues they had to go on. They were no nearer establishing *when* the event might happen either and the longer it went on the more inclined they were to accept it was probably nothing to worry about.

Yet.

10.05pm – Eric's place.

With Dolores tucked up in bed and Sixpack recharging his power cells in the kitchen, the two chums were flaked out in the lounge, enjoying a rare moment alone. Now they had seven successful outings in the bank they were feeling a little happier about the whole superhero thing which had, like everything else in their lives, become a routine.

"So," Hank said, "almost seven weeks down the line and we're still alive."

"Yep, alive and kickin' criminal butt!"

"Feels good doesn't it?"

"Sure does, I wish the cops would be a bit more supportive though."

Eric had taken to buying almost every newspaper and magazine that had mentioned the Avenging Knights and was already on to his second scrapbook. The positive response from the public had given them both a great deal of pleasure, especially Eric. When all said and done this had been his idea, his alone and the fact it had won over the people gave him a warm, fuzzy glow of contentment.

"I can understand the commissioner's reservations," Hank sighed, "we're not exactly in the Captain's league are we?"

"I don't care! We're providing a public service, just as they are and we're not even getting paid for it. You'd think they'd welcome some help."

"Take it easy dude, the people are behind us and that's what counts." As always Hank found it far easier to focus on the positive. "Dolores has come up with a few predictions for tomorrow night by the way, I scribbled them down in your notebook but haven't had chance to try and crack them yet."

Eric fidgeted in his armchair, looking uncomfortable. "Well aren't you gonna take a look?" Hank asked.

There was something on Eric's mind and it was obviously something he wasn't going to enjoy divulging but 'Eric Dorfler struggles to discuss sensitive subject' was hardly headline news. "What is it?" Hank asked resignedly.

"How much longer is Dolores gonna be staying here? I mean, it's OK for you – you can go home at night but I have to take care of her and we both know leaving her with Six during the day isn't an ideal situation – even *with* that maternity chip we installed. I agree it's handy to have her around to predict crimes but you know I'm not very good with kids. The nuns have already got the cops going door to door to try and find her. What happens if they come knocking at my door eh? What am I gonna tell 'em? And don't tell me you're thinking of *adopting* her, being around us is not exactly a stable family environment."

Hank knew Eric wasn't much of a kid fan, indeed he'd been amazed it had taken him this long to voice his dissatisfaction.

"Would you feel better if I took her in at my place?"

"Yeah I would, but it's not fair on you mate, you haven't got the space."

"I'll make space."

"Why don't we just hand her back to the orphanage eh?"

"No way, I'm not handing her back to a bunch of avaricious nuns, besides there's still this big disaster thing to unravel."

"I thought we decided that wasn't worth pursuing?"

"We did but, what if we're *wrong* Eric? What if we can stop it?"

"We don't even know what it is! Dolores's predictions are becoming more and more cryptic and what have we got to go on so far? Broken reflectograms and scary faces, not what I'd call hard evidence bud."

Hank sighed. Eric was probably right, it was a bit flimsy, but could they really just cast it aside? Eric picked up the notebook and pencil from the table; "let's see what conundrums she's left us to decipher shall we?"

"What's the first one?" Hank asked, happy to leave the accommodation issue unresolved for the time being.

Decoding Dolores's predictions was, as Eric had said, starting to get quite tricky. It was almost as if she (or the voice) were testing them, making the clues more difficult as time went on. Eric tapped the pencil against the notepad and frowned.

"Alright, the first one says 'bruises and fists on hungry fish at noon'."

They mulled it over in silence for a few seconds. Eric was right, they were getting more complicated.

"Well, it must be some kind of mugging or assault and it's obviously gonna take place around midday but where? What does 'hungry fish' mean?" Hank said quietly.

Eric had a flash of inspiration and pointing to Hank with his pencil he said:

"I've got it! She means Jaws Street!"

"Nice one man. OK jot that down and...hang on...she could mean Piranha Avenue."

"Damn, it could be either!"

"It's not a major problem, they're only about five minutes apart. Which one do you wanna go for?"

"Let's try Piranha Avenue first."

Yeah right – thought Hank, so I get the blame if we're wrong and if we're right then you can still take the credit because *you* decided to go there first. He smiled at Eric's sneaky move.

"What's next?" he asked.

"Robbery at snake head warehouse on glass slipper drive around 9pm. Oh for heaven's sake, how are we supposed to work that one out?"

Hank did the Cosmopolis Prattler crossword nearly every day, consequently he was quite adept at word based puzzles. Eric only read the cartoons, which is why he was struggling.

"Yeah, that's a tough one, but I'm sure we can crack it. Let's just tackle it piece by piece. It's clearly a robbery that's gonna take place at 9pm. Glass slipper drive? Glass slipper drive?"

He looked to the ceiling for assistance.

"It could be Shattered Drive?" Eric tried. "Ties in with the glass thing, and she's fond of talking about broken glass as we know."

"Hmm, maybe but where does the slipper come into it? Wait! I've got it! She means Cinderella Drive! Remember that old fairytale, where the princess leaves behind a glass slipper or something?"

The blank look Eric gave him suggested he wasn't as familiar with fairytales as Hank was. "I'm sure I'm right, jot it down – Cinderella Drive. Now, snake head warehouse?"

"Cinderella Drive's a fairly small road from memory, there're only a few warehouses down there. Let me think, one belongs to Top Topper's Pizza, there's one for that chemical company Med USA and the only other warehouse I can think of is the one belonging to Skidmark Mac, the air bike dealership."

"I wouldn't have thought anyone's gonna try and rob a pizza warehouse."

"Top Topper's *are* good pizzas though."

"Yeah but come on Eric, what are they gonna do? Melt them down and sell them as kebabs on the black market? No, the other two are far more likely to get robbed, they store valuable stuff. My guess is they'll be after the bikes, chemical stuff is far too well guarded."

"Shouldn't be too hard to spot them anyway, like I said it's a small street, we're bound to run into them no matter which one they go for."

"I think there's one more."

Eric flipped the page over. He read the words then looked across at Hank in disbelief.

"You're kidding me right?"

"I know, difficult innit?"

"*Difficult?* It's gobbledygook! Are you sure this is what she said?"

"Yep, I asked her to repeat it several times."

Eric read it out;

"*'Chain up the Mungle'*. Well – it's meaningless! There's no place, no time, no clue to the crime at all! And what the hell's a Mungle anyway?"

"I don't know. I checked the dictionary and it only had Mung in there, which incidentally is an edible plant. But no Mungle."

"And why does it need to be chained up?"

"I don't *know*!"

Of all the predictions Dolores had given them, this was by far the most obtuse and it had the Knights flummoxed. Hank yawned, he was in serious need of sleep.

"I think we should look at it again in the morning," he said.

His partner yawned back at him.

"Yeah let's do that, I'm beat."

"It could be an anagram," Hank suggested, rising from his seat.

"Whatever, we'll scope it out over breakfast. You wanna crash here again tonight?"

Since their first Saturday as crimefighters Hank had taken to spending Friday nights at Eric's place in the name of convenience.

"Yeah please."

Before retiring to bed (well, to sofa) Hank wrote down the words from the last clue in big capitals, stringing them out at regular intervals to form one long line of letters. He was convinced it was an anagram, his favourite type of word puzzle, but try as he might he couldn't crack it. In the end he submitted to fatigue and dozed off, letting the paper flutter to the floor.

CHAPTER THIRTY-TWO

"Begin challenging your own assumptions. Your assumptions are your windows on the world. Scrub them off every once in awhile, or the light won't come in."

Alan Alda

Saturday 1st October - 7 days til the final.
   9.05am – Bloomissia (a distant planet).

Someone once said 'when you *assume* you make an *ass* out of *u* and *me'*. Other, less articulate individuals, have been heard to say you make an *ass* out of *umption* which, whilst grammatically correct, lacks the necessary impact and misses the point somewhat. Assumptions are a fundamental aspect of life and without them we'd either be extremely smug or utterly clueless. Minor assumptions are often spot on – "I assume by your tone of voice you'd like me to leave now," and "I assumed *you'd* be paying," and "I assume this burger *isn't* 100% prime beef," are perfect examples. But it's the major assumptions that are usually wide of the mark, the real whoppers, such as "the world is flat," and "we are the only intelligent species in the universe."

Which brings us neatly on to the issue of Nature.

Most of us assume that Nature *takes care of itself*, a bit like Time or Space or (in the case of married men) the washing and ironing. But Nature is a complex issue, which is far too unpredictable to be left to itself. Very few people assume Nature is in fact an enormous organisation, with a network of offices and call centres that span the universe in a tireless effort to keep Nature running smoothly. But it's entirely true. Mother Nature, assisted by a veritable legion of managers, department heads, supervisors and field agents, watches over the galaxy, making sure nothing too 'unnatural' occurs. This being 2105, a time when technology and

187

knowledge have left wisdom far behind, the scope for unnatural even *supernatural* occurrences is huge.

And when something unnatural *does* occur, it's down to Mother Nature to put it right. Like any self respecting boss, she often delegates these problems to her subordinates, who in turn sub-delegate to their own underlings until finally the problem has been resolved and all that remains is one unholy scrap to claim the credit.

But the universe is a *big* place and keeping an eye on it is quite a task for just one person – which is why Mother Nature has her 'watchers'. Animal, bird, fish or insect – all are eligible candidates for the esteemed position and there are literally gazillions of them scattered throughout the galaxy. Their ability to communicate with Mother Nature telepathically eliminates the need for extensive travel or lengthy electronic messages and allows the watchers to relay their information in a matter of seconds wherever they may be.

Dibley Spooner had been recently reappointed following a reshuffle at Nature HQ – a sideways move, or at least that's what they'd called it at the time. In his eyes it was akin to a chicken making a sideways move to chasseur. His previous job at the Geology Dept, more specifically Manager of Rockslide and Avalanche Maintenance had been perfect. He liked rocks, they were rugged, tough, unyielding, *masculine* - like Dibley himself. Despite his less than masculine name Dibley was in fact a rock of a man, tall, muscular, broad-shouldered with a serious chin and a voice like gravel. Life had been good at R&A Maintenance and given the choice he would've spent the rest of his working life there. But last month's reshuffle had seen to that.

Sat in his pink leather swivel chair Dibley surveyed his new office. There was nothing manly about it. His predecessor Edna Hogmany-Fortesque had given it the feminine touch and it complemented a man like Dibley the way frogspawn complements a slice of toast. Naturally he had demanded a complete refurbishment but even now, almost three weeks down the line, the decorators were still dragging their feet and had yet to sling a paintbrush in anger. He leaned forward and picked up the brass nameplate that adorned the front of his desk. 'D Spooner – Human Beauty Manager'. He breathed on it and polished it vigorously with his shirt sleeve as though trying to erase the words. They gleamed back at him with renewed enthusiasm, reflecting the 'in-your-face' pink coloured walls of his office. The room even *smelled* pink.

"Beauty," he grumbled to himself. "What the hell do I know about beauty?"

Pretty much nothing was the answer, but Mother Nature had assured him it was essential for his managerial development that he be exposed to new and exciting challenges. New and exciting also meant being transferred from his beloved rock-strewn planet of Granitron to the flower-filled and virtually rock free moon of Bloomissia, a namby-pamby planet if ever he'd seen one. His thoughts about the unfairness of it all were interrupted when Harvey Beedham, his second in command, came crashing into his office. Harvey had been with him at R&A Maintenance and was similarly disenchanted with his new position.

"Hey Harve, what's up?" Dibley muttered, glancing at the piece of paper Harvey was holding.

"Big news Spoon," Harvey said excitedly, "looks like someone finally took pity on us and gave us something worthwhile to do."

"Oh no wait, let me guess, somebody's invented a potion that artificially extends eyelashes."

Harvey laughed, he was well aware of just how much Dibley was enjoying his new job.

"No I'm serious." He waved the sheet of paper around theatrically. "Straight from HQ!"

Dibley sat up, desperately trying to forget he was sitting on a pink chair.

"Let's hear it."

Harvey decided against sitting in the cherry coloured sofa opposite Dibley's desk and remained standing.

"It appears, "Harvey said slowly, "that some bright spark on Earth is building some kind of contraption that can turn people ugly. He's a scientist on some remote tropical island and it just so happens one of Mother Nature's watchers has stumbled across it."

Dibley slumped in his seat.

"And this is your idea of something worthwhile is it?"

"Well...yeah."

"Hardly headline news is it Harve?"

"Wait, there's more. Apparently this machine has the capacity to target entire planets!"

"*What?*"

Harvey nodded.

"Yep. Thought that might grab your attention."

"Right…er…so what the hell are we supposed to do about it?"

"I don't know – you're the boss, it's your call."

Dibley scratched his impressive chin.

"Well, in that case I delegate it to you."

"Aw come on Spoon, that's not fair! You know darn well I've no-one to pass it down to."

"Guess you'll just have to deal with it then."

This was the first significant action they had seen since they'd both moved to Beauty Headquarters and neither of them had much idea about procedures or protocol yet – it had taken them three days just to find the canteen.

Harvey adopted a defiant tone.

"Alright then! I will! And when *I* manage to sort it then maybe HQ will take another look at my transfer request."

This knocked Dibley sideways.

"You've put one in *already*?"

"Yep!"

"But we've only just got here!"

"You know the way it goes Spoon. If you don't ask you don't get."

"Give me the paper!"

"No! I'm quite capable of handling it, boss."

"Give it to me – that's an order!"

Harvey handed it over with a smirk. Dibley scanned the details and said, "look, we'll do it *together*, then perhaps we can both get off this flower stall."

"Fair enough."

"Now obviously we need to get someone down there asap to put this thing out of commission. Who do we have in the way of field agents? Someone who's gonna blend into a tropical environment."

With a smug grin Harvey pulled another sheet of paper from his back pocket.

"Way ahead of you boss," he smiled unfolding the sheet. "There's really only one choice. Seems we have a fella here by the name of Grunter."

"And he is?"

"Very good."

190

"No, I mean what *is* he? Spider? Turtle?"

"Gorilla."

"Perfect! Good track record?"

"Yeah pretty good. He's quite experienced. Remember that genetics lab on Wattoo VIII that got wiped out last year?"

"The one doing the dolphin/pineapple thing?"

"The very same – that was Grunter's work."

"Where is he now?"

"Just back from an assignment."

"Get him in here and bring a translator, we're gonna need to talk to him."

Harvey made for the door. "One more thing Harve."

"Boss?"

"Give those decorators a kick up the arse will you?"

CHAPTER THIRTY-THREE

"Man cannot live by incompetence alone."

Charlotte Whitton

Saturday 1st October - 7 days til the final.
 10.30am – Dr Ticklegrit's office, Perfection Island.

Click!
"Oh come on!"
Click!
"Blast!"
Click! Click! Click!
Max abhorred direct sunlight and no matter which button he pressed on the remote control device he simply could not get the blinds to close. The morning sun poured in through the window, bathing his office in a warm haze. He had been keeping office time to a minimum as best he could, he much preferred the artificial light of the lab or the gloom of the hangar. But he was waiting for an important call, one he had to take personally, which is why he was there.

"What's wrong with good old fashioned curtains?" he mumbled to himself, examining the remote control carefully. He pointed it at the blinds and tried again.

Click!
It was hopeless - there had to be a malfunction. He hurled the remote across the room then jumped as his comm unit beeped at him. Moving his chair into the small shaded area he flicked the switch and answered the call.

"Ticklegrit here."

"Good morning doctor, it's Romeo here from the Cosmopolis lab and I've got bad news I'm afraid."

Max massaged his eyeballs under his glasses. This was all he needed.

"What is it Romeo?"

"Well, you know that list of chemicals you asked for?"

"Yes."

"Well…er…we've arranged for them to be flown over to Perfection Island today as instructed."

"So what's the problem?"

There was a long pause as Romeo summoned up the required courage.

"There's one item on the list I…er…*we* can't get hold of."

"What?"

"It's the tripolytrolyphate."

Max exhaled loudly so Romeo could hear him. Struggling to control his temper he said;

"Romeo, like I told you on Wednesday there's been a change of plan, Miss Tendril now wants me to uglify *everyone in Cosmopolis* on the night of the final. I need those chemicals as a matter of urgency so I can manufacture some more repullium – a hell of a lot more. Repullium is the chemical that fuels the Uglifier and to make repullium I need *tripolytrolyphate!*"

The sentence finished with Max on his feet, bent over the comm unit, screaming the words into the microphone from a distance of two inches. There was another lengthy silence. Back at the Cosmo lab they had drawn straws to see which one of the team would get the job of delivering the bad news. Romeo had come up short and had, after a futile request for 'best out of three', made the call. He'd harboured a tiny granule of hope that perhaps Max would understand and behave in a rational state. Fat chance. Now he was paying the price for his misplaced optimism with the kind of tongue-lashing few people recovered from. Consequently, he had reached the pathetic begging stage rather earlier than anticipated.

"But doctor, please understand, we've looked everywhere and no-one has any! As you know, tripolytrolyphate is only produced on one planet – Krellog XII – and ever since civil war broke out there last month there's been a massive shortage. They're too busy fighting each other you see. Please, we've done everything we can!"

Max paced the office, trying to stay calm – and in the shade.

"Have you tried Drugtastic Inc?"

"Ran out last week doctor."

"Medic Nation?"

"None left."

"Beautiful Pharmaceutical?"

"Fresh out sir."

"Oh come on there must be someone! Med USA?"

"They have some on order but it won't be here for another seven days."

This stopped Max in his tracks.

"When?"

"Next Saturday."

"When *exactly*?"

"They've got a delivery scheduled to arrive at one of their warehouses at noon Cosmo time."

The chemist did some rapid mental calculations while Romeo waited in silence.

"Right! I need the address of the warehouse and as many details as you can find out about the delivery. I need to know how much security there's likely to be, what kind of vehicle is making the delivery and how many people are going to be in the warehouse when it arrives. Is that understood?"

"Absolutely doctor."

"You think you and your imbecilic colleagues can get that information to me asap without mucking it up?"

"No problem sir, I'll get on it right away."

Max brought his fist down on the comm unit, bringing the conversation to an abrupt end. Squinting against the sunlight he gazed outside at the sparkling ocean and let out a deep breath. This was a setback - a major setback which had just sent his chances of success spiralling earthwards. But all was not lost, he could still achieve his objective provided everyone did as they were told and Fate kept its meddling nose well and truly out of it.

He was about to call for one of his engineers when Juliet walked into the office and saved him the bother.

"Oh I beg your pardon doctor," she said politely, "I didn't know you were in here. I was looking for the technical data on the Uglifier's Chemical Displacement Unit."

"Why is there a problem?" Max panicked.

"No, no not at all. I was just doing some routine maintenance and needed the plans. Are you alright doctor? You look rather shaken."

The chemist pulled himself together.

"I'm fine, it's just that some of our amoeba-brained colleagues back at head office are giving me a headache. I mean really, sometimes they make a Flabbergump[†] look intelligent. Anyway, it appears we're going to have to modify our timetable somewhat."

"Modify it how exactly?"

"I was just about to call Victor in to discuss this but now that you're here I might as well tell you."

This news did not gladden Juliet one bit. Whatever had gone wrong had clearly ruffled the chemist and the fact he wanted to 'discuss it with her' meant he wanted to lift the problem off his own shoulders and place it squarely on hers. She cursed her timing, if she had only stopped at the vending machine on the way here she would probably have got away with it.

"What's the problem doctor?" she asked, resigning herself to the responsibility and taking a seat.

Max sat opposite her and interlocked his fingers.

"I've just spoken to Romeo 'two short planks' Jarvis at the Cosmo lab and they've drawn a blank on the tripolytrolyphate. Seems the civil war on Krellog XII has interfered with production and the only chance we've got of finding any is a delivery at a Med USA warehouse on the day of the final."

"That's cutting it a bit fine."

"Quite, I had hoped to have the repullium ready well before the final. Now, we won't have the luxury of going through the time consuming rigmarole of placing an order and paying for it so we're going to have to steal it, then fly it back here immediately. The delivery is expected at noon Cosmo time so if we say one hour to steal it, two hours to fly it over and another hour to formulate the repullium then we should be ready to fire the Uglifier at about 4pm Cosmo time – two hours before the final takes place, provided there are no slip-ups."

Juliet nodded although she wasn't sure why she (an engineer) had been asked to help. Maybe Max just wanted someone else, *anyone* else, to get the job done.

"Should I be writing this down doctor?"

"Not yet, we need a few more details regarding the delivery first, which hopefully, Jarvis and his moronic cohorts will be ringing through soon. Now, I know for a fact that the Industrial Disruption team are the only people in my employ capable of

[†] The stupidest creature in the galaxy, now on the verge of extinction as it often forgets how to breathe.

pulling off a job like this and they're already out on an assignment in Maple (formerly Canada) so as I see it we only have one option."

"You don't want *me* to do it do you?" Juliet cried, ready to give him a huge list of reasons why she would be unsuitable.

"Of course not! I was going to say our only option is to use those plodding Korellians that masquerade as security on this island. Assuming of course that Miss Tendril is OK with it. But I'll need someone to co-ordinate it – you're highly organised and efficient so I see no reason why you shouldn't do it."

"I'm hardly qualified for that sort of thing Dr Ticklegrit, after all I'm just an engineer not a…a…robbery co-ordinator."

"My dear girl if you were *just* an engineer you would never have made it on to my team. You have qualities above and beyond your qualifications, initiative, ambition and drive."

"Thank you doctor but I still think…"

"Of course, if I'm wrong and you *are* just an engineer then I have the perfect job for you. In light of current events I'll be needing someone to travel to Krellog XII to give me a full report on our remote laboratory out there. We wouldn't want any harm befalling it in the wake of this inconvenient civil war would we?"

Working for Max Ticklegrit had its benefits, the pay was good and it was a fairly sure bet you'd end up involved in some groundbreaking research. But there was also a down side. Namely that Max had absolutely no feelings for his staff, no compassion, no sympathy and no respect, in fact he probably didn't have any feelings for *anybody*. Juliet didn't know too much about the civil war on Krellog XII except that 'civil' was unlikely to be an accurate description. Like Max she wasn't much of an outdoors kind of person, especially when the outdoors had bombs whistling through the air and landmines all over the ground.

"OK doctor, what do you need me to do?"

"Well the first thing you can do is show me how these infernal blinds work."

CHAPTER THIRTY-FOUR

"In a time of universal deceit - telling the truth is a revolutionary act."

George Orwell

Saturday 1st October - 7 days til the final.
  8.30am – Eric's place.

Eric went through his usual morning routine. Wake up (eyes partially open and full of crusty sleep) – tumble out of bed (eyes closed again) – brush teeth (eyes still closed) – descend stairs (eyes partially open again for safety reasons). When he entered the lounge (eyes fully open and sleep free) he found Hank laid on the sofa, pouring over the anagram puzzle.

"You've not been trying to crack that all night have you?"

"Oh morning mate. No, I haven't but it feels like it. Think I'm making progress though."

"So what does it mean?"

Hank, who had been studying the puzzle for the last hour, sat up excitedly (crusty eye sleep removed a good forty minutes ago).

"I don't know for sure, but I've worked out that you *can't* make the words Hank, Eric, Sir Prize, Rough Knight, Avenging Knights, Sixpack, Excalibot or Cosmopolis from these letters."

It was early and Eric wasn't ready for mental gymnastics just yet – brushing his teeth had all but exhausted him. Neither Hank or Eric could be described as 'morning people'.

"That's progress is it?" he yawned, sitting down beside his pal.

"I wrote the message out again and put the letters in one big line."

"So?"

"So you can't make any of those words see?"

He handed over the list and Eric scrutinised it through bleary eyes. The following letters stared back at him:

He made a token effort at solving it but the answer didn't immediately jump out at him so he gave it back.

"Nah sorry, I can't suss it."

"I'm convinced it's important, don't ask me how I know I just *know*. It's linked to this big disaster somehow – I know it!"

Eric yawned again – Mr Enthusiasm – then his stomach gave him a nudge.

"Have you seen Sixpack?"

"Yeah, he's making breakfast."

"Groovy, I'm starving," Eric exclaimed and hurried off into the kitchen.

Hank was hot on his heels. Over the last few weeks he'd figured out the best way to get a decent meal from Sixpack's crematorium style cooking was to help yourself to the food before he really got into his stride, when he was perhaps halfway through cooking it. It wasn't long before they were joined by Dolores, who shuffled into the kitchen wearing one of Eric's sweatshirts. Only her head and toes were visible as she rubbed her eyes and took a seat at the table without saying a word.

"Morning Dolores, you want some juice?" Hank asked.

She nodded, too tired to talk – another 'non-morning person'.

Eric looked over his newspaper and said, "any more unfathomable clues for us today D?"

She shook her head and took a gulp of juice, wondering what the word 'unfathomable' meant.

"You're chirpy this morning," Hank joked.

Sarcasm was something Dolores had yet to master and she just sat there looking confused. "Are you alright Dolores?"

"I had a nightmare," she murmured.

Eric rolled his eyes and buried his face in the newspaper, another fine example of his child appreciation skills. Hank was a little more understanding.

"Hey they're just bad dreams, they can't hurt you."

"What was it about this time?" Eric piped up from behind his paper, "more broken reflectograms and scary faces?"

He bit his lip as Hank kicked him under the table – he was wearing slippers too so it was doubly painful.

"You were both in real bad trouble," the little girl said

absently, "fighting a monster."

"A monster?"

"Yeah like a big red dragon, but with no wings and two heads."

There was an exaggerated sigh from the other side of the newspaper as Eric flicked over to the sports section.

"I see Slikkish Brillian set a new record for consecutive touchdowns last night. He's gotta be the greatest Blooball player of all time don't ya think?," he said, trying to bring the conversation into the real world.

Hank ignored him.

"Well there are no such things as dragons, Dolores, not on Earth anyway, so why don't you finish your juice and I'll rescue something for you to eat OK?"

"OK," she squeaked, although she didn't look overly convinced.

Eric peered over his newspaper.

"Maybe we can cook you up a nice bowl of Mungle."

"What's Mungle?" she replied.

"Never mind."

Now the nightmare subject had been dropped Eric got back down to business. Avenging Knight business. "Right, I'm gonna have breakfast then nip down to the basement to print off today's schedule. Six did you clean up Hank's armour like I asked?"

"Yes sir, it is in the garage. I was unable to fully erase the odour though."

It was true – Hank's breastplate had sustained so many hits from the Garbage Shoot it was starting to pong quite badly. "Well, I wouldn't worry about that too much," he said grinning broadly, "Hank's a tough fella, it'll take more than a bad smell to put him off."

"Thanks bud," Hank said miserably.

"Don't mention it. Oh my God!"

"What?"

Eric laid the paper down on the table and read from the page.

"Fire crews struggled to contain a blaze last night at the downtown Waterworld Hi-Rize building. That's where Maria lives."

Hank nodded, frowning.

"What else does it say?"

"Six apartments on the eighty-fourth floor were completely gutted and preliminary investigations have revealed the fire may have been started on purpose. According to eye-witnesses smoke was seen pouring from beneath the door to room eight-four-three, home of Cosmopolis waitress Maria Valentino!"

"Good job she wasn't there."

"We don't *know* she wasn't there Hank!"

"Is there a number we can call or something?"

Eric blah-blah-blahed his way through the rest of the article, tracing the words with his finger.

"Ah here we go. Authorities are pleased to report no loss of life occurred although the damage was extensive."

"That's a relief. Still, she won't be very pleased when she gets back off vacation or wherever she is."

"Maybe we should send her some flowers and one of those 'sorry' cards."

"Doesn't sound like there's anywhere to send 'em now."

"We'll send 'em to Angelo's."

The doorbell made its distinctive ding-dong noise, the way doorbells do.

"Not again!" Hank exclaimed. "This must be the seventh time in as many weeks!"

"At least he's finally managed to find the doorbell."

Eric rose from his seat and marched towards the front door. Hank grabbed his arm;

"Ask him if he knows what *chain up the mungle* means."

Frank Bazonka had indeed made several house calls over the last few weeks all of which had met with the same spectacular failure. Initially Eric had quizzed him about the 'you look so much like his statue' comment from his first visit but the salesman had mumbled his way out of it, claiming Eric must have misheard him. Whatever he was selling it was clear he only wanted to sell it to Eric Dorfler and no-one else. Sure enough Eric came face to face with the salesman when he opened the door.

"Look pal, how many times do I have to tell you? Eric Dorfler does not live here anymore OK?"

"Yes...but...you look *so* much like him!"

Time for another approach, thought Eric, hoping this guy was as gullible as he looked.

"Alright," he sighed, "I'm his twin brother Desmond Dorfler.

We used to live together but we had a falling out over a game of cards. I haven't seen or heard from him in almost twelve months; now will you *please* leave me in peace?"

The salesman seemed to brighten up when he heard this:

"His *brother*, well that's splendid news, could you perhaps tell me his middle name?"

"What?"

"Your brother's middle name, I'm...er...doing a middle name survey for the government you see."

Not exactly the most plausible lie but not bad under the circumstances. Eric's face screwed up in confusion.

"Why do you want to know my middle - my brother's - middle name?"

"Like I said I'm doing a survey for the government."

"Well doesn't the government have a database of everyone's name?"

"Er...they *did*, but some idiot wiped the system by mistake (a far tidier lie). Look, if you can just tell me then I won't bother you again, you have my word as a gentleman."

Eric couldn't see any harm in divulging the information, plus he'd be rid of the pesky salesman/government employee for good.

"It's Jeff."

The salesman retrieved a pad and pencil from his jacket and scribbled it down.

"A thousand thanks sir and please accept my apologies for the inconvenience."

Frank prepared to leave but Eric clutched at his sleeve.

"Just one thing before you go. Does the phrase *chain up the mungle* mean anything to you?"

"Chain up the *what*?"

"Never mind. Anyway, I don't wanna see you round here again," Eric warned, pointing his finger.

"No, no take it from me I'm finished here. I can finally go home."

"Yeah, well, seeya then," Eric mumbled.

He was about to swing the door shut when he noticed something. He stuck his head out the doorway and laughed to himself quietly.

Cunningham had put his house up for sale. Perhaps being shot by his neighbour didn't agree with him.

Thirty minutes later the Avenging Knights were ready to roll. As usual their first stop was Eric's mother's to drop off Dolores – since her arrival Eric had refused point blank to leave the urchin alone in his house and Hank had readily agreed to leaving her in the charge of Mrs Dorfler while they were out tackling crime. This of course had meant letting her in on the whole vigilante story, but they were confident their secret was safe with Mrs D, she was a trusting soul and even if she did let it slip there was a good chance she'd get it wrong – she still referred to Hank as 'that nice man Harold' even after all these years.

8.58pm – Cinderella Drive (inside the Silver Steed MkII)
The day and early part of the evening had been a busy time for the Knights. Using Dolores's clues they had, as usual, managed to prevent a large number of crimes, but they'd had their fair share of unscheduled encounters too. Hank was particularly happy as a) the mugging *had* taken place on Piranha Avenue - as he had guessed - and b) he hadn't been hit with the Garbage Shoot yet. Right now they were parked in an alleyway just off Cinderella Drive as a result of the 'glass slipper' clue and preparing to thwart the theft at the 'snake head' warehouse.

"OK Hank what's the plan?"

"We need a decent vantage point to scope out the warehouses. Did Sixpack bring the Zoom-o-Visions[†]?"

"Why don't you ask him?"

"Sixpack did you…?"

"I have them here sir."

"Right, we'll be needing those. Come on let's get somewhere high, it's almost nine."

The Knights dismounted and began to scale the nearest building via the fire escape. Within minutes they were on the roof, overlooking Cinderella Drive and its three warehouses. Lying on his stomach Hank removed his helmet, slipped on the Zoom-o-Visions and scanned the area.

"See anything?" Eric asked impatiently.

"Yep, an empty street and three warehouses."

"Oh hah bloody hah! Apart from that do you see anything?"

[†] The 2105 version of night-vision binoculars – to you and I they resemble regular sunglasses.

"No, looks pretty quiet."

"Maybe we got the wrong place?"

"No it has to be Cinderella Drive, it has to be."

"It could've been Shattered Drive like I said."

Hank swivelled round to face Eric and got a frightening close up, removing his Zoom-o-Visions he said;

"You still sore that I was right about the Piranha Avenue thing?"

"No!" Eric cried indignantly. "But just because you're in charge doesn't mean you're always right y'know."

"Oh so that's it. It's all about me being in charge is it?"

Down on Cinderella Drive half a dozen Korellians lumbered into view, but the Knights were too busy bickering to notice.

"No! I'm just saying that being leader doesn't make you right all the time!"

"I never said it *did*!"

"Well you sure act like it sometimes!"

Sixpack watched the argument without emotion, he'd begun to accept that this kind of behaviour as commonplace.

"OK Mr Flawless, what do you suggest we do?"

"Give me the Zoom-o-Visions, let me take a look."

Hank handed them over and Eric peered into the street below. Sure enough he spotted the six bipedal reptiles instantly, they had split into two groups and were flanking one of the warehouses, creeping down the alleyways on either side and doing their best to look stealthy – which wasn't easy for your average croc. He scoped out the sign above the warehouse which read; 'Med USA Chemical Storage Depot'. Six crocs – and armed with blitzer pistols too! Undoubtedly their biggest challenge to date (with the possible exception of the Wingnut Gang).

"Well?" Hank hissed.

"You're right there's nothing shakin', but I've got a feeling it might be the Med USA warehouse that's in danger of being robbed."

"Why?"

"It's that clue about 'snake head' it rings a bell; I just can't put my finger on it."

In truth Eric had no idea what 'snake head' meant, he just wanted to get down there as fast as possible, but without a good reason to do so he was stumped. Sixpack came to his rescue.

"Sir, if I may venture an opinion? My former master was well versed in classical literature and I believe the term 'snake head' may pertain to the Gorgons of Greek mythology. They had snakes on their heads instead of hair you see."

Eric and Hank looked at each other in a complete and utter 'what the hell's he talkin' about?' manner.

"Go on," Eric said.

"The most well known of the Gorgon sisters was Medusa, which is another way of expressing Med USA."

"That's it!" Eric spluttered, "I knew I'd heard it before! Come on lets' get down there, we can stake it out before they arrive if we hurry!"

They put their helmets back on.

"Alright, let's move! Well done Sixpack!"

Moving as quickly as they could without 'clanging' too much the three crimefighters made their way back down the fire escape.

CHAPTER THIRTY-FIVE

"Don't be alarmed, ladies and gentlemen.
Those chains are made of chrome steel."

Robert Armstrong in 'King Kong'

Tuesday 4th October - 4 days til the final.
11.10am – Dibley Spooner's office, Bloomissia.

"This, this and this all has to go, along with that, these over here and especially those. I want the whole place slate grey with a stone floor. I've got some ornamental boulders in storage too which I want you to bring in once you're done. Got it?"

The chief decorator nodded slowly. He was looking at a complete refurbishment and had already doubled his initial estimate.

"Twelve weeks pal," he said with a frown.

"*Twelve weeks*? I only want you to redecorate it! You weren't a builder in a former life were you?"

"Look mate," the decorator began, "first you've got your super deluxe Garbantium emulsion, you can't just paint over that stuff you know. It's gonna need to come off first which means you're gonna need your Apocalypse stripper, not easy to come by. Then you've got your double-layered Shockadelic carpet, which is glued to the original floor with industrial strength Stick-o-Fix, the stuff they use on *bridges*. After that there's your boulder problem, you can't just chuck 'em down you know. You're on the fourth floor see? Which is only supported by your standard plasti-steel girders, you're gonna need some reinforcements before you even think about bringing anything as heavy as that in here. And finally, there's your documentation problem."

"Documentation problem?" Dibley gasped.

The only documentation he was considering was the strongly worded letter to the Managing Director of Beauty HQ recommending the decorator be fired immediately, hopefully after a good kicking, preferably by Dibley.

"Documentation," the decorator repeated with a world-weary sigh. "No-one's given me a D76 yet."

"A what?"

"You're new here aren't you?"

Dibley could already visualise his fist flying towards the decorator's teeth. With a huge effort he composed himself.

"What is a D76?"

The decorator increased his chances of extensive dental treatment by shaking his head and adding a patronising 'tut-tut'.

"A D76 is a painting and decorating request form," he said slowly as though talking to a foreigner. "I can't lift a finger without a D76 pal."

Rising from his seat, his temper hanging by the slenderest of threads, Dibley leaned across the desk doing his best to look menacing, which isn't easy when you're surrounded by pink.

"And where would I get a D76?"

"From the Document Office! Cor blimey, some people."

Dentures were looking increasingly likely for the impudent decorator, he was one of those people for whom the phrase 'cause and affect' meant very little. "Get me a D76 and then we'll have another chat." He turned and walked towards the door adding; "personally I don't know why you wanna change this colour scheme. I think it suits you down to the ground."

The paperweight on Dibley's desk was milliseconds from being launched at the retreating figure when the intercom (next to the paperweight) buzzed and spared the decorator a painful visit to the infirmary.

"*YES*?" Dibley screamed, his temper finally finding an outlet.

"Whoa, easy there Spoon," said the voice of Harvey Beedham.

"Sorry Harve, problems with the decorator. What's up?"

"I've fixed up a meeting with Grunter and the translator. Should be ready in about ten minutes."

"Great, I'll be waiting in my office."

"Can't have the meeting there boss."

"Why not?"

"He won't fit through the door. He's a big fella. I've arranged to meet him in the arboretum in the East Garden."

"Perfect, more bloody flowers. OK, I'll see you there." He was about to hang up but then asked; "we don't need to *fill in any forms* before this meeting takes place do we?"

"Not that I'm aware of boss. You will need a D76 though – for your decorating job."

Although he'd had a full ten minutes to calm down Dibley was still seething about the decorator incident when he arrived at the arboretum. The high walled gardens were an explosion of colour and sweet fragrances, the flowers seemed to taunt Dibley as he passed under the stone archway which only made him angrier. But as he approached the lawned area his anger swiftly turned to astonishment when he clapped eyes on the three figures stood waiting for him. It was actually more like three *and a half* figures. First there was Harvey, fussing around a long metal table on which he had strewn various documents. Next to him stood the translator, wearing a crisp blue suit with a yellow tie and looking far too full of his own importance for Dibley's liking.

Then there was Grunter.

He towered over the other men reaching at least seven feet, which was doubly alarming as he was on all fours. Rippling muscle, barely concealed by short, black hair, covered his body and he had a permanent look of annoyance on his face, which had the ability to sap most people's confidence. Dibley swallowed hard, Grunter was easily the biggest ape he had ever seen and for once he found himself in the presence of something tougher and more intimidating than Dibley Spooner. Trying to remain confident under the gorilla's withering stare he approached the trio and forced out a smile.

"You must be Grunter," he said unnecessarily, extending his hand.

Grunter could have shaken Dibley's entire body with one hand.

"I wouldn't do that if I were you Mr Spooner!" the translator snapped.

Dibley's hand shot back down to his side and his feet stopped moving.

"Why not?"

"He may interpret that as an aggressive gesture."

"I'm only shaking hands with him for God's sake. We're all on the same team here aren't we?"

For the second time that morning Dibley ended up on the wrong end of a patronising 'tut-tut' and he realised his first impressions of the translator had been dead on – maybe he was related to the decorator. If shaking hands could be deemed provocative then raising his voice and shouting would probably constitute fighting talk so he decided to try and relax despite being in the face of nauseating officiousness.

"He's a wild animal Mr Spooner. Being a field agent doesn't make him civilised you know."

Dibley thrust his hands in his pockets where they'd be out of sight and unable to gesture aggressively.

"Very well, shall we get cracking then? If that's alright with you Mr...?"

"Terrybeck, Glazwell Terrybeck. Yes, that's perfectly fine. Your colleague here Mr Beedham has already given us a rough idea of what's involved."

"Ah yes!"

This was Harvey's cue and he bolted from his fold-up garden chair, keen to get on with the meeting before Grunter got hungry.

"No sudden movements!" Glazwell hissed.

"Oh sorry."

Dibley glanced up at Grunter's impassive face. He'd barely moved a muscle since he'd arrived and he began to wonder if he even knew Dibley was there.

"What's the story Harve?" he said.

Spreading a map of Earth over the table and trembling a little Harve spoke hurriedly.

"As far as we can ascertain the island on which the contraption is located is here, about a hundred and sixty miles south east of a country called The Underlands (formerly Australia). The island has no name that we're aware of so we're calling it Island X. Basically, we need to get Grunter there and he needs to destroy the machine. According to our watcher's information it's pretty big so he shouldn't have any trouble finding it."

Still, Grunter remained motionless, staring straight ahead.

"Isn't he going to look at the map?" Dibley asked.

"What the hell for? He can't read," Glazwell replied in an obvious tone.

"Well are you going to tell him what needs to be done or are we just gonna stand out here and feed him the occasional banana?"

"He's not very fond of..."

"Just tell him!" Dibley shouted, abandoning his 'gorilla-safe' policy.

For the first time Grunter moved. A slow deliberate turning of the head until he was looking straight at Dibley. Both Harvey and Dibley took a step backwards.

"Keep your voice down Mr Spooner," the translator whispered, "you wouldn't want to antagonise him believe me."

Dibley didn't want to be anywhere *near* the gorilla, let alone annoy him.

"Please, just tell him," Dibley murmured, wondering if he could run faster than Harvey should the need arise.

The translator cleared his throat quietly, turned to Grunter and emitted a comical series of grunts and guttural nonsense. The others gaped in awe as the gigantic ape replied in similar fashion. This bizarre conversation went on for several minutes during which time Dibley got his first glimpse of Grunter's teeth – it did little to ease his fear.

Finally they ceased and the translator turned to Dibley.

"Right-ho. He's got it. We should be able to commission a transporter later this week if we can find the relevant request forms in time. I estimate he'll be on the island in a few days, say…Friday night?"

"Fine by me," Dibley said, hoping this would signify the end of the meeting.

"Anything else he needs to know?" Glazwell asked, grinning pleasantly.

Dibley raised his eyebrows at Harvey who was equally enthusiastic about wrapping things up.

"No, that's it. Just get him there and put that thing out of commission."

"Right then, leave it to us," Glazwell smiled.

"Happy to," Dibley sighed and made for the exit.

"I'll come back and clear this lot up later," Harvey gabbled and strode after his boss the way schoolchildren do when they try to walk fast without running in the corridor.

Grunter and Glazwell Terrybeck waited until they had disappeared.

Then they convulsed in fits of laughter, rolling around clutching their stomachs. Grunter sat up and wiped his eyes.

"Oh man, I love it when we do the 'big and dumb' thing!" he giggled.

CHAPTER THIRTY-SIX

*"It's discouraging to think how many people are
shocked by honesty and how few by deceit."*

Noel Coward

By the time they reached ground level the Korellians had vanished
behind the warehouse, giving the street an air of disguised
innocence.

Hank had absolutely no idea what he was walking into, a bit
like the victim of a surprise birthday party but with rather more
severe consequences.

"Let's try down here," Eric whispered into his helmet mike,
pointing to the alleyway that flanked the left side of the enormous
Med USA warehouse.

He knew there was no way he could be held responsible for
stumbling on to the crocs, if anyone was to blame it would be
Sixpack, he'd been the one to really clinch the deal with his fancy
Medusa theory. Like a puppy on a short leash Eric had been
restrained long enough, he wanted the Avenging Knights to fulfil
their potential once and for all. Pussyfooting around with purse-
snatchers and petty thieves was never going to get them the credit
they deserved. But after this – after bagging a group of *Korellians* –
the police would surely stand up and take note and acknowledge the
Knights as *professional* crimefighters.

The caped trio made its way down the dimly lit alley, Eric
leading the way followed by Hank with Sixpack bringing up the
rear and watching their backs.

"Be ready for anything," Eric whispered barely able to contain
his excitement.

"Relax Eric, we haven't seen a soul down here yet," Hank
replied, suddenly realising he was walking ahead of Sixpack which
put him in the perfect position for another accidental Garbage
Shooting. "Hey Sixpack, why don't you go in front of me and I'll
watch our tails yeah?"

"Tails sir?"

"I'll make sure no-one sneaks up behind us."

"Very well sir."

They swapped positions and Hank drew a teeny piece of malicious comfort knowing that Eric had now replaced him as the prime candidate for one of the droid's notorious misfires. But Eric wasn't bothered, adrenaline was flooding his system. He knew the Korellians could appear at any second, the fact that one hit from a blitzer pistol would rip him (or indeed any of them) in two didn't seem to bother him. The far end of the alleyway appeared through the gloom, it turned right leading to the rear of the building. Eric suspected the crocs were right around the corner and he tensed, readying his weapon.

"Get ready!"

"Ready for what?" Hank asked, bemused.

Then they heard it, just a faint drone at first then, as they drew nearer, they could distinguish individual voices. Hank called a halt, pushed past Sixpack and joined Eric at the front of the line.

"Do you hear that?" he whispered.

"Yeah, it's probably the robbers; let's nab 'em!"

"No wait! We don't want another disaster. Let's creep up to the corner and just listen for a while."

"*You* may creep Hank, I *glide*."

"Whatever."

In the wake of the Wingnut Gang debacle, Eric knew if he jumped the gun again Hank would quit for sure. But the longer they waited, the more chance their quarry had of giving them the slip. Worse still, Hank might decide it was too risky and hit the chicken switch, effectively pulling the plug on the whole event. It was tricky to know what to do next, maybe he could inadvertently kick a loose tin can or give their position away with a poorly stifled sneeze. His thoughts went on ice for a while as Korellian voices drifted into earshot.

"You're sure this is the place?"

"I'm sure."

"Not much security for a medical warehouse."

"Would you prefer it to be crawling with guards?"

"No! I'm just thinkin' we might as well do the job now."

"We can't do it *now* you meathead, the delivery doesn't arrive til next Saturday."

"So why are we here?"

"Didn't you pay attention during the briefing? We're here to case the joint and assess the security. We don't want any unwanted surprises when we come back next week."

"So what's the verdict?"

"Looks simple enough. No guards, no dogs, no cameras, should be a doddle."

"What time does the delivery arrive?"

"Noon."

"Well we've missed it then haven't we?"

"No! No! No! You twerp! It's *next* Saturday! How many times do I have to say it?"

"Hey Danzo who you callin' a twerp? Who do you thinks kickin' your butt in the gorilla shooting contest back on Perfection eh?"

"Oh any fool can pull a trigger Jaggs, besides *I'm* head of security, which means *I'm* in charge so shut yer whining and do as you're told! We're coming back next week and that's final."

Whoever Jaggs was only uttered a mumbled protest, which suggested he had accepted the decision. Around the corner the Knights tried to assess the situation – which wasn't easy.

"Gorilla shooting competition?" Hank whispered, "Who the hell are these guys? And where's Perfection?"

"Maybe they're poachers or smugglers of exotic animals?" Eric suggested.

"But why would they be sniffing round a medical warehouse?"

"How do I know? Perhaps they're looking to broaden their horizons, looking for a fresh challenge."

"Alright, we've heard enough let's go."

"Go! Go where? Let's get 'em now!"

"Eric they haven't committed a crime yet and you heard them, they're coming back next Saturday at noon – we can lay in wait and ambush them."

As usual Eric was desperate to get stuck in, but Hank was correct, right now the crocs were guilty of nothing more than planning a robbery – and abject stupidity. Again he found himself in two minds (both of which were devious). They could wait a week and ambush the gang like Hank said but then what would he say when he saw they were Korellians? Would he beat a hasty retreat? Option two was of course to just pile round the corner and take their chances right here, right now.

"Don't you think we should see how many there are?" he said trying to sound responsible.

"Good point, OK move over I'm gonna take a look."

"No, I'll do it!"

"Fine you do it, but be careful," Hank advised, moving aside to let Eric through. "Sixpack can you please point that thing towards the ground."

"Sorry sir."

Eric took advantage of the distraction behind him and pretended to look round the corner. He turned back to Hank.

"Great news bud, there are only two of 'em. Wimpy guys too, we should be able to nail 'em with our eyes shut."

"Good. Right come on then, let's get back to the Steed."

CHAPTER THIRTY-SEVEN

"Experience enables you to recognize a mistake
when you make it again."

Franklin P Jones

Thursday 6th October - 2 days til the final.
11.14am – The Pitz Hotel, Cosmopolis.

"This is agent number forty…er."

"Hello Frank."

"Hello sir, how did you know it was me?"

"Wild guess – so what's the word?"

"Great news sir, I've got the information. He finally confessed to being the target's twin brother. I guess that explains the resemblance. But he also told me Eric Dorfler's middle name."

"Twin brother? Have you bothered to check the file Frank? He doesn't have a twin brother. The only living relative he has in 2105 is his mother."

"Then how did he know Eric Dorfler's middle name?"

"Because he *is* Eric Dorfler, he's been spinning you a line! Try and use your head for something other than wearing your hat will ya Frank?"

"But…"

"Just tell me the name."

"It's Jeff."

"Is that with a J or a G?"

A dreadfully long pause.

"Er…"

"You didn't ask did you?"

"No sir, I didn't."

"Then you're going to have to go back and ask him aren't you?"

"I can't sir. I told him I wouldn't bother him again, I even gave him my word as a gentleman."

Several million miles and many years away Frank Bazonka's boss tried to control his temper. His next sentence was delivered in a voice close to hysteria, clearly trying to cling to some kind of sanity.

"OK Frank, let's try a different approach shall we? Why don't you look up his mother, her address is right there in the file. She's bound to have the information we need."

"Mrs Natalia Dorfler."

"That's her, think you can handle it?"

"I suppose so sir."

"Of course you can. You seem to lack a certain urgency Frank, may I ask why this is all taking so long? I mean it's been a week since your last report and all you've managed to uncover is another useless lie and an inaccurate piece of data. What the hell have you been doing?"

"Well I thought I'd take some time to try and trace a few of my relatives."

"*What*?"

"All records were destroyed when the planet Earth was…well…when it was…done away with, so I thought I'd see what I could find out."

"Frank you're not there to dig up the family tree! This is an important and *very time critical* mission. We've only two days left man! The engraver is on constant stand-by, he's ready to start chiselling away as soon as you get the information! Now please – *just get it done!*"

"Can't I come back home sir? You could send someone else down here to replace me."

"It's too late for that Frank. Besides, we've been over this already – there's no-one else. You do know what'll happen if you fail don't you?"

"Data Retrieval will be made to look very stupid sir, you've told me a thousand times."

"Yes it will, but what else will happen?"

"I don't know sir."

"We'll leave you down there!"

"What? You can't!"

"Yes we *can* Frank, so I suggest you get your ass into gear and get that information."

"Why don't we just make a guess, I mean it's either a G or a J isn't it?"

"Oh that's great Frank and what if we get it wrong eh? What then? Data Retrieval has a long-standing reputation for its accuracy and attention to detail. At Data Retrieval we don't *guess* and we don't *get things wrong*."

"But we do make mistakes sir."

"Really? Like what?"

"Like sending me down here on this wretched assignment!"

"That's the spirit Frank! Now channel that anger into your job. Go and see Mrs Dorfler and get that data. You don't want to be there in 2108 when Earth gets 'done away with' as you put it do you?

"No sir."

"I look forward to hearing from you soon Frank – don't let us down."

"Very well sir."

Once more Frank slapped shut his inter-planetary, time-splitting communicator, only this time he did it much slower, the way a condemned man might smoke his last cigarette. This was all so unfair – he hadn't even meant to volunteer for this job and they *knew* that! Now he was facing the bowel-loosening prospect of being stuck here, doomed on a planet with a life expectancy of maybe three more years. Why him? He hadn't done anything to deserve this. It just wasn't fair. It just wasn't *cricket*! Emotion got the better of him and, in a rare fit of rage, he hurled the communicator against the wall of his hotel room. It was roughly halfway through its short, yet violent journey when he realised what he'd done. He tried the impossible, running after it in the hope he might be able to catch it before it was too late. The communicator braced itself for the inevitable impact but it was no use, it smashed into a hundred and forty-nine pieces.

Frank stared at what was left of the device. His only way off this planet lay in smithereens on the floor and, to add insult to injury, it had left a large dent in the wall which would doubtless be spotted by the cleaner who would the report it to the manager and then he would lose his deposit. He had no idea how to repair the communicator, he didn't really know how it worked at all if the truth be known and he doubted very much anyone in 2105 would know either. Taking it to an electrical repair shop was not an option – too many questions – most of which would probably come from him. The terrible, cold, hard truth of the situation floated down and covered him like a sheet of despair.

He was stuck here and no amount of tea was going to make him feel better.

CHAPTER THIRTY-EIGHT

*"People need hard times and oppression to
develop psychic muscles."*

Emily Dickinson

Saturday 8th October – 6hrs 30 mins til the final.
11.30am – Mrs Dorfler's house, Cosmopolis.

Eric sat in the Silver Steed, drumming his fingers impatiently on the steering wheel. Dropping Dolores off at his Mum's house every Saturday morning was never easy, she always seemed reluctant to stay there, as though Mrs Dorfler were some kind of wicked aunt – which she wasn't. But today was the worst yet, she had wrapped herself around Hank's leg outside the front door and was clinging to him like a limpet.

"Come on D, you know you have to stay here today," Hank reasoned, trying to prise her away.

"Don't go, please don't go! Not today!" Dolores wailed, close to tears.

Staggering towards the front door, dragging his passenger with him, Hank managed to press the doorbell.

"Dolores please! What's the matter with you today?"

"Bad things are gonna happen!"

Eric jammed his fist against the van's horn several times.

"Come on Hank!" he bawled, "we've only got half an hour to get to Cinderella Drive, the robbery's at noon remember?"

All of a sudden the front door flew open and a spindly droid with a tubular head dashed outside. As soon as he clapped eyes on Hank and Dolores he got very irritated and without warning a weird looking device popped out from a hidden compartment in his chest. There was an air of menace in the way it emerged, which was backed up by the droid's opening gambit;

"Who are you, whaddya doin' here eh?"

Unperturbed Hank sighed heavily and went through the usual

routine.

"Hello Wilfred. My name's Hank Halo, the same guy who's been coming here every Saturday morning for the last seven weeks and I'm here to drop off Dolores like I've been doing every Saturday morning for the last seven weeks."

"Hank what? Hank Halo? Never heard of ya! And how do you know my name – you been spyin' on me?"

"No Wilfred, I haven't."

"You'd better wait here!" the droid screeched excitedly, "I'm gonna fetch the occupant so we can sort out this mess and don't try running off or I'll chase you down and give you a taste of my Shockmaster Deluxe!"

The device protruding from his chest gave a threatening twitch.

"Fine, fine."

The droid disappeared back inside the house. By the time Mrs Dorfler came to the door Hank had succeeded in peeling away one of Dolores's tiny arms.

"Oh hello Harold. Sorry about Wilfred, you know how he can be."

"Hi Mrs Dorfler, that's OK I'm getting used to it. Where the heck did you find such a gung-ho service droid anyway?"

"He's an ex-military droid, formerly a sniper I believe but he was decommissioned a few months ago and reconfigured for domestic service. I decided to snap him up, very reasonably priced I might add."

"Looks like he's still carrying one aggression chip too many to me."

Mrs Dorfler looked down at Dolores and beamed her friendliest smile.

"Dropping off time again is it?"

"That's right, if I can ever get her off my leg."

"Please don't go Hank!" Dolores begged.

It was heartrending to hear but Hank had to get moving if they were to set up their ambush at the Med USA warehouse as planned.

"Everything's gonna be OK, Dolores, now please go inside with Mrs Dorfler."

"Come on sweetie," Mrs Dorfler said soothingly, "I'm just about to start making some doughnuts. Wouldn't you like to come in and help me?"

219

"Nooooo!"

Hank managed to remove her other arm. At this point she burst into tears. With a despairing look to the heavens Hank squatted down so he was face to face with the blubbering urchin. She flung her arms around his neck and sobbed into his metal shoulder pad. "You mustn't go, Hank, please promise you won't go."

There was another impatient 'beep-beep' from the van.

"Alright Eric!" Hank roared, "I've got a bit of a situation here!"

Pulling Dolores from his shoulder he held her by her arms, so she was stood directly in front of him. Tears continued to stream down her face.

"Something really bad is going to happen to you all," she sniffled.

"Listen to me D," Hank reassured her, "we know what we're doing. Yes, I admit that what we do is a bit dangerous but we'll be OK, there's nothing to get upset about. I'll be back in the morning to pick you up like I always do – I *promise*."

This seemed to do the trick and Dolores stopped her blubbing. Using his cape Hank dried her eyes. "Now why don't you go inside and make some doughnuts with Mrs Dorfler eh?"

She nodded slowly and after one last hug she and Mrs Dorfler went inside.

Beep! Beep!

"Oh for crying out loud!" Hank cried, getting to his feet and making for the van.

"'Bout time mate!" Eric blustered as Hank climbed in next to him.

"She's scared Eric, can't you understand that?"

"Yeah, yeah," Eric groaned turning the key in the ignition.

"For God's sake! She's just a kid, a lonely, frightened little kid! There's more to life than the bloody Avenging Knights you know! For your information she's worried about us – you and me! Believe it or not she actually cares about us. Just try thinking about someone other than yourself for once can you?"

Right on cue Eric's face dropped, the way it always did when Hank lectured him. But there was something more in his expression this time, something like panic.

"What?" Hank asked.

Without a word Eric reached down under the steering wheel

and popped the hood.

"I can't get the van started."

"*What?*"

"The van – it won't start! I keep turning the key but nothing's happening and we've only got…" he checked his watch, "…twenty-five minutes to get to Cinderella Drive!"

"Oh great!" Hank exclaimed clambering out of the van.

Eric turned the key again just to be sure. The engine didn't even *try* to start.

"Get out there and help him Sixpack," he whimpered, "we need to get this pile of crap moving pronto!"

Thirty-eight minutes later the Silver Steed screeched around the corner (almost on two wheels) into Cinderella Drive. Eric slammed on the anchors and brought them skidding to a stop. The short journey had been hair-raising to say the least, made worse by the notorious Cosmopolis smog that had begun to descend. Looking relaxed on the outside but quaking within Hank looked straight ahead and said calmly:

"I have to inform you, Mr Dorfler, you have *failed* your driving test."

Eric giggled and unbuckled his seatbelt. "It's no laughing matter Eric!" Hank gasped, trying to prise his hands out of the dashboard, "you tryin' to kill us or what man?"

"Time is of the essence bud!"

Eric knew pitting themselves against a gang of armed crocs would be a stern test, but his mindless optimism kept telling him they'd get through it – and when they did, the police would finally stand up and recognise them as *serious* crimefighters. He also knew that gangs of armed crocs didn't grow on trees so they had to make the most of this opportunity.

"Do you know how close you came to mowing down that pensioner back there?" Hank asked as he disembarked.

"Which one?"

"That old dear on Scarface Boulevard!"

"Oh that one."

"Yes that one! Cripes, if she hadn't been wearing a jet-pack you would've killed her."

Sixpack and Eric piled out of the van and the three Knights regarded the alleyway through the thickening gloom. Being in a fairly remote part of the city there was no-one about and the only thing in the street (other than the Knights and the Silver Steed) was a large twenty-eight wheeler transporter truck with its back to them. It was parked directly outside the Med USA warehouse and doing very little. Eric checked his watch again.

"Damn it, we're late! Alright Six, fetch the weapons, we're going in. I mean, if that's OK with you Hank?"

Hands on hips, Hank surveyed the scene. There were certainly no signs of violence, just a truck sat in the middle of the alley. The warehouse doors were closed in a 'there's nothing to see here' kind of way. With the smog closing in they had to move fast.

"Come on then," he said, putting on his helmet and taking the Web-o-matic from Sixpack, "let's check it out."

CHAPTER THIRTY-NINE

"In life you need either inspiration or desperation."

Anthony Robbins

Saturday 8th October – 6hrs 8mins til the final.
11.52am – Mrs Dorfler's house, Cosmopolis.

"Who are you, whaddya doin' here eh?"

"My name is Frank Bazonka and I need to speak to…"

"Sorry buster, we don't entertain door to door salesmen around here, so clear off. I'd sort you out myself but I've got some domestic chores to finish off, plus you're not much of a challenge are you? Come back with a dozen Brute-Force X-71 Bodyguard droids and I might be interested."

The door slammed shut in Frank's face.

More than a little flustered, he stared down at his feet and then – wondering why everyone he met thought he was a salesman – rang the doorbell again. The obnoxious service droid reappeared.

"Oh so you want a piece of me do you? Alright then let's see what you're made of *woman*!"

With that the droid adopted a fighting stance, fists up and began to circle the bewildered stranger. Mrs Dorfler came to the rescue.

"Wilfred! Will you get back inside and calm down?" she said harshly. The droid lowered his fists:

"We have no idea who this man is ma'am. He could be a mass murderer or a…an insurance salesman!"

"Just get back into the house and let me deal with it."

Mumbling to himself, Wilfred reluctantly padded back inside. "I do apologise," Mrs Dorfler said pleasantly. "Now, how can I help you Mr…?"

"Bazonka, Frank Bazonka ma'am and are you Mrs Dorfler?"

"I am."

"So pleased to make your acquaintance," he smiled doffing his

223

hat. "You don't know me, but I'm looking for your son Eric."

"Well, you've just missed him as it happens, he left here a couple of minutes ago."

"Do you know when he's coming back?"

"He'll be back tomorrow morning, about 9am."

'Too late' Frank thought to himself, 'about fifteen hours too late'.

"Do you know where he is now? It's vital I speak with him."

"Is he in some kind of trouble?"

"No, no, nothing like that, in fact I'm the one that's in trouble."

He opted not to mention the entire planet would be in trouble by 6pm tonight – the kind of trouble from which it would never recover. "Well…er…in that case, would you happen to know the whereabouts of his friend Hank Halo?"

"He's with Eric and his name's Harold not Hank."

"And I suppose Eric's droid is with them too?"

"That's right. What's all this about anyway?"

Frank's thought process stalled. What did he tell her? The truth would be a little hard to swallow. 'Well Mrs Dorfler I need to find them because they're the guys who nearly saved the planet. And now that I've no way of getting back to my own planet, which incidentally is a hundred years in the future, I need to find them and make sure they actually *do* save the planet cos I'm stuck here now. How I'm going to do this I have absolutely no idea.' No – that probably wouldn't work. He'd end up being carted off to the nearest loony bin. In the absence of a decent lie he began to go to pieces.

Until Dolores appeared behind Mrs Dorfler's legs.

"I know where they are," she squeaked.

"Do you?" Frank and Mrs Dorfler said simultaneously.

Dolores just nodded.

"Where are they?" Frank asked.

"Well I don't exactly know where they are but I can take you to them."

Mrs Dorfler did her best to humour the child:

"If you don't know where they are Dolores then how can you take Mr Bazonka to them?"

At the mention of her name Frank visibly started.

"You're *Dolores*?"

Again she just nodded.

224

"My God! You're the one who saw it coming!" he said without thinking.

"Saw *what* coming?" Mrs Dorfler asked, mightily confused.

The conversation was heading down a maze of complexity, which was hardly surprising when you consider the people involved – a man from the future, a psychic six year old and a bewildered mother.

"Please let me take him Mrs Dorfler, I can save them!"

"Save them from what?"

If Eric and Hank were only a couple of minutes ahead of him then Frank stood a good chance of catching up with them, but every second he wasted here at the Dorfler doorstep was critical. He had to hurry things along so he went for the honest approach (which he much preferred).

"Mrs Dorfler I know this is hard for you to comprehend but your son and his friend can save the planet!"

She didn't look very impressed and began to get annoyed:

"What are you two babbling on about? I've never heard such nonsense!"

"Please let me take him Mrs Dorfler!" Dolores pleaded.

"I'm not about to let you go off with some stranger Dolores, you're supposed to stay here with me until they get back! And as for you Mr Bazonka I suggest you leave right now."

He opened his mouth to protest. "...or I'll fetch Wilfred."

Frank's shoulders slouched, it was no use, she wasn't going to listen and he was going to perish right here on this unimpressive planet along with everyone else. What he should've done was assert some authority, demand some action or at the very least ask again in a sterner tone. But at the end of the day Frank was Frank and he had no stomach for confrontation. With a weary sigh he turned away and trudged back to his rental car parked in Mrs Dorfler's driveway. Meanwhile Mrs Dorfler ushered Dolores back inside the house and closed the door.

As he climbed into the car Frank's despair got the better of him and he started to weep. Not a shoulder-shaking sobbing session, just a quiet moment of overwhelming grief. Why him? He wasn't a bad person, a trifle dull perhaps but that was hardly deserving of a fate like this. For several seconds he just sat there, staring through the windscreen and reflecting on just what a lousy hand life had dealt him. What now? Just sit around and wait for the inevitable?

225

With the weight of the world quite literally on his shoulders he turned the key in the ignition and fired up the engine.

He was so wrapped up in his own pity he didn't even hear the rear door being opened and it wasn't until he heard the voice that he realised he had a passenger. A psychic, six year old passenger.

"Quick drive, drive!" she squealed, slamming the door shut behind her.

"Dolores! What are you...?"

"Quick! Quick!"

Frank glanced out the window to see Wilfred stood at the front door looking left and right frantically, Shockmaster Deluxe at the ready. Engaging reverse gear he bolted from the driveway, narrowly missing a passing vehicle as he swerved on to the main road backwards. Spotting Dolores in the back seat, Wilfred came charging after them. Having only learned how to drive a 2105 vehicle a few days ago Frank struggled to get the car to go forwards.

"Come on!" he whimpered, now reduced to pressing buttons at random on the steering wheel. There was a loud metallic thud as Wilfred hurled himself on to the hood.

"Freeze sucker!" he shrieked, "I knew you were a kidnapper the second I laid eyes on ya!"

More through luck than judgement Frank found a gear and the car lurched forwards, its rear tyres smoking furiously. He tried to see past the droid who was blocking his view of the road.

"Knock him off!" Dolores said helpfully.

Unaccustomed to something this exciting Frank didn't react straight away. It was only when Wilfred drew his fist back, clearly intent on putting it through the windscreen, that he finally made his move. Gripping the wheel with both hands he wrenched the car to the left bringing more complaints from his tyres and a squeal of excitement from Dolores. With only one hand to secure himself Wilfred lost his grip and vanished from sight in a rapid sideways move. Kneeling on the back seat, Dolores looked out the rear window to see Wilfred slowly getting to his feet in the distance.

It took a while for Frank's adrenaline to recede and only when he was sure he could speak coherently did he say:

"So where are we going?"

"Not sure yet."

"Well how are we gonna…?"

"I'll just tell you when to turn."

"OK just make sure you give me plenty of warning first. I think you'd better put on your seatbelt too."

The car sped towards the city, making lefts and rights using the fine art of psychic navigation.

CHAPTER FORTY

*"Danger - if you meet it promptly and without
flinching - you will reduce the danger by half.
Never run away from anything. Never!"*

                              Sir Winston Churchill

Saturday 8th October – 5hrs 46mins til the final.
   12.14pm – Med USA warehouse, Cinderella Drive,
Cosmopolis.

The Knights crept quietly down the murky alley and flanked
the enormous transporter vehicle on the left hand side. As they
reached the driver's cab they began to hear noises from within. It
sounded like someone trying to talk through a gag because that's
exactly what it was.

"Alright Eric," Hank whispered, "check it out. But don't shoot
anyone."

Slinging the Inebriator over his shoulder Eric climbed up to the
door and opened it, fully expecting to be greeted by a brutish
Korellian. Sat behind the wheel, her wrists and ankles bound with
rope and a gag tied across her mouth was a gorgeous blonde girl of
about twenty-two. Her blue eyes widened at the sight of Eric and
she managed to communicate a 'get me the hell out of these ropes'
message via various head movements and muffled grunts. Smiling
inside his helmet, Eric shuffled alongside her and removed her gag.
She gasped for breath, then shook the hair from her face.

"Who the hell are you?" she asked.

"Don't you watch the news babe? I'm Sir Prize, one of the
Avenging Knights of Cosmopolis!"

He untied her hands.

"Never heard of you, but I've been off the planet for the last
few weeks. What's with the outfit?"

"It's a *costume*," he replied, reaching down to untie her ankles.

The girl grabbed his hands:

"I think I can manage that myself thanks very much."

"Fair enough, just trying to help – so who are you and why are you in this truck?"

"My name's Cass and I'm the driver."

Eric looked her up and down. She was dressed in a white vest and a dusty black leather jacket with matching leather trousers, black biker boots were on her feet – easily the most unlikely truck driver he had ever seen.

"You don't look like a truck driver."

"I know, but I need the cash – this is just a temporary gig."

"So what happened?"

"Bloody crocs, that's what happened. Six of 'em jumped me as soon as I arrived. They've nicked the entire shipment!"

Reaching under the dashboard she retrieved a battered looking shotgun and 'sha-shakked' a cartridge into the barrel. "Thanks for the rescue Superman, now if you don't mind I need to go and reclaim my cargo."

Not waiting for a reply she squeezed past him and climbed out of the truck.

"Hold your horse's babe!" Eric exclaimed, jumping down after her.

"Whoa! More superheroes?" Cass laughed as she came face to face with Hank and Sixpack.

Eric made the introductions, told them her cargo had been stolen (didn't mention the crocs) then he asked her if he could take her out to dinner.

"I don't think this is the time or the place for courting!" Hank said hastily. "Nor do I think it's a very good idea for you to go running around with that antique shotgun young lady."

Cass was having none of it;

"Well guess what Mr Rough Knight? I don't care what you think, I need to get my shipment back or I'll be fired. So I suggest you back off."

"Oh I like her, she's fiery!" Eric said enthusiastically.

There was every chance the perpetrators were still in the vicinity and Hank didn't want to waste time with this brash young girl. To everyone's surprise he levelled his Web-o-matic at her.

"Just put the gun down Miss and let us take care of it."

Not being the kind of girl that did as she was told Cass began to raise her own weapon. Hank didn't hesitate and squeezed the trigger, sending a strand of sticky webbing straight into her midriff.

"Whaddya doin' man!" Eric cried. "And you call *me* trigger-happy?"

As expected Cass tried to disentangle herself, which had completely the opposite effect. Having been tied up in the cab for the best part of fifteen minutes she was less than impressed to find herself trussed up again so soon.

"What the hell is this stuff? Get it off me!" she screamed.

"Gag her and put her in the back of the truck!" Hank said to Eric.

"What the...why are...?"

"Just do it!"

Cass still wasn't going down without a fight and kicked out at Eric as he followed his orders. Between them they managed to get her inside. They were about to slam the doors shut when Hank reached up and removed her gag.

"You wouldn't happen to know what the phrase *chain up the mungle* means would you?"

"What?"

"Forget it," he said, replacing the gag and closing the doors.

"What was all that about mate?" Eric asked. "She was *babetastic*, we could've let her tag along."

"She's a civilian and she could easily get hurt if she comes with us *and* she was rude."

"Being rude ain't a crime dude."

"Well it *should be*! Impertinence and rudeness three years minimum. Besides, this doesn't look like the work of those 'two wimpy guys' you saw last time we were here. It's a big heist and organised by the looks of things. But where the hell are they?"

"Let's check the warehouse," Eric suggested.

"Yeah, you're right. Alright, keep your eyes out for trouble and fire only on my command understood?"

"Loud and clear?"

"Sixpack do you understand?"

"Yes sir."

"OK, let's go."

The doors to the warehouse were unlocked and Sixpack slid them open with ease. The ground floor was full of boxes and crates all of which were stencilled with code numbers and strange symbols, which is what you'd expect to find in a warehouse. Weapons at the ready the Knights inched their way inside and then spotted a small office to one side. Hank gave the nod and Eric scurried over to it. Kicking the door in was a little unnecessary as it was a) unlocked and b) not very sturdy in the first place. A quick glance inside told Eric it was a security office, TV monitors showed various locations within the warehouse, several clipboards lay on the desk but it was the two security guards sat in the corner that really gave it away. Like Cass they too had been firmly bound and gagged. Eric gave the all clear and was soon joined by his fellow Knights. The guards were de-gagged.

"What happened here?" Hank asked.

Guard One looked up at him with a big smile.

"Holy smoke! It's the Saturday Knights! Hey can I get an autograph for my wife? She loves you guys!"

"Just tell us what happened."

"We got jumped by some crocs!"

"*Korellians*?" Hank gasped.

"Yeah, must've been at least ten of 'em."

"Come off it – there were six," said Guard Two.

"How do you know?"

"I counted 'em."

"Anyway, I think they hijacked a truck outside the warehouse cos when they came in they were all lugging big crates. They went up in the freight elevator over there so my guess is they're probably loading up some getaway vehicle on the roof."

"Eric, we're not equipped to handle Korellians," Hank whispered into his helmet mike.

"Come on Hank, we can't let these guys down. We've got a reputation to uphold," Eric whispered back.

If Hank pulled the plug on this caper it would be a disaster, their one big chance at showing the city just what they were capable of would evaporate. He *had* to convince him to carry on. Meanwhile Hank was running through the options in his head. Leave right now and call the police? The average police response time gave most thieves time to redecorate before they left and there was no guarantee they would turn up at all if they found out they'd be dealing with Korellians. Or stay here and tackle it? That felt like the right thing to do but he also knew just how dangerous crocs could be.

Addressing the two guards (who were still tied up but seemingly perfectly happy about it) Hank said:

"Can you give me a moment to confer with my colleagues?"

"Yeah sure go ahead," said Guard One, "just don't forget that autograph before you leave."

The Knights retreated back into the storage area and concealing themselves behind a few crates held an impromptu emergency meeting. It was a swift meeting, lasting no more than four or five minutes and consisted of Eric mostly begging and Hank saying 'no' a lot. After a while it began to get rather repetitive so Hank brought matters to a close:

"This is way out of our league Eric and you know it."

"How do we know that unless we try?"

"Come on man, I don't need to put a gun in my mouth and pull the trigger to know it's gonna kill me!"

"This is our big chance Hank!"

"For what? A noble death? You *knew* they were Korellians didn't you? You knew all along!"

"Of course I didn't. But so what if they are, there're worse things out there than Korellians you know." Before Hank could say 'like what?' Eric added, "why don't we ask Sixpack for his opinion eh? He's one of the team, he deserves a say. How about it Six, what do you think we should do? Run away or take on the crocs?"

"What is a croc sir?"

"It's slang for a Korellian."

"What is a Korellian?"

"This is getting us nowhere," Hank hissed, "besides, I'm in charge and I say we leave it to the cops."

"That's *worse* than running away!" Eric protested.

Ignoring him Hank made for the office:

"Come on, I've made up my mind, we're out of here. We'll release the guards and that girl and then call the cops."

Eric couldn't believe his ears, they were actually going to walk away from their chance of glory. For a moment he considered taking on the crocs by himself but even he knew six against one had catastrophe written all over it. All he could do was follow Hank and hope he changed his mind some time between now and reaching the office. Desperation gripped him and he searched his mental archives for some convincing emotional blackmail. He'd already tried the 'injured girl' story, maybe he could say he'd seen an old woman

232

with a pushchair walk into the warehouse just as they'd arrived. Too late – they were back in the office.

"We're going to untie you chaps and then call the police," Hank said calmly. "I suggest you get as far away from this place as you can."

"You mean you're not gonna do anything?" Guard One said looking crestfallen.

"See?" Eric blurted out, "our reputation's gonna be shot to pieces!"

"Rather our reputation than us!" Hank replied angrily, dialling the police via the comm unit on the desk.

He relayed the necessary information, deciding not to omit any mention of the Korellians. Resigning himself to the fact they really *were* going to walk away Eric turned his attention to the security monitors.

"Do you have a camera on the roof?" he inquired idly.

"Yeah sure," said Guard One, "just push that green button on the left of the control panel."

Eric scanned the panel.

"I don't suppose either of *you* know what the phrase *chain up the mungle* means do you?" he asked.

They didn't.

He spotted the button in question, a bright green one with the word 'roof cam' printed on it. He gave it a push and watched the monitor flick over. It was hard to make anything out at first due to the smog, but once the camera activated its 'automatic anti-fog filter' the picture became much clearer. Sure enough the Korellians were there, loading large crates on to a transporter ship.

"There they are," he said to Hank with an air of dejection, "committing a crime right under our noses."

"Then let's hope the cops get here soon," was the weak reply.

Hank hated leaving the scene when a crime of this magnitude was taking place, but his logical side would not be denied – they were simply no match for half a dozen armed crocs. As the roof cam panned around left to right and then back again Eric saw there were still a significant amount of crates yet to be loaded. 'We would've arrived just in time' he thought, 'just in time to…' He froze for a second as something caught his eye on the screen.

"Er…Hank," he murmured into his mike.

"We're not going up there! How many more times?"

"No Hank, I think you'd better take a look at this."

Hank turned round to face the screen then saw it for himself – and it made his blood run cold. Scurrying about between the crates, doing a bad job of trying not to be seen, was Dolores.

CHAPTER FORTY-ONE

"There are two kinds of adventurers: those who go truly hoping to find adventure and those who go secretly hoping they won't."

William Trogdon

12.23pm, 5hrs 37mins til the final.

Machines have no appreciation of urgency which is why, despite Hank's frantic pleas, the freight elevator continued to ascend at its usual slow chug. Eric was also frantic – with excitement. They were heading for the roof and that's where the crocs were. Even though Hank had made it clear the plan was to grab Dolores then head straight back down again, he was confident the crocs would spot them and then the fireworks would really start. Sixpack was, as expected, incapable of being frantic about anything and endured the crawling journey in his customary silence. Hank addressed his fellow vigilantes:

"OK listen up. We sneak out on to the roof, nab Dolores then get right back in the elevator understood?"

"Gotcha bud!"

"The smog should give us some cover but on no account do I want anyone to engage the Korellians, got that?"

"Loud and clear."

"Six, you've got that Garbage Shoot safetied, haven't you?"

"Indeed I have sir."

Hank took a deep breath.

"Alright then, get ready, we're almost there!"

Machines also have no concept of stealth; indeed, they have very little appreciation of anything, which is why the elevator doors opened with a resounding clatter. At first the Knights didn't move, they were waiting to see if the inconsiderate elevator had given away their position, but thanks to another machine (the humming engine of the crocs' transporter ship) they remained undetected. One by one they slipped out on to the roof and took cover behind the first big thing they saw – a metal storage container about the size of a school bus.

"I can't see her – does anyone see her!" Hank whispered.

No-one could see her.

"Maybe we should get closer to the transporter ship," Eric suggested.

"Why?"

"Er…I dunno. But you know what kids are like, she probably wants a closer look."

"Forget it Eric, we're staying as far away from that ship as possible. Let's nip over there, behind that container so we can get a better view."

The container in question was about forty feet away and although it did offer a much improved vantage point it meant breaking cover and dashing across the exposed roof. The crocs were busy loading other containers on to the ship, arguing among themselves and generally being obnoxious. After shooting people and paying cheques into the bank this was their favourite activity and they went about it with great gusto. A particularly heated debate had broken out as to exactly who was in charge, providing the Knights with just the kind of distraction they needed. With a quick nod to the others Hank sprinted across the gap. Thanks to the smog and the blazing row taking place by the ship he arrived at the other side without being spotted. He turned to face his comrades and beckoned them to follow. Sixpack was across in a flash but Hank felt Eric could've been quicker and wondered if it had been a deliberate ploy to attract attention.

"You'd better not be dragging your heels on purpose Eric!" he fumed.

"Of course not, I just thought I'd make less noise if I went a bit slower."

Highly suspicious and becoming more agitated by the second, Hank turned his back on Eric and found himself face to face with Frank Bazonka.

"*JEEZUS!*"

"Oh I 'm sorry Mr Halo, did I startle you?"

"Startle me? I nearly dropped my load! What the hell are *you* doing here and…how do you know my name?"

"Look mister," Eric butted in, " I don't know who you are or why you're here but I don't want to buy whatever it is you're selling

OK?"

"I believe I owe you gentlemen an explanation," Frank said politely.

"Not half!" Hank seethed.

"Before I get started, have any of you seen Dolores?"

Hank's brain was beginning to hurt, he was being besieged by rapid-fire confusion, a constant stream of 'whys', 'whats' and 'hows'.

"You brought Dolores here?" Eric said in disbelief.

"Not really, in fact it was more the other way around. My goodness there she is!"

Frank extended a finger and as one the group followed it. Sure enough there she was, walking calmly into one of the open containers.

"I don't know who you are but you'd better stick close to us if you wanna get off this rooftop alive," Hank said seriously.

"Certainly…er…lead the way."

"Alright everyone, follow me."

The container into which Dolores had inadvertently strayed was, like the others, quite large and filled with smaller wooden crates. Hank's concern for her safety seemed to override any fear for his own and he dashed towards the container, not really caring if the others followed him or not. Nor did he care if he was seen by the Korellians, all that mattered was getting to Dolores. As it happened the others did follow him and within a few seconds they were all inside the vacuous container.

"Dolores?" Hank murmured as loud as he dare, his voice echoing around the enclosed space.

No answer.

She had to be in here somewhere he thought and proceeded further into the gloom, Sixpack, Eric and Frank at his heels. Eventually he spied her, hiding behind a crate at the very rear of the container. "D it's me!"

"Hi."

Another 'what' found its way into the conversation.

"What are you doing here? You're supposed to be at Mrs Dorfler's house."

"Ssshh!" she breathed, putting a finger to her lips.

Hank was struggling to avoid starting his sentences with 'what'.

"What's wrong?"

"It's going all dark."

"What do you mea…."

The answer arrived in dramatic fashion as the door to the container was closed, sealing the occupants inside and yes - it did 'go all dark'. "Oh perfect!" Hank sighed.

The container was loaded on to the transporter ship via a gigantic portable conveyer belt along with the others. The Korellians, who had no idea they were carrying five stowaways, continued their argument as they boarded their ship.

"It's quite simple Jaggs, I'm in charge and that's all there is to it!"

"Well I'm sorry Danzo, but I didn't see any memo saying you were the leader for this mission!"

"Of course I am, I'm head of security remember? Besides we don't do memos for these kind of jobs and furthermore, you can't even read."

"I say we put the leadership issue to a vote!"

"We're not voting for anything! Now let's pack up our gear and get outta here."

Mumbling about dictatorships Jaggs reluctantly followed the order and helped the others disassemble the portable conveyor belt. Five minutes later they were ready for take off and still arguing. The ship was not unlike a Korellian itself, big, ugly, hard as nails and low on intelligence. With a shuddering groan of technology it slowly rose from the landing pad on the roof and began its journey to Perfection Island.

CHAPTER FORTY-TWO

*"The path of sound credence is through the thick
forest of scepticism."*

George Jean Nathan

12.34pm, 5hrs 26mins til the final.

The last thing you want when you've been accidentally
kidnapped by Korellians is to let them *know* they've accidentally
kidnapped you – this is why nobody inside the container made a
sound for at least ten minutes. Hot favourite to break the silence was
of course Eric and he did so just as the ship lifted away from the
roof. His voice was somewhere between a whisper and panic but his
fellow stowaways heard it clearly enough.

"I can't see a thing in here! Six, have you got a light?"

"Certainly sir."

The droid obliged by activating his built-in torch, which
extended from his left thumb. The illumination was weak but it
allowed them to see each other. Hank and Eric removed their
helmets.

"Is everyone OK?" Hank asked.

There was no reason why they shouldn't be but he thought it
was worth checking. A few murmured 'yes's' confirmed they were
all fine. "Let's hope we can breathe in here," he added.

There was no sound from outside the container other than the
steady drone of the ship's engine, it seemed the Korellians were
gone, or at least out of earshot. Sat in a corner, with their backs to
the walls of their prison, they embarked on a long overdue Q & A
session. Dolores snuggled up to Hank in the dim light.

"Where are we going?" she said quietly.

Hank had been about to ask her the same question and the fact
she didn't know was a bit of a worry.

"I'm not entirely sure D, maybe our friend here can tell us."

'Our friend' was obviously Frank Bazonka and he shuffled

239

uneasily as all eyes turned his way.

"Erm…well…if my memory serves me correctly we're on our way to a tropical island."

"What?" Eric hissed. "Trop…*what*?"

"Yes, I'm sure that's right…it's…well…er…"

"Just who are you?" Hank said calmly. "And why did you bring Dolores here?" His voice became more agitated. "And why have you been at Eric's doorstep for the last few weeks? *Just what the hell is going on?*"

Frank had been rehearsing this speech for several hours and now that his big moment had arrived he was in danger of gabbling it out in one long burst of nonsense. Composing himself he took a deep breath, sat up straight and let them have it.

"Before I get started I want you to know this is going to be very difficult for you to believe – but I want to make it clear that it's *all* true."

"Try us," Eric prompted.

"Very well, first and foremost you need to know that I'm from the future."

Eric scoffed, it was one of those sarcastic huffs that manages to get across the words 'you're full of it' without actually having to say anything – not the best start for Frank.

"Let's just hear him out Eric," Hank reasoned.

"It's true Mr Dorfler."

"How do you know my…"

"Just let him carry on Eric!"

When he was sure he would incur no further interruptions Frank continued.

"One hundred years in the future to be exact, I'm from the year 2205. My home planet is Harcordia, fourth planet of the Scorus system. Yes, I know what you're thinking, that planet has only just been discovered. As far as you're concerned that's true, but in 2107 work began on colonisation and by 2132 it was a fully inhabited world. My home is a country called Malawinniwa, I live in the capital Vestra-Majora – or I should say I *used* to live there. I can never go back."

"Why not?" Hank blurted out, unaware he was interrupting.

"I'll come to that later, what's important right now is that you understand what happens in the next few hours."

It was tough to know how to explain this next part and Frank clasped his hands before him as if praying for guidance.

"Come on spit it out!" Eric cried, unable to bear the tension any longer.

"According to the historical archives a certain Hank Halo and a certain Eric Dorfler, otherwise known as the crimefighting Saturday Knights, came within a whisker of saving planet Earth."

"From what?"

"From being destroyed – sorry didn't I mention that part?"

Eric threw his arms in the air:

"I think I've heard enough!"

"No!" Frank insisted, surprised at his own assertiveness. "You must listen to me! The story goes like this, in 2105 some crazed scientist unleashed a deadly virus on the planet. I say 'deadly' it was more like 'really unpleasant' as no-one actually died from it, not directly anyway. The virus seemed to have just one purpose, it turned every living thing on the planet hideously ugly – I mean like *repulsive* beyond description. The effect was catastrophic, governments crumbled, wars broke out all over the globe, suicides became an epidemic. Then there was the refugee issue, thinking they would be cured if they left Earth, millions of people fled to the outlying planets. Obviously, no-one wanted them, I mean you wouldn't would you? What if the virus was contagious? You wouldn't exactly welcome infected people on to your planet with open arms."

"So, strict immigration laws were swiftly passed banning *all* Earthlings from *all* other planets. With no cure to be found and nowhere to go the unfortunate blighters had to stay put. At the AGM of 2108, that's the Annual Galactic Meeting, the issue of Earth and its grotesque inhabitants was discussed. I'm afraid to say it was a unanimous decision."

"What did they decide?" Hank gasped.

Frank swallowed hard, he'd heard the phrase 'shoot the messenger' several times and wondered if it would be applicable here.

"They decided to melt it down."

"*Melt it down*?" Eric shrieked, "You can't melt down an entire planet!"

"Yes you can Mr Dorfler."

"How?"

"I've no idea, but they did it."

For once Hank was leaning towards Eric's side, this guy was clearly insane but he opted to humour him. Struggling to keep a straight face he asked;

"What did they melt it down *into*?"

"Have you heard of a planet called Hispaniosa?"

"Of course, it's one of the largest planets in the galaxy."

"That's right and do you know what's peculiar about it?"

Hank and Eric shook their heads.

"It doesn't have a single island, not one. There's just one big ocean on one side and one big landmass on the other. Well the people of Hispaniosa have always wanted an island, several in fact. They've seen them on other planets and quite fancied the idea. So the molten remains of Earth were transported to Hispaniosa, they figured the virus would have perished in the intense heat you see."

"And they used it to make themselves an island," Hank smirked.

"Not just one, I think there was enough for at least a hundred and twelve. They were overjoyed."

"What happened to the people?" Eric asked accusingly.

"What people?"

"The people who lived on Earth?"

"Oh they got melted down along with the planet, hard not to really isn't it?"

Hank pulled Dolores closer to him, she was trembling which he wrongly assumed to be because she was cold.

"Well that's an interesting story Mr...?"

"Oh...er...Frank, Frank Bazonka."

"Tell me Frank, exactly where do Eric and I fit into all this again?"

There was no doubt Frank was losing the fight to convince them, even in this half light he could see their suppressed grins. He battled on regardless:

"Somehow, you found the scientist and very nearly managed to destroy the machine he used to launch the virus. The details are a bit sketchy and I left the file in the car so I can't be exact."

"Wait a minute," Eric said seriously, "If everyone on Earth died then how do you know all this?"

"Simple. Remember the virus was released in 2105 and it wasn't until 2108 that Earth was...er...redistributed. Becoming horrendously ugly doesn't prevent you from communicating

242

y'know. People came to learn of your 'near miss' and they passed it on. If it's any consolation the story of the Saturday Knights is one of the all time great legends of planet Earth."

This was the only part of the story Eric was prepared to believe and he turned to Hank with a broad smile.

"One of the all time great legends bud, I always knew we'd be famous one day!"

"Where do you come in then Frank?" Hank probed.

"Well, back on Harcordia it's the year 2205, exactly one hundred years since you almost saved your world. We're having a memorial to mark the one hundredth anniversary of just how close you came. There's gonna be a parade, speeches, bunting and everything. We've even built two statues in your honour, but there's one problem. We knew Eric had a middle name, it was mentioned in the archives, but we didn't know what it was and the names need to be carved on to the bases of the statues."

"You could've just left it out," Hank suggested.

"No chance, we have to get everything right at Historical Data Retrieval, that's where I work by the way."

"So they transported you back in time, back here, to find out eh?"

"Yeah, I managed to find out it was Jeff but didn't know if it was spelt with a 'J' or a 'G'."

"Couldn't they just have guessed?"

"That's *exactly* what I said! But you don't know what it's like at Historical Data Retrieval, they have to be precise and accurate about every last little thing! To make things worse I've destroyed my inter-planetary, time-splitting communicator so there's no way I can let them know and that means I'm stuck here. They won't let me back til I've got the information you see."

Eric frowned.

"That's a bit harsh."

"Like I said, you don't know what it's like working at HDR."

Silence descended on the stowaways as they allowed the information to sink in.

"What do you think Six?" Eric said eventually.

"About what sir?"

"Haven't you been listening?"

"There are several references and phrases that I do not fully comprehend sir, but I am recording the conversation for analysis at a later date."

"Oh forget it. Look Frank, before we dismiss you as a complete loony, do you have any proof that might make this any easier to swallow?"

Again, Frank had rehearsed this part and had been looking forward to it immensely as it was without doubt the most dramatic section and most people do enjoy a good drama.

CHAPTER FORTY-THREE

*"There is more stupidity than hydrogen in
the universe, and it has a longer shelf life."*

Frank Zappa

12.35am - Perfection Island, 5hrs 25mins til the final.

With half the island's security staff away on their mission to
hijack the repullium shipment in Cosmopolis the remaining six
crocs should have been extra vigilant, especially after Eve Tendril's
rollocking almost two months hence. But there is one fundamental
rule that applies to all admonishments, no matter how harsh, no
matter how venomous it may seem at the time, *all* rollockings have
an effective lifespan and this one had begun to wear off.
Consequently, the guards had slipped back into their slack ways.
With the time approaching thirty-six minutes past midnight they
really ought to have been patrolling the perimeter – but they
weren't. Due to the lack of action on the island, the boredom had
well and truly set in and to pass the time the Korellians had devised
several competitions to keep themselves occupied. The most
prestigious event was the gorilla shooting contest which not only
allowed them to sharpen their marksmanship skills but enabled
them to indulge in mindless violence at the same time. Other
activities included the hardest punch challenge where each croc was
given a single punch to try and knock out an opponent of his choice
until only one was left standing. Another favourite was the glass-
eating contest which is hopefully self-explanatory. But after the
gorilla shooting, the most keenly fought game was surprisingly the
old-fashioned sport of softball. Surprising for three reasons: a) it
was a team game, b) it involved no violence and c) it required a
modicum of intelligence to play. Korellians had always been
designed with fighting in mind and they had been designed very
well. Hurting people, firing weapons and looking fearsome came as
second nature to them.

Playing softball didn't.

From a Korellian perspective, baseball bats were only ever used for one thing – hitting people – and the only things they ever threw were either grenades, very large rocks or other people. As a result they had to train regularly and with nothing better to do that night they had decided to embark on a little midnight batting practice. Hastily erected floodlights bathed the beach in artificial light and the six Korellians were doing their best to whack balls into oblivion without breaking any windows. Their most proficient pitcher, Flink Badduz was currently stood at the mound and had been throwing softballs for the last hour or so.

"Alright it's time I had a swing now!" he barked above the sound of crashing waves.

The others growled their discontent, Flink might be the best thrower but he was a rotten hitter. With Danzo away the most senior Korellian on the island was now Hex Brakkish and he took the opportunity to flex some leadership muscle.

"No way Flink, you couldn't hit the floor if you were standing on it and anything you do happen to connect with could go anywhere."

"All the more reason for me to practice then!"

This was a very valid point and Hex could find no way to argue against it – such was the Korellian intellect.

"Oh…er…OK then, grab a bat and I'll pitch to you, everyone else keep an eye on the ball if he does manages to hit one."

Feeling confident Flink stepped up to his position, took a few practise swings then readied himself to receive the ball. Hex gave him a nice easy underarm pitch, like a Dad pitching to his four year old son. Trying to imagine Eve Tendril's face on the ball, Flink swung at it with all his considerable might – and made a perfect connection. The members of the outfield watched in astonishment as the ball flew over their heads, over the floodlights and eventually came to land with a leafy thud just inside the bordering jungle.

"Holy smoke Flink!" Hex cried, "I didn't know you could hit like that!"

"Me neither!"

"Let's see how you do with this one then," Hex rumbled, picking up another ball. "Hey Flink! Where you goin'?"

Flink was galloping off towards the place his ball had landed, still carrying his bat.

"I'm not letting that one get away," he called over his shoulder, "that's one ball I'm gonna keep forever!"

Finding the ball however, proved to be trickier than Flink had expected. Even with half-decent night vision the croc found it difficult to pinpoint exactly where the ball had come to rest. Using his bat as a makeshift machete he ploughed into the jungle, swishing left and right to clear the vines and creepers that blocked his way. It had to be here somewhere! He'd never hit such a sweet strike in his life and he vowed that if he ever found the elusive ball he'd have it mounted on some kind of ceremonial plinth – probably with his signature on it.

The other crocs dismissed his search as a lost cause and resumed their practise. But Flink was determined to find the ball and hacked his way deeper into the choking vegetation. Slash! Slash! Slash! His search became increasingly frantic until finally he spied the prize. There it was, nestling between two tree trunks and only three feet away. Flink was about to reach down and grab it when one of the tree trunks *moved*. He watched dumbfounded as the tree trunk uprooted and planted itself on top of the ball making retrieval all but impossible. Not quite understanding what was happening Flink allowed his gaze to move upwards, beyond the trapped ball, up the tree trunk, which seemed to merge with a thicker far more substantial object. As he continued to raise his eye-line, Flink's less than developed brain began to click into gear and it dawned on him that trees couldn't just move about like this, which meant it obviously wasn't a tree – it was something else. Your average Korellian stands something like seven feet tall, but even this one had to look up to meet the stare of the thing looking down at him.

It took a good twenty minutes before the crocs realised Flink had not returned. No-one seemed particularly bothered and it was only after the practise session had drawn to a close that they conducted a brief and half-hearted search. All they found was his bat, smashed in two and apparently ownerless. Flink had found his ball they assumed, and had retired to his room to clean and polish it for posterity, the session was officially called to a close and the crocs loped off to their quarters.

Meanwhile, in the dark, unwelcoming confines of the jungle Grunter tramped through the foliage content in the knowledge he had managed to reduce the Korellians' numbers from twelve to eleven.

CHAPTER FORTY-FOUR

"We all have big chances in our lives that are more or less a second chance."

Harrison Ford

When it came to the burden of proof, Frank didn't have an ace up his sleeve, he had no damning, incontrovertible evidence with which to blow away their scepticism – which was a shame because he could really have used one right at that moment - yet he was sure the drama and gravity of the situation would win them over. Pausing for a moment to milk every last drop of tension from the atmosphere he sat back and gave them a wry smile. Hank and Eric exchanged worried looks. Why was he smiling? Did he have some hard evidence? Had he been toying with them all this time? Or was he really a nutcase? Plenty of nutcases walked around with permanent smiles on their faces.

"The proof gentlemen is in several parts," Frank began, still wearing his 'know-it-all' grin, which was beginning to border on the annoying. "The first and most obvious part is 'what have I got to gain by lying'?"

Eric had been hoping for a chance to wipe out Frank's story with one clever, astute comment, but try as he might he couldn't find an answer to that one. He frowned, looking across at Hank who was similarly stumped.

"That's hardly real proof," Hank said.

Frank smiled back at him, his grin now firmly embedded in the annoying category and threatening to spill over into 'infuriating' territory.

"Fair enough, I'll move on to the next part. If you were to take a sample of my DNA and run it through that big new computer...oh what's it called?"

"V.I.N.C.E[†]," Hank replied.

"You'd find that it has no record of me whatsoever – that's because I don't even exist yet."

"That's not real proof either," Eric argued, "someone could've forgotten to input your details, plus we can't exactly do that right now can we?"

Refusing to be beaten Frank moved on to his next revelation.

"Alright then, how's this? According to the archives there was one person who foresaw these catastrophic events, one person who tried to warn the Knights that something terrible was going to happen. Not much is known about this person other than her age and name. She was six years old and called Dolores."

"That's me!" Dolores squeaked.

"Oh my God," Hank murmured. Eric had also worked it out.

"Scary faces and broken reflectograms," they said together.

"I beg your pardon?" said Frank.

Hank could feel something taking a helter-skelter ride around his stomach. For a long time no-one spoke, it seemed the naming of Dolores had really hit the spot. It's not every day someone tells you you've only three years to live and to be honest, they took it pretty well. Eric adopted a somewhat selfish approach and his first thoughts were to list everything he had always wanted to do in life and then try and figure out how to squeeze them into a three year window. Conversely, Hank's immediate concerns were not for himself but rather the fate of the human race. Dolores was slightly too young to understand the full implications and was just pleased her name had been mentioned in the story. Sixpack, well as usual he took the news in his stride and exhibited the same level of emotion one might expect from a toaster. Without a paper and pen handy to make his list, Eric abandoned it and in a flash of inspiration said:

"I know! Of course, it's so simple! We just relocate to another planet right now!"

"You can't just evacuate an entire planet Eric!" Hank

[†] Very Intelligent National Computer Experiment. Rather than have lots of different government computers holding lots of individual bits of data, some official boffin decided to have one big computer holding *all* the data. Six months into its trial run V.I.N.C.E. was doing well with only one minor hitch to date which involved a virus and an ex-government employee who forgot to back-up one night.

blustered.

"Well actually when I said 'we' I meant just us."

"Typical, always thinking about yourself!"

"No I'm not – I'm thinking about *us*!"

The argument began to gather momentum and the volume inside the container increased.

"Why don't you try thinking about everyone else for a change!"

"Hey don't have a go at *me*. It's Futureman Frank here that's bringing us all this good news!"

In one easy movement the argument reached out and pulled Frank into its clutches.

"It's not *my* fault! If you guys hadn't fouled up a hundred years ago everything would be OK!"

Hank didn't like that accusation one bit.

"Fouled up? We haven't even done anything yet!"

"Yeah!" Eric said, suddenly taking Hank's side, "why don't you take your stupid Historical Data assignment and shove it!"

Just as everyone drew breath for another round of verbal sparring a tiny voice from the shadows said:

"Why don't you just make sure you save the planet this time?"

Dolores's big brown eyes stared up at them, a mixture of fear and confusion on her face.

It was a very good question.

"She's right," Hank said. "If we *can* save the planet rather than *almost* save it then everything's gonna be OK."

The animosity between the three men dissolved instantly and they turned their minds to something more constructive – like a plan. Hot-headedness gave way to logic, which is why Hank was the one to get the ball rolling. "Alright Frank, what exactly happened, just how did we almost save the world?"

Even in the gloom of the container they could see Frank blushing.

"Err…I'm not…exactly…sure," he said as slowly as he could.

"Come again?" Eric asked.

"Well, it wasn't part of my assignment. What I mean is, it wasn't essential for me to know the facts surrounding your exploits – the details I mean. I was only told to get your middle name."

Before Eric could wrench the conversation back into an argument Hank said (in his calmest tone):

"Come on Frank, you must know something."

Having left the file in his car Frank was now entirely dependent on his memory and he searched it frantically.

"Now let's see – you definitely make it on to the tropical island which is where the ugly machine is located. You manage to infiltrate the complex and finally find the machine. T-h-e-n...you run into some trouble and I'm pretty sure it's at this point you both get killed."

"*Killed?*" Eric shrieked.

"Oh...er...yes, didn't I mention that either?"

Eric was so desperate to say something profound – *anything*– that he got all tongue-tied and ended up saying nothing. Things couldn't really get much worse but Hank felt he'd better check just in case:

"There isn't anything else you've forgotten to tell us is there Frank?"

"No, I think that's pretty much everything."

There was a very real danger that Eric could explode at any second, he was still looking for a suitable expletive and the effort was sending him into a mental meltdown.

"Just calm down Eric," Hank said soothingly, "we're not dead yet."

With a deep sigh Eric abandoned his search and buried his head in his hands.

"What the hell are we gonna do Hank?" he moaned.

"I'll tell you what we're gonna do, we're gonna find this machine and put it out of commission and none of us are going to die in the process – got it?"

Hank was well aware he (and only he) was holding them together – if *he* lost it then they'd all be in deep trouble and no mistake. Not sure if he really believed it or not he said: "If we approach this rationally we shouldn't have any problems."

"So what's the plan?" Frank asked.

"Well the first thing we need to figure out is a way out of this metal crate. Sixpack we need you to use your torch, check the walls, see if there's any obvious way out."

They got to their feet and made their way to the door, which seemed a good place to start. There were no visible handles or locks anywhere. Eric gave it a push, putting all his weight behind it but it didn't budge. Cursing under his breath he gave the door a kick which sent a clanging sound echoing around the container.

"Eric if it's all the same to you I'd prefer to do this quietly," Hank hissed, "unless of course you *want* the crocs to find us?"

"Sorry bud, I just hate being trapped like this."

A further ten minutes ticked by while they checked the rest of the container, the walls, the floor and the ceiling, but apart from several dime-sized holes in the ceiling there was no clear exit. They sat back down on the floor and tried to think of a solution.

"I don't suppose your droid possesses any kind of welding equipment does he?" Frank said.

"Nah, he's just a regular service droid. He could give the container a good clean if you like?"

With no way out they were in deep, deep trouble. Once the ship landed and the crocs came to unload their cargo it would only be a matter of time before they were discovered – then it *would* be game over – and they wouldn't come close to saving anything.

"Any ideas D?" Hank asked, hoping maybe her psychic voice could offer some assistance.

Dolores shook her head, the voice was clearly asleep or simply not interested. Hank frowned, frustrated at their seemingly helpless situation. "We must get out of this thing before we land," he said, "or we're dogmeat. The Korellians won't…what are you smiling at? Have you found a way out?"

Eric was beaming broadly, a glint in his eye.

"Hank do you realise, I mean, do you have *any idea* how popular we're gonna be if we pull this off? We're gonna have babes queuing up outside the house! Everyone's gonna want a piece of us! And the parties, just think how many parties we'll get invited to!"

"Can't you just focus on the problem at hand for *one minute*! Once this is all over you can party your ass off all you like but right now we're in a bit of a predicament!"

"Oh come on Hank, I'm only trying to lighten the mood. You want a way out of here? You want a plan? OK, here's a plan. We wait til the crocs come to unload the cargo and as soon as the door opens we blast whoever's outside with the Inebriator."

"Do we have a *plan B*?" Frank asked nervously.

"Go on," Hank said.

"Then we all run out of the container as fast as we can until we find somewhere else to hide. If we are supposed to be landing on a tropical island then there's bound to be lots of jungle and stuff –

perfect for concealment."

Hank took a moment to give the plan its due attention, then he made his judgement.

"Sorry Eric, but that's just about the worst plan I've ever heard."

CHAPTER FORTY-FIVE

"Luck, bad if not good, will always be with us. But it has a way
of favouring the intelligent and showing its back to the stupid."

John Dewey

1hr. 44 mins later.

A weird grating sound, similar to that of a malfunctioning
toilet filled the container. Hank addressed his fellow prisoners:

"Sounds like we're preparing to land. Right, we'll go over it
one more time. Eric will be behind this crate here, ready to fire the
Inebriator. I will be here, slightly ahead of him and to the left to
divert the attention of the croc opening the container. Everyone else
will be directly behind Eric ready to exit the container at high speed
once the shot has been fired. When we're off the ship we head for
the nearest patch of jungle to find cover. Does everyone
understand?"

They all nodded – this was after all the ninth time the plan had
been discussed, if they hadn't grasped it by now they never would.
Needless to say Eric was almost dizzy with excitement. Not only
were they about to finally go up against the crocs, but they were
going to do so using one of *his* plans *and* he would get to fire the
first shot! Positioning himself behind the designated crate he
levelled the weapon at the door.

"I wonder what's in these things anyway," he asked no-one in
particular.

"The labels say Tripolytrolyphate," said Sixpack.

"Not much help."

"Sounds like a chemical of some kind," Frank offered.

"Well done Frank, not really difficult to guess as they came
from a medical warehouse."

"Alright Eric, calm down and put your helmet on," Hank
instructed, donning his own headgear.

Scooping up his weapon, he positioned himself as planned,

about six feet in front of Eric and three feet to his left. Behind Eric stood Sixpack and Frank (with Dolores in his arms).

"What if there's more than one croc out there when they open the door?"

It wasn't something Hank wanted to think about but he answered the question anyway.

"We'll just have to shoot them. The important thing is we get off the ship as fast as we can."

Frank didn't look convinced.

"What if they decide to open the container before we land?"

"Frank we can stand here all day and talk about 'what ifs'!" Hank said, losing his patience. "Let's just concentrate on what we're *going* to do shall we? Besides, it sounds like we're getting ready to touch down any minute."

He knew it wasn't a great plan, it wasn't even a terribly *good* plan, but no-one (himself included) could find a better alternative. Surrender was, of course, out of the question, not only would it prevent them from trying to save the world but it was one of those words that just didn't feature in the Korellian vocabulary – they also had no word for 'cuddly'. Surrendering to a Korellian should always be high on your 'to *not* do list', marginally ahead of eating a Bish Bash Rogan Bosh Gullet Stripper further than running distance from a hospital. Waving a white flag to a Korellian tells him one thing – you're unarmed and therefore far easier to kill.

The humans inside the container felt their stomachs rise as the ship lurched downwards, a fine example of the croc pilot's cumbersome flying skills. The ship landed much the same way as an old fashioned parachutist, fast and ungainly with a good chance of injury.

"OK, that's it we're down!" Hank whispered, "get ready everybody!"

Trying to stay relaxed Eric flicked off the safety catch on the Inebriator and turned the dial to 'Banjaxed' – the highest setting. When the ship's engines cut out there was complete silence.

Good fortune was to play a large part in Eric's plan, good job too because without it they would all surely have perished. The person most responsible for this generous slice of luck was the Korellian Jaggs Mixxit. After Danzo Stax, Jaggs was the most senior croc in the team but it seemed second wasn't good enough. He and the other five crocs were up on the bridge. As the ship touched down and the pilot killed the engines Danzo sprang into action.

"Alright you miserable lot, lets get down to the hold and start unloading those containers."

"Not so fast Danzo," Jaggs interrupted, "I wanna discuss the leadership issue again."

"Fine. Here's how it works. I'm in charge so you have to do as I say. Until Miss Tendril appoints someone else head of security that's the way it is. Got it?"

"But what if…what if the others would prefer *me* as leader?"

"*You*? Jaggs, you're too dense to lead. I could count the number of intelligent comments you've ever made on my thumb."

"Saying I'm thick are you?"

"You're damn right I am."

One of the watching Korellians lumbered off down the corridor, making his way to the cargo hold. He'd seen Jaggs and Danzo argue a hundred times before and it always had the same outcome – Jaggs would back down and Danzo would remain their leader. Seeing nothing to indicate this would be any different he decided to get cracking with the task at hand. The other spectators however could see Jaggs's frustration and sensed this time things might not be so easily resolved. Danzo could also feel the tension rising and opted to bring matters to a head.

"Alright, why don't we have a challenge eh? Whoever wins can be leader."

"You're on!" Jaggs cried, clearly fancying his chances.

"Marksmanship challenge OK with you?"

"No problem!"

Jaggs was currently leading the gorilla shooting contest and was indeed a crack shot, capable of shooting the wings off a fire bug at twenty metres, which made Danzo's choice all the more baffling. Yet he seemed to be oozing with confidence.

"What do you wanna shoot at?"

Rubbing his scaly chin with a claw Jaggs considered his options. He peered out of the window at the beach below.

"Something small, something *really* small."

"Mind if I go first?" Danzo asked politely.

"Be my guest."

Danzo calmly drew his blitzer pistol, put it to the back of Jaggs's head and pulled the trigger. The cockpit was immediately redecorated with a splatter effect - a new colour that could only be described as 'dark green and nasty'.

Holstering his weapon Danzo turned to his suitably startled audience.

"I can't think of many things smaller than Jaggs's brain can you?"

One of the crocs managed to find his voice:

"Danz! Do you know what you've just done?"

"What?"

"You've completely wrecked the softball tournament! How can we have six on each team now we've only got eleven players?"

CHAPTER FORTY-SIX

"Adventure is just bad planning."

Roald Amundsen

2.34a.m. - Perfection Island, 3hrs 26mins til the final.

All Hank could do was stare at the locked door. Any minute now one of the crocs (hopefully just one) would open it and their untidy plan would be put to the test. Despite reprimanding Frank for his 'what ifs' he was finding it difficult to avoid some rather alarming questions himself. Firstly, they had absolutely no idea of the ship's layout, which meant they could only hope their container was near the loading door. Secondly, what if the loading door was locked? If they did manage to get out of the ship then what was waiting for them outside? More crocs? Would they be inside a hangar or (even worse) miles from any cover? As usual his main concern was for Dolores. Somehow she had managed to get dragged into this sorry escapade and now she was in grave danger. He put their chances of success at something like twenty to one. He was so wrapped up in thought that the sound of Eric's voice in his headset made him jump.

"Hank, when we get outta this there's something I need to tell you."

"Sometimes you amaze me Eric," he replied shaking his head.

"Why? Because I'm being sentimental?"

"No because you actually believe we're gonna get outta this."

"Oh."

"Why don't you save it til later eh? We've got enough on our plate without....*listen*!"

From the other side of their container they heard a low rumbling sound, something mechanical. Hank prayed it was someone opening the outer door. Then footsteps, heavy and slow and getting louder.

"Get ready everyone!" Eric whispered.

The atmosphere was becoming unbearably tense and it was getting to Dolores who began squirming in Frank's arms. She was also on the verge of tears and already mewling like a distressed cat.

"Keep her quiet Frank!" Hank said as loud as he dare.

But it was no use, Frank's child handling expertise was non-existent and try as he might he couldn't calm her down.

The noise of a large bolt being lifted sent a wave of adrenaline through the group – this was it! The door to their container was being opened! Frank was in all sorts of trouble with Dolores, who was now thrashing around in something close to a tantrum. It was like trying to keep hold of a wet bar of soap. Things went from bad to worse.

The door began to swing open and light streamed into the container.

Eric steadied himself and waited for his target to emerge.

The door opened further and they all saw the Korellian on the other side.

Dolores bit Frank's hand and he dropped her – on to Eric's back.

Eric was knocked sideways and pressed the trigger – hitting Hank.

The Korellian froze for a second, gawping at the bizarre gathering inside the container. Consumed by a haze of intense drunkenness Hank slid down the wall, depressing the trigger of his Web-o-matic as he did so. Another dose of good fortune fell out of the sky as the Web-o-matic spewed forth its sticky webbing – all over the Korellian.

"Holy crap!" Eric cried.

Strong as he was, the croc was no match for the webbing that clung to him. Hank had also left his finger on the trigger and within a few seconds the croc had turned into a giant cocoon. With a groan both Hank and the Korellian keeled over and hit the deck. There was no time to waste and Eric knew it.

"Six pick up Hank, Frank…er…grab Dolores we're outta here!"

Collecting Hank's gun as he went Eric charged out of the container and into the cargo hold, looking round for a way off the ship. He didn't have to look far. The croc had already opened the outer loading door and although it was pitch black outside Eric could feel the air blowing in and could hear the distant sound of crashing surf. "Follow me!"

Leaving the croc twitching on the ground they poured out of the ship and on to a landing pad. Eric pulled off his helmet and tried to get his bearings. Beside the landing pad was an enormous hangar of some kind with another smaller complex beyond it. They were just silhouettes but their angular outline told Eric they had to be man-made structures – or very unusually shaped trees. There didn't seem to be anyone else around but he knew it wouldn't be long before the croc in the cargo hold was discovered. Not entirely sure where he was going he led them down a flight of steps which arrived at the beach. Hoisted over Sixpack's shoulder Hank burbled incoherently. It was only when the moon offered a helping hand by emerging from behind a cloud that Eric spotted the dark, swaying silhouette of the jungle.

"This way!" he said, running along the beach towards the trees.

Breathless and feeling a little better about the situation they eventually made it to the edge of the undergrowth. Beyond the tree line the jungle was just a black mass of tangled vegetation, perhaps not the safest place in which to venture but they really didn't have that many options.

"Six, we're gonna need your torch again."

Still carrying the inebriated Rough Knight, Sixpack activated his torch, which proved to be woefully inadequate as it illuminated no more than a couple of feet in front of them. But it was better than nothing and one by one they slipped into the unwelcoming foliage. It was tough going but Eric insisted they put as much distance between themselves and the beach as possible – just in case. Approximately four hundred metres in he called a halt, deciding this was far enough and that, for the moment, they were safe. They laid Hank down against a moss covered boulder, he was still babbling to himself about pizzas and beer so they decided to leave him be for the time being. The effect would wear off sooner or later Eric told himself, sooner would of course be preferable.

"Alright folks, we'll lay low here for a while," Eric said. "I think we'll be safe until Hank sobers up."

"We're in the middle of the jungle Eric," Frank complained, "how the hell can you say it's safe? There could be anything in here!"

"Just relax Frank; we've still got our weapons. Besides, most of the animals are probably asleep."

"I always thought most jungle animals were nocturnal."

"What the hell do you want me to do Frank? Build you a treehouse? Just chill out, we're gonna be fine. Keep an eye on everyone for a minute will ya? I need to take a leak."

Eric sidled off into some bushes, muttering to himself about alarmists and whiners. He was about to hitch up his chainmail shirt when a movement, off to his right, caught his attention. As his eyes adjusted to the gloom he suddenly found himself face to face with the biggest gorilla he had ever seen.

CHAPTER FORTY-SEVEN

"Revenge proves its own executioner."

John Ford

2.42a.m. – Landing platform, 3hrs 18mins til the final.

Danzo supervised the unloading of the ship without having to do any heavy lifting because (as his team was now very aware) he was in charge. But although he barked out his orders in a confident, arrogant manner he wasn't feeling very sure of himself, far from it. His first worry was that one of his men had been discovered in the cargo hold, trussed up as if a giant spider had attacked him. The story about finding two medieval knights in the container was dubious at best so Danzo had contented himself by assuming they had somehow collected a couple of stowaways in Cosmopolis. Nothing was missing so they weren't thieves or if they *were* they weren't very good ones. Probably just kids looking for thrills.

The second problem had come when he'd spoken to Hex Brakkish. To expedite the unloading Danzo had employed the rest of his security team and this is when Hex had told him about the mysterious disappearance of Flink Badduz. He'd gone to look for a softball in the jungle and hadn't been seen since. With Jaggs rotting in the ship's waste disposal hatch his team was now down to ten members and he knew if Eve Tendril found out there'd be hell to pay. The only positive side was that they now had an even number of crocs, which made the softball teams easier to sort out.

One by one the crates were wheeled into Max's lab, where the chemist made preparations for the manufacture of more repullium. Time was now pressing, he had less than four hours to make the stuff, then get it ready for 'distribution' via the Uglifier. If everything went according to plan he'd have enough time, but if anything went amiss he'd be up against it. One man who was going to *make sure* things went amiss was Cyrus Zifford who had found his way on to the landing platform.

"Successful theft then Danz?" he asked pleasantly, as if discussing the weather.

"Yeah…er…no problems whatsoever."

Apart from having murdered his second-in-command of course.

"You haven't forgotten our little arrangement have you?"

As a rule, Korellians don't do a lot of thinking, they don't need to as most of their issues are resolved in ways that require little or no thought. But in Danzo's case he was having to think of *several* things at once, consequently he was suffering intense mental fatigue.

"Arrangement sir?"

"Yes Danzo," Cyrus sighed, becoming impatient, "the *arrangement*."

The penny dropped.

"Oh *that*! No sir, I haven't forgotten."

"You're sure? You seem a bit preoccupied."

"Well it's been a busy night sir."

The 'arrangement' as Cyrus called it was actually fairly simple (by human standards). Now that Eve had rendered him 'surplus to requirements' he had only one thing on his mind – to hinder Max Ticklegrit as much as he could. His plan called for Danzo to sabotage the Uglifier, nothing too obvious, a snipped wire here, a loose connection there, taking care to remember exactly which wires had been snipped or connections loosened. This would then wreck Max's big moment, dropping him in the shredder good and proper. The way he'd sold it to Danzo had been typically deceptive and had gone something like this:

"Danzo, I've got a little job for you, which if done properly, will not only secure your own employment for the foreseeable future but also portray me as the hero of the hour. It's a fairly intricate plan so I'll go over it slowly and use small words. I need you to get into the Uglifier hangar about an hour or so before it's due to be fired – being head of security this shouldn't be too difficult for you. Then I want you to disable it. Don't blow it up or set fire to it, just cut the odd wire here and there so it won't work. Then, when you've done that, come to my office and tell me *exactly* where you've done the damage – you may want to write it down while you're doing it so you don't forget. Dr Ticklegrit has been ordered to fire the machine just as the televised final begins and

263

when he does, it won't work. What do you mean why not? Because you'll have sabotaged it won't you? Still with me? Good. I'll make sure I'm there to witness the panic and just when everything looks lost I can go over to the machine, pretend to lend a helping hand and solve the problem. How? Because you'll already have told me where to look! Come on Danz, I could get a well-trained chimp to do this for me. Once it's fixed Dr Ticklegrit will look a complete arse and Miss Tendril will proclaim me as her saviour. Then I can get your employment secured by having a quiet chat with her. Got it?"

Naturally, Danzo readily agreed and after writing the plan down and going over it several times they shook hands on it. What Danzo *didn't* know was that Cyrus had no intention of saving the day, he was going to be airborne in his private shuttle at the crucial moment, bound for Cosmopolis. He'd already ordered his pilot to arrive about fifteen minutes before the Uglifier was due to be fired, he'd even cleared his departure with Eve herself, on the basis that if she didn't need him anymore would it be OK to pop back to Cosmo? That way he had a tidy alibi for his own whereabouts if or rather *when* the excrement hit the fan. Would Danzo mention his name? He didn't really care, after all, who would believe a stupid lump like him anyway?

What *Cyrus* didn't know was that between them, he and Danzo would set in motion a chain of events that would ultimately spell doom for the planet - something which only the Saturday Knights could prevent.

CHAPTER FORTY-EIGHT

"Don't judge a book by its thickness either."

Craig Bruce

2.50a.m. – 3hrs 10mins til the final.

Meeting a giant gorilla in the middle of the jungle was something of a shock for Eric (as it would be for anyone, except perhaps another gorilla) but when it *spoke* to him in perfect English his fear made way for astonishment. As luck would have it the beast turned out to be fairly amiable and once they had made their introductions it became clear that he was actually quite a 'good egg'. Eric invited him back to their makeshift camp and, after assuring an ashen-faced Frank Bazonka that Grunter was not going to eat him, made further introductions. Dolores seemed quite taken with the ape and with Hank out for the count he was the next best thing to cuddle up to.

It took Eric roughly fifteen minutes to explain who they were and more importantly why they were here. Consumed by his own importance it eventually dawned on him he hadn't asked Grunter any questions yet. Finding a gorilla in the jungle wasn't what you'd call 'out of place' but the fact he could talk and was five times the size of a normal gorilla did perhaps warrant further investigation.

"So what about you Grunter? What's your story?"

Grunter shifted position slightly to accommodate Dolores who had snuggled into the crook of his elbow.

"Well, funnily enough I'm also here to destroy this big machine that makes people ugly, although I didn't realise it was going to end up destroying the planet."

"Believe me it will," Frank said, "or rather it already *has*, depending on your point of view."

"Who sent you?" Eric asked.

"Sorry, that's classified."

"Aw come on! We've told you everything about us, why can't

you tell us?"

"Cos it's *classified*."

One of the benefits of being so big and fearsome looking is that people don't tend to argue with you very much. Eric didn't fancy it much either:

"OK then, have it your way. So are we gonna pool our resources?"

Grunter looked around him, a battered service droid, a six year old girl, a very nervy bloke who claimed to be from the future and two apparently famous crimefighters – one of whom was too drunk to sit up straight – not what he'd call a resourceful bunch. If he did decide to join forces with them they'd definitely be laying claim to the shallow end of the resource pool. But when all was said and done they would probably be more of a help than a hindrance.

"I don't see why not," he said after a pause, "we're all here to achieve the same objective aren't we?"

"Groovy!" Eric said through a grin.

Frank asked:

"Do you know anything about this island?"

Grunter frowned:

"Not that much, but I have managed to find out a few scraps of information."

"Such as?"

"Well for starters this place is called Perfection Island and is owned by a woman called Eve Tendril, a former beauty queen or something. The Korellians are the only security on the island and there are twelve – sorry – eleven of them, all armed with blitzer pistols. The machine we're after is located in a massive hangar next to the laboratory and it was built by a scientist called Max Ticklegrit."

"And you call that *a few scraps* do you?" Eric said.

"I had some help."

"From?"

"I stumbled upon one of the Korellians and he seemed only too happy to answer my questions."

"You interrogated a Korellian? *And got him to talk?*"

"I think *I'd* talk!" Frank said.

"Yeah but a Korellian! That's some feat man!"

"I'll admit it wasn't easy, but everyone has a weakness. You just need to know what it is."

"Korellians have a weakness? Come on then, spill the beans!" Eric cried.

"Well, like most creatures they have a real aversion to being killed. But with this guy, I just threatened to pull his teeth out, one by one."

Frank's face drained of its colour. After speaking to Grunter for a while (who was quite polite and eloquent for a gorilla) it was easy to forget just how aggressive and violent he could be given the chance. It was a comfort to know they were on the same side. Eric also blanched at Grunter's words, if this guy could bring a Korellian to his knees he would be a priceless ally. He too was glad they were all on the same team. It was definitely time for a plan so he said:

"Right then Grunter, what's the plan?"

"You don't have one already?" the gorilla asked.

"Give us a break! It took us over an hour just to come up with a plan to get out of that container! Plus, we've kind of only just got here so we're making it up as we go."

"OK cool it. Let's get our heads together shall we and think this through *rationally*? If we stick to logic we won't go far wrong."

Eric smiled:

"I can't wait for Hank to wake up, he's gonna *love* you."

After an hour and a half of logical, tactical discussion they arrived at a plan. You may think ninety minutes is a long time to spend on a plan but remember this – it was a plan that could save the world – it couldn't be rushed. Most football teams spend days, sometimes weeks going over their game strategy, so ninety minutes was a pretty respectable amount of time in the grand scheme of things. During this time Hank regained some of his former soberness, which is to say he was now sat up rather than slumped.

"I spotted a stream back there; I'll fetch some water and see if we can't get this guy out of his stupor." Grunter said, clambering off into vegetation.

Taking a rather more direct approach Eric slapped Hank around the face several times.

"Come on man! We need you up and about if this plan is gonna work!"

For the first time since his 'inebriation' Hank opened his eyes, which represented significant progress. Whilst he was no stranger to drunkenness, (he and Eric had enjoyed some monster seshes over the years) he had never experienced anything quite like this. Whenever he turned his head his eyes were a couple of seconds behind and his vision swam like a blurred photograph. The muscles in his neck were fast asleep, which made it nigh on impossible for him to lift up his head and his stomach churned as waves of nausea rippled over him.

And now someone was slapping him.

Although they were in no rush, his senses were gradually returning and he fought through the blurriness to try and identify his assailant.

"Eri...Eric?" burbled.

"Yes! That's right Hank it's me! How ya feelin' buddy?"

"Like a thousand hangovers all rolled into one."

"Can you stand up?"

Assisted by Eric and Sixpack, Hank did his best to get to his feet. It was slow going as his legs were somewhere between jelly and blancmange, but eventually they got him vertical. Dolores ran over and gave him a big hug round the waist, which almost knocked him over.

"Hi Hank!" she squealed.

"Hi D, you OK?"

She nodded enthusiastically.

"Where the hell are we anyway?" Hank mumbled, "and what *happened* to me?"

"It's a long story," said Frank.

Hank took in his surroundings as best he could.

"We're in a jungle. Am I dreaming?"

"Nope, you're awake now."

"So there really *is* a ten foot gorilla standing over there?"

Eric looked over his shoulder to see Grunter stood with a canister of water in his hand.

"Oh yes, Hank meet Grunter, he's here to help us."

It was all too much for Hank who collapsed into a heap, whether from inebriation, surprise or plain old terror was anyone's guess.

CHAPTER FORTY-NINE

*"As much as I'd like to meet the tooth fairy on an
evening walk, I don't really believe it can happen."*

Chris Van Allsburg

4.38a.m. – Max Ticklegrit's office, 1hr 22mins til the final.

Max sat at his desk staring out of the window. Taking a deep
breath to calm his nerves he watched the first traces of dawn creep
inexorably over the horizon. He was nervous, *extremely* nervous.
His finest hour was almost upon him, the moment he had been
waiting for. In just less than and hour and a half his most
magnificent creation – the Uglifier – would whir into life and
deliver its terrible payload on the unsuspecting citizens of
Cosmopolis.

A singular achievement.

It would surely mark the pinnacle of his career at *You Beauty*
and would assure his future with the company. Eve would of course
be delighted and although he was beyond promotion, she would
doubtless shower him with awards and honours. But the crowning
glory would be the victory over Cyrus Zifford, a triumph of science
over sleaze. He couldn't wait to see his face once it was all over. No
more smug grins, no more sarcastic comments, he'd bow at the feet
of the greatest chemist the world had ever seen.

But…before any gloating could be done, Max knew the big
test still lay ahead. He had to deliver the goods. The operation
would have to go smoothly and to this end he had checked the
Uglifier three times before he'd left the hangar. His team was
prepped, the repullium had been manufactured and was already
inside the hangar, waiting to be fired into the heavens and then, via
satellite, into America's capital.

Everything was ready.

All he could do now was wait until the appointed hour. Eve
wanted the machine fired just as the Miss Cosmopolis finalists took
the stage, which would be approximately 6pm (6am Perfection

Island time). Max knew from years of experience not all scientific operations ran smoothly, even when everything appeared fine on the surface there was always the risk of something or someone malfunctioning. He had to remain optimistic, if his nerves filtered through to his team then things could go belly-up. He allowed himself a wry smile, everything would be fine, it would work – it *had* to work! Once more he turned his thoughts to the merciless gloatfest he would unleash on Cyrus once he'd taken care of business. As he leaned back in his chair, dreaming of his impending success, he suddenly felt a shift in the air. Sitting upright he anxiously scanned the room. Then he heard the sound, faint at first but growing louder. Footsteps, running footsteps from the corridor outside his office, but they were light, like a child's. They came to a sudden halt right outside his room. His eyes fixed on the door, more specifically the handle, which slowly began to turn. Who could it be? Was there a problem with the Uglifier? Whoever it was they were taking their time opening the door. Inch by inch the door opened until…there in the doorway…Max found himself staring at what he could only describe as a pixie. Dressed like a medieval court jester and standing less than two feet high the creature skipped inside the room and jumped up on to the desk, nimble as you like.

Max got a good look at the thing. The bright green outfit was festooned with tiny bells, which jingled at every movement. Its face was human enough, with a button nose and sparkling blue eyes. In its hand the creature held a small stick or wand, a miniature jester's head adorned the top. It was clearly a male pixie, the beard proved that. Max leaned away from it, his eyes wide with surprise.

"Hiya Max! How's it hangin' buddy?" the pixie said cheerfully, his voice high-pitched and helium-like.

"Who or rather *what* the hell are *you*?"

"I'm a pixie stupid and my name's Peeble."

"Peeble?"

"Yeah I know what you're thinkin' – it rhymes with feeble, but it doesn't bother me, in fact *nothing* bothers me, I'm a pixie y'see?"

Max regained some composure and sat up.

"Why are you in my office?"

Peeble rolled his eyes, beamed a corker of a smile and tapped Max on the forehead with his wand.

"Cos I'm your personal pixie dummy. Everyone has one, didn't you know that?"

Max could only blink in amazement.

"*Personal pixie?*"

"That's right domehead and why do you keep repeating everything I say?"

"I'm just a little taken aback."

"Well, this is our first meeting so I can't say I blame ya! So how's it going? Everything fine and dandy with the Uglifier?"

"*The Uglifier?*"

"You're doin' it again Max!"

"How do you know about the Uglifier?"

"I know everything about you bozo, favourite colour, how strong you like your coffee...everything!"

Some of the old Max returned, the Max that didn't like being interrupted.

"Look Peeble or whatever your name is, I don't have time to waste chit-chatting to a stupid pixie! Now why don't you clear off and bother someone el..."

Before Max could finish Peeble's entire manner changed. His smile disappeared to be replaced by a look of intense anger, his face reddened to a furious crimson and his hands clenched into fists.

"*You ungrateful wretch!*" he shrieked.

His voice had also changed, now it was much louder, deeper and booming and seemed to reverberate around the room. He was absolutely *livid.* "I take time out of my busy schedule to come down here and introduce myself and all you can do is tell me to *clear off?*"

The change was incredible and once more Max leaned away.

"I didn't mean to offend..." he stammered.

"Too late Max!" Peeble screamed, "now you're gonna *pay*!"

Right before his eyes the pixie began to grow, slowly at first but then faster, his body expanding and changing. Before long Peeble (still on the desk) stood five feet tall, muscles bursting through his costume, fangs replacing teeth, claws replacing fingers. He towered over the chemist, his eyes burning with an insane hatred.

"*Help!*" Max cried, leaping from his chair.

There was no way past the pixie to the door, which left Max with just one exit – the window. Not a very appealing option as he was three floors up and although the sandy beach below would probably be softer than most landing pads he didn't fancy his chances. Nor did he want to hang around and face the abomination (which was *still* growing) stood on his desk. He released a whimper as he saw Peeble's wand transform into a gleaming two-handed sword, blue-silver and crackling with malevolent energy.

"No please! *Help!*"

The monstrosity turned to face him, pointing the tip of the sword at Max's chest.

"*Time to die lab rat!*" the monster roared.

It was going to have to be the window Max decided, grabbing his chair. Using all his strength he heaved the chair through the glass, smashing the window to pieces and making a decent sized hole for him to jump through. Without giving the devil behind him a second glance Max gingerly eased himself halfway out of the window, trying to avoid any sharp edges.

"Doctor!"

"No, you'll never take me!" Max shrieked, wisps of grey hair blowing in the draught.

"Doctor what on earth are you doing?"

It was a female voice, nothing like Peeble's monstrous bellowing. Remaining halfway through the window Max looked over his shoulder. Peeble the pixie monster was nowhere to be seen, instead he was looking at Juliet, one of his technicians. Not surprisingly she was wide-eyed and open-mouthed. Feeling extremely foolish he clambered back inside the room.

"Are you *alright* Doctor?" she asked carefully.

Max surveyed the carnage of his office, straightened his lab coat and said;

"Perfectly fine thank you Juliet. Was there something you needed?"

"Er...no, I just...heard screaming and wondered if you were OK."

"Well thank you for your concern, but as you can plainly see I'm fine, raring to go in fact. Everything alright with the Uglifier?"

Still bemused Juliet looked down at her clipboard.

"Yes Doctor, all systems are 'green for go', we're just waiting for Miss Tendril to give us the nod."

"Very good. I'll call you as soon as I hear anything."

Juliet padded out of the office, not quite sure what she had witnessed but *very* sure she didn't want to witness it again. As soon as the door closed Max collapsed on to the desk. What in heaven's name was going on? Where was Peeble? Had he dreamt it all? He withdrew a handkerchief and mopped his brow. Then it hit him.

He stopped chewing.

Like a technician attempting to diffuse a bomb he reached into his mouth and delicately removed the gum.

Trouble Gum.

He'd taken some about an hour ago to relieve the stress and had forgotten all about it. There was a miniature thud as he dropped it into the wastebasket. He'd had hallucinations with Trouble Gum in the past but never anything this vivid, this terrifying.

Probably best not to have anymore today.

CHAPTER FIFTY

"The machine does not isolate man from the great problems
of nature but plunges him more deeply into them."

Antoine de Saint-Exupery

4.52a.m. – 1hr 8mins til the final.

With the exception of immortals (of which there are very few) one thing in life is certain – it ends. Sometimes it's after a 'good innings', other times it is tragically cut short. Sometimes it's expected, sometimes it comes out of the blue. It can be planned, unscheduled, quiet, loud, violent or peaceful but however it happens – it will always *happen*.

For the two mosquitoes outside the foot of the hangar's west wall, it was violent, unscheduled and a textbook example of being in the wrong place at the wrong time. There's never really a good time for life to be snuffed out but in this case it was particularly poor timing as the two insects were in deep discussion about something very important. Ironically, they were having a chat about life.

"Y'know Desdemona I'm getting a bit sick and tired of this deal."

"What deal?"

"This life we lead – it sucks. No pun intended."

"Well this is why we're here Doris, it's what we do."

"Yeah but look at it will ya? We just buzz around drinking the blood of other creatures, which I might add tastes disgusting, then we lay eggs, then we die."

"Yes but..."

"Not only that, but we only live for a couple of months and that's if we don't get picked off by predators!"

"Yeah I hear Dorothy got nabbed yesterday."

"Bird?"

"Lizard."

274

"That's what I'm talking about! It's so unfair! Two months! It's pathetic. By the time we've figured out what we want to achieve in life it's time to croak!"

"But…"

"And do you have any idea how many diseases are carried in the blood of other creatures? The risk of us catching something is huge! And what's going on with our names eh? Why must we all have names that begin with D? Our entire existence is one big joke! Dixie told me that they even make chemicals designed specifically to kill us! They put them in spray cans apparently, one squirt of that stuff and it's goodnight Vienna."

"Will you just let me speak Doris?"

"Sorry I'm ranting again aren't I?"

"I was chatting to Debs last night and she seems to have found a solution to all our problems."

"What do you mean?"

"She's found a place where there are no predators or spray cans, a place where we can eat whatever we like and she claims the mosquitoes that live there have an average lifespan of at least two years!"

"What place? Where is it?"

"It's a couple miles due south of….*look out!*"

Squelch!

The sole of Danzo's boot came down on the mosquitoes with a solid thump. He wasn't *trying* to kill them – he didn't even know they were there, he was actually on his way to the hangar but – wrong place, wrong time.

Outside the hangar's main entrance was a solitary guard. Perhaps calling him a 'guard' was a little generous, he wasn't armed and had no relevant training, he wasn't even that big. He was in fact one of Max's technicians, a chap by the name of Victor. When he saw the enormous bulk of the Korellian approaching he swallowed hard. Max's instructions had been very simple – *no-one* was allowed inside the hangar without his express permission. Victor couldn't think why anyone would *want* to go into the hangar, especially at this hour and even if they did it would probably be one of his fellow technicians or Dr Ticklegrit himself. But here was one of the fearsome croc security guards, heading straight for him. Was he really going to deny him access? Maybe he just wanted a light for a cigarette. Being a Korellian Danzo was short on manners and heavy on aggression.

"What are you doing here?" he snarled.

Trying to keep the fear from his voice Victor cleared his throat and said:

"Dr Ticklegrit has asked me to watch over the hangar until we're ready to fire the Uglifier."

"Step aside maggot, I need to do a security sweep of the building."

Max's words echoed through Victor's mind.

And when I say no-one, I mean no-one, not even Miss Tendril.

Victor's big weakness was his indecision. His technical prowess, enthusiasm and energy were virtually off the chart but when it came to making choices he tended to dither somewhat. He now had to make an important decision, one that could have drastic consequences – pretty much a life or death kind of deal. It could take him ten minutes to decide what type of cheese to have on his burger, so the chances of a swift decision were looking slim. It boiled down to two options, he could allow the croc access to the hangar or he could tell him that it was off limits, as per Max's orders.

The first option would surely get him fired, assuming Max ever found out – which he usually did. Being fired would catapult him down the career ladder and he'd likely end up working for some two-bit drug store on the dodgy side of Cosmopolis, having to run a gauntlet of muggers and thieves just to get to and from work. His salary would slide into the realms of the downright ordinary which would of course dictate his lifestyle. But at least he'd *have* a lifestyle, because it's very difficult to have a lifestyle without a life – and he was certain that's where option two would take him. This croc wouldn't think twice about wasting him, in fact he'd probably enjoy it. For a man renowned for indecisiveness Victor made a snap judgement, he stepped to one side and said:

"Sure go ahead."

Once inside Danzo got a good look at the machine he was there to sabotage. It was gigantic. He put the height at something like one hundred feet, maybe higher. But it wasn't the height he was interested in, it was the endless coils of wires and cables that snaked their way out of the machine's control panel. The jumble of wires looked like piles of multi-coloured spaghetti and with so many it would be difficult for someone to notice a couple had been severed.

276

Danzo scaled the ladder to the walkway that jutted out from the wall and ambled over to the panel withdrawing a pair of bolt-cutters from his utility belt as he did so. Laying on top of the panel was a manual. It took Danzo only one paragraph to realise he couldn't understand a word of it, but then again he didn't need to. Every single cable had to have a purpose, all he needed to do was cut a couple that looked important. On closer inspection he noticed that each cable plugged into a socket, each of a uniform size and shape. Even better, he didn't need to use the bolt-cutters, he could just rearrange them at random. That would surely do the trick. Making sure he was definitely alone and not being observed he squatted by the control panel and pulled a handful of cables from their sockets. The Uglifier did nothing, didn't move, didn't bleep – nothing. Danzo reattached the cables to the control panel taking care to ensure each one went back into a different slot.

This was the first in a chain of events that, if unchecked, would seal the fate of the planet.

Not appreciating the consequences of his actions the Korellian stood upright and dusted his hands together. He was especially pleased with his lateral thinking – that's why you're head of security he told himself and made for the ladder. Four paces from the door he felt a terrible sinking feeling way down in the pit of his stomach. It was that cold, sharp shock you get when you realise you've done something wrong, when you realise you've given your boss the wrong documents for an important meeting, when you call your wife by the wrong name. In a flash he was back at the control panel, desperately trying to remember which cables he'd just rearranged. But it was no use, he must've reconnected at least half a dozen wires and try as he might he couldn't remember which ones. Why hadn't he written it down like Cyrus Zifford had suggested? What a berk! He removed a notepad and began scribbling down the wires he *thought* he'd moved. Red wire in socket #12 previously in socket #8, yellow wire in socket #9 previously in socket #2 and so on.

After completing his less than accurate notes he trudged back to the door, all former gusto draining away. He'd botched it, a simple straightforward errand and he'd mucked it up. That, he told himself, is why you'll only ever be a security guard.

CHAPTER FIFTY-ONE

*"The battlefield is a scene of constant chaos. The winner will be
the one who controls that chaos, both his own and the enemy's."*

Napoleon Bonaparte

5.01a.m. – 59mins til the final.

"OK one last time, just to be sure."

"Eric we've done this twice now, do we really need to do it
again?" Frank moaned.

"Frank! This could be the most important plan in the history of
plans, we can't afford to goof it up. Now from the top. Grunter...?"

"My fellow gorillas and I create a diversion on the beach to
occupy the guards at exactly 5.15am. Once the security force has
been neutralised I come back here to watch over Frank and
Dolores."

Since his arrival on the island Grunter had made contact with
the other jungle gorillas. They had been only too happy to put in
with him once he'd told them they'd be going up against the
Korellians. They had a score to settle to put it mildly and with
Grunter leading them it evened up the odds.

"Excellent. Frank...?"

"I stay here with Dolores."

Eric waved his hands wildly, encouraging Frank to continue.
"That's all I'm doing isn't it?" he said looking confused.

"You stay here with Dolores *and make sure nothing happens
to her!*"

"Okey dokey."

"Well go on then – say it!"

Like a child reciting his nine times table Frank repeated the
line.

"I stay here with Dolores and make sure nothing happens to
her."

"That's more like it. Sixpack...?"

"Once Mr Grunter's diversion takes place I make my way to the landing pad and try to find a suitable spaceship to facilitate our departure from the island. Once I have found one I come back here to rendezvous with the other members of the team."

"Well done Six. We don't need anything fancy, we might even be able to use the same ship that brought us here, just get us some wings. Hank...?"

It had taken the team a good fifteen minutes to bring the Rough Knight round after he'd fainted away at the sight of Grunter. Still on the groggy side but improving by the minute Hank had allowed Eric to take temporary command of the Saturday Knights until he was operating at something higher than fifty per cent. So far he had been impressed with Eric's logical, even-handed approach, Grunter too seemed to think things through rationally – for a gorilla. It was still hard to believe they were about to try and save the world, but everything Frank had told them had been impossible to disprove. Things had definitely taken a turn for the surreal; here they were sat in the jungle on a tropical island talking to a giant gorilla about the fate of the planet.

"Hank, it's your turn," Frank prompted.

"Sorry, I drifted off there for a moment. Yes...er...during the diversion, Eric and I will infiltrate the main complex to try and locate the scientist Max Ticklegrit. Once located, we will tell him to deactivate the machine, if he refuses we bring him here and introduce him to Grunter. Once the machine is out of commission we meet up back here then fly back to Cosmo in the ship Sixpack will hopefully have commandeered. Grunter's the only one capable of flying it so it's vital he doesn't get killed."

"Groovy! Right then, I suggest we check our gear and get ready. By the way, does anyone know when this machine is due to be fired?"

Everyone looked at Frank.

"Er...from memory it hit Cosmopolis at exactly 6pm today."

"Anyone know the time difference between Cosmo and here?"

"Cosmo is twelve hours ahead of us," Grunter said – he'd done his homework.

Hank stared at his watch, looked at the others then stared back at his watch.

"Oh my God!"

"What?"

"That means we've only got an hour to stop it!"

"*What?*"

"If it hits Cosmo at 6pm and we're twelve hours behind on this island then it's fired at *6am* our time. Look at your watch; it's just gone 5am!"

There was dead silence as the gravity of the situation hit home.

Hank wasted no further time and said:

"Grunter you'd better recruit your chums and get out there, we haven't a second to waste."

"Copy that," Grunter replied and galloped off into the undergrowth.

Hank rubbed his hands together, he was on edge and couldn't tell if the nausea in his belly was due to the magnitude of the moment or the lingering effects of his inebriation.

"You OK D?" he asked to take his mind off things.

She just nodded.

A prediction would have been nice Hank mused, something along the lines of 'you *do* end up saving the world and no-one gets hurt', but no such forecast was forthcoming. Within a couple of minutes Grunter had returned complete with an entourage of a dozen jungle gorillas none of which were his size but looked thoroughly menacing all the same.

"Right we're ready!" Grunter growled.

"Showtime!" Eric hissed, overcome with excitement.

Grunter began leading his team out of the jungle.

"I'm sure you'll hear the diversion once it gets started," he said, "good luck everyone."

Just as he was about to go Eric asked:

"One last thing Grunter."

"Shoot."

Sidling up to the great ape Eric kept his voice low.

"You wouldn't happen to know what *chain up the mungle* means would you?"

"Absolutely no idea."

The nine Korellians jogged down on to the beach, taking practise swings and chatting idly about their favourite acts of random violence.

It was time for a spot of dawn batting practice.

"Where's Danzo?" one of them asked.

Hex Brakkish explained;

"He's involved with that big machine the doctor built; apparently they're firing it today."

"Shouldn't we be up there too?"

"Nah, Danz has got it under control, besides whose gonna mess with it? There's no-one on this island but us."

The crocs fanned out, taking up their positions and the practise session got underway. Hex stood on the mound, massaging the softball in his claws and putting on a mean face. The Korellian at the plate, swung the bat a few times waiting for the pitch.

Whack!

It was a fine connection and the ball went skyward, more up than along. Slightly disappointed he'd been clobbered, Hex watched the flight of the ball, it was arcing towards one of his outfielders, a particularly dull-witted croc by the name of Blox Diggitt.

"Catch it!" Hex cried!

Holding his gloved hand aloft Blox jinked left and right until he was directly underneath the descending ball. Hex groaned as the ball missed the glove and impacted on top of Blox's head. How could he have missed it? He'd been right underneath it! A blind man could've done better. Hex was about to go over and kick the living daylights out of him when he noticed Blox wasn't even looking at the ball. Instead his vision was fixed on the jungle ahead of him.

"Blox you useless pile of monkey dung! What are you...?"

He followed Blox's gaze.

Several gorillas were charging towards them from the jungle, at their head was what appeared to be a giant of some sort. As the distance between them closed Hex saw it was actually another gorilla – but it was monstrous! Instinctively Hex went for his gun but his claw wrapped around an empty holster – this was batting practise, no need for guns. His companions were also 'gunless' but they did have six baseball bats between them. Narrowing his eyes Hex screamed;

"At last! Some action! Come on lads let's get 'em!"

Grabbing the remaining bats the crocs steamed towards the oncoming assault at full pelt.

CHAPTER FIFTY-TWO

"Be willing to make decisions. Don't fall victim to what I
call the ready-aim-aim-aim-aim syndrome.
You must be willing to fire."

T. Boone Pickens

5.08am – 52mins til the final.

The three Saturday Knights had made their way to the edge of
the jungle. From here they could plainly see the battle that had
begun on the beach. Grunter and his gorillas were engaged in a
furious hand-to-hand scrap with the Korellians and from where they
were stood it was hard to make out who had the upper hand.

To their left they could also see the main complex, a
breathtaking structure of white stone and glass bathed in the orange
glow of the rising sun. Beyond the complex was a vast hangar,
which they guessed housed the machine they were here to try and
decommission.

"Guess we'd better get going while Grunter's occupying the
guards," Eric said.

"Yep, it's now or never," Hank replied.

The two friends looked at each other, they knew this was far
and away their most dangerous encounter yet. They were on foreign
soil, unfamiliar with the surroundings, seriously unprepared and
about to enter a complex they knew nothing about to find a man
they had never seen. And yet…the fate of the planet rested on their
shoulders. Eric took a very deep breath;

"Ready?"

"Just promise me you'll be careful Eric. We've come too far to
blow it all now. Don't go charging in anywhere OK?"

Eric could sense the sincerity in Hank's voice.

"Alright, I'll be cool."

"Right then, Sixpack we'll see you back at the rendezvous."

"Very well sir."

With that the trio edged their way out of the jungle. Sixpack hugged the perimeter of the complex, avoiding the melee on the beach, making his way towards the hangar where they thought the landing pad might be. Eric and Hank made straight for the first building they could see, a small one-storey affair annexed on to the main structure – it seemed as good a way in as any.

They arrived at an electronic door with a numbered keypad beside it.

"Oh great!" Eric exclaimed. "Now what do we do?"

Even at this early hour the heat was stifling and the humidity was worse. Hank felt like he had his head inside a blast furnace. Removing his helmet and dripping with sweat he said to Eric:

"I can hardly breathe with this thing on!"

Eric did likewise:

"Yeah me too. Let's take out the headsets though, we can still wear them."

The Knights tossed the helmets into a nearby bush and fixed the earpieces and mikes to their heads. Now looking more like a telesales operator Eric said "testing, tes…"

"Yes I can hear you," Hank said. "Now let's see if we can figure out the code number to open this door."

There was of course no way they could figure it out, they didn't even know how many numbers were needed let alone what the numbers were.

"Let's kick it in," Eric suggested.

"It's obviously an electronic door Eric, it doesn't have any hinges, plus you're likely to wake everyone up."

Before either of them could say another word the door slid open. Standing on the other side was a woman in her mid-thirties dressed in blue overalls and carrying a large plastic bag, which appeared to be full of garbage. She locked eyes on the Knights:

"Who the hell are you?"

Hank had expected the woman to scream for help but she emitted an outward calmness, a kind of 'couldn't care less' attitude.

Eric took a step forward and placed his fist across his chest:

"We're the Saturday Knights, scourge of…"

"We're here to see Max Ticklegrit," Hank interrupted. "Can you tell us where his office is please?"

The woman, who was actually a cleaner about to take her cigarette break, gave them the once over;

"Bit early for Halloween fellas."

"It's supposed to be a surprise; we haven't seen him for a while so we'd appreciate it if you didn't tell anyone."

She lit a cigarette.

"Fine by me," she said absently, "just go through here, past the kitchens, take your second left, follow the corridor for about fifty yards then you'll find the elevators on your right. Take the right hand elevator to the third floor, go left down the hallway until you reach the vending machine then it's your third door on the right, down the corridor, left where the vending machine *used* to be and you'll find his office on the right. You can't miss it."

"Many thanks ma'am," Hank said politely.

She stepped aside to allow them through the door. Without giving her a chance to change her mind the Knights thanked their lucky stars and headed for the interior. It wasn't the best of starts, they hadn't even set foot inside the building and had already been discovered, but this woman didn't seem the slightest bit interested. Just as they were crossing the threshold the cleaner threw her arm across the doorway, barring their way.

"Not so fast!"

Hank winced, he knew it had been too good to be true. Now she was going to start asking questions, she might even bring the house down on them.

"Is there a problem?" he asked nicely.

"There certainly is! I've only just finished cleaning that carpet, you're not going anywhere til you've wiped your feet!"

The Knights did as they were told and wiped their feet on the doormat. Apparently satisfied the cleaner withdrew her arm and they entered the complex. The small corridor led to another door which hissed open for them as they approached. Beyond this was a hallway, nothing too extravagant (this was after all only the servants' quarters) just a few ornamental tables carrying vases and the odd framed picture on the wall.

"Did you follow those instructions?" Eric asked.

"Not really, but we know he's on the third floor somewhere, we just need to find the elevators."

As they stood in the hallway, looking mighty out of place, the smell of food drifted their way.

"Mmmm, smells like bacon to me," Eric said, licking his lips.

"Remember what that woman said? We need to go past the

kitchens."

"Let's follows our noses then. Maybe we can pinch some grub too, I'm famished."

Following the tantalising aroma was easy enough and by the time they reached a set of double doors with two circular windows their mouths were watering. The corridor bent left and right flanking the kitchen on both sides.

"I don't think we need to go *through* the kitchen, we can probably go around it," Hank whispered.

"Are you kidding? I'm starved, can't we just slip in and nab a bacon roll?"

"How many people are in there?"

Very carefully Eric peeped through one of the round windows set into the door. Through the steam he could make out two chefs who were busy rustling up a feast of a breakfast. Behind them, in the centre of the room was a large stainless steel table on which sat a couple of plates already half full of food. A male servant (an oriental chap in his late twenties and dressed in black) appeared through a door in the far side and one of the chefs poured a pan full of mushrooms on to one of the plates.

"This one's for Mr Zifford, the other one's for the prisoner. And when you take Mr Zifford's don't forget the sauces. You know how tetchy he gets when he doesn't have his sauces."

Prisoner? Eric wondered. Had they caught someone *already?* He bobbed down and rejoined Hank, relaying everything he'd just heard.

"Maybe they've caught Sixpack?" Eric said.

"Nah not likely. Besides, they wouldn't be bringing him a hot breakfast would they? Unless they're giving him cooking lessons, which would be time well spent I have to admit."

"Maybe it's...*watch it!*"

The double doors swung open and the servant appeared carrying a plate of food. Hank and Eric flattened themselves against the wall, praying the servant didn't turn their way. Thankfully he didn't and toddled off in the opposite direction.

"Let's follow him!" Eric murmured.

"You can't be *that* hungry Eric, why don't you wait til we find the vending machine."

"No, I meant let's follow him cos he'll lead us to the prisoner!"

"How do you know that food's for the prisoner, it might be for what's-his-name…Gifford?"

"It's Zifford, plus he's not carrying any sauces so it must be for the prisoner!"

"We don't have time to go rescuing anyone, we need to find Ticklegrit. It's already…," he checked his watch, "…quarter past five!"

"Alright then, I'll follow the servant and you can go and find the scientist, we can still keep in touch via the headsets."

"No Eric! We've gotta stick together, this place is huge, if we split up we'll never find each other again."

Trudging around the complex looking for a scientist wasn't Eric's idea of high adventure, but rescuing a prisoner *was*. It might even be a woman, possibly a complete babe, but without Hank on board he was going nowhere. Finding ways to convince Hank to do things he didn't want to do was a skill Eric had honed over the last few months.

"Come on bud, think about it for a minute will ya? This prisoner might be helpful to us. They might know their way round this place, they might know exactly where Ticklegrit is, they might even know how to deactivate the machine. We've got to free her…or him."

Hank thought about it – there was a good deal of truth attached to Eric's words, but he was conscious they were up against the clock. If Eric were right it would expedite matters considerably – it might even save the day. How he wished Dolores were here, a quick pointer in the right direction would be very welcome right now.

"Come on then," he said after much deliberation, "let's follow him."

CHAPTER FIFTY-THREE

"The less effort, the faster and more powerful you will be."

Bruce Lee

Following the servant proved to be extremely straightforward for the Knights. They tailed him down several corridors and even a flight of stairs without being detected. The secret to their stealth was their special surveillance technique. This consisted of a highly sophisticated set of skilled manoeuvres that involved watching the subject from a distance, waiting until he went through a door or round a corner, then scurrying after him as quickly and quietly as possible – this process was repeated until the surveillance was concluded. Of course, it would have been much easier to just follow the whiff of food but the Knights prided themselves on being professional if nothing else.

Eric leaned around the corner and saw the servant had arrived at yet another door, but this time, rather than waiting for the door to slide open, he laid the plate on the floor and retrieved a cardkey from his pocket. Eric rejoined Hank in the corridor.

"This is it! He's unlocking a door, the prisoner must be in that room! How do you wanna play it?"

With precious seconds ticking away Hank knew they couldn't afford to dilly-dally.

"Follow me!" he hissed and rounded the corner.

His timing was perfect, the servant had the plate in one hand and the other on the handle of the door. Creeping up behind him Hank pushed the muzzle of the Web-o-matic in the small of his back and said:

"Hold it right there! Get your hands up!"

The servant froze putting his free hand in the air.

"Can I put the plate down?" he asked.

"Put it on the floor, nice and slow."

"And don't spill any," Eric added.

Bending his knees the servant laid the plate on the carpet as gently as he could, taking great care to keep it level.

"Who's in there?" said Hank.

"A prisoner."

"Don't be a wise ass – who is it? And – *WOORRGHH*!"

Hank doubled up immediately, almost folding in half at the waist. He dropped his gun in the process as a searing pain tore into his nether regions. The servant had moved fast – lightning fast – apparently without effort, Hank hadn't even seen it coming. Whilst crouched the servant had snapped out a straight iron fist punch to Hank's groin and although he had his chainmail shirt there to protect him it seemed to have little or no effect. The pain was *blinding*! Without giving him a chance to recover the servant sprang to his feet and with a high-pitched shriek let fly with a snap-kick to Hank's breastplate. He didn't see this coming either, although his eyes were watering so badly he was having trouble seeing *anything* – except stars. The kick propelled him back into Eric and the two of them collapsed in a pile about twelve feet from their attacker. The servant smiled to himself then bent down and pinched a mushroom from the plate.

"You want some more?" he grinned, bouncing on his toes and chewing his mushroom.

Eric pushed Hank out of the way and got to his feet brandishing the Inebriator.

"Alright tough guy, let's see how you like some – OOOOFFF!"

Again the nimble servant moved with cheetah-like speed, taking two steps then launching himself at his attacker feet-first. The drop-kick catapulted Eric further backwards and he slammed into the wall, the wind knocked out of him. He fell to his hands and knees gasping for breath. "Trust us to find a waiter who can fight like a ninja!" he wheezed.

Stood between the two prone figures the servant laughed to himself, he was having a great time. He turned to face Hank who, like his chum, was now on all fours and crawling towards his weapon. Another shrill scream filled the corridor and the servant lined up for another attack. Hank raised a hand toward him.

"No wait!"

WHACK!

The force of the impact on Hank's chin was too much and for the third time that morning he passed out. Meanwhile Eric was getting to his feet. With his back to the wall he levered himself upright, trying to focus on the three servants that swam before him. The next thing he knew he was being hoisted off the floor. His assailant had him by the belt and the collar and was twirling him round in tight circles.

"Stop!" he cried. "There's something you need to know! We're here to save the *wooooorld*!"

He sailed through the air towards the door the servant had been about to open. On the plus side it was a good job the servant *had* unlocked it, had it remained locked the impact would have been far worse. As it was the door smashed open and Eric continued his flying show into the room beyond. He crunched against the far wall and came to rest in a heap, dazed and pretty sure he was about to pass out. A figure leaned over him and he heard his name being spoken, then the room went hazy and darker – yep, he was definitely out for the count. As he slipped into unconsciousness he had enough clarity of thought to find it strange that anyone should know his name. In a last effort to remain coherent he raised his head to try and identify the figure – he smiled as he realised he was hallucinating, looking down at him was the face of Maria Valentino.

Droids don't believe in luck, they can't, they just aren't programmed that way. As far as they're concerned everything happens for a rational, logical reason. Fortune, fate call it what you will, just does not feature in the droid make-up, which is why Sixpack didn't think twice when he arrived at the landing pad in time to see a shuttle preparing to land. Hidden behind a stack of oil drums he waited until the ship had touched down – then he made his move. The pilot, dressed in khaki overalls and wearing a fetching Kickass Cowboys baseball cap, disembarked and stretched his limbs. Then he saw Sixpack.

"Hey tin pot, run up and tell Mr Zifford his shuttle's here will ya? Whoa – nice cape! What's with the gun? Is that real? Hey quit pointin' it at me will ya? *Hey*!"

Bluff and deception don't feature much in the droid design either, they tend to just get on with things. Sixpack depressed the trigger and watched on impassively as the pilot received a liberal coating of sludge from the Garbage Shoot. "Oh my *God* what is this stuff?"

"It is nothing more than regular household refuse sir, the

weapon has a special feature called the Trash Compacting Putrifier."

"Ugh! The *stink*! Why the hell did you shoot *me* with it?"

"I am terribly sorry sir but I need to disable you."

"You crazy bucket of bolts! I'm gonna rip your rusty head off!"

Once again Sixpack pressed the trigger this time giving the pilot a jet right in the face.

"Ack! (cough!) You…!"

Staggering around blindly the pilot swung his fists in the general direction of the droid. Sixpack realised there was no further need for the weapon and calmly lay it down at his feet. He waited for the foul smelling pilot to get close enough then bopped him on the head with a metal fist – hard enough to lay him out cold. Not wanting to draw any further attention he scooped up the pilot and dumped him behind the oil drums. Now – to business, he walked around the ship assessing it, making sure it would be suitable for the task. Yes, it seemed in good working order, but he was going to need some heavy-duty cutting equipment if he were to get those wings off.

CHAPTER FIFTY-FOUR

"Destiny is a good thing to accept when it's going your way. When it isn't, don't call it destiny; call it injustice, treachery, or simple bad luck."

Joseph Heller

Down at the Battle of the Beach the Korellians were having a hard time of it. Pound for pound they were stronger than the gorillas and certainly better trained and could probably have taken them without too much trouble but there was one thing they didn't have.

Grunter.

He was proving to be the difference. Superior intellect was always a big plus on the battlefield and he co-ordinated his troops tactically, keeping the crocs pinned between them and the sea. Then of course there was his physical advantage. He towered over the Korellians and could comfortably tangle with two at a time – this not only sapped their energy but also their resolve. One could never accuse a Korellian of cowardice, they relished physical confrontation but that was usually because they knew they would win. They often relied on numerical superiority and even if that didn't work they often had more sophisticated weaponry, obviously neither of those factors applied in this skirmish, consequently they were finding it tough going.

Metre by metre the band of apes forced them back towards the surf and it wasn't long before the crocs could feel the water lapping round their ankles. They had also lost all their baseball bats, which were now in the hands of the gorillas. As the most senior croc present Hex Brakkish knew it fell to him to issue the orders. Stand firm, attack or retreat were about his only options, surrender was of course out of the question. He, like his fellow crocs, was exhausted and had, like his fellow crocs, been severely battered about the head and body and was, like his fellow crocs, bleeding badly from several minor wounds. They couldn't take much more punishment and although it annoyed him intensely to have to retreat he knew it was the only wise move, one more punch from Grunter would send him into the next world and he didn't relish that prospect, especially when he still had money in the bank.

"Fall back!" he screamed, more out of anger than desperation, wishing he were holding a really, really big bazooka.

Gradually the Korellians backtracked until they were waist deep in sea water. Of course! Hex thought, gorillas don't like the water, they can't even swim, if they stayed here they'd be safe. Someone *must've* heard the commotion and it was surely only a matter of time before Danzo arrived – with guns! He allowed the tactical withdrawal to continue until they were up to their necks. As expected the gorillas remained on the beach, their orders were only to prevent the crocs from reaching the complex so keeping them in the sea was fine by them.

"Don't worry lads, we're safe here," Hex said reassuringly. "All we have to do is wait for Danzo, then we'll be back in business."

One of the crocs had the presence of mind to look behind him, out towards the open sea.

"Er...Hex."

"What is it Blox?"

"I think we should get out of the water."

"Are you nuts? If we go back on to the beach we'll get minced."

"Yeah but…"

"Oh shut up Blox! Did that softball knock the sense out of you or something?"

"But Hex…"

"I said zip it!"

Accustomed to following orders and handicapped by a severe lack of common sense Blox did as commanded. Again he glanced nervously over his shoulder and as before saw several black fins cutting through the surface of the water.

The sharks were gathering.

Max Ticklegrit reached the hangar at exactly 5.40am. Eve had given him the call and was en route – this was it, show time! A weary looking technician stood guard by the door.

"Everything alright doctor?"

"Yes Victor everything's fine."

292

"Sounds like quite a commotion down on the beach eh?"

"It's probably those imbecilic Korellians fighting among themselves again, anyway we have more important matters to attend to. Has anyone been down here?"

Victor knew he had to lie, if he wanted to keep his job that is. Hopefully Max would be too wrapped up in the moment to get suspicious.

"Nope."

"Good, well the other technicians will be here soon, let's get cracking shall we?"

The two men entered the hangar and scaled the ladder to the walkway. Max cast an eye over the control panel.

"This manual has moved since I left. Are you sure no-one's been in here?"

"Positive doctor. Maybe it was the wind."

"*The wind*? Victor it's at least four inches thick!"

"Err…"

"Never mind let's get on with it. Fire it up."

Victor busied himself at the control panel. He flicked a couple of switches and the Uglifier sparked into life, a few lights blinked on and a low hum filled the hangar.

"Running pre-op systems check," he said to himself.

While the computer ran an internal check Max went back down to ground level and wandered around the base of the machine doing his own personal inspection. Everything seemed to be working correctly and nothing, other than the manual, seemed to be out of place.

"Doctor?"

"What is it?"

Victor was examining the cables frowning.

"I think some of these cables have been switched over."

"*What?*"

"I could be wrong but they don't look like they did yesterday."

Max dashed up to join him, a feeling of intense dread washing over him.

"I need to know Victor, I don't want guesses or estimates I want to know *right now!*"

Grabbing the manual Victor hastily flipped through the pages. This was all his fault – that snooping croc had been messing with the machine. But why? What did he possibly have to gain?

Furthermore how could something as dense as a Korellian know what he was doing? This was state of the art technology, most crocs struggled to operate a calculator. Max was beside himself – what had happened? Had someone snuck in during the night? Was that creep Zifford trying to wreck his big moment? Questions raced through his mind, questions with no answers. He glanced at his watch – 5.46am! Why now? Right at the last minute! Just as his date with destiny was assured. Sweat began to roll down the side of his face.

"Come on Victor!"

He rammed a stick of Trouble Gum into his mouth to try and calm himself down – if he *did* have a bad trip it wouldn't be til after the Uglifier had been fired – but it would be worth it, anything to soothe his shattered nerves. Victor continued to scan through the manual at warp speed, desperately trying to find the right section. The tension was broken by a high-pitched beep and then a computerised voice said:

"System check complete – all systems operational."

Max puffed his cheeks out and dabbed his forehead with a handkerchief. Victor too allowed himself to relax.

"Seems we were worried about nothing," he said, closing the manual. "Maybe we were just a bit paranoid."

"Run the check again," Max said, "we can't afford to take any chances!"

"Having trouble Max?" a voice said from below them.

They look down to see Eve Tendril stood at the entrance. Max spluttered out a nervy laugh.

"Not all ma'am, everything is 'A OK'. Please take a seat."

Against one side of the hangar Max had erected a fold up table. On top of the table was a widescreen TV. Eve had settled on a particularly expensive outfit for today's big event, a designer suit and high-heeled shoes – the power look. The only accessory was a gigantic diamond ring on her right hand, worth more than some small countries. She sat at the table and switched on the TV, then grabbed the remote and cranked up the volume.

"So stick with Channel 12 folks, we'll be right back with the Miss Cosmopolis Final right after these messages."

Eve grinned at the screen – it was all going to happen on live TV and she couldn't wait.

CHAPTER FIFTY-FIVE

"When fate hands you a lemon, make lemonade."

Dale Carnegie

Back inside the complex, Hank was the first to regain his senses. Feeling drained and thoroughly fed up he opened his eyes and immediately realised he was laying on his back, on what felt like a bed – which it was. The whitewashed ceiling stared down at him giving nothing away. He ached from head to foot as though he'd been run over by a train, his groin felt especially tender and the events leading up to his unconsciousness came drifting back. With a groan he levered himself up and turned sideways, resting on one elbow. He was inside a room he didn't recognise or rather he didn't have time to recognise as his attention was fixed on the three other people in the room. Each one induced a different emotional response. When he clapped eyes on the oriental waiter (who was leaning against the far wall with his arms crossed) he felt afraid, which quickly melted away into anger. Then he saw Eric lying on the floor, not conscious but still breathing and he felt anxious. Was he OK? Was there any permanent damage? But all these emotions were eclipsed by downright disbelief when he found himself gazing into the eyes of Maria Valentino.

She rushed over, sat on the edge of the bed and put an arm round his shoulder.

"Hank are you alright honey?"

"I've had better days," he moaned. "What the heck are you doing here anyway? And why is *he* still here?" he gestured toward the servant. "Is Eric OK?"

"One question at a time," she said smiling.

She'd *smiled.*

For Hank it was like a shot in the arm and for a second he forgot all about his aching body, the crucial deadline and the fate of the world. Just for a fleeting moment he was back at Angelo's, sat outside enjoying a summer evening beer with Eric, having a laugh with Maria and the only worry was whether his Captain Uno T-shirt would be clean in time for Wednesday night practise. Somehow all that seemed a million miles away right now.

He was too weary to think;

"It's good to see you Maria," was all he said.

She hugged him tightly.

"You too Hank."

"Just tell me what's goin' on," he sighed. "How come you're *here*?"

Maria explained it all to him. After receiving confirmation she had made the Miss Cosmo Tournament final she had, as many girls would have, gone out on a complete bender to celebrate. She'd returned to her apartment in the wee small hours, extremely drunk but happy about it and had collapsed on to the sofa to sleep it off.

She'd woken up inside this room.

"And you've no idea how you got here?" Hank asked, keeping one eye on the black-belt waiter.

"I was obviously kidnapped."

"But why?"

"I've no idea." She nodded her head towards the servant and gave him a cheeky grin. "I think Wang knows, but he's not allowed to say. One thing's for sure I'm gonna miss the Miss Cosmo tournament now, which is a real bummer."

Hank tried to piece it together but it was like doing a jigsaw puzzle in the dark. Grunter had mentioned this island belonged to someone called Eve Tendril – wasn't she a former beauty queen?

"So what about you? Looks like you and Eric finally decided to play superheroes after all?"

"We're the Saturday Knights," Eric groaned.

Everyone looked round to see Eric sitting up rubbing the back of his head. Maria dashed over and threw her arms around him.

"Eric I'm so glad you're OK!"

"Yeah me too."

Maria suddenly stopped hugging him and held him out at arms length.

"Wait a minute! What did you say? You're the Saturday Knights? *You two*?" She glanced over at Hank who raised his eyebrows and nodded almost apologetically. "I don't believe it! All this time it was you two!"

"And Sixpack," Eric added. "Don't forget Sixpack."

He suddenly realised Wang was stood behind him and sprang to his feet as quickly as he could wincing as his back complained.

"Whoa! It's the ninja waiter servant guy!"

Wang stayed where he was, completely unmoved.

"So what's the deal here *Wang*?" Hank asked.

"Miss Valentino is correct, I am not permitted to say."

Apparently forgetting this man had just kicked his ass, Eric jabbed a finger at him.

"Oh yeah? Then maybe we'll persuade you!"

"Erm…Eric." Hank obviously *hadn't* forgotten. "Just cool it."

"He's actually quite a nice guy," Maria said, "he hasn't mistreated me or anything, in fact he's been nothing but charming the whole time. He's very interesting, knows loads about the Far East."

"Charming?" Hank said in disbelief. "He nearly killed us!"

Wang tut-tutted softly and shook his head.

"I never intended to kill you sir. Believe me if I'd wanted to you wouldn't be talking right now. I would've employed the deadly killer cobra-tongue lethal death strike of certain death."

Hank believed him.

"So what are you doing here?" Eric asked Maria.

She brought him up to speed.

"To say I'm a prisoner it's really not that bad. I get to go out most days, chill on the beach and explore the island, under Wang's supervision of course. It's a beautiful place, have you had chance to look around?"

"We're not here to take in the sights Maria," Hank said adopting a grave tone, "it's a little more serious than that."

This seemed to interest Wang, who appeared to be fixed in the same position, leant against the wall with his arms crossed. He exuded an aura of total cool, there was just something about him that indicated he had wisdom beyond his years. His dazzling martial arts skills only reinforced the perception.

"You said something about saving the world."

Hank held up his hands;

"I know it sounds far fetched but we honestly believe it's the truth. In fact – wait – *what time is it*?"

In all the confusion he'd forgotten he had a perfectly adequate watch on his wrist. Wang looked down at his watch – he even made such a simple action as this look suave.

"It's ten to six."

"*Kerrr-iiiist on a jet-pack*! We've only got ten minutes Eric!"

Eric stood and faced Wang.

"Wang, we need to find someone called Max – what was it?"

"Ticklegrit," said Hank.

"Max Ticklegrit – where is he?"

"He's down at the hangar."

"Can you take us there?"

"Sure." It seemed Wang was perfectly happy to accept the 'save the world' story. "But I must insist that Miss Valentino accompany us. I have orders to keep her within sight whenever she leaves this room."

There simply wasn't time to argue.

"No problem," Hank agreed, "stick close to us Maria."

"What's going on?" she asked.

"Come on," Hank said, heading for the door, "I'll tell you on the way."

Eric stopped them just short of the door.

"*Wait!*"

"What is it now?" Hank fumed, they didn't have time for any of Eric's theatrics.

Eric turned to Maria and Wang.

"Does the phrase *chain up the mungle* mean anything to either of you?"

The way they looked at him suggested it didn't. Without further delay they retrieved their weapons and allowed Wang to show them the way. As he ran (he had made it very clear they *had* to run) Hank felt sick with nerves, they had less than ten minutes to save the planet, unless of course Frank Bazonka was some galactic practical joker – but somehow he doubted it. Eric on the other hand was overjoyed, now that they had saved Maria he was virtually guaranteed a dinner date with her.

CHAPTER FIFTY-SIX

*"Men are liars. We'll lie about lying if we have to. I'm an algebra
liar. I figure two good lies make a positive."*

Tim Allen

How Cyrus Zifford made it down the steps to the landing pad
without breaking his neck was a miracle in itself – maybe it was his
four-wheel drive loafers. Not only was his shuttle late but the pilot
hadn't even bothered to inform him he'd arrived, and now he was
down here the halfwit was nowhere to be seen! He knew the
Uglifier was due to be fired in just over fifteen minutes so it was
vital he got airborne and away from the island as fast as possible.
However, without someone to fly him he was going nowhere.

"Where the hell is he?" Cyrus said to himself, bordering on
hysteria, "and what is that god awful stink?"

Despite the pilot remaining unconscious, he still gave off a
wicked pong from his resting place behind the oil drums. Cyrus
wrenched the shuttle door open and hauled himself up to check
inside.

Nobody home.

With a whimper of despair he jumped back down and scanned
the landing pad, covering his nose and mouth with the tail of his
shirt. From behind a clump of extremely leafy bushes a droid
suddenly appeared – holding a rather large gun. Cyrus was
momentarily lost for words, which didn't happen very often. *What
the hell was going on?* First the pilot went missing and now there
was this droid – wearing a cape and what appeared to be a helmet.
He looked the enigmatic robot up and down, wondering how
dangerous he was.

"Hello," he said.

When in doubt always be polite, especially with droids,
particularly one carrying a gun.

Sixpack kept the gun at his side:

"Greetings sir."

"And you are?"

"My name is Excalibot, I am one of the Saturday Knights."

Part of Cyrus's job was keeping up to date with current affairs.

"Really? I thought your turf was Cosmopolis? A bit off the beaten track aren't you? And where are your chums?"

Turf, beaten tracks, chums – Sixpack just stood there, dumbfounded. "You didn't happen to see a pilot around here did you?"

"Yes sir I have seen him."

"Great! Where is he now?"

"Behind those oil drums."

Informative and brutally honest, but not what Cyrus wanted to hear.

"What's he doing behind the oil drums?" he asked slowly.

"Very little. I subdued him."

Uh-oh. This droid *was* dangerous. Cyrus tried to think his way out of trouble. He knew droids were immune to his usual tactics of toying with people's emotions, they were rational, logical machines.

"Can you fly this thing?" he asked, jerking his head towards the shuttle.

"No."

"Hmm, pity."

"May I ask what your business is here sir?"

"I might ask you the same question," Cyrus retorted, slightly taken aback at the droid's no-nonsense manner.

"I am not permitted to say."

Cyrus began to wonder exactly why the Saturday Knights *were* on Perfection Island. Did it involve Miss Tendril's diabolical plot to sabotage the Miss Cosmo final? Or had they got here by accident? Whatever the reason, he knew it couldn't possibly have anything to do with him. Time was pressing, he had to get off the island pronto and standing here exchanging pleasantries with a droid wasn't going to speed things up at all. Maybe he could appeal to his 'helpful' side, most droids were programmed to assist humans in distress – it was worth a try.

"Alright, I'll tell you. Have you ever heard of the Venomous Green Horned Potato-Head Lizard?"

"Never sir."

It was unlikely he *had* ever heard of it as Cyrus had just made it up.

"Well they're quite rare on a global scale but strangely popular on this island and about an hour ago I was bitten by one. As the name would suggest their bite is highly venomous and, unfortunately for me, we've run out of serum. This shuttle is here to take me to…er…the island of Ziffordania where they have a fully stocked medical centre. Unless of course you happen to have some Venomous Green Horned Potato-Head Lizard anti-venom on you?"

"Sorry sir, I have no such thing."

Cyrus faked a look of total despair and hung his head.

"I guess I'm done for then. Without any serum and no pilot to fly me I'm as good as dead."

"I do have a basic knowledge of first aid," Sixpack offered.

Perfect! Cyrus thought, the droid had fallen straight into his hastily conceived trap. Still he wore his crestfallen expression.

"I'm afraid *basic* first aid won't do it, I need to get to Ziffordania or else I'm a gonner. Shame really, I was so looking forward to swimming with those dolphins on my upcoming vacation…"

Sixpack mulled it over for a while, he was mightily confused as the only solution he could think of meant deviating from his mission – in a *big* way. All droids are programmed with various objectives, call them *priorities* if you like. In Sixpack's case his primary objective (or number one priority) was to do whatever his master told him (Eric wasn't daft), his secondary objective was to preserve human life whenever possible. But an awful lot depended on just *how* he interpreted Eric's instructions. The man in front of him made his decision easier.

"What a minute! I've got an idea! Why don't we use your basic first aid skills to revive the pilot? Then he can fly me to the medical centre."

"My instructions are to bring back some wings for my master. I was going to take the wings from this craft."

Wings? Why just the wings? Cyrus pondered, were they going to strap them to their arms and flap their way off the island?

"I wouldn't worry about that too much. There are dozens of shuttles flying in and out of here all the time, it's a regular spaceport. You just wait a few minutes, the sky will be black with ships you mark my words."

"Very well sir, follow me," Sixpack said.

He led Cyrus over to the oil drums. Sure enough the pilot was there, lying on his back covered in the vilest smelling goo Cyrus had ever had the misfortune to inhale. He brought his shirt up to his face again.

"Uck! What happened to him?"

"I subdued him using my Garbage Shoot."

"Your what?"

"This weapon," Sixpack held it aloft, "is called the Garbage Shoot."

"I see. Alright, lets get down to business shall we? Can you bring him round?"

Unaware he was being duped, Sixpack knelt by the pilot's side.

"Would you be kind enough to hold this for me please?" he asked, offering the weapon to Cyrus.

He took it gladly, smiling behind the droid's back.

Thank you, *thank you very much.*

While Sixpack began to administer some medical attention, Cyrus wrapped two hands around the business end of the weapon. He was sure if he hit the droid hard enough he'd deactivate it. All he had to do was wait until the pilot showed some signs of life and then clobber the robot. It took a mere fifty seconds for Sixpack to drag the pilot back to consciousness. Taking aim at the back of Sixpack's metal skull, Cyrus hoisted the makeshift club over his head, looking all the world like a medieval executioner about to dispense the coup de grace – all he lacked was the black hood. Just as he was about to bring the gun whistling downwards he felt it jerk out of his hands.

He spun round and when he saw who was behind him he almost passed out from shock.

"You gotta be kidding me!" he gasped in awe, "what are *YOU* doing here?"

CHAPTER FIFTY-SEVEN

*"Chaos in the midst of chaos isn't funny,
but chaos in the midst of order is."*

Steve Martin

Danzo Stax, dope that he was, was in danger of being late for the grand finale. The events of the last twenty-four hours had taxed the croc's inadequate brain to such an extent he had dozed off in his quarters. A sudden awakening, a glance at the clock and a surge of adrenaline later he was bounding along the path that led to the hangar. Being so muscular and bulky crocs do not run well, on the rare occasions they do engage high speed they tend to resemble runaway boulders.

Inside the hangar Max now had his full compliment of technicians, Charlie (up by the control panel), Victor and Juliet (both on the ground) were all present. Eve remained in her seat, her eyes fixed on the screen before her. In approximately six minutes she would wreak havoc on the world's most prestigious beauty pageant. *That would teach them to disqualify her!*

"Satellite alignment?" Max said, trying to stay calm.

"Satellite locked and aligned," Juliet responded.

"Repullium status?"

"Repullium stable Doctor," Charlie barked down from the walkway, sounding very important.

"Victor, give me a systems check."

"All systems go Doctor."

He too sounded important but lacked the dramatic flair of Charlie's response.

"OK people, we are Ug Launch minus six minutes, let's stay sharp. Juliet, open the roof."

Juliet hit a switch and the roof split down the middle, yawning apart with a rumble. The first rays of sunlight poured into the hangar.

Eve barely heard it, she was too engrossed in her TV screen.

303

The advertisements were almost at an end – Miss Cosmopolis 2105 was about to begin, showing on at least fifteen different US channels and being beamed to an estimated global audience of four billion.

Man, were they in for a show!

The hangar's main doors burst open and a sweaty, breathless Danzo Stax barged into the room.

"Am I too late?" he panted. "Is everything alright?"

Everyone turned to meet his theatrical entrance. Max was infuriated by the Korellian's sudden interruption:

"Everything's fine you buffoon, why are you here anyway?"

Danzo caught his breath and straightened himself up.

"I run security round here Doctor, I *should* be here!"

Fair point.

"Stax you couldn't run a bath! Just stand there and don't interfere!"

"Is everything alright?" Danzo asked for the second time.

"*Yes!* Everything's alright! Why do you keep asking?"

Danzo frowned, things weren't *meant* to be alright.

"Just making sure."

Eve bolted from her seat:

"Hell's bells you two!" she spat, "how am I supposed to watch this in peace?"

"I do beg your pardon ma'am," Max said.

"Are you *sure* you haven't got a problem?" Danzo said.

"For the last time you bumbling idiot…"

"Right that's it! I'm going to watch this from the comfort of my media room!" Eve screamed, stomping past the Korellian towards the main doors.

With a resounding slam she made her exit.

"See what you've done?" Max seethed.

Danzo's confusion began to make him angry.

"Don't blame me egg-head! You were the one doing all the shouting!"

None of this made any sense – the machine seemed to be working perfectly and wasn't Cyrus Zifford supposed to be here too? What was it he'd said?

I'll make sure I'm there to witness the panic.

But he wasn't.

It took a while but the cold, hard truth eventually came

crashing down on Danzo like an anvil dropped from a skyscraper.

Cyrus had conned him!

No! He wouldn't do that. Would he? Double crossing a Korellian was about as advisable as bedding the sixteen year old daughter of a champion bare-knuckle fighter.

The Uglifier interrupted his muddled thoughts by letting out a series of high-pitched beeps – the kind of beeps that suggested something might be amiss. Up on the balcony Charlie scanned the dials and lights of the control panel, feverishly trying to locate the source of the trouble. Max flew up the ladder to join him, Danzo followed.

"What is it? What's wrong?" Max gibbered.

"I think…er…"

"*What?* Spit it out man!"

"I think someone's been messing with the settings."

"*What?*"

"We're supposed to be targeting Cosmopolis aren't we?"

"Yes!"

"Well, someone's altered the settings to…"

"To what?"

"Doctor, we're currently targeting the entire planet!"

Max pushed the technician aside and looked for himself. The settings had definitely been changed. Danzo smirked, he knew this was probably a result of his rearranged wiring. Cyrus's plan had obviously gone up in smoke so he contented himself with the fact that Max was now in serious trouble – and that made him feel good. He clapped him on the shoulder:

"OK doc, looks like you've got your hands full so I'll leave you to it. I'm off to take care of some business."

With a certain Mr Zifford.

"Business? What kind of business?"

"The unfinished kind."

Not so fast!" Max said. "You're somehow behind all this aren't you?"

The Korellian shrugged innocently.

"Me?"

"It's Zifford isn't it? He told you to sabotage my machine didn't he?"

Charlie's eyes wandered to the control panel, more specifically the countdown display.

"Doctor, the Uglifier is set to fire in four minutes and ten seconds!"

Max's head began to pound – his finest hour was slipping away, his carefully planned operation was threatening to descend into chaos. He chewed furiously, which didn't seem to help.

"Should we abort doctor?" Victor shouted up from ground level.

"No!" Max screeched, his eyes squeezed shut, his hands pressed to his temples. He was losing control, he didn't know what to do!

"Four minutes!" Charlie cried.

Danzo was enjoying himself and broke into a throaty laugh, it was great to see the conceited doctor in such a flap. Max's face was reddening by the second. *It was all collapsing around him!* The sounds seemed to get louder, deafening him, the incessant beeping, Charlie's panic stricken voice, the roaring laughter of the Korellian.

He snapped.

To everyone's astonishment (particularly Danzo's) the scientist lunged for the Korellian. He grasped the startled reptile by the neck and squeezed as hard as he could, which was rather like trying to choke an oak tree to death. More surprised than annoyed Danzo grabbed the doctor's wrists and prised him away.

It was at this point Eric, Hank, Maria and Wang made their entrance.

For a moment everything appeared to freeze as though someone had hit the pause button. The four gatecrashers stood on the balcony that lined the west wall, at exactly the same height as (and parallel to) the walkway on which Charlie, Danzo and Max were positioned. The door hissed shut behind them.

Then all hell broke loose.

CHAPTER FIFTY-EIGHT

"Everybody in their own imagination decides what 'scary' is."

Yvonne Craig

Initially, the scenario was similar to what you see when you kick off the top of a termite's nest.

Total pandemonium.

People started running in different directions, most of them not quite sure why, it just felt like the appropriate thing to do. The two technicians on the ground floor (Juliet and Victor) had the easiest time of it – they just dropped everything and bolted for the hangar's main doors. They had no idea who the new arrivals were and obviously weren't that bothered about hanging around to find out. With the Uglifier operation in jeopardy and Max turning psycho they reckoned the best place to be was as far away from here as possible. Like a pair of gazelles who had just spotted a stalking lion they flew towards the exit.

"Get after them!" Eric screamed, again not really certain why they should pursue the fleeing scientists; it just seemed the right thing to do.

Maybe it was the heat of the moment, or just a desperate need to kick someone's ass again, but Wang sprang into immediate action. With a fluid vault he went over the railing (a good forty foot drop), landed comfortably on a pile of spare cables (like he knew they'd be there), then he was up and through the doors in pursuit of the routed technicians. His instructions to never let Maria out of his sight had presumably taken a back seat, allowing adrenaline to take the wheel.

Hank exercised a degree of common sense and took a second or two to appraise their situation. The mechanical monstrosity in the centre of the room *had* to be the machine they were here to knock out. On the walkway opposite him stood a Korellian grappling with a scientist (quite possibly Dr Ticklegrit) and another technician, who like his associates was making a bid for freedom and was already at the top of the ladder. Instinctively he brought the Web-o-matic up to his shoulder and took aim at the biggest threat in the room – Danzo Stax. Spotting the danger the croc tried to push Max away, he had to reach his blitzer pistol. But Max had well and truly flipped and clung to the reptilian brute like a psychotic barnacle, the madness fuelling his muscles, lending him extraordinary strength.

Meanwhile Charlie had slithered down the ladder in traditional submarine crew style, deciding to give the rungs a miss and sliding down the outside instead – without doubt the fastest method of descent, if you could handle the scorching heat on your palms. Not wanting to follow Wang through the main doors he opted for a less obvious side exit and fled out into the morning sunlight.

Eric took a leaf out of Hank's book and hefted up his weapon, also taking aim at the Stax/Ticklegrit skirmish on the walkway. They turned to each other.

"Ready?" they said in unison.

Taking careful aim they both fired simultaneously. In fairness the target was hard to miss, crocs are big enough by themselves but the added target area of Max Ticklegrit made it an easy shot – even for these two.

They both scored direct hits.

Hank's Web-o-matic had the more devastating effect, it wrapped up the two combatants, locking them together in a comical embrace. Whether or not the Inebriator achieved anything significant became a moot point as the croc/scientist combo bumped into the walkway's railing and then toppled over it.

Into the vat of red, bubbling repullium directly beneath.

Maria cheered as Hank and Eric exchanged high fives.

"Groovy!" Eric said through a smile.

They were now the only ones in the room.

"We need to put that thing of action right away!" Hank said, needlessly pointing to the Uglifier, which continued to beep away to itself. "How long?"

Eric checked his watch.

"Three minutes!"

"We have to get on to that walkway," Maria interjected, "it looks like the machine is controlled from that panel!"

Jumping across the gap was a non-starter, it was way too far and there was always the chance they'd join Danzo and Max in the vat of unpleasantness if they didn't make it. She sped off along the balcony that ran parallel to the walkway.

Where the balcony met the hangar's south wall there was a door.

Where the walkway met the same wall there was also a door.

It was a fair assumption that behind the wall there would be a corridor linking the two.

"Hey wait!" Hank cried after her.

But it was too late she had disappeared through the door.

"What's the plan bud?" Eric asked.

Hank looked at the Uglifier, then gazed up through the open roof.

"How do you think this thing works? Are they gonna bounce it off a satellite d'you think?"

"No idea. What does it matter anyhow?"

"If we know how it works then we've got a better chance of deactivating it."

"Maybe we should just close the roof?" Eric suggested.

Not a bad idea.

"Could do. But we've only got three minutes to find the switch and we don't know how long it takes to close. Nah – we're gonna have to tackle the machine itself. Let's follow Maria, see if we can – oh!"

She appeared at the far end of the walkway, through the door that led into the wall. She had been right, there had been a connecting corridor on the other side.

"Come on you two!" she laughed, hurrying over to the control panel.

Two paces were all they managed before events took a drastic turn for the worst. It stopped them dead in their tracks. The repullium under the walkway seemed to explode, like a geyser of hot water; except it spewed forth much more than mere H^2O, it spewed forth something so abominable it defied description – well almost. From where Eric and Hank were stood it looked as if Danzo Stax and Max Ticklegrit had been welded together – and then turned inside out. Jutting out from the grotesque lump of a double torso they could just about make out four separate arms but only *three* legs suggesting two had merged, making one particularly thick limb. But the head (or *heads*) was the real stomach-turner. First you had what used to be Danzo's head, now twisted, bloated almost beyond recognition. His eyes bulged like bubbles about to burst and his teeth looked somehow bigger, like ivory daggers. Attached to the side of this was a smaller but equally repulsive head that had once been the exclusive property of Max Ticklegrit. Amazingly he still had on his glasses, giving the image an even more bizarre appearance, if that were possible. The entire *thing* looked as though its skin had been peeled off – wet, red flesh glistened in the sunlight, purple veins snaked their way across every sinew and muscle. Slime dripped from just about everywhere.

It was quite simply horrific and would comfortably make it into anyone's horrific images hall of fame.

Which is why Maria screamed as loud as she did.

With her back to the control panel she had nowhere to go, unless she fancied jumping from the walkway, forty feet on to solid concrete. The bunch of cables on which Wang had so conveniently landed was too far away and the ladder was at the other end of the narrow platform – so she'd have to get round the nightmare creature first. It locked eyes with her, or at least Danzo's eyes did, Max's eyes were looking somewhere completely different due to the angle of his head.

She had to find a way past it!

Hank's eyes did saucer impressions – he had never seen anything like it, not even on telly. It was like...like...a big, red dragon. Dolores's nightmare had come true – *a big red dragon with no wings and two heads.*

Dolores.

Where was she right now?

Was she still safe?

No matter which angle he came at it from there was only one that made sense – Dolores was the solution to this entire episode – he was sure of it. She alone held the key. Of all the cryptic clues she had thrown at them only one remained unsolved.

Chain up the mungle.

It was an anagram – it *had* to be. But what did it say? With all that was going on around him Hank found it hard to concentrate. It was like trying to do a crossword in the middle of a crowded disco. Feeling more than helpless he switched his gaze to Maria – who looked directly back at *him*. He could see the desperate terror in her eyes. *Real* terror – not the kind you get from watching a scary movie, the kind you get when you look out the window of the plane to see the wing on fire. There was only one thing for it, he raised his

310

weapon once again.

"That's not gonna work bud!" Eric cried. "Look at it, it's all wet and slimy, the webbing won't stick to it!"

Eric couldn't take his eyes off Maria either, he too was frantic with worry, another half dozen paces and the monster would be upon her. He looked down at the Inebriator in his hands. Fat lot of good this would do. Deep down he knew there was another option which, with a keen eye and a following wind, had a good chance of success. But it meant revealing something he had been hoping to keep secret from Hank. Oh to hell with it! What was he waiting for? The repulsive slimeball on the walkway could tear Maria apart at any second! Dropping the Inebriator he said:

"I've got an idea!"

CHAPTER FIFTY-NINE

*"You have to make difficult choices in your life,
and you just have to be happy with them."*

Lori Loughlin

Chaos reigned supreme inside the hangar. To add to the drama the computer decided to make itself heard. A synthetic female voice suddenly said:

"Warning! The Uglifier will be firing in two and a half minutes!"

It was a calm, placid voice, the kind that wouldn't be out of place at a shopping mall advertising the latest offers.

"Yes we know!" Hank shouted back.

"Just thought I'd make sure," the voice said apologetically.

In a flurry of fabric and chainmail Eric swept away his cloak and dug his hand beneath his shirt.

"What are you doin?" Hank asked, risking another glance at the scene on the walkway – the monster was another step closer to Maria who continued to cower against the control panel.

"Like I said, I've got an idea!" Eric shrieked. "If I don't get to Maria in time, use *this*!"

He tossed something to Hank, then set off at a sprint towards the door at the end of the balcony, the one Maria had left by. Hank caught the object then stared at it.

"I thought you'd taken this back!" he shouted after him, but Eric had already disappeared through the door.

Again he looked down at the small gun in his hand – the Dissolver Revolver – the one Eric was supposed to have returned to Dodger Broadwinkle several weeks ago. Another scream from Maria focused his attention on events atop the walkway.

The beast was only a couple of feet away from her, its arms stretched out in zombie-like fashion, its teeth gnashing together. In anticipation of its conquest it tilted its head(s) to the ceiling and bellowed in triumph – a sound that would leave most people in need of fresh underwear. But Maria used it to her advantage; while the creature was looking up she dashed past it, heading for the door – the only way out. It took the Danzo/Max abomination a second or two to realise the girl was no longer there for the kill. With terrible deliberation it turned on its heels and lumbered after her. Maria was almost laughing with relief when she reached the door; she'd be through here in no time, back along the corridor, then on to the balcony (to join Hank) and away from the awful, slime-covered monster. She slammed her hand against the 'open' button, waiting for the door to slide away.

It didn't move.

She hit it again, then again, the way impatient people do when they're waiting for an elevator.

"*Come on!*" she screamed, "*open!*"

Maybe it only opened from the other side, maybe it was faulty, right now she didn't care *why* it didn't work, she just wanted off this walkway. A series of meaty squelches from behind forced her to look over her shoulder. The thing was coming towards her, faster this time, loping along on its three hideous legs. She spun around to face it, flattening herself against the door, doing her utmost to look like a piece of the wall. She continued to press the button behind her. Of course, the obvious exit was now down the ladder but Maria's brain wasn't working quite as it should – must've been the extreme terror.

Meanwhile Eric was making his way to what he hoped would be the very door Maria was currently so eager to open. He'd expected a corridor to join the two doors, what he found instead was a flight of stairs leading down. There was no time to waste so he dashed headlong down the steps, two flights to be exact until – bingo! – he found a corridor that (if his directions were correct) ran alongside the south wall and which would eventually lead him to the other door. As he sped along, it occurred to him he had absolutely no idea what he planned to do once he got there. Take on the monster? With what? His bare hands? A few choice curses? He rounded a corner, which led to another flight of stairs, this time going up.

"Why didn't they just build a straightforward corridor?" he panted to himself, "why all this up and down crap?"

He clanged his way up the stairs, to his relief he saw the door at the top.

Hank now knew he was armed with the weapon that could save the world. It could also save Maria – but unfortunately it couldn't do *both*. He dredged the far reaches of his memory trying to recall the exact wording of the instruction manual. There was only time for one shot, that much he could remember, one shot every ten minutes wasn't it? So the gun could recharge? Yes, he was sure that was correct. So what did he shoot? He could shoot the monster (assuming he didn't miss) and save Maria or he could shoot the Uglifier (almost impossible to miss) and save the world. Would the gun be powerful enough to dissolve the entire machine? Again he racked his brains – how many cubic feet could it dissolve? Thirty thousand? Forty? Or was it cubic *yards*?

What a choice.

Save a friend or save the entire planet, most of whom were strangers.

If logic prevailed (as it often did with Hank) he would be forced to shoot the Uglifier, which of course meant leaving Maria to the mercy of the multi-limbed eyesore on the walkway. Could he live with that? It would be for the greater good wouldn't it? But he *knew* Maria – she was a friend. Who would bring them ice-cold beers on summer nights if she were to perish? OK maybe that was a bit selfish. One person against an entire world. Hank's brow furrowed and his face creased in distress, as though he had an acute headache.

He *had* to shoot the Uglifier. It was the only real choice. Shoot the machine and hope the weapon had enough 'umph' to get the job done. Holding the feeble looking gun in both hands he took aim at the machine.

"I'm sure you already know this, but just in case you don't...the Uglifier will be firing in one and half minutes!"

"You're not firing anything!" he growled and began to squeeze the trigger.

"Hank! *Help!*"

It was Maria.

As if drawn by magnetic forces he swung the gun around towards the walkway. Six feet was all that separated her from the Korellian/scientist mutation.

Crunch time.

He had about three seconds to make his decision.

His heart made the decision for him. When he saw Maria's

face, the pure, uncut terror in her eyes, he knew when it came down to it, he *couldn't* just leave her to die.

"God forgive me," he murmured.

He took aim at the creature, locked his arms, closed one eye, pulled the trigger…and missed.

CHAPTER SIXTY

*"Heroes take journeys, confront dragons,
and discover the treasure of their true selves."*

Carol Pearson

Eric huffed and puffed his way up the stairs, Mr Cardio-Vascular he most certainly was not, although in fairness he *was* weighed down by chainmail and armour pads. He got to the top, put his hands on his knees, took a big gulp of oxygen then hit the 'open' button.

It was all over for Maria, of that she was in no doubt. The hellish creature was so close she could feel its breath, which made the toilets at Angelo's smell like summer meadows. Too frightened to scream and not brave enough to jump she resorted to good old-fashioned panic. Turning away from the brute she faced the obstinate door again and began to pound it with her fists. Sensing victory the monster closed in for the kill, two pythonesque arms reached out for her. Maria increased her violent assault on the door, which (in about six years) would probably have given way.

Then, in a flawless demonstration of synchronicity, two things happened at exactly the same time and you'll be relieved to hear Maria getting mauled to death by the monster wasn't one of them.

First, the door slid open bringing a breathless Eric and terrified Maria face to face.

Second, the walkway vanished into thin air.

Hank may have missed his target but he hadn't missed everything. In true cartoon style Maria and the beast stood on a platform of absolute nothingness for a split second, then they plummeted. Directly beneath was the vat of repullium which, despite guaranteeing them a soft landing, offered little else in the comfort department. Quick as a flash Eric shot out his hand and succeeded in grabbing Maria's wrist just before she fell out of reach – with his other hand he gripped the doorframe to anchor himself. Now in the movies this looks a fairly simple manoeuvre, but give it a try sometime, it's no bed of roses. Eric was learning this – fast.

When you're holding on to someone with just one hand and that someone is hanging in mid-air they seem to gain an extra seventy pounds.

From below there was a howl of frustration followed by the inevitable splash as, for the second time, Danzo and Max plunged into the nasty stuff.

Maria looked up at Eric, her eyes thanking him over and over again. He gave her a smile – pretty cool really, under the circumstances – and he felt like a million dollars, after all the dragon had been slain and he'd just saved the damsel in distress, like a true knight. This was silky smooth hero stuff, the type he'd always dreamed of. For a moment he forgot the planet's impending doom and allowed himself a brief second of euphoria.

Sadly it didn't last.

Especially when he felt his grip slipping.

Maria's eyes went from 'thank you' to 'don't drop me' in (well yes) the blink of an eye. On the off chance Eric's eye-reading skills weren't up to par she screamed it out loud:

"Don't drop me Eric!"

Thirty or so feet below her dangling feet the repullium swirled and boiled. The monster, thankfully, appeared to be gone for good.

Hank watched the scene in silent fascination, somehow the gods had smiled upon him, he may have missed the target but between them he and Sir Prize had triumphed, or so it seemed. If only Eric could pull Maria up on to solid ground. He too seemed to have shelved the 'save the world' issue for the time being.

"Just a gentle reminder," said a familiar female voice, "but the Uglifier will be firing in one minute."

This wrenched them both back to the present and the very real danger the world was still in. Now bent at the waist and holding on to Maria's wrist with both hands Eric looked across at his pal.

"You've got to stop it Hank, it's up to you buddy!"

Red bulbs dotted around the hangar (previously unnoticed by anyone) suddenly flickered into life and began spinning wildly, a loud, whining alarm like that of an air raid siren accompanied the light show.

It spelt one word – *danger*.

Hank tried to clear his mind.

Chain up the mungle.

It had to mean *something*. This insane caper still had a few loose ends to tie up but Hank somehow sensed the anagram had yet to play its part. And it wouldn't be a walk-on cameo, it was going to play the lead.

"Would you like a second by second countdown or should I just let you know when there are ten seconds left?" the computer asked.

Up on the balcony Hank ignored the question, he was busy trying to focus on the problem at hand.

Chain up the mungle.

"Shoot it Hank! Shoot the damn machine!"

The machine. *The machine.*

Hank's heart leapt into his throat. You could make the words '*the machine*' from '*chain up the mungle*'!

Putting his hands to his temples he tried to envisage the remaining letters. Flashing lights, wailing sirens and the relentless computerised voice did their best to cloud his thinking. God – what he would have given for a pad and paper at that precise moment. The distractions buzzed around his mind like a bothersome wasp that refused to land.

"There're forty five seconds left in case you were wondering," the computer said unhelpfully.

Then came the biggest distraction of all.

It arrived through the open roof, swooping down and landing ten feet away from where Hank stood.

Hank couldn't believe his eyes. Today had been a day of 'firsts', but this took the biscuit.

Standing before him, in full costume, hands on hips, was Captain Uno.

CHAPTER SIXTY-ONE

"I believe it is the nature of people to be heroes,
given the chance."

James A. Autry

So who's *your* idol?

Elvis? Lennon? Ghandi? Madonna? Harrison Ford? Jim Morrison? Maybe even David Beckham?

Imagine meeting them, I mean *really* meeting them. Not during some formal ceremony or anything, imagine they just walked into your living room one day. *Pow!* Suddenly, there they are. It'd be a mind blower wouldn't it?

That's exactly how Hank felt – totally shell-shocked.

On any normal day this would have been a very special moment, one to treasure. But right then, at that given time it was the last thing he needed. Shame really, because this was the one person Hank had been waiting to meet for the last twenty-five years. Call it lousy timing, call it wrong place – wrong time, either way it didn't help the situation one iota.

"Greetings chum," the Captain said brightly, "need some assistance?"

Hank just gawped at him, unable to employ his vocal chords.

Chain up the mungle.

With Herculean effort he tore his gaze away from the world's greatest superhero and focused on the problem at hand. Yes! That was the answer! *He'd cracked it!*

"Sorry Cap, I'll be with you in just a minute!"

Captain Uno frowned as he watched Hank clamber up on to the railing that lined the balcony. People didn't usually react this way, he pondered, normally they would either run for their lives or shower him with praise and adulation (depending on whether they were criminals or regular people of course).

"If there's a problem I can help," he offered. "I am after all Captain Uno!"

As if there were any doubt.

"I know who you are Cap," Hank replied, now balanced precariously on the railing, "but I don't have time to explain!"

Eric couldn't quite believe his eyes either and as he finally hauled Maria up beside him he gasped:

"It's the Cap!"

"What's he doing here?" Maria asked, one arm around Eric's waist, just in case.

"It's the Cap!" Eric repeated, awestruck.

With great difficulty he returned his attention to Hank and his balancing act. "What are ya doin' man? Just shoot it!"

Clearly, the 'one shot every ten minutes' rule had slipped his mind in all the confusion.

"What's he doing?" Maria said.

"I dunno. Looks like he's gonna jump or somethin'!"

Hank looked across at the Uglifier and readied himself, if he really *had* cracked the anagram (and he was convinced he had) he would need to get down on the ground as fast as possible. Hanging from the ceiling were several long chains, what purpose they served was anyone's guess but for Hank they were mightily convenient. He bent his knees and sprang from his perch, arms out, hoping to catch one of the dangling lifelines. Lady Luck had obviously taken a bit of a shine to Hank and he silently thanked her as he felt his gloves clasp around solid metal. His momentum carried him forward and just like Tarzan he swung across the gap between the balcony and the Uglifier, his cape billowing behind him.

"The Uglifier will be firing in forty seconds," said the computer. "I thought I'd break it down into ten second intervals from now on."

As his impressive swing neared the machine Hank let go of the chain, again he flew through the air assisted by nothing but his own impetus. With a clang he landed on the side of the machine. Wires and cables entwined themselves around the structure and it was these that Hank used to secure himself to the Uglifier. Then he began to descend as quickly as he could, like a young boy climbing down an apple tree after being spotted by the farmer. He jumped the last few feet and landed on the ground with a thud.

"What's he doing?" Maria asked again.

Eric just shrugged.

Captain Uno leaned over the balcony for a better view. Why

didn't they want his help? He could've flown down to the ground in an instant without the need for daring acrobatics. Whoever this caped daredevil was he clearly knew what he was doing.

"Thirty seconds, I'll do the second by second thing when we get to ten if that's alright with you?" the computer said politely.

Down on the ground Hank began a desperate search for what he needed. There had to be one main cable somewhere! The floor was littered with wires and cables, some led into the machine others seemed to lead nowhere. There were also plenty of spare parts and debris lying about which made the search doubly difficult. Then he saw it – one thick black cable that led away from the base of the Uglifier.

"Twenty seconds," the computer advised him.

Hank followed the black cable, it snaked away to the edge of the hangar, towards the wall. Half walking, half running he tracked it through the jumble of mechanical litter that covered the floor.

The computer's voice sounded positively thrilled;

"OK here we go! Ten...nine...eight..."

The Uglifier began to whine ominously, the red bulbs seemed to spin faster – this was it.

In his haste to find the other end of the black cable Hank tripped and went sprawling among the junk.

"...seven...six..."

Now slithering forward on his hands and knees he scrambled towards the edge of the hangar.

"...five...four..."

Then he saw it and with a final effort, lunged for the wall.

"...three..."

The cable ended at an enormous plug, which was inserted into the wall of the hangar. Clasping both hands around it he gave it an almighty tug and wrenched it from the socket.

"...two...ooooo...ooo..." the computer said, its voice dropping several pitches to a deep moan and slowing to a complete stop.

The bulbs stopped spinning, the beeping ceased, every light on the control panel went out and for a moment there was silence. Hank sat with back against the wall, his chest heaving, drenched in sweat, his hands still clutching the oversized plug.

"*Unplug the machine,*" he gasped to himself.

He tried a smile and it seemed to fit perfectly, then he began to

321

laugh, quietly at first – just a chuckle – until the full impact of what he'd done washed over him. Then he was guffawing heartily, looking up to the ceiling and roaring with laughter.

Up in the doorway Eric and Maria were laughing too, hugging each other and nearly crying with relief.

"He did it!" Maria cried, "he stopped it!"

Eric gave Hank a big thumbs up.

"Groovy man!"

Captain Uno applauded enthusiastically.

"Bravo!" he shouted.

The euphoria continued for several seconds until they were all laughed out. Hank threw the plug aside and got to his feet.

"Come on, let's go find the others," he shouted up to Eric.

"How do we get down?" Eric asked.

Having been uninvolved in the climactic events of the last minute, the Captain finally did something useful. He flew over to Eric and Maria, placed an arm around each of their waists and glided slowly to the floor. Maria flung her arms around Hank.

"I'm so proud of you two!" she giggled. "You really were like a couple of superheroes!"

Hank just smiled, he was too exhausted to do anything else, on top of everything the earlier laughing had worn him out. Then he found himself face to face with Eric. Were those tears in his eyes? Eric took a pace forward and extended a hand:

"Way to go bud."

"You too, " Hank replied, shaking his hand firmly.

"We did it didn't we? I mean we *really* did it! We saved the world!"

"Yep, I guess we did. Kind of appropriate we did it on a Saturday too eh?"

Then they were hugging each other, neither one quite able to believe they were actually still in one piece.

"You know, saving the world is usually *my* job," the Cap said through a grin.

"Sorry to muscle in Cap," Eric said earnestly, "but it was just something we had to do. How did you get here anyway?"

"I flew naturally."

"No, that's not what I meant. I mean how did you know the machine was here?"

"Your droid told me, what's his name – Sex Pest?"

322

"Sixpack!"

"Oh yes, that's right."

"Yeah but…how…?"

The Cap beamed a perfect smile and clapped Eric's shoulder.

"Come on let's rejoin your friends, I'll tell you on the way."

"Er…hang on a sec," Maria said. "Are you just gonna leave that thing as it is? What if someone plugs it back in?"

Whoops.

"Maybe that was the part where we *almost* saved the world," Eric smiled.

"Mind if I step in here?" Cap asked.

"Be our guest."

Happy he was at last significantly involved, the Captain flew up on to the Uglifier, or rather *into* it, landing softly in the middle of the giant satellite dish that formed the machine's head. Eric, Hank and Maria watched in awe as they heard the awful grating sound of metal against metal until finally the satellite dish came loose. The last two months of relaxation had recharged the Captain's super powers; they weren't back to their vintage best but still sufficiently super enough for something like this. Dragging the dish behind him he flew out through the roof into the open air above the hangar. With a mischievous smile he transferred the huge metal bowl to one hand and turned to face the ocean. Then, like a champion Frisbee thrower, he hurled it towards the horizon as hard as he could. After clocking up an impressive three miles the dish began to descend until it hit the water, bounced a couple of times then sank without trace.

CHAPTER SIXTY-TWO

"Punishment is justice for the unjust."

Saint Augustine

Eve popped another luxury, calorific chocolate in her mouth, a triple Cappuccino Delight to be exact. This was going to be a great day, so great that even *she* would temporarily abandon her strict diet and make way for a spot of indulgence. The viewing monitor almost filled the far wall of her media room and the sound assailed her ears from a dozen carefully placed speakers. What next? Champagne Strawberry Truffle or Cognac Nut Swirly? Choices, choices. The Champagne Truffle eventually went off in search of its Cappuccino cousin.

The Miss Cosmo Final had just started and Eve knew that any second the tournament would be plunged into chaos.

"Nobody disqualifies Eve Tendril," she said to herself.

The Swirly was put to the sword as she cranked up the volume a little.

It took a little over two minutes for her to realise something was amiss. Max had been told to fire the Uglifier as soon as the final got underway, not sixty seconds afterwards, not two minutes – *as soon as it got underway!* So why was nothing happening? She reached for the intercom and was about to dial when she remembered the hangar had no communications equipment of any kind. There was no way she was going down there, despite the final being recorded for posterity she knew that if she left her seat she'd miss the big moment as she was halfway down the stairs. Another number was dialled and within seconds a servant was in the room.

"Yes ma'am?"

"Get down to the hangar and find out what's going on. And be quick about it!"

"What's going on in the hangar?"

"Not a lot by the look of it!"

"I meant what is *supposed* to be happening in the hangar?"

"Just get down there and tell Max Ticklegrit to pull his finger out! And be sure to tell him *I* sent you!"

"Very well ma'am."

Five minutes dragged by and as time wore on Eve became more and more uneasy. What the hell was Max playing at? He was normally so punctual. She was also suffering the after effects of annihilating the chocolates so quickly and she let out a groan of indigestion. The servant reappeared, somewhat out of breath.

"Well? What did he say?"

"I didn't tell him ma'am."

"Look, we both know you're not employed for your brain power but it was a relatively simple errand. Most carbon-based life forms would've been able to manage it. Why didn't you tell him?"

"He wasn't there."

"*What?*"

"No-one's there, it's empty."

Eve hurled the empty chocolate box at the monitor and sprang to her feet.

"*Imbeciles!*" she screeched and pushed past the servant.

She hurried to the hangar as fast as her heels would allow, slowing every so often when her stomach cramped from chocolate overload. Once inside it became worryingly obvious the servant had been correct, the place appeared deserted. More alarming still was the sight of the Uglifier, or what was left of it. The entire top section was missing! She'd only been away from the hangar for seven or eight minutes, how could they possibly have dismantled it in that time? Furthermore, *why* would they dismantle it? There was no sound to disturb the calm other than the low bubbling coming from the vat of repullium. She scanned the room – there were no signs of violence and nothing seemed to be out of place as far as she could see (apart from the headless Uglifier). One thing was for sure, the whole 'wreck the Miss Cosmo Final' idea had dissolved like so much moisturiser. Her master plan to exact revenge on the tournament organisers lay in ruins. Confusion and anger combined to tip her off the scale.

"*MAX?*" she bellowed, half expecting to see him emerge sheepishly from the shadows.

Nothing.

Even though she was fairly certain there was nobody in the

room she decided to search it anyway. The clicking of her heels echoed off the walls, accompanied by the odd groan of intestinal disquiet.

Then she discovered the plug.

Without thinking she plugged it back into the socket. It seemed the obvious thing to do – if you see a telephone off the hook you put it back on the cradle don't you? The red bulbs danced back to life, spinning wildly and the annoying high-pitched whine made a return. So did the computer:

"Aah, that's better. Now where was I? Oh yes I remember, two….one…fire!"

The siren increased to deafening proportions and Eve was forced to cover her ears. A deep rumble from somewhere inside the machine shook the hangar – the Uglifier was discharging its payload. But what Eve *didn't* know was Captain Uno's decapitation of the machine had completely destroyed the C.D.U. (chemical displacement unit), the fancy gizmo that converted the repullium from its liquid state to the laser beam that was supposed to bounce off the satellite. Consequently, the Uglifier was bursting at the seams with liquid repullium and with the C.D.U. defunct it had nowhere to go. Metal pipes inside the supporting structure began to swell under the pressure the way a garden hose does when you step on it. Eve wanted to run; right now running for the door as fast as humanly possibly was a very appealing option. But she couldn't, the spectacle seemed to root her to the spot. All she could do was stand and stare as the Uglifier bulged and complained.

Jets of steam burst from the machine's innards, hissing like a weightlifter trying to lift too many kilos. Eve had a pretty good idea what was going to happen next but still her feet refused to believe it. Her eyes widened in perfect concert with the pipes. Something had to give and suddenly…it did. At first it was nothing more than a thin spurt of red liquid, just a tiny hole in the pipe's exterior. It landed by her woefully inactive feet and she gazed down at it, spellbound. Another minor puncture and a second pipe yielded to the pressure, more repullium spewed out on to the floor. With every fibre in her body screaming at her to flee Eve remained motionless, the dam was about to collapse and all she could do was stand there and watch it.

And then it happened.

Quite fed up with trying to contain its bladder the entire

machine exploded from the inside, showering the hangar in a fountain of red repullium. Instinctively Eve covered her head with her arms, but it was no use, the chemical coated her from head to foot. The shower continued until finally, with a sigh of relief, the machine allowed the rest of the liquid to drain away and the explosion subsided, spilling out the remainder of the repullium, which spread to the four corners of the room. The hangar (and Eve too) looked as though it had been dipped in red paint. Repullium ran down the walls and dripped from the rafters, the floor a good two inches deep in the foul stuff.

A low moan escaped Eve's lips. She now cut a very different figure, no longer the haughty dictator, more the dishevelled, pathetic weakling. Red, slimy repullium dripped from her body, her hair hung in soaked clumps, sticking to her face. She coughed and spluttered as she inadvertently swallowed some of the toxic goo. She knew what this chemical was, she knew what it was designed to do, she'd seen the results close up – and she knew there was no antidote.

She was screaming long before she felt her muscles start to mutate.

CHAPTER SIXTY-THREE

"A hero is an ordinary individual who finds the strength to persevere and endure in spite of overwhelming obstacles."

Christopher Reeve

Warm morning sun cloaked the quartet of adventurers as they made their way on to the beach. There was no sign of Grunter, his gorilla chums or indeed the Korellians, just a lot of churned up sand near the water's edge. They failed to notice the sea had a decidedly red tinge to it about twenty feet out.

"Looks like Grunter did his bit," Eric commented.

"Yeah, he should be back at the rendezvous with Frank, D and Sixpack," Hank added.

"Who on earth are Grunter, D and Frank?" Maria asked.

Hank smiled:

"You'll be meeting them soon, they're all part of this insane caper."

"So how did you find your way to us then Cap," Eric asked, "are you psychedelic or something?"

"Psychic," Hank corrected.

"Whatever."

They rounded a curve on the shore and the edge of the jungle appeared ahead of them. They'd be back at the rendezvous in less than five minutes.

"Not quite," the Captain explained, "as you probably know I retired a couple of months ago and decided to kick back and enjoy the good life for a while. I took out my luxury yacht and went on a bit of a jaunt around the globe, relaxing, fishing, trying new beers. Anyway, I'd always fancied visiting the Underlands, which as you may or may not know is about a hundred and sixty miles north-west of here. I anchored not far from this island a day or two ago, turns out the fishing here is *amazing* by the way. Anyhow, sometime after 2am this morning I was awoken by this unholy din coming from outside, I checked it out and sure enough there was this enormous spacecraft, heading for the island."

"That must've been the ship we arrived on," Eric said.

"It seemed a bit strange for such a big craft to be coming *here* so I checked out the island using my on-board navigation computer and guess what? According to the computer, the island was purchased some years ago by a private individual, a former beauty queen no less. Now what would a former beauty queen want with a ship like that eh? I decided to go back to sleep and check it out at sun-up."

"But how did you find your way to the hangar?" Eric asked.

"Let him finish Eric," Maria scolded.

Large footprints had appeared in the sand, stretching out towards the jungle tree line, Grunter and his ape gang had obviously come this way.

"Go on Cap," Hank prompted.

"So I flew over here at daybreak. I found the landing pad easily enough, but there were *two* ships, the one I'd seen earlier plus another smaller shuttle. That's when I bumped into your droid Sixpack – great name for a droid by the way."

Eric beamed – praise from Captain Uno – life didn't get much better.

"Do you know if he managed to get us a ship?" he asked.

"Stop interrupting!" Maria cried.

"He'd already defeated the shuttle pilot and was talking to a fellow I now know to be called Cyrus Zifford. Turns out I made it there in the nick of time, Zifford was about to take your droid's head off, but I…well…I talked him out of it. Sixpack told me the whole story, so I went off in search of the hangar."

"Can I speak now?" Eric asked Maria.

She elbowed him in the ribs and gave him a killer smile. "So how 'bout it Cap? You gonna come out retirement?"

There was a lengthy pause as he considered it.

"Sounds to me like you're doing a pretty good job of things in Cosmo in my absence."

Hank and Eric rose about ten feet – how cool was this? A pat on the back from Captain Uno himself!

"Yeah but, we don't have any super powers," Eric pressed, "we're just regular guys with some fancy toys."

"You've got much more than that, Eric, you've got the desire to fight crime, to right wrongs, to bring some much-needed justice back to the people. Sometimes that's all you need. I mean look at you – between you, you've just saved the world from a terrible disaster – you didn't really need my help."

"I guess you're right," Eric mumbled. Then he got all excited again, "just wait til we get back Hank! We're gonna be so famous, parties, interviews, chat shows!"

Hank smiled faintly, as usual he'd given it a little more thought:

"I hate to be the one to tell you this Eric, but has it occurred to you that no-one's actually going to *know* we saved the world?"

"We'll just tell 'em!"

"And who's gonna believe us? I mean, where's our proof? The only credibility we've got is Frank and he's not exactly Mr Believable is he?"

"We'll get the Captain to tell 'em. They'll believe him."

Captain Uno was about to speak but Hank beat him to it:

"Can't you just content yourself with the fact that we saved the planet? We don't need all the fame and fortune do we?"

"Fortune and glory isn't everything it's cracked up to be," the Captain added, "I used to live for the limelight, but in the last few months I've come to realise I don't miss it, in fact it's nice to be left alone."

"But…it doesn't seem fair!" Eric blustered. "We've risked our necks on this mission and now you're telling me no-one's gonna know?"

"I'm afraid that's the way it has to be Eric, you'll just have to accept it. I think the important question now is – do we carry on?"

"*You wanna quit?*"

"No – I'm just saying, how can we possibly top this?"

They had arrived at the edge of the jungle. "Let's discuss it later shall we?" Hank suggested.

They pressed through the undergrowth until they saw their friends, duly waiting at the rendezvous point. Grunter was there, together with Frank and Dolores, but no Sixpack.

"Is that who I think it is?" Frank asked, gawping at Captain Uno.

"Sure is," Eric said proudly.

"Wow, the one and only Captain Uno. People s talk about you in the year 2205 y'know?"

"That's nice to know," Cap said.

"Well, don't you want to know how we got on?" Eric asked.

"You did it," Frank said flatly.

"How do *you* know?"

"Dolores told us."

"Oh."

Dolores burst from behind Grunter's legs and threw herself into Hank's arms. He scooped her up, gave her a hug and sat her on his shoulders.

"You OK D?"

"Yes, I'm really happy none of you died!"

"Me too."

The remaining introductions were made – which took a while.

"Crocs give you any trouble?" Hank asked Grunter.

The colossal ape grinned.

"Piece of cake actually, we forced them into the sea and the sharks took care of the rest."

"Nice."

"Hey, where's Sixpack?" Eric asked, suddenly concerned.

"We assumed he was with you," Frank replied.

"I left him back at the landing pad," Cap said, shrugging.

"What did you do with that Zifford guy?" Hank said.

"He's at the landing pad too, but I wouldn't worry, he's not going anywhere."

Eric picked up his Inebriator:

"Right, wait here folks I'm gonna go and find Sixpack."

Hank lowered Dolores to the ground.

"I'll join you."

"I think we should all stick together from now on," Cap advised.

Nobody was going to argue, so as one they trudged out of the jungle.

CHAPTER SIXTY-FOUR

"You and I will meet again, When we're least expecting it, One day in some far off place, I will recognise your face, I won't say goodbye my friend, For you and I will meet again."

Tom Petty

The search for Sixpack did not last long – less than two minutes to be exact. The group spotted him as soon as they made it on to the beach. He was some three hundred yards away and appeared to be dragging something behind him, like a caveman bringing home lunch.

As they got closer they could see he had his back to them, taking one slow step at a time, bent at the waist and pulling something of considerable weight. They broke into a jog until they got near enough to make sense of it. Detecting their presence the droid lay down his load and turned to face them.

Eric could scarcely believe what he was seeing:

"Six!" he almost laughed, "what on earth is that?"

Resting on the beach was an enormous piece of flat metal, easily the size of a regular family saloon. A thick furrow in the sand stretched away into the distance as far as they could see.

"It is a wing sir."

"A wing?"

"Yes sir."

"What would I want with just a wing?"

"I do apologise, sir. Perhaps I did not make myself clear, I can see how it may look strange. This is only the first of *two* wings. I could not manage both at once so I plan to go back for the other after I have delivered this one."

Hank chuckled to himself:

"You and your slang Eric, when are you gonna learn?"

"Eh?"

"*Just get us some wings* – that's what you told him wasn't it?"

"Oh…yeah."

A chorus of laughter rippled through the group.

"Am I to understand this wing is no longer required sir?"

"Six, please tell me there's another ship at the landing bay," Eric said.

"Yes sir, I believe it is the same ship that brought us here."

"And does it s have its wings attached?"

"Yes sir."

"Groovy! OK everyone, I suggest we make for the landing pad asap!"

A few minutes later they were stood by the transporter ship. Next to it stood the wingless shuttle, its other wing lying beside it.

"Where's Zifford?" Hank asked.

"Behind those oil drums, together with the pilot of this shuttle. They're...er...taking a nap," Cap explained. "I'll be alerting the Underlands authorities once you've gone, they can tidy up this mess. From what Mr Zifford told me this was quite an operation, I see lengthy jail terms ahead for some people."

"Will you at least tell them *we* apprehended them?" Eric pleaded.

"Sure thing Eric. In fact we could have some more candidates right here."

Captain Uno pointed up at the main building. Marching down the steps towards them were four people, three dressed in white, the fourth in black.

"It's Wang!" Maria exclaimed.

There was slightly too much glee in her voice for Eric's liking. But she was correct, Wang was leading three sorry-looking scientists (Charlie, Victor and Juliet) down to the landing pad. They were cuffed at the wrists. As he approached Eric stepped forward:

"Thank you Mr Wang, we'll take it from here!"

Wang, s looking incredibly cool, said:

"Has anyone seen Miss Tendril? I've been looking all over and she's nowhere to be found."

Nobody had seen her. Eric herded the scientists away from Wang.

"You can toddle off now Mr Wang, everything's under control."

"Sorry I can't do that. I have to take Maria back to her room."

With Captain Uno stood behind him Eric discovered a new level of courage.

"Look buddy, I've a mind to turn you in with the rest of these losers if you don't make yourself scarce!"

A cocky smile, a narrowing of the eyes and then:

"OK, come and get me."

Hank walked between the two of them.

"Alright! Alright! Just calm down you two. Wang, it's clear you don't know the full story here and whilst you're clearly batting for the wrong team I've no wish to get you caught up in it. My advice would be to leave this island as quickly as you can before the cops arrive. My *other* advice would be to try and solve any future problems with a conversation rather than a Cobra Killer Death Strike or whatever you call it."

Hank 'Diplomacy' Halo strikes again.

"Fair enough," Wang said after a brief silence. "Can I leave these goons with you?"

"No problem."

"Goodbye Maria, it's been a pleasure."

"Same here."

Hank grabbed the collar of Eric's cloak in the nick of time.

"Cool it!" he hissed in his ear.

With that Wang trotted back up the steps and disappeared into the main residence. The focus shifted back to the matter at hand.

"Reckon you can fly this thing?" Hank asked Grunter.

He peered inside the cockpit and said:

"I'll have to rip the seats out just to get in, but I think with a few minor alterations I should be alright."

Hank turned to Captain Uno.

"Well Cap, I can't begin to tell you what a pleasure it's been to meet you."

They shook hands warmly.

"The pleasure's been all mine I can assure you."

"Don't forget to tell the Underland cops it was the Saturday Knights that foiled this plot will you?" Eric asked, shaking Cap's hand.

"I won't."

"Fancy a beer to celebrate? I'm sure they'll have some up in the kitchens."

Cap shook his head.

"I don't drink anymore."

This raised a few eyebrows.

334

"I don't drink any less either!" he laughed. "Seriously though, I'll wait til I get back to the boat before I crack open a cold one."

"One last thing Cap – can I get an autograph?" Eric asked.

Delving into his cloak Eric retrieved a pen and pad. Hank rolled his eyes – he could've really used that back in the hangar.

"I've got some signed photos back at the yacht if you like?" Cap asked.

Eric looked wistfully at Hank.

"No Eric, we really ought to be going."

Crestfallen but not altogether unhappy Eric handed the pad to the Captain.

"*To Eric and Hank from my good friend Captain Uno* will do just fine."

The Captain scribbled it down and handed the pad back.

"Anyone else?" he asked, smiling.

It looked as though Eric and Hank were the only die-hard Captain Uno fans until Maria said:

"Oh go on then!"

After a quick discussion it was decided that Captain Uno would take care of the prisoners until the police arrived – he'd made a call from the main building and, after persuading the operator this wasn't a crank call, had finally been put through to the chief of police.

The cops were en route.

The scientists, Cyrus Zifford and the shuttle pilot were incarcerated in one of the nearby storage bays and Captain Uno had the only key.

It was time to part company.

Grunter had performed a few interior modifications to the transporter ship and was getting ready to fire her up. Frank, Dolores and Maria were in the cargo bay. Having now met the legendary Captain Uno, Eric was reluctant to say goodbye.

"Can't we have a go on his yacht?" he whispered to Hank as the Captain said farewell to the others. "Just for an hour or so?"

"I think everyone's bushed Eric, they just wanna go home."

"Home? Dolores is an orphan – living at *my* home I might add and Frank's home is a hundred years in the future!"

"And Maria?"

"Her apartment got cremated remember? Besides, seems to me

she'd probably prefer to stay here! With Wang!"

"Ooooh, jealous eh?"

"No!"

"She's not your girlfriend Eric."

"I saved her ass…her life…back in the hangar, if that doesn't get me a date I'll eat my ha…" he stopped and a look of alarm spread across his face.

"What's wrong!"

Eric chose not to explain, instead he turned to Captain Uno and shook hands vigorously.

"Cap, it's been amazing to meet you. If you're ever in Cosmo feel free to look us up – 99 Fargo Drive."

"You can count on it."

"I've got one last thing to do, you'll probably be gone when I get back so once again, it's been a privilege."

"Take care of yourself Eric."

Before anyone could stop him Eric went hurtling up the steps, heading for the main complex.

"I'll be back in a few minutes!" he bawled over his shoulder.

Cap turned to Hank:

"Where's he going?"

"No idea," Hank admitted, hoping he wasn't off to look for Wang.

"Well, I'd best be off. I'm gonna bring the yacht round, then wait for the police. I hope you and Eric keep up the good work back in Cosmopolis. Remember, the city *needs* you. The heart of American justice must keep beating."

"Hmm. I dunno. I'm sure Eric won't want to hang up the cape just yet, he's having far too much fun. We'll see."

They shook hands.

"Bye Hank."

"Seeya Cap."

With a flurry of red and silver the Captain launched himself skyward and out over the open sea. Hank watched him go with mixed feelings. Their time with Captain Uno had been brief, there were so many things he wanted to ask him, but at least he'd finally *met* him, something he thought he'd never achieve. That was the part that made him warm all over.

Grunter hit the ignition and the engine spluttered into life.

"Ready?" he asked Hank.

"Yeah, just wait a minute til Eric gets back will ya?"
"Where's he gone?"
Hank answered him with a shrug of his shoulders.

CHAPTER SIXTY-FIVE

"Home is any four walls that enclose the right person."

Helen Rowland

Hank wandered to the edge of the landing platform, leaned forward resting his forearms on the railing and looked out to sea. It was an idyllic scene. The sun reflected off the water, palms swayed in the early morning breeze and the refreshing smell of the ocean filled his nostrils. He inhaled deeply, this was the last breath of unpolluted air he'd taste for a long time – a million miles from the grime and grubbiness of Cosmopolis. It was exactly the kind of place where he dreamed of living; winning the inter-galactic lottery and retiring to somewhere like this would do just fine thank you very much. His daydreams came to an abrupt end as a mosquito (named Daphne in case you were wondering) alighted on the back of his neck and hunkered down for a bite. He slapped it into the next world and began to wonder where Eric had disappeared to. Other problems dogged him too.

Problems with no obvious answers.

Where would Maria stay once they got back to Cosmo? She had no family to put her up, no obvious place to go, unless she had a friend with a sofa. And what about Frank? He couldn't spend the rest of his days in that crumby hotel, he'd have to find a job so he could rent an apartment. But what would he do? A guy from the future with no apparent skills other than a knack for being pathetic – it didn't bode well. Finally there was Dolores and this problem bothered him the most. What was her long-term future? Staying with Eric was only a temporary arrangement and, for Eric, it couldn't be temporary enough. Would Mrs Dorfler take her in? With that lunatic droid Wilfred in the house it was only a matter of time before something drastic happened.

Questions, questions.

He pondered over these nagging uncertainties for several minutes, until he heard Eric return. Wandering back to the ship he

338

saw his pal charging down the steps. Just before Eric reached the platform Hank hauled himself up to the cockpit;

"No offence Grunter but you *can* fly this can't you?"

"Don't worry, I've been trained. I have nearly two hundred hours of flying time."

"Really?"

"Yep, I've been yanking and banking for over two years."

"OK, like I said no offence."

"None taken."

He hopped back down to ground level and as Eric approached he at last understood what he'd gone back for.

"Couldn't go home without these!" he puffed.

He carried the two helmets they'd discarded before entering the complex. Hank gave him a weary smile:

"Yeah, I'd forgotten all about those."

He detected a mischievous glint in Eric's eye, the kind that usually meant they were about to find themselves in deep excrement. But there was no danger here, not anymore. "Alright, what've you done?" he asked in a knowing tone.

"Whaddya mean?"

The innocent schoolboy with the catapult behind his back – as usual.

"Come on dude, I know that look."

"I went back for the helmets!"

"You didn't bump into Wang while you were up there did you?"

Thinking about it, if he *had* bumped into Wang he probably wouldn't be walking – or talking.

"No."

"So why the cocky smile?"

Eric checked himself – was he smiling in a cocky fashion? Well actually yes, he was.

"Come on lets get outta here," he said, unable to suppress the cheeky smile that had given him away.

Hank moved to the cargo area, s convinced his fellow knight had been up to no good. Eric joined him and slid the door shut.

"Say goodbye to paradise, folks," he said as the ship began to rise.

Grunter turned out to be a first rate pilot and they were soon cruising comfortably at twenty-thousand feet. The plan was fairly straight-forward. Drop the others off at Cosmopolis, somewhere out of town and then Grunter would return to Perfection Island to await extraction by a Nature HQ spaceship which would return him to Bloomissia. Frank had plonked himself in the cockpit and was chatting to the great ape about time travel. Back in the cargo hold Maria and Dolores were fast asleep, Sixpack was recharging in the corner, leaving Hank and Eric to chat by themselves – in private. They found a quiet corner and leaned against the wall, facing one another.

"Alright, tell me," said Hank, folding his arms.

"Tell you what?"

"I've known you too long bud, you've got that look like you can see right through my poker hand. Come on give it up."

Eric feigned innocence for a moment longer then bowed to Hank's intuition. He said:

"Have you noticed how there are s a few loose ends Hank?"

"Yeah, I was thinking about that earlier."

"Well, I've been doing some thinking and I may have come up with a solution."

Eric thinking – always a dangerous thing.

"I'm listening."

"OK, but hear me out before you butt in."

Hank spread his hands, encouraging Eric to continue.

"Right, well as I see it, the biggest problem we face is one of accommodation. When we get back to Cosmo you and I will be the only ones with anything like permanent homes."

As per Eric's instructions Hank said nothing, in fairness he had nothing to say at this stage anyway. Eric took a deep breath before continuing – another bad sign.

"Remember how my neighbour Cunningham put his house up for sale before we ended up here?"

Hank nodded.

"Well, I was thinking maybe we could buy it."

This was the perfect time to butt in with a loud *whaaaat?* But Hank remained silent, much to Eric's surprise.

"I know what you're thinkin' – how could we possibly afford it right?"

Again Hank nodded.

"The other big question is why would we *want* to buy it."

Another nod, although holding his tongue was now becoming a real effort.

"The reason is this – as you know our houses are semi-detached, only a wall separates my house from his. So if we were to buy it then we could knock it through and make one big house."

Hank's pact of silence reached breaking point.

"Wait a minute Eric."

Amazed he had managed to keep quiet this long Eric permitted the interruption:

"What's up?"

"Do you have any good answers to the two questions you've posed?"

"I think I do. I'll answer the 'why' question first. Maria, Dolores and Frank have nowhere to go. My house ain't big enough nor is your apartment. Frank and Dolores are the critical cases, neither have any potential for getting settled without some kind of assistance. I know you've taken a shine to Dolores and the last thing you want is to see her back at the orphanage."

"And you've taken a shine to Maria."

"Come on pal, I've always had the hots for her."

"And you think she'll move in with you? Just like that?"

"Well I was gonna ask you first."

"I dunno Eric, seems a big step for you both."

"No, I meant I was gonna ask you to move in with me first."

This stopped Hank in his tracks.

"Me?"

"Only if you want to."

Putting aside the cost issue for a moment Hank mulled it over. He had no great love for his crappy apartment and hadn't he always envied Eric's house? It was in a better neighbourhood and it would be nice not to share a bathroom. – some of Hank's fellow residents had toilet manners that would curl your toes. If they could somehow afford to annex Eric's house to Cunningham's there would be double the space, more than enough – lots more. Saturday Knight activities would also be much easier to co-ordinate if they were both under the same roof. He could ride with Eric to and from work, no more commuting on the suicidal subways. He was also touched by the gesture, Eric didn't often make these kind of offers unless he had an ulterior motive and, as far as he could see, there wasn't one here – yet.

341

"There's more to this, isn't there?" he asked after a while.

Eric smiled; it was kind of nice that Hank knew him so well.

"If we had twice the space there'd be room for us all."

"All?"

"Yeah, you, me, Six, Maria and Dolores. We'd be like one big family."

"What about Frank?"

"We could put him up until he found a place of his own."

"When did you come up with this idea?"

"As I was coming back down the steps."

Nice to see Eric hadn't changed his policy of thinking things through thoroughly. But the more Hank thought about it the more he believed it *could* work. It would be good for Dolores to have a woman around the house, they might even get some decent meals if Sixpack was relieved of cooking duties. But it was all academic, there was no way they could afford to buy Cunningham's house.

"I have to say it sounds like a cool idea Eric, but how were you planning to fund it?"

"Why don't you let me worry about that?"

"No Eric – I need to know now."

Eric peeked out into the storage area, the girls were s snoozing and Six was recharging his power cells in 'stand by' mode.

"I found something while I was fetching the helmets."

"Found or stole?"

"Found!"

"Do you swear?"

"Nearly every day."

"Come on man! Do you swear?"

"On my Mother's life."

What did you find? An enormous suitcase full of money?"

"Better!"

He dug into his shirt and withdrew a gold ring sporting the biggest diamond Hank had ever seen.

"Where did you get that?"

"Like I said I…"

"Found it! Come on Eric, people don't just leave diamond rings lying around!"

"Like I said Hank, I swear on my Mother's life. I went back for the helmets and saw these weird red, wet footprints all around the front of the complex. Right next to the wall I saw this. It's not stealing!"

Hank sighed, it was a little late for recriminations now and maybe Eric was telling the truth, he had just sworn on his Mother's life after all (twice), not something he did a lot – a bit like telling the truth.

"I don't suppose the owner will be making any complaints to the police will they? Can I see it?"

Eric handed the ring over and Hank scrutinised it as though he knew what he was looking for – which he didn't. One diamond was much like another to Hank. "If this is a genuine diamond we'd be able to buy a dozen houses!"

"We only need Cunningham's. I've got plans for the rest of the money."

Uh-oh.

"Like what?"

"I thought we'd plough it into the Saturday Knights. Think about it, a new vehicle, much more hi-tech and powerful, more sophisticated weaponry, military chips for Sixpack, new outfits, we'd be a force to be reckoned with! Plus we could have a few belting parties to celebrate!"

"Calm down big spender," Hank laughed. "We don't know how much it's worth yet. Plus we need to run all this past the others."

"OK, we'll ask them about it when we land, but you're with me on this aren't you?"

Hank gave him a reassuring smile:

"Yeah," he said quietly, "I'm with you bud."

CHAPTER SIXTY-SIX

"Saturday night's alright for fightin', get a little action in!"

Elton John

Six weeks later.

3am – a murky alley somewhere in Cosmopolis.

Whispered voices.

"You sure this is the right place?"

"Sure as I can be."

"That's not exactly a comfort."

"Dolores said it would be a bank raid on a road at the end of the world – if that's not Armageddon Street I don't know what is! I mean look, there's the Deep-Debt Bank building right there."

"How many did she say we'd be up against, again?"

"Whoa, careful there Eric, you're almost planning ahead."

"Very funny, how many?"

"You should pay more attention at the briefings y'know."

"Just tell me!"

"Five, maybe more."

"Is Sixpack in position?"

"Yes, he's on the roof with the Entangler Deluxe."

"Groovy."

The Rough Knight and Sir Prize were crouched in an alley opposite the front of the bank waiting for their quarry to arrive. Their attire had been updated and improved. Dark, lightweight, laser-proof plating covered their bodies at strategic points and they surveyed the scene through night-vision visors built into their shiny new laser-proof helmets. Silk capes flowed down their backs. It's fair to say that (for once) they looked pretty damn cool. They tensed at the sound of an approaching vehicle.

"Get ready!" Eric hissed.

The garbage truck drove right past them and into the distance.

"It's just a garbage truck," Hank chuckled.

"Are you *sure* this is the right place?"

"They'll be here, just give it time."

A minute passed in silence then Eric said:

"Did Maria leave supper out for us?"

"Yeah...er...beef curry I think. We'll have to nuke it though."

"Excellent, I'm so hungry I could eat a...wait!...listen!"

Another vehicle was approaching, a battered van, and this time it pulled into the alley adjacent to the bank.

"This must be them," Hank said calmly.

"Party time!"

"Simmer down Eric. Six you got 'em?"

"I see them sir, thirty feet below me in the alleyway."

"Alright, stick to the plan. Wait til they get out then net as many as you can."

"Roger that sir."

"*Roger that*?" Eric laughed.

"Seems military chips give you the full package," Hank said. "Here they come, look sharp!"

Two men disembarked from the front of the van, another four piled out of the back. They wore balaclavas over their heads and carried various items, ranging from laser rifles to welding equipment – they were clearly not here to wash the windows.

"Six of 'em," Eric murmured, "we'd better *both* go."

"OK Sixpack, give 'em the bad news," Hank whispered as they broke cover and raced across towards the van.

Now fluent in slang thanks to a custom-made (and very expensive) jargon chip, Sixpack made his move, leaning over the roof and firing his Entangler Deluxe into the group beneath him. A wide, flexi-steel net with specially weighted corners flew from his gun and landed on the goons below. It was a perfect shot and three of the bank robbers were suddenly ensnared inside the net, which began to constrict, rendering them completely immobile.

"Three targets neutralised – reloading!" Sixpack reported.

"Nice going Six," Hank said, "just stay where you are, we'll take the rest."

"Copy that sir, reverting to back-up status."

"I love it when he talks like that!" said Hank.

The Knights crossed the empty road and approached the remaining hoodlums. Eric flicked on his recently installed voice modifier and issued the challenge;

"*ALRIGHT SCUMBAGS! WE'RE THE SATURDAY*

345

KNIGHTS, NOW DROP YOUR WEAPONS AND KISS THE
PAVEMENT!"

It carried a terrifying air of intimidation and was loud enough
to illuminate a few neighbourhood lights as inquisitive civilians
were roused from their slumber. Like most criminals the goons had
heard of the Saturday Knights and (like most criminals) decided not
to obey the command. One bolted for the van, another ran in the
opposite direction while the last thug readied his rifle. Hank took
control:

"The shooter's mine!" he screamed. "Six, take out the runner
going for the van, Eric the other runner's all yours!"

Sixpack scurried over to the corner of the roof, took aim and
fired. Another direct hit sent the fleeing perp into a net covered
heap.

Eric flicked a switch on his wrist-mounted control panel and
felt the satisfying warmth on the soles of his feet as his booster-
boots ignited. He catapulted into the air, blue fire spurting from his
heels and guided himself towards his target. Like a lion bringing
down a zebra, he landed squarely on the back of his assailant,
dropping him to the pavement with a dull crunch. In seconds the
cuffs were out and the robber lay writhing on the ground, his wrists
secured behind his back.

Meanwhile Hank was tackling his own opponent. The thug
hadn't been expecting real trouble, he'd brought along the laser rifle
as a precaution and nothing more, which is why he hadn't charged it
up. Through his helmet's enhanced sensors Hank heard the tell-tale
whine of the battery, he had about four seconds before the laser was
ready to fire.

Plenty of time.

In a flash he levelled his Limited Edition Super Sucka at the
stranded hoodlum. Of all the weapons they had purchased in the last
few weeks this was his favourite, a nice non-lethal piece of
hardware that always took his enemies by surprise. The barrel was
larger than most standard weapons, some ten inches in diameter. He
pulled the trigger and watched through a smile as the hooded man
across the street began to move towards him. He resembled a novice
ice-skater as he gathered speed, sliding forwards, his arms flailing
wildly.

"What the...?" he managed to say.

Hank transferred the Super Sucka to his left hand, spread his

346

feet and braced himself for the impact. With a solid 'thunk' the thug was drawn into the weapon, he could feel his skin being pulled into the muzzle where it met his stomach. Using his free hand Hank swung a mailed fist into the perp's chin. It had the desired effect and he hung limply from the end of the gun, his arms by his sides, his head lolling around. Hank smirked and deactivated the weapon, the bank robber collapsed at his feet.

"All clear here," he said into his helmet mike, slinging the Super Sucka over his shoulder.

"All clear!" Sixpack replied from the rooftop.

"Piece o' cake!" Eric cheered.

Holding the unconscious thug by the collar, Hank dragged him over to the battered van.

"Alright, let's call the cops and tell 'em they've got a collection to make," he said. "Six, get back down here and fetch the Steed." And then to himself, with a smile, "the heart of American justice beats on."

Not long afterwards they were heading home in their new chariot, a sporty, sleek roadster brimming with hi-tech gadgets and capable of breaking any speed limit the Department of Transport could throw at them.

"Not a bad night's work," Eric said cheerfully. "How many we rack up tonight Six?"

Sixpack made a left on to the Multiplicity Mega-drag and said:

"Plenty sir, do you want exact figures?"

"Yeah go on – indulge me."

"Very well sir, today's tally stands at sixty-nine. That's twenty-six muggers, nineteen car thieves, fifteen burglars, six bank robbers, two arsonists and a granny-jacker."

"Y'know we really oughta consider doing this full time," Eric suggested. "Sooner or later the criminal element is gonna cotton on and they'll just stop committing crimes on Saturdays."

"We've been through this before bud, we don't get paid to do this, how are we gonna make ends meet? Plus, people are gonna figure out who we are before long."

"There's s a ton of cash left from the diamond sale, we could use that."

"No way, we said we'd save that for Dolores, college fees are pretty steep."

"She's only a kid, Hank, she's a long way off going to college."

"We agreed Eric."

"Okaaaay. Say. did the decorators turn up this morning?"

"I think so."

"Good, I want that basement refurbished as soon as possible. Then we'll have a real HQ, one to be proud of!"

Eric was buzzing. The Saturday Knights were really making a difference, especially since they'd had a serious cash injection and upgraded their equipment. "Did you clear out the basement like I asked Six?"

"Yes I did sir and…"

"And what?"

"I've been meaning to ask you about this sir. I located several items which I did not recognise. I am sure they do not belong to you."

This statement seemed to send Eric into a minor panic.

"Never mind that Six, probably just some old stuff I owned before I purchased you. Anyway…er…what about Frank winning all that dosh on the Bloodball Final last night? Who would've believed it eh? A fluky touchdown in the last second! He'll be renting his own place in no time."

He knew he'd said it much too fast, he just prayed Hank was too busy to notice.

"But sir I am familiar with every item you own. I performed a full inventory before we purchased the Cunningham residence."

Eric could feel the sweat forming on his brow. Damn it Sixpack, why can't you keep your mouth shut!

"Like I said Six, don't worry about it."

Please don't worry about it.

But Hank's curiosity had been pricked.

"What did you find Six?"

"Look!" Eric shouted, pointing out the window, "isn't that the place we nailed those car jackers last week?"

It was too late; his attempted diversion only heightened Hank's suspicion.

"What did you find Six?" he repeated.

"Various household items sir, an old Dust-Zucker vacuum cleaner, a TV, some bowling trophies…"

"Stop the car Six!" Hank said evenly.

"Right here sir?"

"Stop the car *now*!"

The street was bathed in a red hue as the vehicle's brake lights glowed into life. Hank turned to face Eric who was looking very uncomfortable in the back seat. "It was *you* wasn't it?" he said.

"What do you mean?"

Catapult behind the back – same old story.

"*You!* It was *you* that burgled my apartment that night! So I'd change my mind about becoming a superhero! You stomped off in a tantrum remember? I didn't get home for a least another hour and a half, you had plenty of time!"

Eric considered sticking with his innocent approach, but the look in Hank's eye told him that was probably not a good idea. Hank would be down the basement like greased lightning as soon as they got home, then he'd find all his stuff. He hadn't seen Hank this angry since the Wingnut Gang episode, so he did what he usually did in these situations – he fled. Wrenching the door open he clambered out of the roadster and set off at high speed down the deserted highway.

"Son of a…!" Hank seethed and flung his own door open.

Sixpack watched them in contemplative silence. Then he eased the car forward, trying to catch up with the two grown men dressed as medieval knights chasing each other down the street.